Also by Allison Brennan

THE
LOST
GIRLS

Allison Brennan

St. Martin's Paperbacks

This is a work of fiction. All of the characters, organizations, and events portrayed in this novel are either products of the author's imagination or are used fictitiously.

THE LOST GIRLS

Copyright © 2016 by Allison Brennan.
Excerpt from *Make them Pay* copyright © 2016 by Allison Brennan.

For information address St. Martin's Press, 175 Fifth Avenue, New York, NY 10010.

ISBN: 978-1-250-10509-7

Our books may be purchased in bulk for promotional, educational, or business use. Please contact your local bookseller or the Macmillan Corporate and Premium Sales Department at 1-800-221-7945, ext. 5442, or by e-mail at MacmillanSpecialMarkets@macmillan.com.

Printed in the United States of America

St. Martin's Paperbacks edition / November 2016

St. Martin's Paperbacks are published by St. Martin's Press, 175 Fifth Avenue, New York, NY 10010.

10 9 8 7 6 5 4 3 2 1

To Mike & Erin Pettingill, missionaries,
who left successful careers to serve the less fortunate,
first in Honduras, and now Equatorial Guinea.

ACKNOWLEDGMENTS

The Lost Girls was an emotional book to write, and required more research than I initially thought. I think Google maps has become my best friend!

First and foremost, I want to thank Mike Pettingill, a friend of mine who used to work with me in the California State Legislature. The year after I left the legislature to write full-time, Mike and his family became full-time missionaries with Missions to the World. Mike answered all my questions about what it's like to be a missionary, the joys and the fears. I wish I could have used everything I learned. It takes a truly special person to give up everything they own to serve others.

Once again, Deborah Coonts—author, pilot, and all-around extraordinary woman—helped with the plane details. If I got anything wrong, it's because I messed up.

I was thrilled when my cousin Jason Gifford married the amazing Dee—for more than because I like her. She's also a nurse! Dee helped me tremendously with a pivotal scene in this book that, without her guidance, wouldn't have been half as good. Thank you so much, Dee.

Crime Scene Writers led by the wonderful Wally Lind is always my go-to place for all types of crime questions—

this time I needed information about warrants, foreign nationals, extradition, witness protection, and more. Thank you to all the cops, lawyers, medical examiners, pathologists, and P.I.'s who are extremely generous with their time and talent to help writers "get it right." I may have taken a few literary liberties, but I try to stay as close to the truth as possible—while still keeping the story entertaining.

Always, thank you to my agent Dan Conaway who keeps me grounded, and my editor Kelley Ragland at Minotaur who helps each book reach its greatest potential. This time she outdid herself and forced me to dig deep into the emotional well to make *The Lost Girls* hit all the right notes.

Last but not least, my family—for understanding my crazy schedule, for being patient, for letting me bounce around ideas, and for making me laugh.

PROLOGUE

Father Sebastian Peña sat up in bed early that morning, mindful of every ache in his arthritis-ridden joints. Disease didn't care if you were a saint or a sinner or—like most of God's creatures—somewhere in between.

Sebastian had always been an early riser. The sunrise was his favorite hour, peaceful, unlike any other moment of the day. But it wasn't quite five, early even for him. A rustling outside had him thinking a wind was picking up. But then he heard nothing. No wind, no cars. What had he heard in that dream state before waking; what had him rising before the sun?

As soon as his feet touched the cold floor he sought his slippers. He turned on the dim light, then wrapped a thin robe around his broad but frail shoulders. Sebastian had once been a large man. He'd played football in college, before he received his calling. He had been a wild young man, but like Saint Augustine, once he was called, he kept his vows. Still, he wondered at times—as inappropriate as it was—if God had afflicted his joints because of the prideful athlete he'd once been.

That sound again, faint but distinct, came from outside. He parted the blinds and peered out the window into the darkness. A small house behind Our Lady of Sorrows served as the parish rectory, which he shared with Father Peter Mannion. Father Peter was a young priest who had taken over the parish when Sebastian retired last year. Sebastian had both longed for and dreaded retirement. He was tired, very tired, but he loved his church. The families he'd seen week after week, from baptisms to weddings to funerals. The joys and the deep, deep sadness. Our Lady resided in a poor, rural community halfway between San Antonio and Laredo. Sebastian had been in the Laredo Diocese for years, but the last thirty he'd spent here, in this small parish, in this impoverished town. He was here only for a few more months, to help with the transition. By January he'd be settled into a retirement home in Tucson, Arizona—a great relief from the Texas humidity, which worsened his arthritis.

But he didn't want to leave.

A clang of metal on metal made him pause. A chest-high wrought-iron gate circled the property—easy enough to climb over if someone felt compelled to vandalize or rob the church. Perhaps it was the garbage cans, a cat or opposum in the trash again. Father Peter was far too forgetful. How many times had Sebastian told him to secure the lids?

Sebastian walked through the house. The living and dining areas had been converted to the parish secretary's office and his private office. No, not his anymore . . . Father Peter's.

"Forgive me, Lord," he muttered as he turned on the entry light. Yes, his pride and jealousy were coming through. He had thought he'd conquered those vices decades ago, but turning over his parish to another, younger priest had brought back emotions he thought he'd never feel again. Along with the sick sensation that his life was over.

For seventy-one, Sebastian was a healthy man. He

drank in moderation, had never smoked, and exercised regularly—except on days like today when his arthritis would prevent him from doing much more than walking. His life wasn't over. He could still celebrate Mass during the busy seasons, he could still participate in the church, he could volunteer. Play golf. He almost laughed at the thought. He'd never picked up a golf club in his life. Perhaps he could volunteer at a church high school as a coach. He would enjoy that, working with youths and teaching them. There were options. He wasn't dead yet.

Sebastian unlocked the door and stepped onto the small porch. It was a chilly morning, the first sign that autumn was approaching. Later that day it would again be hot, but the morning was refreshing.

He looked around. His body may be failing, but his eyesight was not. The streetlights in front of the church didn't reveal anything suspicious. No one was climbing over the section of the fence he could see. Father Peter was still sleeping: as he'd walked through the kitchen, he'd noticed that the coffee had yet to be made. The young priest would rise by six to prepare for the morning Mass. Sebastian had never acquired the taste for coffee, though he enjoyed tea.

He heard a faint cry—it sounded like a baby. This early in the morning? A parishioner, perhaps, needing solace?

He walked slowly down the porch stairs. Out of the corner of his eye, he saw a flash of light in the dark. He turned and looked down. It wasn't a light; it was a white cloth, left under the statue of Saint Elizabeth.

Sebastian bent down to pick it up. At the same time he noticed there was something moving beneath the cloth, he heard a murmur.

The murmur turned into a weak cry.

Dear Lord, what is this?

Of course he knew.

A baby.

A newborn.

Sebastian ignored the pain and creaks in his joints as he knelt in the dirt and picked the baby and the blanket up from the cold earth. Holding the infant close to his chest with one large hand, he used the statue as leverage to rise again, then walked back to the house. The child's cries were muted. Sebastian barely gave the mother or circumstances a thought, not then. The poor soul in his arms was his immediate concern.

Headlights approached from the south end of the street. The high beams were on and the car drove slowly. Sebastian hurried back inside and closed the door. He bolted it, not quite certain why his heart was pounding. He didn't turn on any lights, over and above what he'd already turned on before going outside. He didn't want to draw attention to the small rectory behind the church.

The baby started crying again, its sound weak and sickly. Or was it? Sebastian knew little about babies. He'd blessed babies, he'd baptised babies and—on sad days—buried babies. Was the child hungry? What did one feed a newborn when there was no mother?

He took the baby across the hall to his room and turned on his nightstand light. He put the baby on the bed and opened the cloth. It was a shirt, not a blanket—and there was a lot of blood. He prayed without realizing the words were coming from his lips as he inspected the infant. The child didn't appear to be bleeding, though the umbilical cord was still attached. It had been tied off, but looked unusually large and swollen. Was this common?

He took a clean undershirt from his drawer and wrapped the baby. She was a girl, a perfect, small human child. So delicate, so fragile . . . who would just leave her on the cold ground? Did the blood come from her mother? The umbilical cord was tied, which meant someone had cut the cord, tied it as a doctor or nurse would. But this baby had no wrist or ankle band; this baby hadn't been born in a hospital. This baby had been born tonight, possibly only hours ago.

"Saint Elizabeth, please pray for this child laid at your feet tonight," Sebastian said as he picked up the baby. He held her close. He had never had a child, but the protective instincts must have been granted to all God's creatures, because Sebastian felt that he would do anything for this little soul. "Elizabeth," he whispered and rocked the baby stiffly in his arms.

Sebastian looked down on the bed. Tangled in the bloody shirt that the child had been wrapped in was a necklace of some sort. He picked it up.

A simple, oblong silver locket hung from a long chain. On the front was a cross, on the back an intricate design. It looked familiar, but Sebastian couldn't imagine where he'd seen it before.

He opened it. There were two pictures inside. On the right was a photo of two Hispanic girls who looked almost identical standing outside a small church that was unlike any he'd seen in the area; on the left one of the girls had her arm around a tall white girl wearing a wide-brimmed hat. They were in a field somewhere, but the details were lost in the miniature picture.

One of the photos was loose. As he tried to close the locket, it slipped in the catch, and then slipped when he opened it again. Something was written on the back. He searched for his reading glasses.

Ana, Siobhan, me.

Under the names was a phone number, but he couldn't make out all the numbers. They were faded. Maybe someone with better eyes could read them.

He picked up the phone to call 911. Then he saw that the shirt had writing on it, in the blood.

He spread the shirt out.

Trust no one.

He put the phone down.

CHAPTER ONE

The house on El Gato Street appeared empty, save for a lone beat-up van in the weed-choked driveway and a pickup truck parked on the dead lawn behind the house. Photojournalist Siobhan Walsh had been watching the place for two hours, taking photos and zooming in to analyze every detail. She'd seen *something* inside. Movement behind the thick drapes.

Patience was her strength, and she would sit in the neighbor's house as long as it took to get proof that her friends—two sisters who were practically family—were here.

Siobhan adjusted the zoom lens to focus on the van. Again. She'd already taken a series of pictures. The filthy Texas license plate was near impossible to read, but she used the technology built into her state-of-the-art camera to expose the numbers. She already had them memorized, but if she was right—and the van belonged to human traffickers—the number would lead nowhere.

She would follow up nonetheless.

Siobhan had good instincts, but there were times when she had to go against her gut in order to do the right thing. More often than not, she came out of such a situation not only unscathed, but with the result she wanted. Kane Rogan had once told her she was a cat on the last of nine lives. She scoffed. Some things were worth the risk. Of all people, Kane should understand.

Finding Marisol and Ana was *definitely* worth the risk.

It wasn't as if she were going to confront the bullies who were holding the young women; she needed evidence. Pictures. She would expose the bastards for the world to see, while giving law enforcement information they needed in order to do their job. She'd been burned in the past when she turned over unverifiable information to local cops. It took them too long to mount an investigation—they wouldn't act solely on her word that a crime had occurred. They wanted proof. By the time they had actionable evidence, the traffickers had moved out, taking the girls with them.

Or worse, the girls had been sold or killed.

Siobhan couldn't take the chance that this particular enterprise would shut down overnight, not when it was the closest she'd come to finding the sisters. She'd take photographs of every person and car coming and going from the house, then she'd walk away. She'd have to, no matter how hard it would be to leave.

Unless she saw them with her own eyes. Then she would call 911 and say anything to bring in the police.

I'm not the idiot you think I am, Kane Rogan.

Siobhan stood and stretched. Two hours and her joints were creaking from sitting still for so long. She rolled her neck and lamented that she couldn't break herself from the imaginary conversations she had with Kane. It had started years ago, almost from when she'd first met him, but the habit had grown worse since she'd left him in that hospital room three months ago.

I didn't leave you, Kane; you kicked me out.
Jerk.

She had contacts *other* than Kane Rogan. He wouldn't jump through hoops to help; he wouldn't think this was his problem. He didn't work cases in the United States; he much preferred the dark underbelly of Mexico where he didn't have to play at being a diplomat, where life was cheap, where he could kill a cartel leader and walk away unscathed. Kane Rogan was perfectly willing to save a kidnapped American being held for ransom by a two-bit cop in the middle of Nowhere, Mexico, but he'd damn well make sure you knew how stupid you were while he saved your ass.

Siobhan sat back down and looked again through her camera lens. She was losing light. In an hour it would be dark, and she wouldn't be able to see much of anything.

The small, broken-down houses were set far apart, most rented by migrant workers or longtime residents who couldn't afford much. No air-conditioning in the hot summers; faulty heat in the cold winters. Dismantled cars cluttered dirt yards; metal and other large items that most would call junk—most of it *was* junk, Siobhan thought— littered the area. Refrigerators with and without doors, some chained and bolted. But the house across the street was cleaner than the others; it was not in as sorry a state of disrepair.

There was activity every day—when Father Sebastian first talked to Mrs. Hernandez, she'd said there were many people coming and going, men and women of all races, many of them pregnant. If Father hadn't spoken at Mass about the baby left at the rectory, Mrs. Hernandez probably wouldn't have even approached him. But Siobhan convinced him to release the information. Mrs. Hernandez was the only one who stepped forward. The only one who was willing to help, even though Siobhan saw fear and guilt in the eyes of others.

Father Sebastian had wanted to come with Siobhan

tonight, but she wasn't going to risk an old priest with arthritis so severe he could barely stand upright.

Right now, this was her only lead other than the baby herself. Father had called her Elizabeth, and the nurses in Laredo had kept the name. Siobhan couldn't wait to return to the hospital and see her again. She'd promised Elizabeth that she would find her mother. There was no doubt in her mind that either Marisol or Ana had given birth to that small, beautiful child.

She stared out the window. Nothing had changed, except it had grown darker.

She needed something.

Please, God. Don't let me leave with nothing.

Mrs. Hernandez came into the bedroom where Siobhan was sitting in the semi-dark, waiting for someone to exit the house across the street.

"Enrique will be home soon," the woman said. "Please, you need to go."

Mrs. Hernandez had been nervous from the moment Father Sebastian had convinced her to let Siobhan in, and those nerves had steadily increased. But she'd been the one who called Father when the van arrived two hours ago. She wanted to help, but she was scared.

Siobhan had faced people like Mrs. Hernandez many times.

"Ten more minutes, *por favor.*" What would ten minutes do that the last two hours could not?

"No more, no more," Mrs. Hernandez said, a catch in her voice. She walked out.

Of course the woman was fearful—that's what these bastards did. They scared people into silence. Good people, who recognized evil, didn't want to face it down. They didn't want to be hurt. Close the doors, shut the blinds; if they couldn't see the bogeyman, the bogeyman couldn't see them.

A false and dangerous sense of security.

She'd already searched property records. The property across the street was owned by a business in San Antonio that was most surely a front. That would be her next step—tracing the business. Even if she found Marisol and Ana . . .

When. Even when you find them . . .

. . . she would track down these people and expose them. Her camera had never let her down.

Siobhan tried to put Mrs. Hernandez out of her mind and once again turned her attention across the road. There were no streetlights anywhere she could see; if she couldn't get a good photo of someone in the next thirty minutes, she'd have to leave even if Mrs. Hernandez didn't kick her out first. She could only do so much without a flash.

A car was coming down the broken street, headlights on in the dusk. At first Siobhan feared it was Mr. Hernandez, but the black Escalade pulled into the driveway across the roadway.

An Escalade certainly didn't fit into this neighborhood. The vehicle practically screamed *Illegal activity here!*

Siobhan zoomed in and clicked several photos of the license plate, then zoomed out and kept shooting as two people emerged from the Escalade: a man in the driver's seat and a woman in the passenger seat. The man looked like hired help: broad, physically fit, Caucasian, well dressed. Far too well dressed for this neighborhood. The woman was older, wore makeup and a sleek pantsuit. A glitter of jewelry caught Siobhan's eye, but she was too far away and the lighting too poor for her to make out much detail. The camera, however, would catch it all and she'd go through the images carefully. A black sedan drove up and stopped in front of the house. No one emerged.

The man and woman walked to the back of the house and disappeared from her view. Movement behind the upstairs window caught Siobhan's eye. She aimed her camera at the house and watched the scene through her telephoto lens: upstairs and downstairs and all around. She silently took pictures, her camera purring in her hands. She wasn't looking for an artistic shot, she wasn't framing an image or trying to capture the best lighting. But her skill was natural, born out of the love of film and years of experience, from the moment her father gave her a nearly indestructible point-and-shoot camera when she was five. Now her camera did most of the work. Four thousand dollars—between the camera and the lens she'd chosen for this stealth mission—was a lot of money, but it was worth it. The camera captured license plates. Profiles. Gestures. Clothing and shoes and jewelry and the way people parted their hair. Still, she'd inspect every detail later, because her eye could see things the soulless camera could not.

Then the front door opened. Two goons whom Siobhan suspected had come with the van earlier, before Mrs. Hernandez called, followed by the well-dressed man. The three of them stood on the brown grass, as if waiting.

The curtain moved again and caught Siobhan's eye. She was shooting before the camera focused. She caught a glimpse of a face, female, then it was gone and she prayed her camera had caught her image, that she could bring out the detail on her computer.

It could be Marisol or Ana. It could be . . .

Two of the men began to argue in front of the house, but Siobhan couldn't hear what they said—words lost in space, only the occasional angry curse coming through.

The door opened again and the well-dressed woman came out; this woman was not scared. She was in charge, an older, marginally attractive Hispanic woman with a sleek bun and round cheeks. The men avoided her gaze. She was admonishing them for something—perhaps the argument they were having in public. She raised her hand and another, much younger, woman came out. She was very young, rail-thin, and pale—nearly as pale as Siobhan—with short, dirty-blond hair. She carried a bundle in her arms—a bundle in a white blanket. Siobhan kept taking pictures, but she was distracted by the young girl who was clearly carrying a baby.

Her heart skipped a beat. This couldn't be Baby Elizabeth. She was safe in Laredo, an hour away. The nurse promised to call Siobhan if anyone came to claim the baby. One of the advantages of having a mother who'd been a nurse was that Siobhan knew the lingo, knew how to get them to help her.

Another baby? Mrs. Hernandez told Father Sebastian she'd seen "many" pregnant women; when pushed, she'd said she'd seen three or four different women, all pregnant. There was no sign that this was a sanctuary for single mothers who needed a helping hand.

Yet it could be.

You really believe that, Siobhan? That these people are helping pregnant women? You're not that *stupid.*

"Get out of my head, Kane," she muttered.

The blonde climbed into the Escalade with the two goons. The older woman walked to the sedan and the driver emerged, opened the rear door for her; she slipped in. The man she'd arrived with walked around to the passenger side, and almost immediately they drove off. A fourth man Siobhan hadn't seen before came out of the back of the house, opened the driver's door of the Escalade, and drove off with the goons, girl, and baby.

That left the beat-up van at the house, but six adults and the girl had left. There couldn't be anyone else inside, could there be?

Siobhan flipped rapidly back through the digital photos until she found the series she'd taken of the window. She vaguely heard a rattling truck on the road and glanced up, but didn't see anything. She focused again on her camera.

A woman's face was clear. She wasn't Marisol or Ana, but she could have been their cousin. Young, not more than twenty. Beautiful, with the same exquisite, almost exotic features. Whiter than most Mexicans, with thick silky hair and almond-shaped eyes. She was definitely from the same region as the de la Rosa sisters.

And she had been crying.

The bedroom door burst open again. "You must go. Now. Enrique is home. Now, now!"

Siobhan quickly packed up her equipment and put her backpack on her back. "Thank you."

"Go!"

A door opened and closed in the house.

Mrs. Hernandez put her hands to her mouth. She ran out and Siobhan followed. Maybe she could explain to Mr. Hernandez the importance of her work, that she was trying to help . . .

He stared at Siobhan, angry and worried, the same fear and worry that had been on his wife's face.

"Who is this?" the man said in rapid Spanish.

"No one," the woman said. "A friend of Father Sebastian's."

"You're lying to me." He glared at Siobhan. "Do you know what you do?" In rapid Spanish he said to his wife, "I told you not to say anything, do nothing!" He turned to Siobhan and in broken English said, "You take advantage, this old woman."

"No, señor, I'm leaving now. I'm sorry."

"And will you be here when they come for us in the night? When they shoot us in our sleep? When my wife cries as they hurt her? Where will you be? Where will God be?"

He was as scared as he was angry. Siobhan understood

him; she understood the fear that made good people look the other way.

Maybe Kane was right and she ran tilting at windmills, ignorant, getting herself and others in trouble; but if not her, who? If she didn't fight to help those who were abused and dying, what right did she have to call herself a daughter of God? Kane didn't believe; she didn't know if he ever had. But she did. She had a calling, she knew it as clear as day, and she would never turn her back on those who through no fault of their own were brutalized by evil people.

Siobhan said in Spanish, "God bless you both."

"Pray for us," Mrs. Hernandez said. "If they find out, we will be punished."

"Just go," Mr. Hernandez said, the veins in his neck enlarged from his barely controlled anger. "Go and never come back."

"You will be in my prayers every night," she whispered. She left through the back door.

They slammed it behind her.

CHAPTER TWO

Siobhan debated for five minutes what she should do—go back to the rectory, go back to Laredo, or help the girl in the window.

Okay, she debated for five seconds. She had to help. If she didn't, she'd never forgive herself if something bad happened. And the girl might know Marisol and Ana.

But Kane's training—wanted or not—kicked in. She needed a backup plan. After locking her bag in the trunk of her rental car, she called Father Sebastian.

"Our Lady of Sorrows, Father Sebastian Peña speaking."

"Father, it's Siobhan Walsh."

"My child, are you okay?"

"Yes. Mrs. Hernandez's husband came home, I had to leave. But I saw something at the house. I need to find out what's going on."

"I do not think that is a good idea."

"A young woman may be in danger. If you don't hear from me in an hour, I need you to call a friend of mine. He's in the FBI, I trust him. Do you have a pencil?"

"Siobhan, I don't think—"

"Please, Father, I need you to take down his name and number."

He sighed. "I have a pencil."

She gave him the private cell phone of Rick Stockton, then hung up before Father could argue with her anymore. Rick was one of the few people she trusted explicitly, and unlike Kane and RCK, he would always answer his private phone. He was dependable that way.

Why couldn't you have fallen in love with Rick? Loyal. Dependable. Brave. A decorated war veteran. As solid as they come.

But he wasn't Kane. It was as simple as that.

She locked her rental vehicle and walked back down the street, silently approaching the intersection. Flat, no sidewalk, few trees. In the heat of the summer, it would be unbearable, but now that it was nearly fall, the evening was comfortable.

No one was out tonight. Yellow lights behind closed blinds. Dogs barking in the distance. Chickens already hiding in their pens from four-legged predators.

There were no other cars at the house except the truck in the back. The goons had left, as well as the older woman and the well-dressed man. Plus the scared young girl with the infant. A mother and child?

The mother. Marisol and Ana were young—nineteen and eighteen now—and one of them had given birth, Siobhan knew it the moment Father Sebastian had called her three days ago. Her number, on the back of a photo in Mari's locket. Siobhan couldn't help but think that all the flyers, the interviews, the energy spent following leads that led nowhere for two years were a waste. That it was the locket Siobhan had given to Mari all those years ago that had led Siobhan to here and now.

The baby had been born three days ago, left at Our Lady of Sorrows. Father had taken her directly to the hospital, then contacted the police. He and his fellow priest, Father Peter, claimed they didn't know anything for certain, but

Siobhan suspected they didn't trust the local authorities. The hospital was in the adjoining county. Siobhan had tried to talk to the police, but they wouldn't give her anything, other than telling her it was an active investigation. She'd almost called Rick then, but knew what he'd say.

I can't send in agents unless I have something tangible. It's a local case.

He'd also tell her to be careful, and she was trying, but since she'd arrived yesterday she'd run against brick wall after brick wall. Father Sebastian was scared but determined to find the mother of the child he'd called Elizabeth, and this house—this woman—was her best lead.

Siobhan couldn't stand on the street too long; she didn't want anyone to notice her. Even though she'd stuffed her long curly red hair under a baseball cap and wore faded jeans and a black T-shirt, it was clear that she was a stranger.

She touched the old crucifix beneath her shirt. It had been her mother's; she'd wanted to bury her mother with it, but her father had said Iona wanted her to have it.

"She lives in your heart, she lives in your compassion and hope. Don't let her death lead to your despair."

Her mother should never have died; her mother was stubborn and strong and had the biggest heart in the world. Siobhan knew she'd been sick, and still she'd gone to the States because her mother had promised her father that when Siobhan was fourteen, she could choose. Siobhan chose high school in America. The chance to spend a few years with the father she barely knew, but loved with all her heart.

A year later her mother was dead.

Siobhan shook away the memories. Now wasn't the time or place.

She walked around to the back of the house, past the old truck that looked inoperable, sticking to the shadows as best she could, easier now that it was nearly full dark. All the windows were nailed shut from the outside, Siobhan noted. Dark curtains covered them. The two doors, front and back, had security screens that looked more like prison bars.

Father Sebastian was right—this mission was foolhardy at best and dangerous at worst—but that girl was in trouble. If there was any sign of another person inside, Siobhan would leave. But if it was just the girl, she had to try to help her.

Siobhan wasn't a novice in rescuing girls from the sex trade, but she wasn't as experienced as those who actually worked in the field. She was aware that some girls were so brainwashed that they would do nothing to help themselves and, in fact, might even resist a rescue. Some had been threatened with the lives of their families if they left their captors. Some were convinced that this was the only way of life. But Siobhan had to try. She had to do *something*, because doing *nothing* was not an option.

She walked almost entirely around the house, except for the side yard piled high with junk, metal pipes, and moldy furniture. She stood in the back and listened.

Silence.

Then she heard something. A faint sob? Maybe. Or was that wishful thinking?

Siobhan tried the back door; locked. She bit her lip and considered her options. She didn't know how long she had before the people returned; could be an hour, could be days. She didn't know if someone else was inside, other than the woman. But if she left to find help, whom would she ask? She didn't know any of the police here; they were in a small county, an hour from the border town of Laredo. Father Sebastian seemed to think there was corruption in the small sheriff's department but wouldn't discuss it with her. What about the deputy she'd spoken to in Laredo yesterday? He seemed aboveboard, though he hadn't shared anything with her.

For a split second Siobhan felt lost and depressed, the kind of lost she'd felt after her mother died, when she didn't know what she should do; when the simplest of decisions had seemed impossible. Where were these emotions coming from? Lack of sleep? Worry about Marisol and Ana? Frustration that Kane hadn't even once called her to say he was okay and out of the hospital and she had to hear it thirdhand from a mutual friend?

Stop it, Siobhan.

She couldn't do Mari or Ana any good if she didn't have the courage to do what was right. She refocused her attention on the house; the sights and sounds.

She saw no one, heard nothing. No cries, or voices, or movement.

Before she could change her mind, Siobhan pulled a lock pick out of her front pocket and worked on the screen. It was a new lock—odd, for this prewar house—and it took her a couple of minutes to get it open. The door was also locked, but that latch popped easily.

The door creaked as it swung open. She froze, listened. Heard a television somewhere—in a basement? It was low, a sporting event maybe, but she couldn't make out anything but mumbled dialogue. She closed the door behind her as quietly as she could.

To the left was a small, tired kitchen with an ancient sink and stove, and a refrigerator with rounded corners that looked like it was from the 1950s. The wallpaper had mostly peeled off revealing soot-stained walls. But the counters had been wiped down, and the dishes had been washed and stacked in a drying rack. A bowl of fresh fruit sat in the middle of the table, bright and colorful in the dingy house. The house smelled clean, both lemony and antiseptic, neither pleasant nor pungent.

To the right of the back door was a staircase. Straight ahead she could see the front door, with a room off each side she couldn't quite see through the wide openings. Two closed doors framed the hall.

The floor creaked when she stepped forward, and she winced. Waited. Didn't hear anything else, except the television. If the girl was still here, she was upstairs, so Siobhan turned up the staircase, trying to keep her heart from pounding so loud she couldn't hear what was around her. She kept her feet on the edge of the staircase to minimize sound.

Upstairs there was a small landing with doors to the left and right, and an open door straight ahead into a bathroom, with the same 1950s decor as the kitchen—chipped tile and rusty sink but smelled clean.

Cautious, she opened the door to the left and peeked in.

The room had a single bed neatly made with a worn, handmade quilt. An empty bassinet—clearly new in a room of old furniture—stood against one wall. Neatly folded towels were stacked on the dresser along with one package of newborn disposable diapers and three un-opened packages of white infant T-shirts. Two chairs crammed one corner, but the oddest thing was next to the bed in place of a nightstand—a medical tray with sealed, sterile medical instruments and a box of latex gloves.

Everything necessary for a midwife to help birth a child in the comfort of one's home. Siobhan had helped her mother, a nurse who worked with missionaries in Mexico, deliver more than a dozen babies. This setup was far nicer and cleaner than many of the villages Iona Walsh had been in.

Maybe there was nothing nefarious going on here. What if it was all a mistake? What if Siobhan was wrong, if Mrs. Hernandez was mistaken? What if Marisol had never been in this house?

But there *was* something odd going on. She *had* seen the woman crying in the window. Those men and that woman and the girl with the baby . . .

She left the door open and turned to the other door in the hall. A lock—on the outside. As quietly as possible, she slid the lock open and turned the knob.

This room was three times the size of the other, but there were eight beds set up dorm-style. Siobhan barely noticed the cramped quarters—or the fact that all the beds, except one, were empty. The room smelled clean, but it was an artificial clean, antiseptic, and very warm. A lazy fan blew in the corner. Back and forth. Back and forth.

There was a woman in here; she was sitting on the bed closest to the window. When the door opened, she whirled around, her hands going to her large stomach. She was pregnant.

"No!" she cried.

Siobhan put her hand to her mouth. "Shh!"

She wanted to ask where the other women were—it was clear from the folded clothes and blankets on each bed that other women lived here.

"I can help you," Siobhan whispered in Spanish.

The woman shrank away from Siobhan and spoke in Spanish, but a dialect that Siobhan didn't understand. She thought she heard the word *baby* but she wasn't positive.

"Let me help you," Siobhan whispered. "Is there anyone else in the house?"

She wasn't certain the young woman understood her. Siobhan had lived most of her childhood in Mexico and half of her adult life, and she could understand more dialects than she could speak, but she could usually make herself understood by sticking with the basics. Siobhan said clearly, "Come with me."

The woman wasn't a child—she looked to be in her early twenties. She stared at Siobhan with wild, fearful eyes. She looked healthy and clean, if a little thin. She was clearly more than halfway through her pregnancy, probably around seven months.

"My name is Siobhan, I work with the Sisters of Mercy. The sisters can save you and your baby."

The woman shook her head.

Siobhan took a few steps closer. "I'm a friend of Marisol and Ana. Do you know them?"

The woman scowled, eyes wide, pure rage on her face burying any fear that Siobhan thought she'd seen before. "Go away!" she hissed. "Go away!"

She stood, and that was when Siobhan heard a rattle and looked down.

The woman was shackled to the bed.

The chain appeared long enough for the woman to reach the bathroom. But the sight of the bindings surprised Siobhan.

"Let me untie you," Siobhan said.

"More problems! More trouble!" the woman cried out. At least that's what Siobhan *thought* she'd said. "Satan!"

That was clear.

Siobhan heard movement downstairs. Gut instinct had Siobhan fleeing as fast as she could—there was no way she could unchain and get the pregnant woman out, especially since she was so unwilling to be helped. If only Siobhan had more time!

She ran down the stairs, not caring about noise. She opened the door to the back just as a hall door she'd barely noticed before swung open. A tall, young man emerged and Siobhan didn't take the time to explain herself. She pushed open the back door and ran.

She had to run down the driveway to get back to the street and her car. She thought she'd make it, but the front door opened and the man ran after her. He was a teenager, she realized as he tackled her.

He slapped her and pinned her arms down. He might look young but he was as strong as a grown man.

Siobhan fought back and kicked him in the balls. He howled in pain. She scrambled up and started running again, but slower—her ankle was sore, maybe sprained, maybe just bruised, but she jogged as fast as she could.

A police car came around the corner and Siobhan immediately thought that Father Sebastian had called them, worried after her call to him. She ran up to the vehicle. "Officer!"

The deputy stopped his car and opened the door, car running. The teenager approached.

"Officer, there's a woman being held against her will in that house!" Siobhan said.

"Deputy Jackson," the teenager said, "this woman broke into my house."

"What's your name?" the cop asked her.

"Siobhan Walsh."

"You don't live in this neighborhood."

"No, I'm visiting a friend, and I saw a woman crying in the window. She's chained to a bed."

"How do you know that?"

"Deputy," Siobhan said, her worry returning. *Father told you he didn't trust the police.* "I know what I saw."

"Deputy Jackson, I don't know what she's talking about," the teen said. "My sister is upstairs. The house was locked, and I heard something and saw this woman running out the back. I don't know how she got in. She must have broken in. I've never seen her before."

"Ms. Walsh, please put your hands on the car."

This was all wrong. Dammit!

But she complied. The deputy had a gun; she did not.

"We had a call about someone lurking in the neighborhood," Jackson said. He frisked her, patting her breasts heavily. She wanted to hit him and fisted her hands, but resisted the urge to lash out.

He chuckled in her ear. "You like that, don't you?" he said and pinched her nipple.

"Touch me again and I *will* file a report against you."

He laughed out loud this time. "What's this?" He pulled her lock pick from her pocket. "I'm inclined to believe young Pete here." He took her wallet from her back pocket and flipped through it. "Siobhan Walsh from Chantilly, Virginia. You're a long way from Virginia, missy."

She didn't speak. She already knew what was going to happen, and was so glad she had locked her camera in her trunk.

He continued to flip through her wallet. Found some money, her credit card, her press credentials. He frowned. "Who do you work for?"

"I'm a freelance photographer."

"Where's your camera?"

"I didn't bring it with me."

"Stay here. If you move, I will arrest you."

He moved away—along with the teenager. They walked far enough off that Siobhan couldn't hear what they were saying, then Deputy Jackson got on his cell phone.

This was all wrong. Damn her red hair, she hadn't kept a low profile since she'd arrived. She'd been at Mass this morning when Father talked about the infant left at his door. Any number of people could have seen her; someone would eventually connect her with Father Sebastian. She itched to call him and tell him to be careful, but the deputy had taken her phone as well as her car keys.

What had she been thinking? Of course, Kane Rogan would have said she *wasn't* thinking, but what was she supposed to do, turn her back on someone who needed help? It wasn't in her nature.

A pregnant woman . . . and a baby carried by a young girl . . . what was going on? Most of the time when a girl in the sex trade got pregnant, they forced her to have an abortion.

Siobhan's stomach fell. What if these girls weren't forced to have abortions, because the babies were being sold? She didn't know much—okay, she knew next to nothing—about illegal adoptions, only that they existed.

But even that didn't make sense to her—there was money in illegal adoptions, but there was more money in human trafficking and the sex trade, with less risk.

Still . . . something was different about that house and these people. The location? Maybe . . . this wasn't an ideal place to house girls working in the business, voluntarily or not. It was in the middle of nowhere. A way station of sorts? Maybe . . . but why here where they'd stand out? Why not in downtown Laredo or a big city where they could blend in? Why in the middle of a poor, rural Texas community?

Jackson was talking to someone . . . and he kept glancing over at her. They wouldn't kill her, would they? She didn't think so . . . more likely they'd tell her to get out of town.

The conversation went on for several minutes, making her even more nervous. Finally, he hung up and walked over to her. "Ms. Walsh, you're under arrest for breaking and entering."

"I didn't!" Yes, she was lying, but they couldn't prove anything. Even the kid hadn't seen her *in* the house. Well . . . he did see her leaving. "I heard someone crying and I thought they were hurt. The door was open."

Shut up, Siobhan! Don't talk without a lawyer.

Amazing that everything she knew went out the window when she was stuck between a rock and a hard place.

"Put your hands on top of your head. Now, Ms. Walsh."

She didn't want to spend the night in jail, but it was after nine and there was no way they'd let her out if this was the route they were going. She would have to make the best of it. Jail was better than the morgue. They'd give her a call, right?

She slowly put her hands on her head. Deputy Jackson took one wrist and pulled it behind her back and cuffed it. He stood so close behind her that she could feel his breath on the back of her neck. She grimaced. "I'm just playing with you, missy, lighten up and enjoy it," he said.

He reached around the front of her shirt and squeezed her breasts again. She wasn't expecting it and swung out with her free arm, catching the deputy in the face with her elbow.

"Shit! Fuck!" he screamed. He pushed her to the ground and roughly cuffed her. Blood dripped from his nose. "We'll add resisting arrest and assault of a peace officer to the charges. You'll be doing some serious time, missy."

Siobhan closed her eyes. She was so screwed.

Okay, Kane, you were right this time.

I always am, sugar.

She heard Kane's voice as clear as day and glanced around to see if he was standing there.

He wasn't.

CHAPTER THREE

FBI SSA Noah Armstrong spent the first thirty minutes of their two-hour drive south talking on the phone to Zach Charles, the analyst for San Antonio's Violent Crimes Squad. Lucy tried not to eavesdrop, though it was difficult considering she was sitting in the passenger seat. Noah was going over active cases with the ease and confidence of someone who'd been running the squad for years instead of two months.

"Kincaid is with me," Noah said. "I sent Quiroz a message that I had to pull Lucy from the double homicide they've been working with SAPD. I've assigned Agent Cook to replace her." He listened to something Zach said, then continued. "If Agent Cook has an issue with the assignment, she can call me and discuss it." He hung up a moment later.

Lucy itched to discuss the case with Noah, but thought better of it. She'd barely spoken to Elizabeth Cook in the nine months she'd been in the San Antonio field office. The only thing Lucy knew about her was that she was divorced, had two daughters, and planned on retiring early at the end of next year at age forty-five, after putting in twenty years. Lucy'd never worked a case with her, and Cook rarely went out into the field. The Violent Crimes Squad handled a variety of crimes, but as their official name—Violent Crimes and Major Offenders—suggested, most of the cases dealt with physical crimes against people. Multi-jurisdictional homicides, kidnappings, special circumstances cases, and similar situations. They worked extensively with other law enforcement agencies to pool resources. Cook tended to assist more than investigate, and primarily from the office. While most agents abhorred desk work and writing reports, Cook preferred it.

Three months ago, the local DEA and the San Antonio PD—as well as the FBI to a lesser degree—had been decimated after a major corruption conspiracy was uncovered. Five DEA agents and two prison guards were murdered, an SAPD cop arrested for attempted murder and conspiracy, and FBI Agent Barry Crawford's injuries were so extensive he was still on disability and would likely never return to active duty. Juan Casilla, Lucy's boss, left on paternity leave after his wife nearly died in childbirth. Nita was still ill, and while he had a month more of official leave, the rumor was he would either be taking a sabbatical or resigning.

Noah Armstrong had come to San Antonio from Washington, DC, the first week of July as the acting SSA of Violent Crimes, but he was also here to liaise with other agencies as everyone had to clean house and rebuild. Lucy liked working with Noah, who'd been her first training agent last year before she'd entered the FBI academy. They'd become friends and Lucy greatly respected him. But in the ten weeks he'd been here, they hadn't worked together on a case. Though she didn't like passing off her current case to another agent, she was glad he wanted her help on this new case in Laredo.

"Ask," Noah said.

"Excuse me?"

"You're biting the inside of the your cheek, which tells me you want to say something. But I won't discuss personnel issues."

"It wasn't that." Well, yes, in part it was, but she'd never have asked about Elizabeth Cook and why she didn't work in the field—or why Juan went along with it. "You haven't told me why we're going to Laredo."

"I'm sorry, I assumed you knew." Noah passed a slower driver and maintained his speed. It was still early, the sun barely up, and Lucy wanted more coffee.

"I'm good at my job, but I'm not psychic."

He glanced at her with a half smile on his face. "You sure about that?"

"Pretty sure."

"I got a call from Rick Stockton late last night. A photojournalist, Siobhan Walsh, was arrested and is being held in Freer, about an hour from Laredo. He hasn't been able to get any information out of the locals, and he wasn't allowed to speak to Walsh. I assumed you knew because Rick said Walsh is tight with the Rogans."

"I know of her, I've never met her."

"There's more going on than a simple arrest. Rick was alerted to Walsh's disappearance by a local priest who said she'd given him Rick's number in case she didn't return from taking photos—at least that was Rick's understanding. Though the priest didn't seem to trust Rick and didn't want to give too many details over the phone, Siobhan's arrest may be related to a newborn baby who was left at the church last week."

A baby? "Why wasn't the FBI brought in earlier?"

"Rick did some research and learned that early Thursday morning, a baby was left at the door of Our Lady of Sorrows, a rural parish between San Antonio and Laredo. The two priests at the parish didn't call police, but drove the infant to a hospital in Laredo—in another county.

The infant is being kept there while the police and Child Protective Services conduct their investigation."

"Is this a Baby Moses case?" Different states called their laws different things, but *Baby Moses* in Texas meant that mothers could leave their infants at designated safe places without reprisal.

"No—the church isn't a safe haven. There's been some jurisdictional issues—the local police want to investigate because the baby was left in their jurisdiction, but the Webb County sheriff's department is also investigating because the hospital is in their jurisdiction. Our office wasn't notified or called."

"What does this have to do with Siobhan Walsh and her arrest?"

"I don't know yet. Once we have Walsh in our custody, we'll find out if her arrest connects to the infant. She'll have more answers, at any rate." Noah glanced at her, then sped up to pass another driver. "Rick wants the FBI to work this case, which is why he didn't call RCK to get Walsh out. But I sensed he was torn."

"Rick isn't someone torn over difficult decisions."

"You're right, so I want to get him answers today. I need someone who speaks fluent Spanish, which means you, Emilio, or Ryan. But you're the only female on the squad who's fluent, and we don't know exactly what we're dealing with."

He didn't need to explain that some victims much preferred talking with female agents, and Lucy was well trained in working with victims of sexual assault.

"If a woman left her baby at a church, she could have feared for her life and her baby," Lucy said. "Perhaps trying to protect the baby from its father."

"I was thinking something along those lines. Rick didn't ask me to bring you along, but he implied you'd be the most helpful."

"I appreciate his faith in me."

"It's not faith, Lucy. You earned it."

She didn't say anything.

"What?"

"Nothing."

"Hardly."

She didn't want to talk about her place in the office, how awkward it had been over the last three months. She just wanted to do her job and do it well. When she'd first arrived in San Antonio, she felt like she fit in. She'd made friends on her squad, closed tough cases, and had immersed herself in the city.

She'd grown to love San Antonio and to think of it as her home. She and Sean had settled into their house, and while Sean hadn't taken a regular job, he had enough freelance security assignments to keep him busy. And now they were planning their wedding . . . or, rather, Sean was planning it. He seemed to enjoy it, so she let him do most of the work—within reason. She didn't want anything fancy or big, though considering they each had a large family, she couldn't do much about the size of the wedding.

But now . . . nine months after moving here . . . she felt like she'd lost something. She knew why. People didn't trust her. Not because they thought she was corrupt, but because they thought she was a magnet for trouble. Maybe she was. Trouble seemed to follow her. Maybe she went looking for it. Some people believed so.

She'd made mistakes—at least in the eyes of others. And on the nights she couldn't sleep, she considered other ways she might have been able to do things. There were always options. But in the end, she had to accept that she'd broken rules—and perhaps, made mistakes—because someone was in trouble. She couldn't sit back and watch a tragedy happen if she could stop it, even if that meant bending—or breaking—the rules.

It had taken her a long time to get to this point. She believed in the system, she believed in justice. But what happened when the system and justice didn't align? Which was more important? The system that upheld justice but sometimes faltered or the idea that justice could always be obtained, though sometimes at a price?

"You've never walked an easy road," Noah said after a minute. "I think you know that."

"I do."

They drove in silence awhile longer, but it was a comfortable silence. Noah said, "I received your wedding invitation over the weekend."

"I hope you're still in town at the end of October."

"Not sure, but if not I'll fly out. You deserve to be happy. You and Sean have made yourselves a nice life here."

"We like it. I love my family, but this is the first time I've felt like I'm truly on my own."

"I was an only child. I've always felt like I was on my own."

He sounded a bit sad about it, but before Lucy could ask questions, his phone vibrated. He answered. "We're almost in Freer," Noah said. "Ten minutes or so." He listened. "That's serious. How—" He stopped talking, listened, then said, "I'll talk to the priest first. But don't you think—" He stopped again. "I understand. Can you send her file to Lucy? Thanks." He hung up. "That was Rick."

"You sound concerned."

"Rick didn't wait for us—truthfully, I wish he'd have let me handle this situation in person. Apparently he and Walsh have been friends for a long time." He hesitated, as if he was going to say something else, then cleared his throat and said, "Anyway, he spoke to the sheriff after getting the runaround. Walsh was arrested for breaking and entering, assault on a peace officer, and resisting arrest. She'll be arraigned at ten this morning." It was just after eight now. "Rick tried to speak with her, but the sheriff said no, she had a public defender and would be allowed to make a call after her arraignment."

"You sound—irritated."

"Over and above that Rick just tipped our hand? He's smarter than that." Noah typed the address for Our Lady of Sorrows into his GPS. The computer shifted their route and gave them eighteen minutes to destination. "Rick wants to know what Walsh and the priest were doing last night—before she's arraigned. I suspect he's going to try to get the charges thrown out, though how he can do that I have no idea. Rick's sending you information on Walsh."

Lucy pulled out her phone. Rick's email had just come through. She opened and scanned the file, giving Noah the highlights. "Siobhan Walsh, born in Chantilly, Virginia, to a US Marine Lieutenant Colonel Andrew Walsh and Iona O'Malley, of Galway, Ireland. Has a half brother, deceased, killed in action in Afghanistan. A half sister, Andrea Walsh, stationed at Quantico." That named sounded familiar to Lucy, but she didn't remember why. "Thirty-four, carries dual citizenship. US and Ireland." She glanced up. "That's unusual."

"Her mother was an Irish citizen."

She looked back at her phone. "Siobhan has an active US passport, most recently came in through San Antonio from Mexico City on Friday morning. She's a freelance photojournalist, has sold photos to it appears every major newspaper and television network. Won several awards."

"Rick said she was a big deal in that world, but focuses on missionary work."

"She has an affiliation with the Sisters of Mercy, a group of religious social workers based outside Monterrey, Mexico, who primarily do missionary work in southern Mexico and Central America. Some dangerous areas, it seems." Lucy scanned. "Most recently she had a series of articles in the *New York Times* Sunday edition about a village in Guatemala that the charity helped rebuild after an earthquake caused a mudslide that cut off the only road. Oh."

"Oh, what?"

"She has a record—she's been arrested twice for assaulting a law enforcement officer. Once in DC and once in Los Angeles. No details here. She was arrested for trespassing multiple times in three different states, got time served. In the last twelve months, she's only been in the States for seven weeks. Her permanent address is in Chantilly, Virginia, in a house she co-owns with her half sister."

Lucy put her phone down. "Siobhan grew up mostly in Mexico with her mother, who was a missionary for the Sisters of Mercy. She was a nurse, though there's nothing that says she was also a nun—which is doubtful since she was married." She paused. "Actually—there's nothing in here that says her parents were married. That's probably irrelevant. Anyway, when Siobhan was fourteen she moved to the States to go to school and live with her father, and a year later her mother died. No cause stated. That must have been so hard for her."

"When did she return to Mexico?"

"It doesn't say—she attended the University of Virginia for a year, then a school in Ireland for two years. She seems to do a lot of fund-raising work for the Sisters of Mercy, which originally started as a missionary group from Ireland that worked in several countries, but as their numbers shrank, they're only active in Mexico."

Noah glanced at his GPS and turned off the highway. Almost immediately the roads became bumpy. He slowed down. "Let's see what the priest has to say and then make sure we're at the courthouse before ten."

Morning Mass had just ended when Noah and Lucy arrived at Our Lady of Sorrows. A young priest was in the vestibule, but according to the diocese website Father Peña was seventy-one.

They approached the priest and introduced themselves after the small group of parishoners left.

"You're looking for Father Peña," the priest said. "I'm Father Peter Mannion." He motioned for them to follow him to the rectory behind the church. "Father Peña has been very concerned about the infant left here, but his actions—well, I don't think he's thought things through. He's one of most honest, sincere priests I have met, and I fear he's letting his emotions cloud his judgment."

"How so?" Noah asked.

"I have faith that the authorities can handle the situation," Father Peter said. "This is a poor church in a poor parish. Father is retired, he's moving in January. I think he's holding on a bit tightly."

"How long has he been the parish priest here?" Lucy asked.

"Thirty-some years. His insight into the community has been valuable." He stopped walking and gestured to a statue of Saint Elizabeth. "This is where the infant was left. Poor child. The doctor told us that she was less than a day old."

"Why did you take her to the hospital directly instead of contacting the authorities?" Noah asked.

"Father Peña insisted—I asked why, he said he felt the child would be safer in Laredo at the children's hospital there. That they could care for her needs better than our small county hospital."

Reasonable, but there could be something more—

especially since Father Peña had been in the community for so many years.

Peter led them up the stairs and opened the door. "May I get you anything?"

"No, thank you, we can't stay long. We need to talk to Father Peña about Siobhan Walsh and what he can tell us about why she's here."

Father Peter opened his mouth, then closed it when he saw Father Peña enter the room.

"Sebastian, these people are from the FBI. Agents Armstrong and Kincaid."

"Armstrong," Sebastian said. "Yes, the gentleman I spoke with said you would be coming down. Please, let's sit."

"I need to return to the church and take care of a few things," Peter said. He left, and Sebastian sighed and rubbed his eyes, but didn't say anything.

"Is Siobhan okay?"

"She's being arraigned this morning," Noah said. "We need information, Father."

"What would you like to know?"

"First, how do you and Ms. Walsh know each other?"

"Do you know about the infant?"

"Yes," Noah said. "You found her early Thursday morning."

Father nodded. "So small, so innocent. She was wrapped in a bloody shirt, not her blood. She didn't have a mark on her . . ." His voice faded. "I gave everything to the hospital. Including the locket and the note."

"A note?"

"*Trust no one*," he quoted. "It was in blood, on the shirt she was wrapped in. And the locket was a picture of three girls—a woman, Siobhan, and two younger girls. The photo was old. But the back—it had Siobhan's name and her number. It took me getting a magnifying glass before I could read the phone number. That's how I knew to call her. But Father Peter insisted that I turn everything over to the hospital, and they gave everything to the police, I believe."

"The police in Laredo?"

He nodded. "I've tried to get more information—and Siobhan tried all day Saturday—but there isn't anything to get, I suppose."

Noah said, "You were with Ms. Walsh last night?"

"No—she came to Mass yesterday morning, asked that I talk to the parishioners about the infant. One parishioner, Mrs. Hernandez, told me about several young women, all pregnant, living in a house across the street from her. I thought perhaps one was the mother of Elizabeth—"

"Elizabeth?" Noah asked.

"I—I called the infant Elizabeth. She was left under the statue of Saint Elizabeth, and it seemed fitting. No child should be born without a name. The locket had been left with the baby. Wait a moment." He rose, left the room, and came back a few minutes later. "Siobhan gave me this flyer. She'd sent it to many churches in Texas, New Mexico, and south of the border. I hadn't seen it, but this is the locket that was with the baby, and the photo that was inside."

Lucy looked at the flyer. A photo of two young girls with a tall, curly redhead that had to be Siobhan was at the top; at the bottom was a photo of a locket with a Celtic cross.

MISSING GIRLS
Marisol & Ana de la Rosa
Now 18 and 17
Disappeared after work from Monterrey, Mexico
Possibly in southern or western Texas
Marisol is fluent in Spanish, English, and French; she has an oblong birthmark on her right forearm. She's approximately five foot four, with black hair and hazel eyes.

Ana is deaf in her right ear. She is approximately five foot five, black hair and hazel eyes.

Both girls are devout Catholics and if in trouble, may seek help from a church, priest, or nun. Both girls wear a unique sterling-silver locket with a Celtic trinity circle on one side and a cross on the other. Inside the locket is this photo plus a photo of their parents, who died in a mudslide six years ago. They went to work in Monterrey to earn money to help rebuild the village and disappeared seven months later.

Call Siobhan Walsh, Sisters of Mercy, with any information. Can remain anonymous. $1,000 reward for verified information.

"You called Ms. Walsh because of the number on the back of the photo in the locket and she came?"

"Yes, I called her late Thursday, after we returned from the hospital, and she was here Friday night. I met her at the hospital; she wanted to see the baby. She is staying in Laredo, but has been here each day. Yesterday I told Siobhan about what Mrs. Hernandez said, and she went to talk to her."

"You didn't go?"

"She said she wanted to do it alone. She called, said if she didn't call me again after an hour, for me to call Mr. Stockton and gave me a number."

Noah was taking notes. "Just to make sure I understand correctly: You found the baby early Thursday morning. You took the baby to the hospital in Laredo, which is nearly an hour away. Then you returned, contacted Siobhan Walsh because of the number on the locket. She came immediately."

"Yes. These girls"—he tapped the flyer—"Marisol and Ana. They are her friends, she's very concerned about them. No one has heard from them in over two years.

Siobhan said this is her best lead. That one of these girls left the baby, the locket, her number."

"So you don't have any pregnant women in the parish who may have left the baby?"

He shook his head sadly. "This is a small, old parish. There's a new community being built in town, and we're getting younger families, but most of my parishioners are older. We have one girl who's pregnant, but she is a longtime parishioner. I baptized her, married her ten years ago, this is her second baby. I know her, her husband, her parents, his parents—and as far as I know, she hasn't had the baby. She told me she's due in November, wanted to make sure I would still be here to baptize the child."

He sighed. "That will likely be my last. I move to Tucson, to retire, in January."

Noah stood. "Thank you for your time. I appreciate your help, and we may call with additional questions."

"Anything I can do to help, Agent Armstrong, anything."

Lucy and Noah left.

"Thoughts?" Noah asked.

Lucy had many, but they were still forming. "We should talk to the doctor, the police in Laredo, find out what they know."

"Agreed. Let's find out what Ms. Walsh has to tell us and see if we can keep her out of jail."

CHAPTER FOUR

This wasn't the first time Siobhan had spent a night behind bars. It could have been much worse—like the time she'd been "detained" in Chiapas. Or when she'd been arrested for trespassing in Brazil . . . though the guards there had been extremely polite. But she'd hardly slept last night out of worry and frustration. Worry about that young woman in the house . . . worry about Marisol and Ana and the baby. Frustration about, well, *everything*. She didn't trust the police in this small town, so she kept her mouth shut and waited for her arraignment. They'd assigned her a public defender, whom she also didn't trust—not because she thought he was working for whatever organization had been keeping those women, but because he didn't even look old enough to be out of high school, let alone possess a law degree.

They would arraign her, she'd post bail (though she was loath to call her sister, she didn't have enough money in her pitiful savings account), and then she'd deal with the fallout. She might be prevented from leaving the country until the charges were dropped or she paid a fine, but at this point she believed that Marisol and Ana were in the

United States and she didn't plan on going anywhere until she found them.

She just wished she had more information. Why had one of them—or both of them—left the baby? Where were they now? Why did they leave her phone number with the priest instead of calling her themselves?

I wrote the number. Years ago . . . maybe they didn't even remember it was there.

The only way she'd find answers was to find the girls.

The guard came in. Siobhan jumped. There was only one other person in the four-cell jail, and he was sleeping off a night of heavy drinking.

The guard unlocked her cell. "Please come with me, Ms. Walsh."

Siobhan was suspicious.

Thank you, Kane Rogan, for making me always think the worst of everyone.

She shook it off and complied with the guard.

"Isn't it too early for the arraignment?" she asked. "They told me ten a.m. I haven't spoken to my lawyer since last night. Don't I—"

"You're being released, Ms. Walsh. We need to return your belongings and log you out."

"Released?"

"The charges have been dropped."

"Dropped?"

The guard almost smiled. "Did you want to stay with us?"

"No, no, but—" She bit her lip and stopped talking. Something weird was going on . . . Rick! Father Sebastian must have talked to Rick. That man could move heaven and earth if he wanted. She owed him big.

The guard didn't cuff her, which was a relief. They went down a short hallway to a locked room. The guard walked around to the other side of the desk, unlocked the bottom drawer, and took out an envelope with her things. There wasn't much because she'd only had her wallet on her. Everything else was in the trunk of the rental car, and she hoped that it hadn't been towed. Everything seemed in order—her US passport, her Virginia driver's license, her international driver's license, a little over one hundred dollars in cash, her credit card, her hotel card key in Laredo, the key ring with the rental car key.

And her locket. The same locket that Mari and Ana had.

Siobhan put the locket on, though she hadn't worn it in years. She'd bought three matching lockets, each with a Celtic cross, nearly ten years ago when she was visiting her grandmother in Galway. She'd given them to Mari and Ana as presents, and given the third to their mother, Tilda. Tilda had been young when she had the girls, marrying at the age of fifteen. Siobhan was two years younger. She'd helped deliver Ana, the younger sister.

Tilda and Jesus had died in a mudslide. Siobhan hadn't gone on the last annual pilgrimage to their village with the Sisters of Mercy . . . she'd been busy, too busy she'd convinced herself, even though these were the same people who had cared for her mother when she was ill. Siobhan had loved Tilda like a sister, but she'd been so excited about new assignments—taking jobs from others rather than going where she wanted.

And then the mudslide. The population of the village— unnamed on any map—went from 110 to 67 after that horrific tragedy. The villagers called their home Vala Vida, which loosely translated to "Valley of Life" because it was located between two rivers, one of which flowed year-round. It was near nothing; the closest town—of less than five hundred—was Ayotuxtla, which was half a day's walk because of the rough terrain.

Siobhan hadn't visited, always thinking there would be more time. And then they were gone.

"If everything is in order, please sign here . . . and here."
He pointed on the form attached to a clipboard.

She signed and put all her things back into her wallet
and her wallet into her back pocket. "Thank you," she said.
Why was she thanking the guard? Well, he *had* been kind
to her. Unlike the deputy who'd arrested her.

"Come with me, Ms. Walsh."

"Can't I just leave?"

"There are two federal agents who want to speak with
you."

That was the last thing she expected. Sure, Rick could
make calls and get things done, but send two agents
for her? Her heart skipped a beat. What if he'd called
Andie and these agents were assigned to take her back
to Virginia? Andie had told her the last time she was
arrested—again, not her fault—that if it happened again,
she was grounded.

As if Andie could ground a thirty-four-year-old woman.

Siobhan never wanted her sister to worry. Andie already
had a difficult job, and she had been heartbroken when
their brother was killed in action ten years ago. Then losing their dad . . . Andie's mother had died when Andie was
five, and she'd been twelve when Siobhan was born. Now
they were all they had left by way of family. Siobhan had
her elderly grandmother in Galway whom she visited at
least once a year, but she was all Andie had.

But . . . Siobhan wasn't going back to Virginia. She had
to find Ana and Mari; she was so close! Closer than she'd
been since they disappeared. Andie *had* to understand. She
would. Andie might complain and worry, but she would
understand better than anyone.

Resolved to talk her way out of this—after all, unless
they arrested her, she didn't have to go with the feds—she
went with the guard to the lobby.

The feds were quite obviously FBI agents—the male

was probably close to forty with conservative-cut sandy-blond hair. He wore a light-gray suit and stood like he'd served in the military. Maybe it was just that he had that military *look* that Siobhan knew all too well. The woman was younger, maybe thirty or so, with her black hair pulled back. Siobhan assessed her features. She'd traveled extensively in the Western Hemisphere, she could generally discern where someone was from. She was Cuban, maybe—at least a quarter, but probably half Cuban.

"Agent Armstrong," the guard said.

The man approached and thanked the guard. He extended his hand to Siobhan. "I'm Supervisory Special Agent Noah Armstrong. This is Special Agent Lucy Kincaid. You're free to go, Ms. Walsh, but we'd like to talk to you first."

"Sean's Lucy?" Siobhan asked. She smiled broadly and hugged the woman. Lucy didn't hug her back—a little aloof—and she seemed surprised. Siobhan couldn't help herself—she'd always been a touchy person. "Wow! I'm so glad to finally meet you. Sean told me he was getting married, but that was after that whole thing with Kane down in Santiago—I didn't have an opportunity to come up for a visit."

"Nice to meet you," Lucy said, a bit on the formal side. She was pretty, a bit standoffish. Reserved, Andie would say. In fact, she was a lot like Andie. No wonder Kane had so much respect for her. "I've seen your work—it's amazing."

"Thank you, I appreciate that." They walked out of the police station and to a sedan. Noah opened the rear passenger door for Siobhan. She said, "I'm so sorry about all this. I really didn't think I would run into a problem. I didn't mean for Rick to send two agents to get me out."

"That's not the only reason," Noah said and closed the door.

What did that mean?

As they drove away, Siobhan said, "I'm not going to Virginia."

"Okay."

"Okay?"

"We need to talk about what you discovered, and how it connects to the abandoned infant."

"Oh. Well. I don't know yet, I'm still working that out, but when we get my camera—do you think I could trouble you to take me to my rental car? I parked a few blocks from where I was arrested. I hope they didn't tow it. I mean, I didn't rent the best car on the lot, I wanted something to blend in, but I still have to pay for damages."

"Tell me where," Noah said.

Siobhan rattled off the intersection, and the fed typed it into his GPS.

"We spoke with Father Sebastian. He told us your theory."

"Well, such as it is. I'm close. I know it. The locket." She reached up and touched the locket that had been Tilda's. "Neither of the girls would have just gotten rid of it. If Elizabeth isn't the daughter of one of them, her mother knew the sisters." She looked at her watch, then just spilled everything she knew. This was *Sean's* Lucy Kincaid, and Siobhan trusted the Rogans. Siobhan needed help—help, not replacement—and hopefully Lucy would let her stay involved.

"Mari and Ana have been missing for two years," Siobhan said. "They each had an identical locket—one of which Father Sebastian found on Baby Elizabeth—that I had given them." She pulled her locket from under her shirt. "This one belonged to their mother, Tilda, who was my friend. She died . . ." She shook her head to clear it. She still regretted so much . . . she should have been there,

helping before the mudslide. She should have said good-
bye to Tilda. And then she was gone.

"Eight months ago," Siobhan continued, "it was early
February, I think, though I can check my notes, one of my
reporter friends did an undercover exposé on a brothel in
Del Rio. Most of the girls he spoke with were underage,
most illegal immigrants, most hadn't been trafficked but
didn't see any other way to earn a living. However, one
of them gave my friend a story about six girls who'd
stayed at the brothel for three days. This was a year ago
last June. They closed the place—why would they do
that? And the regular girls were paid to stay away. What
brothels that use underage girls pay them for a vacation?
The girl recognized the photo of Marisol, but more
than that—she said that Mari spoke French. Mari has a
knack for languages—Spanish is her native language,
but she speaks and understands multiple dialects, speaks
near-perfect English, French, and was learning to read
French before the mudslide." Siobhan shook her head. I
know it was her. But after those three days, the six girls
disappeared and no one seems to know what happened
to them.

"Anyway, I've been looking for them for two years,
but couldn't do much until I got that lead. The number
on the locket is my cell phone—I don't give it out to
many people, and the village didn't even have electricity,
but I wanted to make sure if there was an emergency
that they could reach me." It felt like a lifetime ago. "I'd
sent out flyers, I'd called, I made sure I was always ac-
cessible. I know Mari and Ana as if they were my own
sisters . . . they would escape if they could. They'd find
a church. They don't trust the authorities—their village
is in the middle of nowhere, but the few run-ins they had
weren't pleasant."

"What happened to them? Were they kidnapped?" Lucy asked.

"I don't know. Six years ago, there was a mudslide. Nearly half the people in their village were killed, including their parents. Tilda was one of my friends, and I didn't even know about the disaster for weeks because I was on assignment in Chile. By the time I got there . . ." It had been awful.

They were still recovering bodies. The Sisters of Mercy had come to help with the cleanup and burial, but there was so much work to do, and so much sorrow. And there were no young sisters, not anymore. Siobhan shook her head, clearing her thoughts. "We started rebuilding, but donations are difficult these days. One of the sisters heard about a business hiring bilingual employees, and she helped Mari get the job in Monterrey. Ana went with her, safety in numbers, and she worked for the same company. They were vetted, I talked to the owner—he was upset when they went missing. Distraught—I don't think he was faking." She knew he wasn't faking, because she'd called in Kane—Kane had talked to him. Kane said their employer had nothing to do with their disappearance. How he was so certain, she didn't know . . . but she trusted him.

"I'm certain their roommates know something, but I couldn't get anything out of them." Neither could Kane, and he was far more intimidating than Siobhan. But Kane tracked them until they disappeared—dead or in hiding, he couldn't say, but he'd spent a lot of time helping her. "Now they're gone, too."

"Did you run it through RCK?" Noah asked.

"You know of . . . of course you do. You know Rick and Kane and Sean. No one filed a missing persons report on the roommates, but things are handled a little less . . . formally, you could say, down south."

"Do you think someone misled the girls? Maybe enticed them with more money, and then tricked them?"

"Not Mari," Siobhan said. "She was too smart to fall for anything like that. And she wanted to go home. The job was supposed to be for two years. She was translating for the company to help them gain more business in the US. They manufactured children's toys. Wooden puzzles, mostly. Ana . . . maybe. She was sweet. Mari wanted to go home, Ana might have been a bit more excited about Monterrey." Siobhan hesitated. "I'm the one who took them from their village, traveled with them, got them to Monterrey. The job. And left them there. I should have checked up on them more often, made sure they were okay."

"They could call you, right?"

She nodded. "They knew that."

"Then stop blaming yourself," Lucy said.

Siobhan sighed. "I'm not." But she was.

She leaned forward as they rounded the corner and she saw the rental car. "Thank God," she said and crossed herself out of habit. "It's still here."

Noah parked behind it and Siobhan got out. So did Noah and Lucy. "I want to show you the house. I know, you can't go in, but you should still see—" She opened the trunk and frowned. Her camera case was on the right side of the trunk and she was positive she'd put it on the the left side, like she always did.

She opened up the case and checked her camera. It was gone. "Well, dammit."

"What happened?" Noah asked.

"Someone took my SD card."

"Are you certain?"

"Of course. I locked my camera in the trunk; the camera is here, the memory card is gone."

Lucy raised an eyebrow. "You don't sound all that upset that you lost all your pictures."

"I didn't *lose* anything. They save automatically to the cloud through a phone app that your brilliant fiancé set up for me ages ago. But that SD card was the best I had, costs two hundred bucks a pop."

Siobhan was even angrier that someone had gone through her things. She glanced through her satchel and backpack—nothing else appeared to be missing. She'd left her laptop in the hotel safe. It was a bold move to grab her SD card—could they have also taken her hotel card key and gotten into her room? Maybe . . . though they wouldn't know what room she was in.

"Are you certain you didn't misplace the card or drop it?" Noah asked.

"Of course I'm certain," she snapped. She rubbed her eyes. "I'm sorry, I didn't mean to get snippy with you. I know, you can't prove that deputy came here and stole my SD card. I just *know* that he did. Or he gave my key to someone else. No one broke in, and the car and trunk were locked."

"Wasn't the evidence bag sealed with your belongings?" Lucy asked.

"Yes, but they didn't have me sign it or anything. They could have put everything back in a new envelope. I just verified nothing was missing." She glanced at Noah. "I need to go back to the house."

"Since they let you go so quickly, I suspect they already cleaned out the place."

"There'll be something! You can do forensics and stuff, right? Get fingerprints?"

"We'd need a warrant."

"Okay."

"It's not going to be that easy to get," Noah said.

"But I saw a pregnant woman in that house with her ankle chained to the bed! Locks on the outside of the doors!" Were all cops like this? So rigid about rules? Someone was in trouble. A pregnant woman was in danger. Why didn't that trump everything else?

"And you illegally entered the house."

"I saw her in the window and she looked to be under duress." That was all truth. She'd swear to it on a Bible.

"It might fly, but it's not going to be a slam dunk."

Lucy said, "Would it hurt to stop by and see if we can talk our way inside?"

Siobhan looked at Noah. "Please?"

Noah nodded, but he didn't look happy about it. They all got back into Noah's car, and Siobhan directed him the three blocks to the house.

"I'd like to see the pictures you took as soon as possible," Noah said. "We can run the images through the federal database and possibly ID one or more of the individuals involved. If there's an arrest warrant, that'll help me get a search warrant."

"I can download them to my phone or on my laptop. I just need to see if that young woman is okay. She was upset, angry with me, angry—" Siobhan paused.

"Did she say something?" Lucy prompted.

"Her Spanish was street-level, very lowbrow, I guess you'd say. Slang. I didn't really understand her, and that's unusual because I know Spanish better than most gringos. I mentioned Marisol and Ana, hoping to forge a connection with her, and that's when she started shouting. She called me Satan. I thought she said *more trouble*, but I could be mistaken."

"She didn't want your help," Noah said flatly as he parked directly in front of the house.

"Girls like her are brainwashed. Her family could have been threatened. She was scared—yes, angry, but also very scared. I've met girls like her. She needs our help, even if she thinks that being bought and sold like cattle is normal."

Who was this guy and why had Rick sent him? Siobhan

didn't think she should have to explain this to a federal agent.

Lucy put a hand on Noah's forearm, and Siobhan could practically see them speaking telepathically. They must have been partners for years to be able to just know each other that well.

Lucy turned to face Siobhan in the backseat. "Stay here."

"But—"

Lucy repeated, "Stay. We're going to check it out, but we don't know what we're facing, and you don't want to get out of this car. Understood?"

"Fine."

Siobhan watched from the rear window. The truck that had been parked in the back was gone. Noah knocked on the door. There was no answer. He and Lucy walked around the house, then returned several minutes later and got back into the car.

"No one's home."

"Maybe they're just not answering."

"We have no cause to enter. All the doors are locked. There is no vehicle in the driveway."

"Mrs. Hernandez will know. She's home. I saw her looking through her blinds. She's not going to talk to you, you're cops. She'll tell me."

Noah glanced at Lucy. Again, the unspoken communication.

Lucy said, "I'll go with you. It's not up for discussion."

"You sound like Kane," Siobhan snapped and got out of the car.

Lucy followed her to the house kitty-corner from their location. "Was that an insult or a compliment?" Lucy asked her.

"Both," Siobhan said. She knocked on Mrs. Hernandez's door. No one answered. She knocked again. "Dolores, I know you're in there, I saw you. Please, I need your help. I need to know what happened to the woman across the street."

It took a long minute, but the door opened. Dolores Hernandez didn't unlock the screen. "They're gone."

"When?"

"Last night. They left." She eyed Lucy suspiciously.

"What time?"

"Late. Midnight. Maybe a little earlier."

"Did someone come back for the woman?" Siobhan said. "What about the pregnant woman? Was she okay? Did you see her?"

"That's all I know. Leave."

Siobhan was growing increasingly frustrated with this entire situation. How could she be so close to Mari and Ana and still not find them? It wasn't fair!

Lucy cleared her throat and said in clear, perfect Spanish, including a slight accent she didn't have when she spoke English, "Mrs. Hernandez, *por favor*. The young woman Ms. Walsh saw yesterday was pregnant and appeared in poor health. Father Sebastian is very concerned about the health and welfare of both her and her unborn child. We don't care about her immigration status, we don't care about any crimes she may have committed. We just want her to be safe. Did she leave with someone?"

Mrs. Hernandez nodded.

"A man or a woman?"

"A man. A young man, I see him many times. He drove the truck, the pregnant girl was with him. She walked out on her own. She wasn't hurt."

"Did they pack anything up? Suitcases?"

She nodded again. "She had a small bag. He had a suitcase. No one has come back since. I'm glad, but Enrique is worried they'll come back and know we let her in." She glared at Siobhan. "I don't want trouble."

"No trouble from us, I promise you," Lucy said. "Do you know who the boy was?"

"Pedro. That's his name. He talks about his parents, but I never see them. He's always there. He's seventeen, I know this, because I asked him once why he's not in school. He said he doesn't need school, he's seventeen." She shook her head. "My boy went to school. Went to community college, too. Now has his own restaurant. Education is important."

"How long was he living there?"

"Since the week after Easter." She crossed herself. "Please, that's all I know. I told Father Sebastian everything I knew, that they all left Thursday night. I didn't know there was anyone else there, other than Pedro, until you came." She glared at Siobhan. "I don't want trouble."

"Thank you for your time. God bless," Lucy said.

Siobhan wanted to ask her more questions but Lucy led her away.

"That's all you're going to get from her," Lucy said. "They're gone."

"No!"

"But we have information we didn't have before. You said you know how many girls were there?"

"There were eight beds, and they all appeared to have been used."

They got back into the car and Noah drove back to Siobhan's rental car.

"And Mrs. Hernandez saw three or four pregnant women. There may have been more. It all changed after the baby was left at the church. They took everyone away on Thursday, except for that one girl. She may have been too sick to travel, or about to give birth, or there was another reason."

"But Mrs. Hernandez was wrong—there was another baby. I have no idea how old, but I saw a girl—she couldn't have been more than twenty—carrying a baby out of that house. Surrounded by several goons. And a well-dressed woman who didn't fit into the neighborhood." Siobhan straightened her spine. "I have the pictures. I can prove everything I said."

"Proving their existence doesn't mean anything illegal was going on," Noah said.

"But you know there *was* something going on. Why else would someone steal my SD card and not the four-thousand-dollar camera it was in?"

"Let's see what you have," Lucy said, "and maybe we can find out exactly what's been going on."

CHAPTER FIVE

An hour later, Lucy and Noah arrived at Siobhan's hotel room with takeout from a nearby fast-food restaurant. It wasn't a five-star resort, but it was a nice, clean residence-style hotel with in-suite kitchenettes, laundries in every wing, and a work area. Siobhan unlocked the safe in her room and pulled out a small, thin laptop. She sat at the desk while Noah and Lucy sat at the two-person table.

Siobhan quickly booted up her laptop and downloaded the photos from her cloud account. She worked quickly and efficiently. "I'll pull out the best photos—the ones that clearly show facial features. I also have license plates. But then I really need to go to the hospital. You should come, too—see Elizabeth, talk to her doctor. I'm worried about her."

"Is she sick?"

"No—she was small, barely five pounds, but was at term or close to it. Beautiful. Perfect. But the hospital has already had inquiries about her. What if someone tries to claim her?"

"The police would have questions. CPS would need to verify—"

"But she's my *only* connection to Mari and Ana. She

was left at that church for a reason. She was left with the locket for a reason—and that reason was for the priest to call me. She *wants* my helps. *Needs* it. I can't walk away, and I can't let anything happen to Baby Elizabeth." She took a deep breath and turned back to the photos. Siobhan was certainly passionate.

Noah's phone rang, and he excused himself and went into the hall.

"What's his story?" Siobhan asked Lucy, keeping her eyes on the computer.

Siobhan seemed genuinely interested, though it was clear to Lucy she'd been frustrated with Noah. Lucy appreciated that Siobhan said what she thought and didn't play games. Her methods were straightforward. She wanted answers because she cared—not just about Marisol and Ana, but about the girl who had been chained to the bed.

"Noah is one of the best agents I've ever worked with," Lucy said. "We knew each other in DC before I went to the academy."

"And he's in the San Antonio office now?"

"Temporarily. Long story."

"Something to do with what happened in June?"

"In part."

"He just seems very . . . suspicious. Very cop-like."

Lucy almost laughed. "He can be serious. He's methodical and organized. He's a good person to have watching your back because he doesn't get flustered. He's a by-the-book agent, but can be flexible. He was my mentor when I was in DC."

"By-the-book? I'll bet he and Sean butt heads."

"They did. They're fine now." At least, they were friendly. *Friendlier.* They'd never be best buddies, but Lucy appreciated that they both made an effort.

"Good. That would be pretty uncomfortable if your partner and husband didn't like each other."

"Husband," Lucy muttered.

Siobhan laughed. "Get used to it."

"I am. It just sounds . . . strange." Lucy had never believed she'd get to this point. That she'd fall in love, live with a man, get married. It was overwhelming and exciting at the same time.

Siobhan clicked a few keys then tilted the computer screen so Lucy had a better view. "These are the best shots of each person."

Lucy leaned over the desk and studied the photos with Siobhan.

"I don't have a photo of Pedro, the teenager who called the cops on me. The deputy, by the way, called him Pete. But there are four other men, the woman, the young girl carrying the baby. I don't have a great shot of the woman upstairs, but I can work on it."

"That's her baby." Lucy pointed to the blond girl carrying the infant.

"How can you tell?"

"Well, she's wearing a maternity blouse for one thing—see those straps? They unbutton for nursing. Then look at her arm—she recently had an IV."

Siobhan enlarged the photo. "You have a good eye. I hadn't noticed that. I was focused on their faces."

"She's so young," Lucy said quietly. Eighteen, nineteen maybe. Not much older.

"Maybe someone is looking for her," Siobhan said. "I have to believe that. I can't believe that all these girls are unwanted. Unremembered."

Lucy didn't recognize any of the other people, but the older, well-dressed woman was put-together—the whole package. Jewelry, makeup, clothing, shoes. She was clearly in charge. The way the men stood around her, they deferred to her. The man who came with her, the one in the suit, was her bodyguard—Lucy could tell by the way he looked around, the way he stood next to her. Observant. Protective.

"Send those files to me and Noah," Lucy said. "He'll get them to the right people."

"Get what?" Noah said, stepping back in.

"The pictures."

He nodded. "I'll have Zach run them."

"Send the girl to NCMEC," Lucy said. "She's young, possibly underage. She might be a runaway or a kidnapping victim."

"Do you still have contacts there?" Noah asked.

"Yes."

"You do it, then—your personal connection will get our request to the top of the list."

Lucy started composing a message to her friend at the National Center for Missing and Exploited Children.

Lucy stared at Baby Elizabeth through the window of the nursery.

She was beautiful.

"My life is too unpredictable to have a baby," Siobhan said quietly. "But I would adopt a child in a heartbeat. There are so many young children who need homes. Babies are in high demand, so they get adopted much easier. It's the older kids, the ones that parents think are too much trouble, or they can't mold, or they have problems because they lost their entire family."

Lucy turned from the infant to Siobhan, surprised at the sudden kinship she felt with her. "I feel the same way."

The difference was that Lucy couldn't have children—she'd had an emergency hysterectomy when she was eighteen. Growing up, the idea of having children was a given—not something she actively thought about, but one of those *Down the road I'll get married and have kids* things. But when she realized that she could never have her own child, it felt like she'd lost something. How can you grieve for something you never had, never could have?

"Mari and Ana have a little brother. He'll never know his parents; he was a toddler when they died in the mudslide. All he has is his sisters and his grandmother, but she's much older. It's a hard life in the valley, but it's beautiful. A paradise, until the mudslide. They can rebuild, but it'll take time and people and money. Many have left for other homes. Mari and Ana were their hope, and when they disappeared, some lost hope. I have to find them, for the village, for their family, for a way of life. For that little baby in there. Elizabeth. I just have to."

Lucy understood the need to solve crimes. Most of the crimes she solved were homicides. Justice for victims who couldn't speak for themselves because they were dead. There were other victims, though. The victims of sex trafficking. Their families. The lives of those the evil of human slavery touched.

The baby sleeping in the bassinet.

"Noah and I are here," Lucy said. "I don't give up easily."

"When I lost track of them after they disappeared in Monterrey, I almost gave up. In fact, for months I put them out of my head because I would have gone crazy. I exhausted every lead. Kane helped for a while—he doesn't give up easily, either. But there were no leads."

"Kane's a good man."

"Yeah. Though Kane will do everything in his power to make you think he's not."

Lucy raised an eyebrow but didn't comment. She wasn't someone who noticed interpersonal relationship issues until they hit her over the head or someone more astute, like Sean, spelled out a situation. The realization that Siobhan had feelings for Kane maybe wasn't of the hit-on-the-head magnitude, but strong enough that Lucy recognized the tone.

"That's Kane," she said lightly.

"Absolutely impossible," Siobhan muttered. "Thick-headed, stubborn, arrogant mule." Then she said something in Gaelic. Lucy knew several languages, but Gaelic wasn't one she'd picked up. She only recognized the cadence.

"There's Dr. Davidson," Siobhan suddenly said and strode off down the hall.

Lucy sent Noah a quick text message that the doctor was available, then followed Siobhan. She wondered where he'd gone off to in the first place, but running the Violent Crimes Squad was time-consuming. Juan had rarely left the office to investigate, though he often supervised major operations. Noah was definitely more hands-on. And if Lucy was going to be honest with herself, she much preferred working with him than with anyone else. There was a comfort and confidence working with a partner who not only knew you, but whom you trusted explicitly.

Perhaps that wasn't fair. Lucy hadn't really had the time to get to know the other agents. Nate Dunning had become friends with Sean, and she liked him fine, but since they were both rookies, they couldn't partner up. Ryan Quiroz used to be a cop and he reminded Lucy of her brother Connor—a bit hotheaded, but rock-solid. But the other agents she'd only worked with on the periphery, and she had the distinct sense that no one particularly wanted to partner with her. The sad thing was she'd thought she'd been making friends before the shit hit the fan in June.

Siobhan introduced Lucy to the doctor. "Any news?"

Dr. Davidson said, "Elizabeth is healthy. She was small, but all organs are functioning properly. She weighed in this morning at five pounds, six ounces.

"I also got her blood work back, and she's healthy in every test we run. Her mother must have eaten well and likely took prenatal vitamins. The only thing I'm a bit concerned about is a slight wheeze, though her lungs seem clear. We're watching it, in case it's an allergy or develops into a bronchial infection, but all the tests are normal."

"That's great news," Siobhan said.

"CPS wants to know when they can place her into foster care. There are several homes approved for newborns."

"No," Siobhan said emphatically. "Laurel, I told you, I know her mother. The FBI is here, we're going to find her."

"Be that as it may," the doctor said, "I can't keep her here indefinitely. Maybe twenty-four hours longer."

Noah approached them. "Doctor, I'm FBI Supervisory Special Agent Noah Armstrong. Before you release the child, please call me—my boss is working on putting the child into protective custody."

"Really?" Siobhan said, eyes wide and optimistic. "You can do that?"

Noah glanced at her with a frown. "Doctor, may I speak with you privately?"

They walked down the hall. Siobhan turned to Lucy. "That was really rude."

"Trust him," Lucy said. "He has the infant's best interest at heart. Let's look at her again."

Lucy led Siobhan back down the hall to the nursery, where they could watch the babies through the window. A nurse was rocking Elizabeth and feeding her. "It's just, why can't he tell me?" Siobhan said.

"It's a complex legal matter," Lucy said, "and there could be other factors. We don't know, but Noah understands the situation."

"He didn't seem to at the hotel."

"He's doing everything he needs to do, and more."

Siobhan sighed and sat down in a plastic chair. Lucy sat next to her. "You're right, I know you are. Where are they? What's really going on here? Because this whole thing is so unfamiliar."

"We'll find the truth."

Noah came back down the hall without the doctor. "Siobhan, I understand you're frustrated and worried. We're not letting anything happen to that baby. The doctor agreed to increase security for the next forty-eight hours, and I'm hoping by that time we'll have a custody arrangement that will keep the infant safe until her mother can be located. Lucy and I have an appointment with the assistant sheriff in Webb County. I'll be happy to drop you off at your hotel."

"Thank you," she said, "but I think I'll stay here for just a little longer."

"I thought so. I also cleared it that you can have access to Elizabeth in the neonatal unit, under supervision. Not that I don't trust you, but no one is allowed to be alone with the baby except the nurses assigned to this floor and her doctor."

"You did that for me?"

"Not just for you."

Noah and Lucy walked out. "That was nice of you," Lucy said.

"I need her occupied. Siobhan is driven and intense and while her insight has been valuable, she's focused on the wrong thing."

"Why were there multiple pregnant women in that house and where did they go?"

"Exactly. And I tracked down that reporter who gave her the info on the girls in the first place. I'd rather she wasn't around when we talk to him." Noah pulled out of the hospital parking lot. "Check your email, read the report from Zach. He has property records, license plates— I didn't have time to review it. I had a talk with Agent Lopez, the SSA running the Laredo office." The FBI's Laredo office was a Resident Agency under the San Antonio umbrella. "They're swamped right now, but set us up to talk with the assistant sheriff, who may have information on a related case."

"How so?"

"Woman, suspected illegal, gave birth at the hospital, then disappeared with the baby—even though she was granted temporary residency. It may have nothing to do with this . . . but Lopez said there were other suspicious things about the case. He only knew about it through interdepartment communications, not because he worked it."

Lucy looked through Zach's reports. Thin, but at least they had a direction. "All the vehicles are registered to a business," she said. "Except the truck. Odd."

"Odd what?"

"The house is also registered to a business."

"Shit."

"What does it mean?"

"It's going to be a shell game."

Lucy had no idea what Noah meant, but it didn't sound good.

CHAPTER SIX

"Thank you for staying after your shift to meet with us," Noah said to Assistant Sheriff Adam Villines.

"It's not late—my wife will tell you we eat promptly at six every night, but by the time the kids get back from practice and clean up and whoever is supposed to be cooking actually cooks—we rotate between the kids—it's closer to eight. Which is fine with me, because my seven-to-five shift rarely ends at five. And it's Monday. Which means Isabelle is cooking, so help me."

He motioned for them to sit across from his desk, then he closed the door and sat in his seat. "Tim Lopez from your Laredo office gave me a heads-up, says you're sharp. I'll admit, I'm not a fan of the feds. We get a lot of that here, between the DEA and ICE and FBI, pushing in, causing more problems than they solve. Tim and I are both local boys, I trust him. He says you're okay, you're okay. But what I want to know is why isn't Tim investigating this case, why bring in someone from DC?"

"I'm working out of the San Antonio office indefinitely while SSA Casilla is on leave," Noah said. "I spoke with Agent Lopez earlier, he'll be assisting, though Agent Kincaid and I are running this investigation. As you know, the

Laredo Resident Agency is a small office, they don't have the time or resources with their current cases to take the lead. I'm keeping Lopez in the loop, however."

Villines nodded his approval.

Noah continued. "Ms. Walsh spoke to you this weekend?"

"I've already had two visits from Ms. Walsh. Tenacious. I know all about the missing girls—she said they were her friends—and what she thinks she knows about the case. To be honest with you, we're not seeing any foul play here. Not on the surface. We can assist in finding the infant's mother, but because the baby was left in the county next door, I don't have any jurisdiction to dig around. I made a call to the sheriff, she says she'll look into it."

"Not on the surface?" Noah repeated.

Villines nodded. "If Ms. Walsh wasn't so dead positive that the baby belongs to one of her friends because of that locket, I would have thought it was left by a poor, young girl overwhelmed by the idea of motherhood. Devout, leaving it at the church. Figured it would be cared for. Or an immigrant who was concerned about her status, maybe unwed, scared. And then the note."

"What note?"

Villines opened a file, showed Noah. Lucy glanced over. The photograph of a bloodied white T-shirt seemed odd. Lucy tilted her head and saw the message.

Trust no one.

"*This* is why the priest brought the infant to the Laredo hospital, he knew it was a different jurisdiction."

"Do you know a Deputy Jackson?" Noah asked.

Villines grunted. "I'm not going to talk shit about another cop. Let's just say he wouldn't be working under me."

Noah said, "Three months ago, a young pregnant woman was dropped off at a hospital here in Laredo. The staff suspected she was illegal, but the baby was in duress and they delivered it by emergency C-section."

When had Noah learned about that situation?

"Correct. It's a common situation—we're a border town. The woman would have died across the border, as well as the baby. Desperate times, Agent Armstrong."

"Dr. Davidson treated that woman as well."

That must have been why Noah wanted to talk to the doctor without Siobhan. Lucy wished he would have clued her in earlier.

"And you think these cases are connected?" Villines asked.

Noah shrugged. "The mother and baby disappeared."

"They were given temporary residency—thanks to the hospital staff who know the ropes—but walked away from a shelter two days after they were discharged," Villines said. "It happens."

"Dr. Davidson said you have the mother's prints and belongings."

"There wasn't much—she packed up and left—but yes, I ran her to make sure she had no criminal record, a requirement of the shelter. It's a church-run group for un-married women with young children. She was clean, but I didn't add her to the criminal database when she dis-appeared. She wasn't accused of a crime."

"I want to run her prints against all databases," Noah said. "I'm getting a warrant for the house where we suspect Baby Elizabeth's mother was staying before she left the baby at the church. I'm going to print the place." Noah leaned forward, put out his left index finger as he counted. "One abandoned baby at a church." Put out another fin-ger. "One pregnant woman Ms. Walsh saw inside the house." He put out a third finger. "One young girl carry-ing an infant leaving the house yesterday evening." And his pinkie finger. "And three months ago a mother and infant disappear even though they were given food, shelter, medical care." He leaned back. "Dr. Davidson said the woman didn't speak much, that she'd clearly received prenatal care, and she filled out the birth certificate with false information. She had no identification on her."

Villines considered. "I had two deputies called out to a house fire shortly after the woman disappeared. The fire department was able to contain it to one dwelling, but there were a few oddities. Four cribs in one room, several twin beds in another. No fatalities or injuries—the place was empty, and no one claimed any belongings—though there was little left. The fire investigator ruled it arson. The structure was unstable and demolished, but there are photos. You're welcome to a copy of the file."

"Who owned the house?" Lucy asked.

Villines glanced at her as if he'd forgotten she was there. "I don't remember. A property management company? It was some sort of business on the records."

"Was it Direct Property Holdings?"

He raised both eyebrows. "I think it was."

Lucy glanced at Noah and said, "They owned the house outside Freer." To Villines she added, "The house where Siobhan Walsh saw the pregnant women."

"I don't believe in coincidences," Villines said.

"Nor do I," Noah said. "We're running all property in the area owned by the same company, but I was hoping you might be able to spare a deputy who knows the area to help run them down."

"I'm sure we can handle that. Get me the list."

Noah made a note then stood. "Thank you for your help. I'll keep you in the loop."

Eric Barrow, Siobhan's reporter friend, lived outside Laredo in a dumpy apartment building. There were eight units—four up, four down—and he lived in the north upstairs corner.

Lucy researched Barrow during the drive and shared it with Noah. The reporter had sold a few stories to major papers—most of them with photos by Siobhan Walsh—but the overwhelming majority of his work was published for NAN, an Internet news feed that focused on the Southwest, Texas, and Mexico. She had no idea what the acronym stood for; it wasn't on their masthead or website. Eric clearly had an agenda: He didn't like law enforcement, he hated politicians, and he wasn't fond of the military. He seemed to relish catching people of authority in compromising positions. In fact, the exposé he wrote on the brothel he'd alerted Siobhan about was a classic example: He outed a local elected official—who'd run on a pro-family, conservative platform—as a patron of hookers. He skewered the guy—Lucy felt he deserved it not only for his actions but also for his hypocrisy—and took down two other elected officials at the same time.

But once the story was over, he didn't follow through on what happened to the women in the club, whether they'd been arrested or let go or given assistance. It made Lucy wonder if his concern was more about challenging authority than it was about helping the girls who suffered as a result of such corruption.

Barrow wasn't a bad writer, but he had an edge that Lucy found unappealing. It was completely opposite from how she viewed Siobhan. She wondered if Barrow and Kane had had any run-ins. She thought about sending Kane a text message asking about Barrow, but then decided against it—not without running it by Noah. Though Noah's problems with the Rogans and the way RCK operated had been mostly resolved over the nearly two years Lucy had known him, she didn't want to create any new friction. She was about to ask him when they reached Barrow's apartment and Noah cut off the ignition.

"The guy rubs me the wrong way and I haven't even met him," he said. "Cover the back. I'll give you twenty seconds."

Lucy hurried to the back of the building and identified Barrow's apartment from the rear. He had a balcony and it would be very easy for him to run.

A group of kids, boys and girls all under ten, were playing in a makeshift playground on the edge of the parking lot. There was a plastic slide that had seen better days; a sandbox with gravel instead of sand; a box of broken sidewalk chalk that two young girls were using to draw some elaborate but unidentifiable landscape on the broken pavement. The kids all noticed Lucy and stared, but didn't seem scared or nervous.

The sliding glass door above her slid open less than a minute after Lucy positioned herself. Noah had been right—the jerk was running. Lucy stayed in the shadow of the building until Barrow dangled from his balcony and dropped to the ground.

"Shit," he muttered as he fell on his ass. By the time he got up, Lucy stood two feet in front of him.

"Mr. Barrow, I'm FBI Special Agent Lucy Kincaid. We need to talk."

He stared at her, glanced behind him, took a step back. "I—uh—"

"Don't," she said. "I would hate to arrest you in front of those kids over there. But I will take you down if I have to."

Barrow's pale-green eyes darted right and left. He ran a hand through his shaggy sun-bleached hair as if wondering if he could outrun her or if she would shoot him in the back. Then he smiled, showing perfect teeth. "Hey, sugar, anything you want."

"Sugar?" she said. "Really?"

Noah came around the back. He was irritated, and Lucy didn't blame him. Barrow looked at Noah and the smile disappeared. "I didn't know who you were," he said.

Noah glared at the guy. "Let's go."

"Why?"

"I don't want to have a discussion here."

"I'm not going anywhere with you."

"Your apartment."

"I don't want you in my apartment."

"Then let's talk at the station," Noah said. "Villines said we could use his interrogation room, right, Kincaid?"

"He did," Lucy said.

"Okay, look, I don't know what this is about, but—Kincaid? Kincaid . . . you're not really feds, are you? Well shit, I can explain. I was on a story, a hot story, I didn't mean to get your guys in trouble, I really didn't know there was a situation . . . I mean, we're talking two years ago, and no one got hurt, right?"

Lucy raised an eyebrow.

"Why am I not surprised," Noah muttered. He pulled out his badge. "FBI Agent Noah Armstrong. FBI Agent Lucy Kincaid."

Barrow was wholly confused. Lucy almost laughed. Small world, but Jack had spent nearly twenty years based out of Hidalgo, Texas. She wasn't surprised that Barrow knew her brother.

"Your apartment or the sheriff's department," Noah said, "I don't really care, but I'm not playing games."

"Jack's not around, is he?" Barrow asked Lucy.

"I can call him if you want," Lucy said.

"That's okay. Don't tell him where I live. We had a disagreement a couple of years ago, he can be a prick, you know—oh, don't say I said that. He's a very nice prick."

Lucy was really enjoying this conversation. She couldn't

wait to call Jack and find out what had really happened with Barrow.

"We'll go to my apartment," Barrow said. "But, I'm not in any trouble, am I?"

"I don't know, are you?" Lucy asked.

"What does Siobhan see in this guy?" Noah asked as he motioned for Barrow to walk in front of them.

"*Siobhan?* Why didn't you tell me? Where is she? Is she okay?"

He walked back to the front of the building. An older woman was struggling with her door on the first floor while she juggled three grocery bags in gnarled hands. Barrow immediately went over and took the bags from her. "Hey, Miz T, I said to call me."

"I didn't want to be a bother," the old woman said in broken English.

"No bother."

The woman unlocked her door and Barrow went in with the bags. Lucy thought for a second that he was going to bolt again out the back, and so did Noah, who walked over to get a better look. But a second later Barrow came out. "Thanks, Eric, dear," Ms. T said. "There was someone looking for you yesterday."

Barrow immediately looked panicked. He was up to something, Lucy could feel it.

"Who?"

"Big guy. Tattoos." She tapped her knuckles. "All over. No good."

"Thanks."

"Be careful." She glared at Noah and Lucy, then closed her door.

Barrow led them upstairs. "I'm going to have to disappear for a while," he said as he unlocked the door.

"I don't think so," Noah said.

"You don't understand." Barrow closed the door behind them.

The place was cluttered and Barrow immediately grabbed a bong and small bag of pot and put them in a cabinet. He could do nothing to diminish the scent of weed. He had a high-end computer on a desk that took up half his living room. There were books everywhere, mostly nonfiction.

"I know I haven't done anything to piss off the FBI lately," Barrow said, "but a little while ago I ran with a story that some people aren't happy about. The guy with the tats on his hands? Bet it's Gino Salvatore. I ran a story exposing his brother for taking bribes. Look it up, Salvatore was an ICE agent, turned his back on some nasty shit for money. How did Gino know where I lived? Fuck, I like this place. But I like my face more."

There wasn't much to like, other than it was quiet.

Barrow kept rambling, shuffling things around, seemingly haphazardly, but Lucy suspected he was hiding notes or drugs. "ICE was pissed off, too. Didn't like having one of their own shown to be a bastard. I don't much care, they probably knew about him, turned the other cheek. There's few good feds, but some really rotten ones." He glanced at them. "I'm sure you're fine, being Jack's sister and all."

"Enough," Noah said. He rubbed his head. "Sit. Now."

Barrow sat at his desk and leaned back. "What's up? You said Siobhan, right? Hot. I mean, we're not involved—God, no, I mean, I would totally hit her up, but she's off-limits. But she's totally cool." He looked concerned for the first time. Really concerned. "She's not, like, hurt? You told me she wasn't hurt or anything. She's not in trouble, right?"

"Eight months ago you gave Siobhan a tip that one of the girls she was looking for was seen at a brothel in Del

Rio," Noah said. "She took you at your word, but you didn't give her any real evidence. I want the evidence."

Barrow stared at him. He might have acted the airhead stoner type, but he was shrewd and calculating.

"I gave Siobhan everything I knew about Marisol and Ana. I'm no saint, but I wouldn't keep anything from her if it would help."

"Photos," Noah said. "You went undercover, you talked to the girls, you took photos. You didn't get any of Marisol and Ana because the story you told Siobhan was that they'd come and gone by the time you got there."

"It wasn't a story. It was the truth. Someone else told me about Siobhan's lost girls."

"You published photos of the politicians that used the brothel. You must have taken others. We want them for an active investigation."

"No." He crossed his arms.

Lucy stepped forward. "No? Really?"

"They're not going to help you. You're fishing for something. I'm not going to let the feds run around through a back door to get dirt on someone who may not be a total shit. My sources trust me that I'm not going to screw them—people I care about, at any rate."

Noah opened his mouth, but Lucy cut him off. "You are as much of a hypocrite as the people you skewer in the press. We are trying to find not only Marisol and Ana de la Rosa, but also an at-risk pregnant woman who was chained to a bed so she couldn't escape. We know one or both of the sisters was in Freer last week, and you told Siobhan that they were in Del Rio over eight months ago. You have photos of everyone who came in and out of that brothel for weeks. If the girls are still in the area, they are in danger. I want the pictures and I want your notes, now."

Barrow opened his mouth, then closed it. He finally said, "Look—"

"No excuses. Either you're one of us or you're one of them. There is no middle ground in this war. Those girls are being trafficked, abused, tortured. They trust no one because they were likely abducted in another country and taken far from their homes, their families. Statistics say that they will be dead before they're thirty, and if you don't share what you know, you're as much responsible for their deaths as the bastards who took them."

Barrow was torn. Lucy saw it in his eyes. He looked at Noah, almost as if to plead with him, but Noah maintained his cold cop stare.

"It's not that simple," Barrow said. "You're not going to know what you're looking at. These people don't play in the same pool. The FBI is all domestic shit, these are the international bastards, and really, you can't trust ICE. Not all of them. That report I did on Salvatore was just the tip of the iceberg." He smiled. "Hey, that's good." He scribbled something on a piece of paper.

"Don't worry about what we're looking at," Noah said. "We have our own resources."

Barrow grunted. "Right. As soon as you put their faces into your precious database, somebody's gonna know. You guys just don't get it. There's a mole in every fucking office. You think not? Look what just happened in San Antonio this summer! DEA gutted from the inside out by one of its own. Poetic justice."

Lucy wanted to hit him. "You have no idea what happened in San Antonio."

"Yeah, I do. A fucking corrupt agent went in and cleaned house. How many in all? Someone in the FBI, couple in the DEA, couple in SAPD, you think they got them all?" He snorted. "Hardly."

"I'm from the San Antonio office," Lucy said. "And you know shit."

"I call them as I see them."

"Then you're blind."

"How do I know you're not here trying to protect someone? Grab my pictures to protect some fucked agent?"

"Because I told you why we're here."

"Why not have Siobhan ask me herself? Maybe you're just using her like your people use everyone else."

"Knock the chip off your shoulder, Barrow," Noah said.

"Then you won't care if I call her."

"Go ahead," Noah said.

Barrow hesitated, just for a moment, then pulled his cell phone from his pocket, scrolled through contacts, and dialed.

"Hey, Siobhan, it's Eric . . . all's well. I'm here with two feds, Armstrong and Kincaid. Know them?" He was silent for well over a minute. "But, don't you think—" He was quiet again. Then his face paled and he stared at Lucy. "Oh. No, sugar, I just wanted to make sure they were legit. They want some of my photos from Del Rio." He turned around and mumbled something Lucy couldn't hear.

Noah stepped closer to her and whispered in her ear, "Want to bet she mentioned that you're marrying a Rogan?"

"He should help because it's the right thing to do," Lucy said.

"Fear is a more powerful motivator."

"You know I'd do anything for you, Siobhan—you just have to ask. But—you know, it would help if you told him I helped you out. I want in on a raid . . . I won't screw him, you know that, scout's honor . . . Okay. Thanks." Barrow hung up. He started typing on his computer, then stuck a CD into one of the drives. "I'm copying all the photos to a disk. It'll just take a minute."

"Why the hell do you want in on one of Kane's raids?" Lucy asked.

Barrow looked like a deer caught in the headlights. "It'd make a good story."

"You would screw him over in a heartbeat for a story, wouldn't you?"

"I wouldn't."

Lucy didn't believe him.

"Luce," Noah said in a low voice.

She walked out.

Five minutes later, Noah joined her. "What was that about? You had him, then you nearly blew it."

"Because I know exactly what he wants. He wants in so he can expose mercenaries. The good, bad, and ugly."

"You don't know—"

"I spent the thirty-minute car ride skimming a dozen articles that he wrote. He hates people like us, and people like Jack and Kane. Jack was a good soldier and a good mercenary. People like Barrow want to make them all out as being corrupt or corruptible. He might be able to play the game for a while, and he might have some redeeming qualities, but I don't trust him."

"Do you honestly think that Kane would take him on any of his operations?"

Lucy opened her mouth, then closed it and shook her head.

"Siobhan would know that, too, don't you think?"

"Probably," she admitted.

"Your future brother-in-law can take care of himself, especially with a guy like Barrow. Let's get back to Siobhan's hotel and look at these pictures, see if there's anyone we recognize. If not, we'll send them out."

"Do you think he's right about ICE?"

"He could be. I don't know. But Rick has a few people he trusts that he can go to on the QT, so that's where I'll start."

The drive back to downtown Laredo went faster with commuter traffic easing up, and they made it to Siobhan's hotel twenty minutes later. Noah was itching to get back to San Antonio, but he wanted to make sure that Siobhan didn't start investigating on her own. "I don't care what you have to say to her," he told Lucy, "but we have to contain her. This is dangerous, and she is friendly with that ass of a reporter."

"I'll take care of it," Lucy said. "We're coming back tomorrow, right?"

"I don't see how we can avoid it," he said.

"Why do you sound skeptical?"

"Because we don't have much yet. I want to run the photos Barrow gave us, and we may have a drive to Del Rio ahead of us. I wish I could pull in the Laredo office, but Barrow was right about one thing—there's a problem with ICE here, and our office is providing assistance. Headquarters is well aware of the problem, and they're handling it. The last thing we need is to tip their hand and jeopardize their internal investigation."

"How'd you find out?"

"I've known since I got here." He glanced at her as he pulled into a parking slot. "Part of being not only the boss, but tasked with cleaning house. But what it means for us, if Rick wants us on this investigation, I have to pull from my squad—and that means shifting and prioritizing other cases. I don't have to tell you we're severely understaffed."

Not only were they down an agent, but the Violent Crimes Squad in every FBI office had been cut back drastically when the FBI reprioritized counter-terrorism as their number one focus.

As soon as they got out of the car, Siobhan exited the hotel and ran up to them. "I just got back from the hospital. Someone broke into my hotel room and stole my computer. *And* my camera. But we're going to find those bastards. I have GPS tracking on both."

CHAPTER SEVEN

Marisol was sleeping in an old barn when a sound woke her. She didn't know what time it was; she didn't know how long she'd been sleeping. She feared she had an infection. She was hot and achy and had no energy. Everything she'd planned was falling apart. She didn't know how long she'd walked, how many miles, but she'd found this barn after two nights and knew she needed to sleep.

Light flitted through the beams. Either the sun was rising or the sun was setting. She didn't know which way she faced.

Two men were talking outside the barn. She froze. They'd found her.

They spoke English, clear as day.

"The damn tractor broke down again Friday. I just said what the hell, but I can't afford a new one."

"I can fix it, Dad. I wish you'd called me earlier."

"You're busy, son. I didn't want to bother you."

"I'm not so busy I can't fix your tractor. What do you think is wrong with it?"

"I thought the alternator, but that's not it. Checked the oil and fluids and all that. It turns on, but it doesn't have any umph."

"So technical." The younger man laughed.

The doors of the barn opened and more light came in. Marisol didn't move. She was partly buried under the hay; maybe they wouldn't see her.

They were chatting, a father and son who cared for each other. Metal clanged against metal. The tractor started up. It sounded as sick as she felt. "I see the problem," the son said. "I'll just need to get a couple parts. I'll pick them up tomorrow after work. Won't take me more than an hour or two."

"I appreciate it, Johnny. Really, I do."

"Next time, call me before you start dicking around with the engine. I don't mind. It feels good to get my hands dirty again."

There was some rustling. "Dad, did you cut yourself?"

"No."

"This is blood."

Marisol began to shake. Oh God, they were going to find her. How could she save her sister if she was in jail? Or what if the bad police sent her back to those people? She couldn't trust anyone. Who would believe her? Who would know the truth when the truth was so difficult believe?

"Dad."

The voice was right there, right in front of her. She opened her eyes. Everything was blurry, but she saw him. The son. He was tall, so very tall. He dressed well, had his sleeves rolled up. There was a grease mark on his white shirt. His dad stood behind him. Also very tall. Dressed in old jeans and a faded plaid shirt.

"We're not going to hurt you." The son squatted. "My name is John Honeycutt. This is my dad, George."

"I'm sorry," she said. She used English, because she didn't want these people to think she was an immigrant. That she needed to be deported. She *wanted* to be deported, she wanted to leave this country as soon as possible, but not without Ana. She couldn't leave without her sister.

And she couldn't leave without her baby.

"It's okay," John Honeycutt said.

"I'll tell your mom to get a plate ready," George said.

"No, I'll go. Please, I don't want any trouble." Marisol sat up. Too quickly, because she felt dizzy and stumbled.

John reached out for her, but she pulled back and fell into the hay.

"What's your name?"

She didn't want to answer.

"You're flushed, you have a fever. When have you last eaten?"

"I have food," she said and glanced over at the bag that she'd been using as a pillow.

"John," George said. The two men looked at each other and spoke without saying anything. The same way she and Ana could communicate.

"Please, I'll leave, I want no trouble. I'm sorry, so sorry."

"We can get you help."

"No!" She didn't want to shout at them, but they didn't understand. There was no one to help. No one to trust. "I beg you, do not call the police. I—" What could she say? She couldn't fight these men. She could barely speak. She was sick, she didn't know what to do.

"All right," John said, "I won't call the police."

She didn't know if she could believe him.

"If you let me take you inside, give you some food and water, then you can leave in the morning."

She glanced outside. It was dusk.

She nodded. "Can I—can I use a phone?"

"Of course you may." He held out his hand to help her up.

She took it and winced. She was so sore, so shaky on her feet.

"What happened to you, girl?" George asked.

"Dad," John said quietly.

"Marisol. My name is Marisol." She looked down at her torn dress and the sweater she'd stolen from a car she'd passed near the church. She saw what they saw—the blood. So much blood.

"You need a doctor."

"No. No. I'm okay."

"Dad, go ahead and tell Mom we're bringing Marisol in."

George left. John helped her walk across the field to the house. She hadn't realized when she arrived how close the house was. She'd come in the middle of the night . . . how long had she slept in the hay?

"I'm a teacher," John said. "I teach math and science in town. I'm not going to hurt you, but you need help. If you want to talk, I'm a good listener. So are my parents. They're good people. We won't let anyone hurt you. Do you believe me?"

She nodded, surprised that she did believe him. No one had shown her such kindness in years. "Thank you," she whispered, leaning on him, surprised she wasn't more terrified. "I have someone to call. Someone who can help. Just—please don't call the police. Please. My sister's life depends on it."

CHAPTER EIGHT

"She can stay with us indefinitely." Sean Rogan looked at the time—already eight at night. "Are you leaving now?"

He glanced over at Nate Dunning, one of the agents in Lucy's office, who had stopped writing his to-do list for the wedding and was listening to their conversation.

"Noah is wrapping things up with the deputy," Lucy said. "Processing a motel room is next to impossible—I don't think they're going to get much from here. Siobhan has GPS on her equipment, and we tracked them. Destroyed. We have to come back tomorrow, though. I'll find her a safer hotel to stay in—this motel is clean, but the security is nearly nonexistent."

"Not surprised. I have a few ideas—I'll work on them before you get here."

"You're wonderful."

"I know."

She laughed lightly. "I have to go—I'll fill you in on the details when I get home. I love you."

"Love you, princess." He hung up and frowned.

"Trouble?" Nate asked.

"Maybe. Nothing they can't handle. It's just the case

itself—possible human trafficking. Lucy and Noah think the bastards are selling babies."

"That's fucked."

"You said it. Someone left a newborn at a church last week. It may have been a young woman Siobhan Walsh knows."

"Isn't she a reporter or something? The one grabbed in Santiago in June?"

"Photographer. And yes—she was used as bait for Kane."

His brother was still recovering from his injuries. He'd had a kidney removed, but it wasn't the organ that gave him the most trouble. Most people could function normally with one kidney. He'd also been shot in the leg, and he was only at about 90 percent three months later. He refused pain meds because he claimed they made his head fuzzy. But of course he'd gone back to work. Kane was stubborn.

It ran in the family, Sean supposed. But Sean had never worried about his big brother before—Kane was tough. This time, he wasn't bouncing back as fast. If he wasn't at full strength, he was vulnerable.

"They've all been busy today," Nate said. "Zach has been running backgrounds and photo IDs nonstop." Nate stood. "I think I'm good to go here. Lucy is definitely going to be surprised."

"I hope in a good way."

"Oh yeah."

"She's not big on surprises."

"This is a good one."

Sean smiled, appreciating the reassurance. "Thanks for your help, buddy."

"Anytime."

Sean walked Nate to the door then reset the security system. He went down the hall to check the guest room and make sure it had everything Siobhan would need. At first Sean had been happy that Lucy called him earlier to say she'd be home late; it gave him and Nate time to finish some last-minute wedding details. But now it *was* late, and he wanted to see her. Lucy had sounded exhausted.

He'd already surprised her by asking her brother Patrick to be his best man. For Sean, there had been no other choice. He could have asked his brother Kane, except Kane would show up for the wedding and disappear right after. And Duke—Sean loved his other brother, but he and Duke were just now getting along. They'd had a falling-out last year and Sean was having a harder time forgiving Duke for things he'd said than he'd realized. It had gotten better, but Sean wanted his wedding to be fun and as stress-free as possible. Patrick would be part of the festivities, he'd help with anything, and he'd already planned on coming down a week early to help pull everything together and mediate between the large Rogan family and the larger Kincaid clan. And of course, there was the bachelor party. Besides, Sean already considered Patrick his brother.

Lucy had a more difficult time picking her maid of honor. She was closer to her sister-in-law Kate than she was to her two sisters, but family meant everything to the Kincaids. It ended up that she asked her sister Carina, and Kate and Lucy's closest friend Suzanne Madeaux from the New York FBI office were her bridesmaids. For Sean it was much easier—his brothers Duke and Kane. If Kane bailed after the ceremony, no worries. And if Liam—his other brother—got his nose out of joint, he could just deal with it. Besides, Sean didn't think he and Eden would even show up. Fine by him; the drama that would follow his brother and sister was more than Sean wanted to deal with, especially on his wedding day.

October 29 had to be perfect.

Once he'd freshened up the guest room, Sean sat back down at his computer and went through his checklist.

Everything that had to be done was done. The invitations had gone out a bit later than they should have, but they'd had less than five months to put the wedding together. When Lucy started to feel overwhelmed and talked about postponing it, Sean took everything for himself to do.

All you need to worry about is finding your dress. You could wear a burlap sack, for all I care. You'll still be the most beautiful woman in the church.

He knew for a fact that Lucy had found a dress—she'd flown home to San Diego for a weekend, and Carina and their mother had taken her shopping. All Carina had done was text Sean a thumbs-up sign and he knew it was all good.

Not that he was worried. He wouldn't be looking at the dress.

His doorbell rang and he opened the security panel on his computer to see who was paying him a visit.

He stared.

Her blond hair had darkened with age, and instead of hanging long and straight down her back it was cut into a sassy shoulder-length bob, but Madison McAllister had not changed in the thirteen years since Sean had last seen her.

Campus security stood inside his dorm room. Sean was required to pack up his belongings and be escorted from campus before five p.m. that day. It was Sunday and he'd spent the last three days in jail. He was angry and humiliated and he considered emptying his bank account and disappearing. He would never forgive Duke for cutting a deal with the feds. They should be giving him a fucking medal for exposing the pedophile, not putting him on probation and expelling him from Stanford.

"I called in a favor. You're going to MIT." Duke stood in the corner of the dorm room, arms crossed, because Sean told him not to touch his stuff.

The damn feds had already seized his computer equipment.

"Fuck you."

"You'll thank me later."

"You had no right."

"I'm your guardian. For two more weeks, at any rate. You have no idea what you've done here. You haven't even apologized!"

"There's nothing to apologize for!"

"You had other options. You could have come to me."

"Right. Because we know the system always works."

"I would have helped you."

"Then no one would have realized how flawed the FBI security program was."

"You embarrassed your university, the FBI, and yourself."

"I'm not embarrassed. I did the right thing. I accept the consequences."

Duke threw his hands up in the air. "If you'd accepted the consequences you would have been in prison!"

"Trial by jury, brother. No one would have convicted me."

"Your looks and charm aren't always going to save your ass, Sean. And frankly, I don't find you very charming right now."

Sean sensed more than saw someone in the doorway. He whirled around, ready to unleash his anger.

Madison.

She stared at him, worry in her eyes. "Is it true? You're really leaving?"

Duke glanced from Madison to Sean. "I'll be downstairs," Duke said.

He left, and Sean looked over at the campus security guy. "Hey, Joe, can I please have five minutes of privacy?"

Security wasn't supposed to let him out of their sight,

but Joe liked him. He could tell. Joe winked and closed the door.

Madison ran to him and wrapped her arms around his neck. He hugged her back. Damn, this situation was so fucked.

"Hey, sit down." He pulled out his desk chair for her. He sat on his bed and held her hands. "You are a sight for sore eyes, Maddie."

"I tried calling you and you never answered. I saw the police take you away in handcuffs, and everyone was saying you were going to jail and . . . is it true? Did you hack into the crime symposium? And expose Dr. Smith as a pedophile?"

"Yes." It was easier not to explain everything. Madison was smart, but she didn't understand technology. She could barely use her cell phone even though her daddy bought her the best tech out there.

"And they expelled you? Are you really going to jail?"

"Yes and no. I'm sorry I couldn't call and explain what happened."

"I understand."

But he could tell by her tone that she didn't.

"Hey, Maddie, it's going to get better."

"But it's true."

"So? Smith is an asshole. He had hundreds of child porn videos on his computer. I don't regret what I did."

"But you were arrested!"

"Probation. That's it. Well, and the university didn't really like the fact that I didn't tell them first."

"I—Sean, I—"

"Hey, I'm going to be okay."

"Where are you going?"

"Duke pulled strings and got me into MIT. Banishing me three thousand miles away. What do I expect?"

Sean had probably complained to Madison far more

than she wanted to hear about Duke and his heavy-handed ways. His brother had been his guardian for nearly four years—ever since their parents were killed—and Sean couldn't wait until the end of the month when he'd be eighteen and finally on his own. Control of all his money— most of which he'd earned himself, but couldn't access. Control of his inheritance. Control of his life.

He'd give MIT two weeks, but if it wasn't for him, he'd walk. Liam and Eden would take him in. They were living in London now, and Liam was always telling Sean that he could use someone with his skills. Sean hadn't even seen his brother and sister since their parents' funeral, though Liam called him all the time for tech help.

"You don't have to go. You can stay here."

"Maddie—I care about you so much, you know that. But I can't stay. Stanford expelled me. Being on the East Coast is probably a good thing. Get away from here, away from my brother."

"But didn't you say you hated college? That you could get a job at a start-up company in the Silicon Valley?"

He had said that, but he didn't really hate college. He didn't like some things about it. But he'd started school a year early. He wasn't even eighteen yet. He had never really fit in—he'd been younger than nearly everyone, and smarter—and maybe he'd acted it. It was hard to deal with the pompous jerks on a campus filled with smart people when he knew he could run rings around most of them.

But Madison had helped. When he started dating her six months ago, she'd kind of legitimized him, in a way. He'd made friends. Found a place to belong.

Until he blew it.

"After this, I don't know if anyone would hire me."

And he didn't want to work for anyone else. If he was going to work for a start-up, he was going to start it himself. He had plenty of ideas, plenty of smarts, and could raise the capital necessary or write another video game. He didn't particularly enjoy writing game code, but he was good at it, and he could sell the code for a small fortune.

But not now. Not when he was shy of eighteen, expelled from Stanford, and on three years' probation.

He would never forgive Duke for cutting this deal.

Madison started crying. Sean ached—he didn't want to hurt her. He hugged her tightly. "Hey, I'll visit."

"You know it's not the same. You'll be there, I'll be here—it's over, Sean."

He'd known it would be, but it still stung. "Maddie, don't say that—"

She jumped up. She couldn't look at him. "I love you, Sean. But it's over."

His heart stopped. Love? She loved him? Oh, God, he'd really hurt her. He never wanted to hurt anyone, especially Maddie.

"Maddie—"

"Don't say it. I don't want to hear it, because you won't mean it."

He wasn't going to say it. He liked Madison a lot, he cared about her, but love? He was seventeen. His life was fucked up. He was moving to Massachusetts. Love? Really? He didn't even like himself *half the time, how could he love anyone else?*

"Let's just see how it goes, okay?" he said. "You don't know that we can't make this work."

"Good-bye, Sean."

"Maddie—don't leave like this."

She left.

He didn't go after her.

Sean hadn't seen Madison since that Sunday afternoon. Until now. Almost thirteen years later to the day.

CHAPTER NINE

What the hell was Madison McAllister doing on his doorstep?

The bell rang again, forcing Sean to his feet. He strode out of his den and opened the front door.

"Madison."

She smiled at him, a perfect smile, but it didn't reach her eyes. Madison McAllister had been unattainable. He'd thought . . . well, what had he thought? He'd been two weeks shy of his eighteenth birthday when he was expelled; Madison was two years older. They'd had fun, which was all he'd wanted at the time. It was all she wanted. That was a lifetime ago.

"I should have called first, but I wasn't certain you'd speak to me."

"How did you get my address?"

"I can be persuasive."

"That isn't an answer."

"May I come in?"

He hesitated, just a fraction. She sensed his indecision and said, "I would never have flown out here if it wasn't an emergency. I need your help, Sean. You're the only one who can help. You're the only person I can trust."

A bit melodramatic, but his curiosity was piqued. He had cared for Madison once upon a time. They'd spent the better part of his freshman year together. She'd been a sophomore when they'd met in a French literature class. Sean hated French, but it was better than the alternative language requirement. Madison loved French. It was the only class Sean had ever struggled in, but he'd ended up with a B largely because of Madison.

"Come in," he said.

She looked around, her back to him. "You have a lovely home."

"Yes, we do."

She was surprised. "You're married?"

"Almost." He closed the door behind her.

When she turned to face him, tears leaked from her eyes. He hated seeing tears; it always hit him in the gut. The last time he'd seen Madison she'd been crying, too.

"My husband is in trouble—but I wouldn't come to you if it was just about Carson. It's my son, Jesse. I didn't want Carson to take him to Mexico—I told him no, it's the beginning of the school year. But he talked me into it, said he'd only miss one day of school. They flew down Thursday afternoon. He promised me they'd be back Sunday."

"Yesterday?"

She nodded.

"And he wasn't."

"I called Saturday because he didn't tell me what flight he'd be on, but he didn't answer. An hour later he forwarded me his itinerary. They were supposed to be in at eleven fifty Sunday morning. They weren't on the plane! And the airport said they never boarded. I tried calling, no answer. I haven't spoken to him or Jesse in forty-eight hours. Jesse's phone goes straight to voice mail. I'm terrified."

Madison was panicking. Sean steered her to the living

room and she sat on the couch. Though she was dressed impeccably, with perfect clothes and makeup, she was playing with her fingers, twisting them around. Her fingernail polish had been nearly all scraped off, and all of the nails had been bitten to the quick.

"They may have lost their phones," Sean said. "And I won't lie to you—Mexico can be very dangerous. Depending where they are, they could have had their luggage stolen, or been pickpocketed; Carson could have lost his wallet."

She was shaking her head. "I called the resort and they would not tell me whether they were registered! Said it was against policy, but I'm his wife! I flew down to Acapulco and finally the manager told me the truth—they'd checked out on Saturday. *Saturday.* Not Sunday. I've been calling and calling and sending emails and . . ." She took a deep breath and reached for Sean, squeezed his hand. "Sean, I called Carson's employer. He works for a start-up in Orange County. They said he'd taken vacation time. That he wasn't in Mexico for *their* business. I didn't know what to do. I know your family rescues h-h-hostages."

"Stop. You don't know what's happened, do not assume the worst. Did Duke give you my address?"

Why would his brother just share that information? And not tell Sean about it?

She shook her head. "I called Quentin. Told him I wanted to mail you some pictures I'd found, asked if he had your current address."

Of course Quentin would give it out. The guy was as honest as the day is long and the least suspicious person Sean had ever met. He was the only friend from Stanford that Sean had kept in touch with, they'd worked on some computer systems together—he'd even invited him to the wedding.

Sean was going to have a talk with him. He worked for

one of the biggest computer gaming companies in Seattle. He should be more security-conscious.

"Madison, you don't know—"

"Yes, I do. Something is wrong and I need you to find them."

The last thing Sean wanted to do was go to Mexico to find his ex-girlfriend's husband and son. Yet . . . they could be in trouble. Kane was itching for work. If this job seemed tame enough, Sean could ask Kane to do it. But he needed more information.

"How is your marriage? Are you separated? Divorcing? Any reason for Carson to leave the country with your son?"

All standard questions Sean would ask any potential client—even if he had no intention of taking the job. Kane would ask him, and he needed the answers.

"No, we're fine."

He raised an eyebrow. "Are you sure?"

"Yes! I'm *positive*."

"Why are you coming to me? Your father can hire the best PI in the business."

"Rogan-Caruso is the best."

That was certainly true, but Ronald McAllister hated Sean, and he would never let her hire RCK. Still, there were a couple of other firms RCK could refer her to.

"Truthfully, if it's a kidnapping, you need to talk to my brother Kane. He works south of the border. The best way to reach him is through JT Caruso. I'll call him for you, but I don't work for RCK anymore."

Her lip quivered. "But I need *you*."

"Madison, this just isn't something I can do." He wasn't going to work for his ex-girlfriend six weeks before his wedding. Not only because it was awkward, but because he had a wedding to organize. And a honeymoon. He wanted—needed—to be home at night for

Lucy, especially when she was working a difficult case like the one in Laredo.

Madison scraped off the last of the nail polish on her left thumb. "I think Carson got involved in something he can't get out of, and now my son is in the middle of it. I'll die if anything happens to him."

Against Sean's better judgment, he asked, "What exactly did your husband get involved in?"

She knew, he could see it in the way she avoided looking him in the eye.

"Madison, you need to be completely honest with me."

She stood up and paced. Madison had always been a beautiful woman—the kind of beauty that was graceful, classic, almost like a porcelain doll. Age had improved her.

But he also knew her tells, the way she avoided his gaze, the way she wrung her hands, the scraping of the polish, so discreet, as if no one would notice.

She had a secret and she didn't want to tell him.

Sean walked to the door. He didn't have time for games. "I'm sorry you came all this way, but we're through."

She spun around, a flash of anger in her vivid green eyes. "Do you think this was easy for me? Coming here, asking for your help?"

"Then why did you?"

She tilted her chin up. "Carson is a lawyer for a start-up. But he made some bad investments a few years ago and refused to go to my father to bail him out. He has a strong sense of pride—a lot like you, Sean."

That grated. Their breakup had been more or less mutual—he'd been expelled, after all, and moving cross-country. Long-distance relationships rarely worked, especially not as teenagers. And then there was his anger—that Madison's father had forbidden her to see him and they snuck around, that he'd been expelled in the first place even though he'd done the right thing, that his brother Duke had made an agreement Sean didn't want to sign, but had no choice because he was still a minor and Duke was his legal guardian. Sean had a lot of anger buried under his happy-go-lucky, partying lifestyle.

"Don't compare me to your husband, Madison."

"He took a freelance accounting job—before he went to law school, he was an accountant. He didn't lie to me— he told me he was going to Mexico on business. I just think it wasn't for the start-up—it was for this other business."

"What other business?"

"I don't know! I'm telling you the truth, Sean. I never asked. Maybe—I didn't want to know. Carson is a good man, but over the last couple years he's become sullen. We had more money than ever before, but it didn't seem to make him happy."

"Money doesn't make anyone happy."

"You don't understand!"

"I understand a lot more than you think. He's a lawyer *and* an accountant. Freelance? He was laundering money for someone. It's as clear as day."

"No."

But there was no venom in her voice. She'd thought the same thing.

Sean rubbed his face with both hands. He didn't want to turn Madison away, but he couldn't be involved with this bullshit.

He said, "Put together everything you know about Carson's travel plans, his businesses—legitimate and illegitimate. We'll need a recent photo, passport numbers, phone numbers, credit cards, bank accounts. I'll make you a list. We'll get on a conference call with JT tonight and he'll put together a team to find Carson and Jesse."

"So you will do it." She sighed in relief. "Thank you, Sean."

"No, I'm not touching this." Of course she didn't understand; Madison McAllister always got her way. But there was no way he could go to Mexico now. "I'm getting married next month, I don't have time. But I'll help you with the details. JT and Kane are far more capable of handling something like this anyway. Kane has rescued hundreds of Americans, those who were in danger and those who just didn't want to come home and face the music. And I'm only helping because there's an innocent child at risk. I couldn't care less what happens to your husband, Madison. He made his own bed. That he dragged his kid into the mess makes him ten times worse."

"He couldn't have known that something might happen—he wouldn't do that to Jesse."

Sean shook his head. "Get your head out of the sand, Madison."

"I need *you* on this. Only you care enough."

"Maddie, I'm sorry, but believe me when I tell you that my brother is just as good as me. Better, in situations like this."

She opened her purse and took out her phone. She stared at the screen, then walked over to Sean and showed him a photo. "This is Jesse."

Sean stared at the image. The boy was older than Sean had thought he'd be. Older . . . and he knew. As soon as he looked into Jesse's deep-blue eyes, he knew.

He couldn't speak. His hand began to shake. Jesse had dark-blond hair, darker than his mother. He had his mother's smile.

But he had Sean's eyes. The same color, the same shape. And if that didn't convince him that Jesse was in fact his son, the dimples did. Madison's smile, but Sean's dimples, one side deeper than the other.

He didn't need to ask her if Jesse was his son; he could see it in the boy's face. That's why she'd come to Sean.

He could hardly speak. Waves of anger and sorrow and a cold disbelief washed over him. "How dare you." His voice was barely a whisper. "How dare you keep this from me." He'd scream if he didn't control his growing rage.

"I didn't have a choice."

"A *choice*? He's mine."

"He's *my* son."

He stared at her, took a step forward. She stepped backward.

"You—you didn't give me a chance," he said. "Do you think so little of me that you thought I would have walked away from my responsibility? From my own child?" Now he was shouting. He had to get these emotions under control. He couldn't think. He couldn't do anything except feel a deep loss.

You have a son who doesn't know who you are.

"I wasn't going to be a *responsibility*. We were young, we were stupid, I didn't even know I was pregnant until the night you told me you were going to MIT. Do you actually think we could have been parents together?"

"Yes!"

"What, you would have married me?"

"I wasn't impoverished, Madison. I've done well."

"We didn't love each other."

"So you lied to me?"

"You didn't love me. I knew it that night when you told me you were leaving."

"I never lied to you. I cared about you, and I would have done everything for you and our baby. Dammit, Madison! You should have told me! I should have been a part of Jesse's life from the beginning!"

"And you would have what? Dropped out of college? Worked where? Done what? Resented me and Jesse because we forced you into marriage?"

"You have no idea what would have happened then because you didn't give me a chance." His voice cracked. He swallowed; his mouth was dry as sand.

"Because you are known for making smart decisions. Like embarrassing the university and the FBI when you hacked into their database."

"I had a right to know. He's my kid. My *son*. And you had no right to keep him from me. No right!" He was repeating himself but he didn't care.

"I had *every* right. It was *my* choice to have him, I didn't ask you for *anything*. No money, no child support—"

"That has nothing to do with it! I would have supported him. You *know* that!"

"I didn't need you."

Sean felt like his heart had been turned inside out. He wanted to slap her. He'd never wanted to hit a woman so badly as right now. He backed away, overcome by the intensity of his emotions.

"That came out wrong," she said.

He didn't respond. He couldn't even look at her.

"Sean—my father—you know how he is." Her voice was softer. Through his overwhelming emotions, he knew she was manipulating him. Trying to calm him down. Trying to get him to do what she wanted. "You'd been expelled. It . . . tainted you. Us. I didn't want it to come back on my son."

He didn't regret his decision, but it had come back to bite him in the ass so many times that he was beginning to wonder if he should have just turned his back on the pedophile.

Of course, that wasn't the issue—the issue was how he'd exposed the bastard. He'd embarrassed the university and law enforcement. In hindsight, there were other ways to yield the same result. But at the time . . . he liked to prove how much smarter he was than everyone else. He was a teenager. A showman. A genius with too much anger and the need to prove himself to . . . to everyone.

He didn't have anything to prove to anyone anymore.

"I was weak, Sean. I couldn't go against my father."

That he believed. Ron McAllister was a narrow-minded bastard who had never thought Sean was good enough for Madison. They were kids, they should have been going out and having fun, but it was as if Sean were always on trial for something. It didn't matter that Sean started college early, that he had a genius-level IQ or had made six figures designing a top video game before he'd turned eighteen. All that mattered was that he didn't come from a "good" family, that he had gotten in trouble as a kid. Trouble? No one knew the half of it. The three years after his parents died . . . Sean could have killed himself a dozen times over. That he didn't was a miracle—and Sean didn't believe in miracles.

"Forgive me, Sean."

"No. No way in hell am I ever going to forgive you, Madison."

He turned to face her. Silent tears ran down her face, but they had no impact on him.

"Please. Sean. I can't lose my son. I don't have anyone else to turn to."

"I can't believe you kept me from knowing *my son*. He's twelve years old. *Twelve*. I lost out on *twelve years*. Does he even know I'm his father?"

Slowly, she shook her head. "I—I told him I didn't know."

"Am I on his birth certificate?"

Again, she shook her head.

Sean didn't think he could feel any worse, but he did. His son—his child—out there, not knowing him, not knowing his heritage, who his father was, what he was made of. A blank line on a birth certificate. How could Madison have done that? How could she have done such a thing to Sean? To her own son?

Instead of hitting Madison, Sean swung out and knocked over a decorative vase. It shattered on the tile floor. He stared at the pieces of glass. He and Lucy had gone to a craft fair one Sunday afternoon and bought the handblown vase. It didn't really match the house, but they both loved it. Like his heart, it was broken.

What could he do? Leave his son—*his son*—down in Mexico, without knowing his fate? With a father—a *stepfather*—who had put Sean's child in jeopardy because of his own selfish needs? What was Carson up to? Were they already dead?

Could he turn his back on Madison and Jesse as if he had never known the truth?

Sean turned to face the woman who had betrayed him so deeply he didn't know how he was going to climb out of this pit. "I will not lie to Jesse," he said.

Madison released a sob but nodded.

"Whatever I say is gospel. You do everything I tell you. You do not lie to me about anything, from this moment forward. Understand?"

Again, she nodded.

"Get out of here. Right now. I can't look at you."

"But Sean—"

"I'll email you everything I need to get started. But I need you gone. Lucy will be home soon and I have to talk to her."

"Lucy . . ."

"My fiancée. The love of my life. If I have to leave the country to find my son, then she needs to know what I'm facing."

Madison opened her mouth but to her credit didn't say a word.

"I'll leave in the morning."

"I have to come."

"No."

"But—"

"You will not come with me."

He couldn't talk anymore. He had to act. To do *something*.

Sean opened the front door and didn't look at Madison as she crossed the threshold. She turned and faced him. "Sean, I *am* sorry."

"No, you're not. If Jesse wasn't in trouble, you would never have told me."

He slammed the door. He had a son. And his son was in danger.

CHAPTER TEN

Typing the formal memo to Madison asking for all the information he needed to begin the search for Carson and Jesse calmed Sean down. At least enough for him to think clearly. She'd already sent the preliminary information—Carson Spade's full name, social, employer, recent photos—but there was much more Sean needed.

He sent off the email, left a message for Kane to call him immediately, and then called JT Caruso. He needed cover from RCK in case things went south in Mexico.

"Are you certain you want to do this?" JT asked after Sean told him the basics. "She should hire RCK and we'll put together a team. I can have good people on site in eight hours."

Sean almost told JT about Jesse, but decided to keep that information to himself, at least until he told Lucy. Right now, it was need to know . . . and JT didn't need to know.

"I have to do it. I left Kane a message—I want to use him, but we need to be partners on this. I'll pay RCK rates."

"I'll pretend you didn't say that," JT said. "I don't have

to remind you how many operations you covered at your own expense. Jet fuel isn't cheap."

"You know I don't care about that."

"We could solve all your problems if you come back."

"I don't have any problems, if you can give me cover."

"Sean." JT didn't say anything else; he didn't have to.

Sean sighed and rubbed his eyes. Sure, he and Duke had mended fences, but every time there was something critical, something where it might seem that Sean was going to the dark side, Duke assumed the worst. Sean couldn't live like that anymore. "You know why I can't."

"Won't. Not can't."

"That's a conversation for another day. I wouldn't ask for help if it wasn't important."

"You're not telling me something."

"True, but it's not important to you right now. I'll fully brief Kane."

"Fair enough. I hope this girl is worth it."

"I don't give a shit about Madison McAllister Spade. And her husband sounds like an ass. It's the kid, JT. He's in danger and I can't turn my back on him."

"That I understand. Kane's in Hidalgo right now, so he should get back to you quickly. He's pissed at me because I won't let him take any major assignments, so this will be a good transition for him before he gets back to the job."

"I can't promise it won't be dangerous."

"No one can promise we'll live to see the sunrise in the morning. What else do you need?"

"A plane. I don't have the contacts here that I do in Sacramento. I have a new plane on order, but it won't be delivered until the week before I get married."

"I never thought I'd hear you say those words—and without fear."

"It's Lucy. What can I say."

"I'm glad I didn't fall in love with Jack's sister." JT laughed and Sean, as usual, felt that little twinge of panic at the mention of Jack. The guy scared him. He shouldn't— Jack and Kane were two peas in a pod. But Lucy wasn't Kane's baby sister. "I'm kidding you, buddy. Jack is a man of few words, but he used them to sing your praises after you took out Rollins and Tobias."

Sean didn't want to relive that nightmare, so he went back to the subject at hand. "In addition to the plane, I need some research."

"You've never asked for research assistance. Jaye's going to lord this over you for the rest of your life."

"She's good. I want to get out of here first thing in the morning—I'd go tonight, but I need to talk to Lucy first. I'm sending you the information Madison gave me already, plus the research I've started. I'm expecting more info. My gut tells me Carson Spade is laundering money, but I don't have the time to trace who he's working for and verify the data. The more I know, the better chance I have of finding him."

"We'll take care of it. Be careful, Sean."

Sean hung up and glanced at the clock. It was nearly ten, and Lucy still wasn't back. He sent her a message.

Have you eaten?

He pushed back from his desk and went down the hall to the kitchen. He looked through the refrigerator thinking about what he could put together. There wasn't much. He had planned on doing the shopping tomorrow—he'd actually grown to like his weekly excursion to the grocery store.

His phone vibrated and he read Lucy's message.

We ate in Laredo. Home in less than thirty. Love you.

Thirty minutes—that would put them in well after ten. He doubted either Lucy or Siobhan had eaten much of anything, not with everything that was going on. And he knew Lucy—when she was working, food was the last thing on her mind.

Eggs, tomatoes, mushrooms—he'd make omelets when they got back. Find a way to get Siobhan off into her room so he could talk to Lucy.

How was he going to explain this to her?

And then there was Noah . . . maybe he'd just drop Siobhan and Lucy off, and Sean wouldn't have to talk to him.

Noah Armstrong was a bit of an enigma for Sean. They hadn't liked each other when they first met nearly two years ago. That was certainly an understatement. Noah was the type of self-righteous, rule-of-law cop that Sean despised. Yet . . . Noah had bent when he needed to bend. He and Noah had learned to get along, largely because of Lucy. And, Sean had to admit, when he and Noah had worked together on an undercover case where Sean infiltrated a hacktivist group, Noah had come through big time.

Noah had been Lucy's trainer before she entered the academy, and he'd been very supportive of her career. Yet even though Noah hadn't made any blatant moves on Lucy, Sean knew he was attracted to her. Hell, Noah had admitted it to Sean. But Noah was too honorable to go after another man's girl.

Still, Sean was more than a little happy that now that Noah was in San Antonio—even temporarily—there was an engagement ring on Lucy's finger.

Of course, Lucy was oblivious to Noah's feelings. For a woman who could see and understand the smallest detail at a crime scene, a woman who studied criminal psychology and was a shark in interviews, she was clueless when it came to how men viewed her. It wasn't even her looks, it was the package. The way she moved, the way she played with her hair, how she frowned when studying a complex problem. To Sean, she glowed. He wasn't naturally a jealous lover, but with Lucy he got the pang. Sometimes. Especially around Noah Armstrong. Okay, only around Noah Armstrong.

Maybe because Sean sometimes felt he wasn't good enough for her.

Sean shook the thought from his head. He prepared everything for omelets, but didn't cook. His phone rang as he covered the vegetables.

He answered, "Rogan."

"It's Kane. I just talked to JT."

Sean was relieved to speak to his brother. He was glad he didn't have to repeat everything. "I'll send you what I sent him."

"He already did."

"I can't do this without you."

Kane didn't say anything for a long minute and Sean thought he'd been disconnected. Then Kane said, "How old is Madison's kid?"

"Twelve."

"It's yours."

His stomach flipped. "I didn't know until tonight."

"Of course you didn't. I know Madison's type. I knew it thirteen years ago. I have a plane. I'll be in San Antonio at dawn."

"Thank you."

"He's a Rogan. We're going to bring him home. I need to make some calls about this Spade. I know a security guy in Acapulco who can help."

"I confirmed that they flew into Mexico City, then transferred to Acapulco on Thursday night. They had return tickets direct from Acapulco to Los Angeles for Sunday, but never used them. Madison said the hotel manager told her they checked out Saturday evening, even though their flight wasn't until the morning."

"I'll have more answers tomorrow. Watch yourself with that woman—she's lied to you for thirteen years, there's no reason she isn't keeping something else from you now."

"I asked Jaye to run a deep background."

"I know." Kane hung up.

Sean sat down and put his head in his hands. He felt a deep loss inside that he couldn't explain. He'd missed the first twelve years of his son's life. He hadn't raised him. He wasn't there for his birth. He wasn't there to teach him to ride a bike or skateboard or play baseball or video games. He didn't even know if Jesse liked any of those things. What was the kid going to think when Sean showed up? How was he going to tell him? Because Jesse had to know the truth—that if Sean had known about him, Jesse would have been a part of his life.

How was Lucy going to take this news? She was a rock . . . but she'd gone through so much in her life. Sean would make sure that she knew there was nothing between him and Madison—Lucy trusted him, but more than that, Sean trusted Lucy. She would understand; she would support him. They'd get through this—together. Because with Lucy, he could get through anything. Do anything. Face his son, tell him the truth.

I'm your father, Jesse. If I had known about you, I would have been there.

Would he have? He hoped so. He'd been young and wild, he'd partied hard and dated lots of women and never wanted to settled down, until Lucy. Yet . . . he would have taken responsibility. He would have been there for the important events. Talked to him. Traveled with him. Insisted on joint custody. Jesse had a right to know who the Rogans were, what his grandparents had accomplished in their short lives, what RCK did and what his legacy was. Sean would never have forced any one path on his kid—he might have even discouraged it—but Jesse needed to know that he had options, that he had heroes for uncles and a noble background of family who always fought for the right thing, even when it wasn't easy. Even when it was dangerous.

Sean's son was being raised by a criminal. Money laundering meant one of three things: drugs, human trafficking, or organized crime. Southern California? Sean was betting drugs, but he couldn't count on it. Any of the big three would put Jesse in danger.

It put Madison in danger as well . . . but Sean couldn't concern himself with Madison right now. Once he found Jesse, brought him back along with Carson Spade—whom he would turn over to law enforcement—he would think about Madison and Jesse's future security.

And Madison had better damn well listen to him.

A beep told him that someone was on the front porch accessing the keypad. It must be Lucy. Sean went to meet Lucy at the door as she opened it. Noah wasn't with them, and Sean was relieved. He didn't know why.

Both Siobhan and Lucy looked exhausted.

Sean kissed his fiancée, then gave Siobhan a hug. "I'm glad you came back with Lucy."

"I didn't want to," Siobhan said. "I wanted to stay."

"It's not safe for you right now," Lucy said. "We'll go back tomorrow." She turned to Sean. "I may be gone for a day or two."

"That's okay—I have a case." Suddenly he didn't want to go. "I'll be busy. Are you hungry?"

Siobhan shook her head, but Lucy said, "Siobhan only picked at her food."

"I'm so angry. They took everything. I mean, I have my photos, but they took everything else. My camera. My computer. We tracked them down—destroyed! And they went through my stuff."

Sean exchanged glances with Lucy, then put his arm

around Siobhan's shoulders and led her down the hall. "You can shower, change, I'll whip up an omelet. Breakfast food is about all we have in the house right now."

"You don't have to do anything for me," Siobhan said.

"Nonsense." Sean stopped in front of the main guest room. "I'm serious."

Siobhan smiled at him, though it didn't reach her eyes. "How's Kane? Better?"

"You haven't talked to him?"

She shook her head. "Not since the hospital."

"He's good." Sean frowned. "Better than you, it seems."

"I've been looking for Mari and Ana for over two years—I should have been looking harder."

"Don't do that to yourself. There is no one who's looked for those girls harder than you." He tilted her chin up. "Take a shower, then come and eat."

"Okay." She gave him another hug. "By the way, Sean, I absolutely adore Lucy. I see why you love her."

Sean waited a minute until he heard the shower running, then walked back to the living room.

Lucy wasn't there. He went upstairs and found her ready to get into the shower. "Join me," she said. "I missed you today."

Sean hesitated, just a second. He should tell her about Madison and Jesse right now—but she was so tired, so forlorn. Later, after she relaxed, ate, had some peace. Then he could tell her. He touched her face, kissed her warmly.

"Ten minutes, Sean. Of you, me, and water. I need to clear my mind, regain my footing so I can look at this case objectively."

"Anything, princess."

Thirty minutes later Siobhan entered the kitchen, her curly red hair wet and hanging down her back. She looked a million times better than when she'd first walked in. So did Lucy. Sean finished the omelets and dished up three plates.

"You didn't have to do this," Siobhan said.

"Nonsense. I know Lucy doesn't eat right when she's working, and you had a difficult couple of days."

"Jail certainly wasn't fun."

Sean stared, mouth tight. "No one told me you were in jail."

"I didn't know the details until we got down there," Lucy said. "Trespassing, breaking and entering, assault—"

"He pinched my nipple," Siobhan said bluntly. "On purpose. My elbow in his nose was a knee-jerk reaction. I didn't *mean* to break it." She paused. "Not that I feel guilty about it."

"You shouldn't," Lucy said before Sean could speak. "Charges were dropped, but Siobhan uncovered something potentially big. We're going back tomorrow—we have several leads."

"And I'm worried about Elizabeth."

"Elizabeth?" Sean questioned.

"The baby," Lucy said. She had a faraway look on her face for a second, then shook her head. "We believe that Marisol or Ana gave birth and left her infant at a church."

"The baby was wearing a locket I gave to each girl," Siobhan said. She pulled her necklace out and showed Sean. "The locket was Marisol's because of the photo and what she wrote on the back, so I'm inclined to think Elizabeth is her daughter, but we don't know for certain."

"A baby?" he said. Sean was watching Lucy. She stared at her plate, not looking at anyone.

"She's beautiful," Siobhan said. "You know what happened to Marisol and Ana de la Rosa, right?"

Sean nodded. "They've been on the RCK hot sheet since they disappeared."

"Hot sheet?" Lucy asked.

"Individuals, regardless of nationality, who disappear in Mexico or the US under certain circumstances, such as sex trafficking. It's a long list, but it helps in case Kane and his team comes across a group or individual."

"I helped them get the job in Monterrey," Siobhan said. "They were saving money to rebuild their village. They wrote and called several times . . . wrote their grandmother—and then it stopped. Kane and his team helped initially, but there were no leads. Nothing. It was like they vanished into thin air." She took a bite, washed it down with water. "When Eric—a friend of mine who's a reporter—heard a rumor that Mari was in a brothel in Del Rio, I sent out flyers to every church in the area, then branched out to border towns in both Mexico and the States, thinking maybe they'd been grabbed for sex trafficking, or maybe took illegal jobs in the US. I don't really know what I was thinking, except they had to be somewhere." She took a big breath.

Lucy said, "Noah and I talked to the reporter. He gave us photos from his report into the brothel. Zach is running the images against our database and against the photos Siobhan took last night. Webb County has been very helpful, but the adjoining county less so."

"Jack lived in southern Texas for a long time," Sean reminded her. "You should reach out to him, get the information about the small-town cops. Who you can trust, who you can't."

"I might do that. It was too easy getting Siobhan out. Dropped charges an hour before her arraignment. They'd made up their mind before we even arrived."

Siobhan said, "Rick can be very persuasive."

Both Sean and Lucy knew Rick well, and if Lucy thought something was off, something was off. "Trust your instincts, Luce."

"Noah and I are on the same page. We think this is a black-market baby operation."

This time, Siobhan stared at Lucy. "What? No—it's set up to be a typical sex shop. A house to lock up the girls when they're not working."

Lucy didn't waver from her opinion. "It's not typical. The house wasn't in a major city. It was in an unpopulated rural area. You saw a young girl with a baby, another girl pregnant, and Father Sebastian found Elizabeth. There was also another young mother who was left at the emergency room in the middle of labor and needed an emergency C-section—we believe that may be connected to the same group. She left without giving any information, but police traced her to a house that had been set up just like the one in Freer. Also abandoned. Now she's in the wind as well."

"I don't have to leave," Sean said quietly. "If you need me, I can stay."

She shook her head. "I'm okay. Really—we have leads, we're going to find out what's going on down there."

Sean didn't want Lucy to go back to Laredo. And he didn't want to go to Mexico. Something about this case bothered him. Or maybe it was his own situation, not wanting to leave the country when Lucy was involved in something like this.

Lucy asked, "How long will you be gone?"

"Hopefully not more than three days."

"So back by the weekend. Perfect, I'm not on call this weekend, and one thing I've learned this last year is not to work on my days off." She squeezed his hand, but even her little smile was sad. He wanted to talk more about this case, what she saw, what she was thinking, because he could see Lucy's mind at work. She always internalized her cases, unable to put them aside to give herself some peace. It made her good at her job . . . but it took its toll.

"What kind of case are you working?" Siobhan asked Sean.

Sean didn't want to explain the situation until he had a chance to tell Lucy in private. "An old friend from college came by today—her husband and son disappeared while in Mexico. The husband may be involved with something shady. Kane and I are going to look into it."

"I didn't know you were working with RCK again," Siobhan said. "It's about time."

"I'm not with RCK, but since I know Madison, and a child is at risk, I feel I need to help. Kane knows the area and people better than I do, but considering he had major surgery three months ago, I'm not going to ask him to go alone."

"He knows everything," Siobhan said with a touch of sarcasm. "Stubborn jerk," she muttered.

Lucy glanced at Sean, eyebrows up. He shrugged. "Rogans tend to be stubborn," he said.

"Some more than others," Siobhan countered.

"Seriously, though—I'll be available by phone. If you need anything, call me."

"Will do." Siobhan rose and stretched. "I'm going to sleep. Noah—what a genuine guy, even if he's a bit gruff—said he'd pick us up at seven to beat traffic. I'm setting my alarm for six forty-five. It doesn't take me long to get ready, and I really need a good night's sleep."

She hugged Lucy and kissed Sean on the cheek. "Thank you for letting me stay."

"Mi casa es su casa."

She laughed. "Your Spanish is pathetic, Sean."

She left the kitchen and Lucy cleared the plates. "I'll take care of these tomorrow," Sean said. "Tell me what's wrong."

Lucy sat back down. "Siobhan doesn't believe it—but Noah and I agree. Multiple women, multiple infants, multiple pregnancies. Marisol and Ana disappeared a little over two years ago, and one of them gave birth to Elizabeth, but left her wrapped in a shirt at a church. The other pregnant women, the other house in Laredo that was shut down at the same time as the house outside Freer opened, I think one of two things is happening. What if these are all girls in the sex trade who get pregnant and instead of forcing the girls to terminate the pregnancy, they force them to deliver and then sell the babies?"

Sean tensed. "Lucy—"

"Or," she continued, "this is the plan all along. Not sex trafficking. Maybe when these girls find themselves pregnant, they are convinced to give up their babies. Taken from their friends and family, leave voluntarily, I don't know. Maybe they think it's a legitimate adoption. But so many are embarrassed, or unmarried, or illegal immigrants, or young and they don't know who to turn to. They're being used. Manipulated. The mother in the hospital three months ago—she could have told the doctor everything, she would have been given help. The ob-gyn is someone Siobhan vouches for, she seems to have a good head on her shoulders and has been very agreeable to all of Noah's suggestions. Security, keeping Baby Elizabeth longer and under protection."

"What happened to the woman three months ago?"

"According to the report, she was put in a shelter for unwed mothers, but left two days later, with the baby. Just vanished."

Lucy looked down at her hands. She was tense and shaking.

Sean pulled back her hair, made her look at him. "Honey, what is it?"

"I can't stop thinking about Elizabeth—that's what Father Sebastian named her. Innocent. Pure. Left at a church by a desperate mother . . . where did she go? Why didn't she ask Father Sebastian for help? She trusted him enough with her baby, why not with her own safety? What if these babies *are* being sold? What if they're being sold to . . . to . . ." A sob escaped Lucy's throat.

"Don't go there," Sean said, harsher than he wanted. "You can't go there."

"I can't help it." Her voice was small. "I want to believe that rich people who can't adopt legally are buying these babies and will love and take care of them. That maybe they're not bad people. But you and I both know that there are sick people in this world, and who is going to protect these babies? If we can't find the others . . . I don't know. I see everything that can happen and it makes me feel so damn helpless!"

Sean gathered Lucy up in his arms. "Don't. You're going to do your job and do it well, better than anyone else. Noah's on this, and you trust him—he's a good cop. Between the two of you, you'll find these people and stop them."

"And what about the babies? Are we going to find them?"

Sean couldn't answer that; if he said yes, Lucy would know he was placating her. If he said no, he'd destroy her hope. "Have faith, Lucy."

She seemed unusually fragile. Sean turned off the lights and wrapped his arm around Lucy's shoulder. He walked her upstairs. Put her to bed. She was asleep in minutes, snuggled against his chest. Safe.

He was almost asleep when he realized he hadn't told her about Jesse.

CHAPTER ELEVEN

Siobhan woke up at four that morning after nearly five solid hours of sleep. She didn't want to get up—the bed was the most comfortable she'd ever slept in, with smooth sheets and a thick down comforter. She sighed, stretched, then relaxed and checked her phone for messages. One from her editor she'd been ignoring for days. He wanted to know what she was working on. She wasn't—she hadn't been doing much of anything since she got the call from Father Sebastian about the locket. She'd planned to visit a Habitat for Humanity site in El Paso—they were building a series of town houses that would eventually house twelve families. Each of the families was required to help, and Siobhan wanted to explore their stories in a photo journal of the entire project.

She liked to think her mom would have been proud of the path she'd chosen. Siobhan's mother, Iona, had planned to be a nun from when she was little. The Sisters of Mercy didn't require their members go through a convent, though most were nuns, but they required a three-year commitment and a devout lifestyle. It was at the end of the three years that Iona had met Andrew Walsh . . . but she didn't want to leave her work.

Siobhan's dad loved them, he wanted to marry Siobhan's mother, but Iona didn't want to settle in the States. She wanted to continue doing what she felt God called her to do. She never once called Siobhan's birth a mistake, though considering Iona and Andrew weren't married until Siobhan was five, the pregnancy was certainly unplanned. It was that year, when Siobhan was five, that Iona took a year off from the sisters and brought Siobhan to the States. She'd met her half sister Andie, her half brother Bobby—who was already in the Marines—and they lived on a horse farm in Virginia. Siobhan loved it. The house, her family, the horses, that she had her own room! She'd didn't want to leave, but she didn't want her mother to leave, either.

Siobhan didn't know exactly what happened between her parents, but they got married that summer and then Iona took Siobhan back to Mexico to work with the sisters. Her father visited for two weeks each year, wherever Iona was working, and Siobhan spent a month every summer in the States—but Iona never joined her. Her dad wrote to her often, and Siobhan took photos of everything that interested her and sent them to him. When Siobhan turned fourteen her mother said that she could choose—to go to school in the States or stay with the sisters.

Siobhan chose the States. She missed her father. She liked living a missionary life—she knew how to grow crops, deliver a baby, treat almost any injury, and she was the best fisherman among the sisters, much to the frustration of Sister Bernadette who had taught her. Her mother taught her English and even some Gaelic; she learned Spanish from the sisters and the locals; she taught English to the younger kids. Sister Gretchen, from Germany, had been a physicist before she got her calling. Siobhan learned math up to calculus by the time she was fourteen because Sister Gretchen was such a great teacher.

But Siobhan missed her dad. She wanted to experience *more*—the States, movie theaters, limitless books. She wanted to talk to people and see what they were like. She wanted to go to museums and see a big city and not be scared anymore.

Because for all the joy the missionary life gave her, there was fear. Great fear. Of men with guns, of the cartels, of corrupt police and executions.

She'd learned that fear came in all shapes and sizes; that the grass was always greener on the other side of the border, but in the dark of night you had to know in your heart that you were on your path, not the path forged for you by someone else. It wasn't until her father died, joining her mother in Heaven, that she searched her soul, searched her heart, and knew what she should do. And the last ten years—through violence, through illness, through heartbreak—she had a deep inner peace because she was on the journey she was meant to be. It wasn't the path of her mother, or her father; it was her own.

When the digital clock changed to five o'clock, Siobhan got out of the warm, soft bed and dressed in layers as she habitually did. Lucy had been kind enough to let her use her laundry room, so she pulled all her things out of the dryer and repacked her lone backpack. It was durable, military grade, and could hold far more than it appeared from the size.

But she felt naked and lost without her camera.

It wasn't just the cost of the equipment. It was state of the art, for certain, and it would be difficult and costly to replace, but without her camera she felt incomplete. She'd had a camera since she was five years old; she itched to hold one right now.

She walked down the hall to the light in the kitchen. Lucy was there, pouring herself coffee. Siobhan had been thrilled to finally meet the girl who'd won Sean's heart, but she wished it could have been under better circumstances.

"Coffee?" Lucy offered.

"Thank you. Black." She used to drink it with cream and sugar, but when she was on the road with the sisters, she couldn't be guaranteed either, so she grew used to drinking it black. Fresh-brewed coffee itself was a luxury—she really despised the instant kind. "Well, maybe just a sprinkle of sugar."

She sat down and looked around the kitchen. "This is really a terrific house. And the neighborhood is so quiet. I get itchy when I'm in a city after living so many years in the middle of nowhere, but this doesn't feel like San Antonio."

"It's an established neighborhood. Sean picked it out." Lucy put the coffee in front of Siobhan and sat across from her. "I thought it'd be too big, but we've had a lot of company. Kane stayed here for three weeks after his surgery."

"I'm glad he took time off—I was afraid he'd go right back into the trenches. He's not getting any younger."

"I think he realized that."

"Sean has always been there for Kane, but Kane is hard to get close to." That was an understatement. Siobhan wanted to throttle him half the time and kiss him the other half. Kiss him? She wanted to do a lot more than kiss him.

But Kane was stubborn. Stubborn with a capital S.

"How long have you known the family?" Lucy asked, sipping her own coffee.

"Forever," she said. "Andie, my half sister, was Kane's commanding officer when he enlisted. I was a kid, didn't meet him until I was seventeen and Andie was awarded a Purple Heart and a Medal of Honor for saving her unit and a bunch of civilians. Kane was at the ceremony, came back to the house. He reminded me of Bobby, my half brother. He'd been killed in Afghanistan the year before, and Andie missed him tremendously. I thought for the longest time that Kane and Andie were involved, but they're just friends." She didn't know much about her sister's private life. All she knew was that she'd been in love once and he'd died. She never talked about it, and Siobhan didn't ask.

Then seven years later, Siobhan saw Kane again. Under far more dangerous circumstances than a party at the house.

"Anyway," Siobhan said, shaking off the memories, "I started college in Virginia, then went to Ireland. I had no intention of going back to the Sisters of Mercy. My mom died when I was fifteen, after nearly twenty years of serving, and I didn't have the same calling. But . . . well, long story short, I've always loved photography. There's something the camera sees that we don't. The sisters' numbers were shrinking, they had fewer resources. I'd been working for *National Geographic* and traveling all over the world and I loved it. Then Sister Bernadette reached out to me. She asked if I would join the sisters for six months and help rebuild a village that had been destroyed in a flood. I could take pictures and document their work, bring attention to the plight of these small communities, and also help the sisters with their fund-raising. It was the least I could do, after having lived my first fourteen years with them. That was ten years ago. Now I spend three or four months each year with the sisters. The rest of the time I travel through Mexico and South America, primarily, freelancing for a couple magazines. *National Geographic*, *Life*, *Photography*, whatever I can sell to. Sometimes the *Times* if I can get a good Sunday feature story worked out. It's a good balance for me."

Sean walked in. "You were up early, Lucy," he said.

Lucy leaned up and kissed him. "You didn't sleep well last night. I thought I'd let you sleep longer."

Sean took out a pan and started preparing scrambled eggs. He got out tortillas, sausage, salsa, and cheese. "Spicy or sane," Sean asked Siobhan.

She laughed. "Spicy."

Sean moaned. "You and Lucy. It's a wonder your taste buds aren't fried by now."

"You don't have to cook," Lucy said. "We can get something at Starbucks."

"Sit. At least you'll have one good meal today."

"You're not hearing me complain," Siobhan said.

Sean left for a minute, then returned with a small black bag and put it in front of Siobhan. "It's not what you lost, but it should work until you can replace your camera."

"What?" Siobhan stared at the bag, then looked at Sean.

"Open it."

Lucy crossed over to Sean and kissed him. "You're amazing," she said.

Siobhan opened the bag case. Inside was a digital camera. Almost as nice as the one she'd lost. "I can't take this."

"It's a loan, until you get yours replaced. Seriously, I rarely use it. I configured it like your old one, so it should work with your phone app."

Siobhan jumped up and hugged first Sean, then Lucy, then Sean again. She blinked back tears. "You guys are so, so . . . wonderful. Thank you."

There was a beep at the door that startled Siobhan. "What's that?"

"Our security system." Sean typed in a code on a small tablet that was attached to the wall. "Oh, he has the code."

"You gave Noah the house code?" Lucy asked.

"Of course not. Kane."

Siobhan froze. "Kane's here?"

"Yes I am," a deep voice behind her said.

Her heart raced as she whirled around to face him.

Kane looked like he always did—hard, handsome, rough around the edges. He'd lost weight, and he'd never been overweight. His jaw was still square, firm, defiant. He had a touch of gray at his temples. His dark hair was still short, but a little longer than the military cut he usually kept. He wore khakis and a black T-shirt. He dropped his duffel bag just outside the kitchen entry.

He stared at her, his dark-blue eyes unreadable because he was good at shutting down his emotions.

I've always loved you, Kane.

She had, from that day when she rescued the little girl and he saved them both. He was impossible, arrogant, condescending, loyal, and brave. He cared more than he showed, more than he could say, about the plight of others. He acted, always acted, to stop bad people from hurting innocents. He didn't want to care, he said he didn't, but she saw that those who talked cared less than those who acted.

Kane didn't talk much.

He could deny his attraction until his last breath, and she wouldn't believe him. She'd spent too much time with him, on and off, over the years. She knew he loved her. Knew it as deeply as she knew the truth about her own feelings. He would come to accept the truth—though seeing him now, after what happened after his surgery, how he'd *ordered* her to leave as if she were one of his soldiers . . . that had hurt. She tried to tell herself it didn't, but it had. How was she going to get through to him?

"Just in time for breakfast," Lucy said, breaking the awkward silence.

"Seems you're not surprised to see me," Siobhan said to Kane.

"I'm not." He didn't elaborate. What did he know about

the baby? Marisol and Ana? She opened her mouth to ask, but he cut her off.

"We need to leave, Sean."

"Breakfast first," Sean said.

Siobhan frowned, looked from Kane to Sean and back again. Silent communication.

Lucy took Sean's hand and pulled him from the room. Siobhan glanced over her shoulder, wistful. They loved each other and told each other often. They didn't stop touching. The little things. Sean brushing by her shoulder, planting a light kiss on her lips. Lucy rubbing his biceps. They couldn't pass each other without physical contact. Why couldn't she have that? Why did she have to fight for everything?

Kane took over where Sean left off and slipped Siobhan a breakfast burrito. Then he pulled out aluminum foil as if he knew the kitchen well and made two burritos to go for him and Sean. He dished up the remainder of the food for Lucy, put it on the island, and popped a bottle of hot sauce next to her plate.

"I like her," Siobhan said, hating the silence between them.

"She's one of the best."

"From you, high praise."

"Don't do anything stupid, Siobhan."

She bristled. "Don't start."

"You were arrested." He turned around and stared at her. There was a flash in his eyes, heat and ice, and she almost couldn't speak.

"I did what had to be done. You would have done the same."

"I would never have been caught."

"I'm just not as good as you then," she snipped. "Where are you and Sean off to? Someone disappeared in Mexico, Sean said?"

Kane opened his mouth, then closed it. He glanced over Siobhan's shoulder, and for a moment Siobhan saw indecision on his face. Kane was *never* indecisive.

"Businessman disappeared with his son," he said. "Friend of Sean's."

Kane put the breakfast burritos and several water bottles into a small cooler and zipped it up. He was about to walk out when Siobhan reached out and touched him.

"Kane."

"Good-bye."

"I meant what I said three months ago, and if you think I've forgotten, you're an idiot. I certainly know *you* haven't."

He walked out.

"Well, dammit, that didn't go well," she muttered and ate her breakfast.

Kane drove, which irked Sean—he much preferred driving.

"You didn't tell me Siobhan was at your house."

"Problem?"

No answer.

"She was pretty shaken last night. What was I supposed to do, tell Lucy to leave her in Laredo after her motel room was ransacked?"

"Why didn't she call us?" Kane said.

It took Sean a full minute to understand what Kane was talking about. "You mean, why did she call Rick and not JT?"

"The feds are ill equipped to handle this situation."

Sean had second—well, *tenth*—thoughts on leaving Lucy this week. "Lucy told me about the case."

"She doesn't know the half of it."

That angered Sean. "Then give her something. She trusts you, Kane. If you keep something important from her because of some stupid jealousy thing, that's on you."

"This has nothing to do with jealousy, little brother. I talked to Rick. This isn't sex trafficking. It's black-market babies."

"Lucy is good at her job. She already figured it out."

"I didn't say she wasn't."

"What's with you and Siobhan?"

"She finds trouble. Actively seeks it out. If she had a lead on the missing sisters, she should have contacted RCK. Rick chose his side long ago. He's good, but he and his people can't do what needs to be done."

Sean's phone rang, cutting off this infuriating conversation. He glanced down and swore under his breath before answering. "Madison."

"Where are you? What's going on?"

"I told you last night that Kane and I were leaving first thing in the morning."

"And I told you I need to come with you!"

"And I said no. Go back to California, Madison. There is nothing you can do except slow us down. If you hear from Carson or Jesse, call me at this number. Otherwise, I don't want to hear from you at all."

"Sean—don't be like this."

That was rich, coming from a woman who'd lied to him for thirteen years. Lies of omission were still lies. "I'm serious. If I need something, I'll call." He hung up. "Don't say anything."

Kane didn't speak. Sean was angry, but more angry with himself. He had wanted to talk to Lucy, but when? In front of Siobhan? Wake her up in the middle of the night? Damn, he couldn't sleep most of the night, but he must have crashed late because he hadn't even heard Lucy get up.

He was embarrassed by his past behavior. His irresponsibility. Angry at Madison for keeping this secret. Worried about Jesse, a kid he didn't know, depending on a man he thought of as his father who was a criminal. Sean wanted his son in his life, but what would he say when he met the kid? *I'm your dad, I love you.*

And he felt selfish and then guilty for feeling that way. Why did this have to happen *now*? Why six weeks before his wedding? Why couldn't this have happened two years ago, before he met Lucy? Or in two months, after they were married and back from their honeymoon.

There was no good time to be told you had a half-grown child.

"You didn't tell her, did you?"

How did Kane know things he shouldn't know?

"There wasn't time."

"Call her."

"I'm not telling her over the damn phone." And that was that, subject dropped.

Kane turned into the small private airport that Sean used. They checked in with the desk, filed a flight plan that was as vague as they could get away with, and Kane walked over to the edge of a runway. "Wow. Nice ride. Where'd you get it?" Sean couldn't help but admire the Piper Seneca.

"Friend of JT's. He knows everyone, and everyone seems to owe him a favor."

"Who else knows?"

"I haven't told anyone, but the kid looks just like you, Sean. JT didn't ask. He didn't have to."

"I fucked this up."

"You did shit. This is on Madison. What you do from this moment forward is on you."

Sean said, "I'm flying."

"Good, because I didn't sleep last night."

Sean got himself familiar with the Seneca. He asked Kane, "You talked to Rick—what does he know about the situation in Laredo?"

"Nothing more than Armstrong and Lucy know. I gave him information about my search for the girls when they

first disappeared. The guy they worked for is clean. Believe me, I pushed. He gave me access to his employees, I
found a few lowlifes, but no one with ties to the girls or to
trafficking. I tracked law enforcement, they didn't find
anything—no bodies have popped up that could be the
girls." He paused. "I know they were grabbed in the middle
of the night. Their roommates were paid off by some lowlife to disappear. I think they're dead."

"Siobhan didn't tell me that."

"She doesn't know because it led nowhere. I tracked
down the lowlife. Throat slit. Whoever he was working for
took care of loose threads."

Sean hesitated. As if Kane could read his mind, he said,
"Rick—and you—vouch for Armstrong. And I planted
some seeds in Rick's head that they may want backup they
can trust down there, that this case could either disappear
with no leads or blow wide open."

"Nate."

Sean would feel better if Nate was watching Lucy's
back.

"I could send in my people, but we're spread thin right
now. Partly because I've been out of commission. Let's
get your kid back on US soil and then we can both be
involved."

"Lucy absorbs everything. These investigations—yes,
she's good, I trust her, but she can lose herself."

"You love her. I get it." Kane closed his eyes. "It's why
I don't get involved."

"You don't? Really?" Sean would have laughed if he
weren't so worried. "Then what was that thing with Siobhan in my kitchen?"

Kane didn't respond. Typical.

Sean finished getting himself familiar with the plane
so he could take her up.

* * *

Madison McAllister Spade paced the hotel room. How could she go back to California when her son was missing? When her husband wouldn't return her calls? When her entire world was falling apart and she could do not one thing to stop it?

She had never wanted Sean Rogan to know about Jesse. In a perfect world, she would have stood up to her father and told Sean from the beginning . . . or, maybe not. She'd been nineteen. Sean wasn't even *eighteen* when they were dating, though he was far more mature, and a lot more fun, than anyone her age. They'd been silly and stupid and she knew exactly when they conceived Jesse. Four weeks before Sean was expelled, the first weekend after classes started, Sean had flown them to Las Vegas, bought quality fake IDs, and they gambled and drank and went to shows for two amazing nights. Sean had won a huge amount of money at blackjack, and she suspected he was counting cards—he was that good. And it was that weekend he'd told her about the professor who had child porn on his computer.

She'd told him to turn the professor over to the university. Then he admitted that he'd hacked the computer to play a prank on the guy because he was a jerk and that's when he found the videos.

"They won't care about that—if he has child pornography, you might get a slap on the wrist."

"I think they'll bury it. Remember the fraternity that was accused of feeding girls mickeys at that blowout party last spring? Slap on the wrist because no one could prove who was behind it. Big institutions want to make problems disappear. Then there's the fact that he's a tenured professor."

"Sean—what are you going to do?"

"I don't know yet. But I'm going to expose him, one way or the other."

What would she have done if Sean hadn't been expelled? If she didn't have an excuse to keep her pregnancy secret? Would she have stood up to her father and told Sean about the baby? Would she have expected a wedding? A commitment? He hadn't loved her. Not then. Maybe he could have learned to . . .

She could lie to herself all she wanted, but he didn't love her like she loved him, and she didn't want to be the burden. The girl who *had* to get married. The girl who roped a guy into a family. They had fun, and that's all it was. He was smart and exciting, he treated her very well, he was considerate . . . but he didn't love her.

As it was, she'd left school after the semester ended, before she started to show, and transferred to UCLA. Because even though Sean went to Stanford for only a year, he had made a lot of friends. She didn't keep in touch with any of them. She rebuilt her life in LA.

She'd gone through a litany of emotions from grief to embarrassment to anger to sorrow. She considered an abortion—had even made an appointment—but in the end, she couldn't keep it. This baby was part of *her*, and deep down she knew that no matter what her father thought of Sean Rogan, he had good genes. He was attractive and smart. He was a genius. If she'd gone to a sperm bank and checked the boxes of what she wanted in a donor, Sean Rogan would have been at the top of the list.

Carson Spade was the opposite of Sean in so many ways, though just as handsome and just as endearing. But Carson wasn't wild. He was five years older than her, stalwart, a businessman who cared about image and status. She wanted to tell herself she didn't care about those things, but that would be a lie. She did because her father expected it. He wanted the whole package, not just money, but stature, respect, *respectability*. Carson Spade was everything her father wanted in a son-in-law, so when they started dating a year after Jesse was born, he'd gone from boyfriend to fiancé in a matter of months. He loved Jesse as if he were his own son. And that was one of the reasons Madison loved Carson. He loved Jesse unconditionally. He didn't care who his father was, and didn't hold it against her for keeping the information from Sean.

It wasn't until Jesse was eight and came to them with some simple addition and subtraction that they told him the truth—at least, part of the truth. That Carson wasn't his biological father, but he loved him as much as if he were.

Madison put her hand to her stomach. She felt sick. She should never have told Jesse that his father hadn't wanted him. She should never have told Jesse that his father was a wild college boy and she'd had a lapse in judgment. That it had been a one-night stand. She didn't say that, exactly—she had to phrase it so an eight-year-old would understand—but Jesse got it.

She just hadn't expected that Sean and Jesse would ever meet.

Her phone rang. It was a blocked number, but she answered it immediately.

"Hello?"

"Mom?"

"Jesse! Oh God, are you okay?"

"I'm fine, Mom. Sorry I didn't call sooner, we couldn't get a signal. Dad wants to talk to you."

There were muffled voices, then Carson came on the phone. He said to Jesse in the background, "Go grab me a bottled water, will you please, Jess? Then you can talk to your mom again."

A second later Carson said in a low voice, "Madison, what have you done?"

"What have *I* done? You disappeared with our son! I waited at the airport, thinking you missed your flight, but you didn't call, didn't text. You weren't on *any* plane and you checked out on *Saturday*. I have no idea where you've been for *three days*! What the hell is going on, Carson? Why haven't you returned my calls?"

"Stop. Please, Madison. Just calm down."

"*Calm down*?"

"You panicked. You're putting us all in danger. Someone has been sniffing around, a PI making calls. Did you hire someone to find me?"

"Yes! Yes I did because I thought you were kidnapped or . . . or worse."

"Dear God, Madison, you're going to get us all killed! Call them off."

Madison sank down into the hotel desk chair. Killed? *Killed?* This could not be happening. What was her husband doing?

"Are you being held? For ransom? Do they want money? I have money—my dad—"

"No, Madison, nothing like that! Jeez, girl, your imagination is out of control. This is just business."

"This is *not* just business! Carson, tell me, or I swear, I'll send an army after you."

"It's nothing I can't handle. Just a little money problem. I'm fixing it, and then we'll be on the next flight home. But you have *got* to call off the dogs. Right now. You'll freak out people we don't want to freak out. You're lucky I found out about it before my employer did."

"I cannot believe this, Carson." Madison was going to hyperventilate. She could feel it building and tried to force herself to *calm down*. Panicking was not going to get her son back. "You have *my son* in the middle of something this dangerous?"

"It's not dangerous! Just someone else's mistake I need to fix. Trust me, Madison. I love you, I love Jesse. This is just a small glitch and I'm the only one who can fix it.

Nothing is going to happen to him, but you're panicking, and that's not good for any of us."

"You should have told me from the beginning. You should never have brought Jesse down there."

"I'm taking a risk calling you now. If everything goes right, I'll be done here by Thursday, Friday at the latest."

"Where are you?"

"Honey, I'd tell you, but right now you're not thinking straight, and the last thing I need is you showing up here. Or sending a damn PI after me. Call him off. I mean it. I love you, Maddie."

He hung up. He *hung up on her*!

She was torn. Carson was obviously in the middle of something potentially dangerous, which put Jesse in danger. But she'd just spoken to both of them, and they sounded *fine*. They were alive, they were healthy, Jesse didn't sound like anything was wrong. She wanted Sean to bring her son back . . . but she didn't want to get her husband hurt.

"How could you do this to me?" she screamed in the silence of her hotel room.

She had to trust Carson. They had celebrated their tenth anniversary in April. She loved him. Her father respected him. He'd provided for her, took another man's son as his own, helped her build her own business—antiques, something she loved and was good at. She had a *life* and Carson and Jesse were a part of that life. They *were* her life.

Coming to Sean Rogan was a mistake. Carson was right, she'd panicked. Why had she even come here? What had she hoped to gain?

Because you hadn't spoken to your husband and son in three days and Carson lied to you.

Damn damn damn!

Why hadn't she called her father?

She knew why. Her father would know then that Carson was moonlighting. He would know they had financial problems that Carson had taken a second job to remedy. And Carson wouldn't forgive her. He may never forgive her for talking to Sean. Why had she called Sean? She could have found someone else . . .

Punishment. You were mad at Carson for scaring you, for taking Jesse when you really didn't want him to go . . . and then lying to you. So you went to the one person you should never have seen again.

"It's okay," she told herself, as if speaking out loud would make it true. "Jesse is my son, I would do anything to protect my son."

Carson and Jesse were safe. For now. She had to call off Sean. To keep them safe.

She grabbed her purse and cell phone and ran out of the hotel.

Jesse brought his dad the water bottle. He'd already drunk half of another on the way back from the kitchen. "Here," he said. "Where's Mom?"

"The phone cut out—cell reception is terrible here."

"She sounded really worried. I thought you said she was fine with us staying longer."

His dad drank some water. "I thought she was, but she worries, you know that."

Jesse shrugged and sat down on the couch. His mom was moody all the time lately. His dad said it was girl hormones, but Jesse thought it was something else. She'd seemed sad when he left last week. "I should call her back—or maybe we can just go home? Do we have to stay until Friday?"

"This is important, Jess. You're right—I should have left you at home, but I thought this would be good for us to have some guy time. You have straight A's, it's not like you're going to miss anything if you miss school for a week. And I talked to Dom, they have season tickets to the football team here. They're playing tonight."

"Really?" Jesse loved soccer. He'd been playing since he was six. But he'd never been to a professional game.

"I may be able to wrap up everything by Wednesday. We'll leave as soon as I'm done."

"Sure. Whatever."

"You're having fun, aren't you?"

"Yeah. Just bored. I wish we didn't have to leave Acapulco."

"I can't let you just go out and explore—it's pretty safe here, but you know how Mexico can be. We need to be smart."

"I know." Jesse finished his water bottle. "Can I go swimming?"

"Of course. You can go anywhere on the property—Dom has forty acres to explore. But come in before noon, the sun can be murder."

"Okay." Jesse put his DS on the charger and left the suite of rooms Dominick Flores, his dad's boss, let them use. He already had his swim trunks on—he'd been swimming every morning and night since he got here. But he was bored. There were no other kids, everyone was serious except for Gabriella.

Two of Dominick's bodyguards asked him where he was going. "Swimming," he told both of them.

It was weird to be here in a house full of armed guards. His dad said that Dominick was extremely wealthy and there was always the threat of kidnapping for ransom or thieves. And they were in Mexico. So why not just stay at the resort? At least there was a lot to do—they had a totally badass game room.

Jesse went outside and around back to the pool. It was early, but hot. It would be sticky and gross later.

He swam for thirty minutes or so, but it really wasn't that much fun. Everyone seemed to stay up real late and sleep in . . . so except for his dad and the guards, he hadn't seen anyone. Dominick's younger brother Jose was sort of cool—he had a totally sick gaming system in his apartment and had let Jesse play with him last night. But then he and Gabriella had gone out.

Jesse dried off, pulled his T-shirt over his head, and went to the back door. It was locked. He walked around the side of the house—the place was a mansion. It had to be like ten thousand square feet. Maybe more. The kitchen door was often open because the cook liked to go out for a smoke like every ten minutes. Yeah, Dominick was rich—he had his own personal chef.

The kitchen was open, but no one was inside. Jesse picked a muffin off the cooling rack—the cook was a jerk, but he baked the *best* muffins and pastries. He went through the dining room, down the hall, through the foyer, and thought he heard his dad in the library. The door was partly open, and he almost walked in, but then he heard Dominick raise his voice.

"I hope you're right, Carson. I can't afford any scrutiny right now. Neither can you."

"I'm sure it's nothing," his dad said. "We're on track, but I need to get to the bank today, set up the new accounts. By tomorrow—Thursday at the latest—I'll have moved all the money. Even if the feds track the old accounts, they'll be shut down."

"You'd better be right."

"I am," his dad said. "But I've added another layer of security. In three months the new accounts will automatically be converted into yet another new account. I can set it up in advance. So even *if*—and it's a big if—they track us, by the time they figure it out, the money will be gone."

"I like the plan in concept—but it had better work."

"Dom, I've been doing this for years. I set up the contigency plan in the first place, and it served you well, didn't it?"

Jesse heard two people walking down the main staircase, so he quickly turned into the closest room and shut the door. The room was empty—a sitting room. Dominick had a dozen sitting rooms all over the house. Double doors led into the atrium in the center of the house. Jesse waited until he thought the people had passed, then walked through the double doors and into the atrium. There were lots of plants and even full-sized trees in the huge room. Dom had a lap pool in here, too, but it was for family only, Jesse had been told.

"Swimming so early, little man?"

He jumped and almost stumbled halfway up the stairs. Gabriella stood in the middle of the atrium looking up at him.

"Yeah," he said. "Before it gets hot."

She walked up the stairs and stopped on the stair beneath his. Looked him in the eye and said, "Be careful, Jess. There are a lot of eyes—and ears—in this house." She then smiled, patted him on the shoulder, and said as she passed him on the stairs, heading toward her apartment, "Next time you go for an early swim, let me know."

CHAPTER TWELVE

"I'm ready," Sean said to Kane as he slowly started taxiing out of the hangar. His phone vibrated on the console next to him. It was a long text message from Lucy.

I'm on the road, but right before we left, your friend Madison Spade called the house—about 10 minutes ago. She sounded upset and wanted to know what airport you were at. I told her to call you, but she said she tried and couldn't reach you. I don't know what her story is, and I didn't want to tell her, but she said that she has important information about her husband and son that you have to know before you leave, so I sent her to the airfield. Be careful. I love you.

"Well, shit," Sean said and stopped the plane. He showed Kane the message. "What is Madison up to?"

"No good," Kane responded.

Sean called Madison's number. She picked up immediately. Before he could get a word out, Madison said, "Don't leave! I'm almost there!"

"You are not coming with me."

"No, no, it's not like that. I talked to Carson. He and Jesse are fine. You don't need to go."

Every instinct in Sean's body told him either she was lying or not telling him the entire truth.

"Did he call you?"

"Yes! I spoke to both of them. Please—I just got to the airport. Your girlfriend told me where you were."

"I know. She told me."

Madison clearly wasn't expecting that answer.

"You should have called me."

"I didn't think you'd talk to me! You were very mean when I called earlier. I have to see you. I'm canceling this whole thing. They're *fine*. I just panicked. But they're fine, really."

Sean hung up. He did not believe this. "Watch the plane," he said to Kane and climbed out of the cockpit. By the time he dropped to the tarmac, he saw a white sedan racing toward him. She screeched to a halt only feet from the tail of the plane and jumped out of the car. "Thank God you haven't left."

She looked frantic and took a deep breath. "Carson called me thirty minutes ago. He and Jesse are fine. I talked to Jesse. They're fine, they were robbed. They'll be back on Friday."

"Robbed?"

"Yes, that's why he couldn't call me, didn't get my messages. Their passports were stolen, they're at the American embassy. That's where they called me from."

He didn't believe one word.

"The American embassy where?"

"I don't know. I didn't ask. Probably Acapulco."

"And he couldn't call you for three days."

"He didn't have time to explain everything! He just told me they were fine, they were at the embassy and straightening everything out. I talked to Jesse myself."

That he believed. She had talked to her son but he didn't

know whether that was to verify he was alive, or because he was really safe.

"Give me your phone."

"What?"

"I'm tired of the games. Give me your fucking phone."

"I'm not hiring you. I'm *unhiring* you. You can't do this. Just leave it *alone*."

He yanked her purse from her hands, retrieved her phone, then tossed the purse back at her. He walked back to the plane.

Sean said, "Spade made contact." He tossed Madison's phone to Kane, who grabbed it with one hand. "Plug that into my tablet and break her passcode." He reached into his go-bag and pulled out a phone. He wrote the number down on a pad, then walked back to Madison.

She stood exactly where he'd left her, eyes wide.

He handed her the burn phone. "This is how I will contact you."

"You don't understand . . ."

"What did he say?" Sean stepped forward and Madison stepped back. He didn't care if he looked or sounded threatening; she was lying to him and now he knew for certain that her no-good husband and *his* son were in danger.

"They're *fine*. They'll be back on Friday."

"And?"

"And . . . that's it. Please don't go. I should never have come to you. I should never have told you . . ."

"You're lying."

She straightened her spine and stared him in the eye. "Who are you?"

"If you don't tell me exactly what your husband said, you're putting your son in greater danger. *My* son. And I will do *anything* to protect my son."

"I'm not lying, Sean. Carson called me and said they

were fine, he just has more business, and he will be home on Friday."

"And?"

Her eyes darted toward the plane, just briefly, before looking Sean in the eye. "And . . . nothing."

"So the whole story that they were robbed and at the American embassy was a big fat lie." Sean turned and started walking away.

"No!" Madison ran after him. She grabbed him and he shook her off. "Please, Sean, trust me."

That was *it*. "Trust *you*? You lied to me for thirteen years. I have a son. He doesn't even know who I am. You kept that from me. I will never forgive you. I will never trust you. And now you're lying to me *again* to protect your husband, putting *my* son in danger. *Your son.* You know what I think? I think your husband is laundering money, and if he's in Mexico, that means he's doing it for the cartels. And if he's laundering money for the cartels, you and Jesse already have a target on your backs."

She was shaking. "I-I talked to J-Jesse. He's f-fine."

"No matter how many fucking times you tell me Jesse is *fine*, he's not *fine*. I will bring him back. At this point, I don't give a fuck what happens to your husband. But Jesse is not going to be used as a pawn between Carson and the cartels or whoever the hell he's screwing around with. And there is nothing you can do or say to stop me."

Sean returned to his plane. He was shaking. Fear and anger. He started the plane again and rolled forward.

"Blocked number. Six-minute conversation."

"And?"

"Your program said it originated within fifty miles of Guadalajara."

"If he calls again, I'll run a program to trace it."

"We have a meeting with security in Acapulco."

Sean didn't say anything.

"We need intel."

"Four to five hours to Acapulco, and that's pushing it if we have to hop back on the plane for another three-hour leg to Guadalajara. We'll need to refuel someplace."

"We're covered. Sean, don't change the plan."

"We have no fucking plan because we don't know what the fuck is going on or where the fuck they are!"

Sean turned toward the runway. He glanced once back toward the tarmac. Madison was standing right where he'd left her.

Kane didn't say anything as Sean built up speed and lifted off. If this was any other day and any other trip, Sean would have appreciated the state-of-the-art plane. The comfort. The speed. But today . . . now . . . he just wanted to find his son.

His son.

Kane said, "Control your emotions."

"I am."

"Bullshit."

Sean spent more time than necessary playing with the gauges and controls. Kane knew what he was doing. Getting his shit together.

"We landed on somebody's radar," Sean said. "That's why Carson called her."

"I talked to one person who I trust. But he may have tripped something getting details on Spade. Who did you talk to?"

"No one except you and JT and Jaye." Sean paused. "I dug around in Carson's finances."

"Trip anything?"

"Doubtful, but I didn't have time to be extra cautious. The only way he would know I was digging was if he was watching real-time or had a program that knew exactly what to look for in a hack."

"How likely?"

"Well, I'd say highly unlikely unless he's working with top tech people. Or he had someone like me set it up for him. Or if he was suspicious. And if he's laundering money, he would be suspicious."

"We tipped our hand. One of us—you or me. Or Jaye. You have her running backgrounds and financials?"

"She's just as good as me when it comes to covering her tracks."

There was only so much they could do. If someone was monitoring finances live and they were smart, they might see something odd. If they were up to no good, they would be suspicious of anything out of the ordinary.

Kane continued. "My security guy in Acapulco is pulling feeds from the resort Spade was at. We'll know who, if anyone, he met with. What he did. What he fucking ate for breakfast and when he took a shit. We need that intel, otherwise we're going in blind. So stay on course, Sean." He paused. "Jesse is a Rogan, we're not going to leave him behind. I promise you that. But we're not going to be stupid about it, just like you weren't stupid when you rescued me outside Santiago."

Kane was right. Of course he was, he'd been doing these kind of rescues for twenty years. It was in his blood. Sean was just the driver—or pilot, as the case may be. He had to trust his brother.

"She lied. In part. I'm sure she talked to Spade and Jesse, but he told her something else. Something that freaked her out so much that she came to the airport and tried to stop us."

"The question is, did she tell Spade who she hired?"

Sean considered the conversation he'd just had with Madison. "My guess is no. She wouldn't want him to know she came to me when the going got tough. Carson must know I'm Jesse's real father. And Madison is trying to salvage her life right now."

"We'll go on that assumption, but you have to remember, Sean—the Rogan name is akin to God in some places, and Satan in others. We're certainly not in Kansas anymore."

Sean glanced at his brother with a half smile. "A joke. Really."

Kane smiled, closed his eyes, and went to sleep.

Sean flew. And thought about the lost years.

CHAPTER THIRTEEN

Lucy, Noah, and Siobhan arrived in Laredo just after nine thirty Tuesday morning. Lucy had spent the two-hour drive reviewing notes from their analyst regarding the properties managed by Direct Property Holdings.

TO: SSA N. Armstrong
FROM: Z. Charles, Analyst III
RE: Case 16-T4022209-A
CC: SA L. Kincaid

The two properties in question are owned by different entities, but run by the same property management company out of San Antonio as I forwarded yesterday. Direct Property Holdings—DPH—has no identifiable employees, but I've sent a request to access tax records. DPH is owned by Direct Business Management registered in Reno, Nevada; I've requested the corporate filings from Nevada but based on what I've learned so far, I suspect that there will not be any individuals listed on those records.

I have, however, backtraced seven additional properties managed by DPH that are within a hundred-mile radius of the Freer property. There may be more, and I will continue to work this angle. The list is attached. I will trace these companies as far as I can, but I've seen this before and it's far out of my skill set. I would like to bring this to the attention of our White Collar Crimes Division who may have additional insight into how this is set up and how the operational tree is organized. However, because this is a highly sensitive issue I wanted your approval first, and if there was a specific person I should discuss this with.

I've begun the search of all individuals in the photographs you forwarded. It'll take some time. The brothel pays under the table, so I have no employment records. I'll forward positive identifications as I receive them. The first is attached: Leo Musgrove. He has a record and was easy to find.

Lucy looked at the list of addresses. Two were in the Laredo area. One was in Del Rio. It was familiar. She started flipping through her notes.

"It's the same place," Noah said.

"Excuse me?"

"You're looking at the list of addresses. I already confirmed that the Del Rio address is the brothel that Barrow investigated. There are three in the San Antonio area, and Nate and Kenzie are going to check them out today if they get a break in their current caseload; otherwise we'll check on them tomorrow. In the meantime I've asked Rick to smooth over some ruffled feathers."

Lucy couldn't imagine what she'd done that upset anyone.

Noah laughed. "It's not you. Jeez, Luce, do you always think you're the one making waves?"

"Lately," she said.

"This time, it's me, and I'm not going to apologize. I don't have to—I'm not going to be in San Antonio forever. You know Dean Hooper, right?"

"Heard of him, never met him."

"He's pretty tight with the Rogans and with Rick," he said. "He's also the former assistant director of White Collar Crimes at national headquarters. He took a demotion, of sorts, into an ASAC position in Sacramento after he got married, but still consults with DC because he's the foremost expert we have in financial crimes. He's sharp, and we need sharp on this." He hesitated. "You know how I feel about bringing in civilian consultants."

"I wouldn't ask. And Sean respects ASAC Hooper tremendously, from what he's told me."

"I already asked Rick if I could bring in Sean if needed. I'll talk to Sean tonight, because Dean already asked if he could use him locally. Our San Antonio office just isn't as advanced in white-collar issues as we are in the other divisions."

"Sean is out of town for the next two to three days."

"Business?"

"A friend asked him to find her husband and son, who disappeared while on a working vacation in Acapulco." She hesitated, then added, "Kane went with him."

"You sound worried."

"Sean wouldn't have left if it wasn't serious." He'd been worried about her last night; she'd sensed it the minute she walked in. She must have looked like death warmed over. She did her best to show him that she was all right. And she was . . . she'd miss him, but she was a big girl. She needed to learn to decompress on her own. Lucy internalized her cases, and it sometimes got to her, resulting in little sleep and long nights. She found it both beneficial and terrifying that she often understood killers, that she could get inside their heads and emotionally dissect them. Sometimes, that was the only way to stop them.

But it took its toll. Insomnia, poor eating habits, lack of emotion—Lucy could psychoanalyze herself until the cows came home, she understood her defenses, but that didn't help when she found herself alone and thinking too much about her cases.

Her last partner, Barry Crawford, had told her she didn't know how to turn off the job. This was true. Sean could do it for her. He would take her hand, smile, and know exactly what to say or do to shut it down. Whether it was a quiet night at home, a dinner out at their favorite restaurant, or inviting friends over for a game of poker, Sean had this uncanny way of knowing exactly what she needed and when.

She was spoiled. She was going to miss him the next few days.

A phone rang in the backseat. Siobhan answered it. "No, that's not necessary. I'm serious—I'm with Lucy and another agent . . . Don't. I'm *fine* . . . I promise. One problem, I'll call . . . I said I promise . . . And you know what? Next time Kane wants to know how I'm doing, have him call me direct."

Siobhan pocketed her phone. "Impossible," she muttered.

Lucy exchanged a glance with Noah. "What's going on?" Lucy asked Siobhan.

"Kane told Ranger everything, and now Ranger's worried." To Noah she said, "Ranger works with Kane in hostage rescue. Ranger and his team are in Honduras escorting a medical unit through a dicey area. Far more dangerous and necessary than babysitting me. But Ranger said he'd drop everything if I needed help."

Lucy didn't quite know what to say. She'd seen the exchange between Kane and Siobhan that morning, before she and Sean gave them some privacy.

She was about to comment when Siobhan continued. "It's the principle of the thing. Yes, I appreciate his help, but it's Kane being dictatorial. Thinking I'm going to get in trouble. I lived and worked in Mexico for *years*. I know how to take care of myself. And he called Andie. *Again*."

"Andie—your sister."

"Now she's worried. I mean, I know, I'm not a cop, I'm not a soldier, I don't even like guns all that much—but I can hit the target when I have to. Andie made sure of that. But I'm not a child, and I resent being coddled and scolded like one."

"They care about you," Lucy said. "I am a cop, and I like guns, and my family still worries about me."

Siobhan rubbed her eyes. "You're right. I just . . . I'm stuck. I don't know where else to look."

"You don't look anywhere," Noah said firmly. "That's why Lucy and I are here. You're involved because you know these girls and you have contacts in the community, but you are not to go out on your own. Do you understand?"

"You're a cop *and* military, aren't you?"

"Air Force, ten years."

"One of the nice guys."

"Excuse me?"

"Air Force guys were always the nicest. There was one Airborne unit, after the mudslide in Mari and Ana's village, who came in with extra medical supplies and water. And they brought me—there was no getting in and out of the village on foot because the bridge was taken out. It was risky—Vala Vida is remote and pristine and the cartels and rebels leave them alone, but to get there we have to go through some dangerous areas. There's only one way in and out. Anyway, a unit raised the money on their own to bring in the supplies. It wasn't the first time the Air Force came through for one of the sisters."

"Okay, I'll take being a nice guy."

Lucy laughed.

Noah mocked indignation. "I am."

"You are," she agreed, glad for a little levity.

Noah pulled in front of the address of the hotel that Sean had reserved for Siobhan.

"No way," Siobhan said. "This place costs a fortune."

"The security is good," Lucy said. "And Sean paid for it. You'll hurt his feelings if you don't stay here. Not to mention he'll find out, tell Kane, and Kane will probably send Ranger up here. I know how they think."

Noah parked in ten-minute parking and got out, opened the door for Siobhan. "I agree with Lucy. You stirred the hornets' nest, and whoever was running the house in Freer knows you're still looking for Marisol and Ana."

"It's just—it's too much." She looked pained.

Lucy picked up Siobhan's backpack and started toward the door. Noah escorted Siobhan inside. They were greeted almost immediately by hotel security. "Ms. Walsh, it's a privilege to have you with us. I'm Horatio Peterson, the head of security."

"How do you know me?"

"Mr. Rogan said you'd be checking in this morning. Your safety is my number one concern. Our hotel has state-of-the-art security systems, and we monitor visitors closely. We've had many important people stay here—actors, musicians, presidents even—and I can assure you as long as you are here, no one will disturb you." He handed his card to Siobhan, Noah, and Lucy. "Agents, I'm at your disposal if you need anything during your stay here."

"We're not staying," Noah said.

"Nonetheless, there are two rooms adjoining Ms. Walsh's suite also reserved for the week." He handed out card keys. "It's a long drive to San Antonio."

Noah glanced at Lucy and shook his head, but she could see a slight smile on his face.

"I don't know whether to shoot him or hug him," Siobhan said.

"I often have that feeling," Noah concurred.

Peterson said, "If you need to go anywhere, I have a driver at your disposal."

"It's a lost cause," Lucy said. "Just enjoy it. And you're close to the hospital."

"Fine," Siobhan said. "I'm going to owe Sean big time."

"You owe him nothing."

"He loaned me his camera. This hotel. Everything."

Noah and Lucy left Siobhan at the hotel. Noah pulled out and said, "We're going to pick up the files from the sheriff before we head out to Del Rio and track down Leo Musgrove." The sheriff's department was on the way. "Sean shouldn't have done all this. We're not going to stay—at least, I hope not."

"He wanted to. Really. He didn't want to go to Mexico, I think he was feeling a little guilty that he didn't turn down the job."

After they picked up the files of the mother and infant who'd disappeared three months ago, and the subsequent arson fire, they turned onto the highway heading to Del Rio, which was nearly three hours northwest.

"This could be a total bust," Noah said. "I wish I could have sent a local team, but the terrorism alert is on high— ICE caught more than a dozen questionable Middle Eastern detainees attempting to cross in Laredo last month. They have backgrounds to run and heightened security to deal with. I can't pull them off for this."

Violent crimes in the FBI took a far back burner to counter-terrorism, counter-intelligence, and cybercrime. In fact, Lucy had the distinct feeling that Violent Crimes had moved to the bottom of the list. While on the one hand she understood that the FBI and other law enforcement agencies had stopped terrorist attacks before they occurred— planned attacks that they often didn't share with the public—violent crime affected so many people. What was happening to these girls in Freer and Laredo was heartbreaking.

Noah muttered, "This is when I wish I owned my own airplane and made enough money to pay for fuel."

"What, the FBI wouldn't reimburse you?" Lucy teased.

Noah was on the phone most of the drive talking to nearly every agent on the Violent Crimes Squad seeking updates on cases, as well as giving Dean and Rick updates on their case. Lucy turned her attention to the thin file Zach had sent them on Leo Musgrove.

Born in Austin, Texas, to a science teacher and a nurse, Leo's parents divorced after he graduated high school and moved to different states; he stayed, went to state college, dropped out after a year, and had taken a variety of odd jobs. He was suspected of dealing drugs, had been arrested multiple times, but charges didn't stick until the third arrest when he served fourteen months of a two-year stint in minimum security for possession with intent. Good behavior, no problems, and he disappeared when he was released.

Now he was thirty-four with conflicting affiliations—Del Rio local law enforcement put him in a gang, while federal law enforcement marked him as an associate of one of the Juarez-based cartels. But Leo had kept his nose mostly clean, popping up on police radar as a middleman, then disappearing when the heat came down.

There were no recent photos of him, except the pictures Barrow had given them.

Lucy hadn't liked Eric Barrow, but it appeared that his exposé on the brothel had resulted in its being completely shut down. On the one hand, that was good—most of the women there were forced to work, and many were illegal immigrants who'd been threatened or kidnapped or couldn't find any way out of the sex trade. They didn't trust law enforcement and they didn't trust the system. They were considered property by the people who ran the brothels, brutalized because they didn't have anyone to turn to for help. On the other hand, what had happened to them? Did the organization close up shop here and open elsewhere? Or was their fate worse?

Maybe that's why Lucy didn't like Barrow. He came in, wrote his story, and left. Let the pieces fall where they may, he didn't care. No help for the girls, just expose a corrupt system and *adios*. How had he and Siobhan become friends? They were so different. In attitude, values, goals.

As they neared Del Rio, Noah took a call from the local resident agency in Del Rio. "It's about time he called me back," Noah muttered before he answered.

By the sounds of it, the conversation didn't go well. Noah tossed his phone on the seat and slammed his hand on the steering wheel as he turned off the highway into town.

"We're on our own."

"Del Rio should have eight to ten agents. They don't have anyone to assist?"

"Four are on a joint operation with border patrol and the others are spread thin because of it. The SSA never heard of Musgrove, said he's not on their radar, and they can't spare anyone."

"What about the brothel?"

"Confirmed that it was shut down after Barrow ran his story, but said it opened up again—only this time they rotate locations. He's sending me a list of possibles, but it would take days to investigate and there is no viable lead that the de la Rosa sisters are there."

"I don't think they're here," Lucy said. "Barrow indicated that the brothel had been shut down so a group of women could be brought in. New girls? Special business arrangement? We don't know, but they didn't stay around, according to Barrow's source. If the source was right and

Marisol de la Rosa was one of those special women, she's not here now." Not if she just gave birth. "Musgrove will know."

Noah parked a block away from their target address. "Are you wearing a vest?" he asked.

"Yes."

"Isn't that uncomfortable?"

"You get used to it."

Noah went around to the trunk, took off his jacket and shirt, and slipped on the thinnest available Kevlar vest over his undershirt. Then he buttoned back up and put on his jacket.

"I hope we don't need them," Noah said.

"If Leo Musgrove has been involved for years, and this brothel is connected to the house in Freer, he'll know the people in Siobhan's photographs. We need to find the woman."

"You think she'll cave? Did you get that just from her photo?"

"No—I think she's in charge. Or is close to who's in charge. When I was looking through the photos again, I couldn't help but notice how the men deferred to her. It was subtle, the way they stood, they way they treated her as if she were their mother or someone of importance. The way she held her head—as if she owns everything in her path."

"Okay, I can accept that. I trust your judgment."

"Thanks."

"Lucy, we've worked together often enough that you don't need to thank me." He smiled as they walked around the corner to a dive bar over which Musgrove lived. "We check the bar first, then go upstairs. Be alert—if he bolts, you take the back."

As soon as they walked into the bar, they were made—

two men sitting in the corner, neither of whom was Musgrove, slipped out the back.

Musgrove was at the bar drinking coffee, his back to the door, but he locked eyes with Noah in the mirror. Then he glanced at Lucy. Assessing both of them. He slowly rose from his seat and walked across the bar, past Noah and Lucy, and toward the back.

"Mr. Musgrove," Noah said.

He didn't stop. He didn't run or slow, he just kept going.

Noah nodded to Lucy, who ran back out the front and sprinted to the alley. She encountered the two men who'd left getting into a beat-up truck. She ignored them, even though she felt them watching her as they pulled out of the rutted dirt parking lot. Her instincts, always knowing when someone was staring at her, had saved her ass many times. This time it didn't matter; the truck drove off.

Musgrove exited and walked right over to Lucy. "You trying to get me killed? Walking in like you own the place?"

Lucy stood her ground, keeping his hands in view. He was likely carrying.

Noah was right behind him. "Leo Musgrove, we need to talk."

"What do a couple of feds want with me?" He was jittery. "People will think I'm a snitch. And right now, being a snitch will get you dead. Who told you where I was?"

Of course he'd pegged them as feds, even before they ID'd themselves. Criminals had a sixth sense about cops.

"I'll put cuffs on you, make it legit," Noah said.

"Fuck that." He was backing away from them, not overtly looking for an escape route, but he definitely didn't want to be talking to them.

"You run, we'll haul your ass in," Noah said. "It's too fucking hot out here to play this game." He motioned toward the bar. The back wall was shaded. "Against the wall, Musgrove."

He was weighing his options.

Noah stepped toward him. "I'm in much better shape than you are, Leo. Wall. Now."

Leo swore and backed against the wall.

"Turn around."

He complied.

Noah searched him. Removed a knife and a small gun. Slipped them into his pocket. "Turn around."

"I'd better get those back," Leo said. "I'm no longer on probation, I can carry a fucking gun."

Noah said, "Eight months ago you moved a small group of young women, ten to twelve of them, into the brothel on Seventh Street that was subsequently shut down after an investigative reporter exposed a bunch of cops and politicians using the place. But before that, the whole place came to a halt for three days while these girls were there. Who did you move them for and where did they go?"

Leo stared at Noah like he was asking him to drink cyanide.

"I don't know what the fuck you're talking about."

Lucy handed Noah the thin folder with photos of Marisol and Ana.

Noah showed Leo the de la Rosa sisters. "Seen them?"

Leo didn't even look at the photo. "No."

"Look again."

Leo waved his hand over the photo in dismissal. "Girls like them are a dime a dozen. In and out, working girls. I don't know who they are, what they do, nothing. *Nothing.* Got it?"

Definitely protesting too much. Out of fear or because he was protecting someone?

"These girls were taken from Monterrey, Mexico. Which means this falls under border security issues. The fact that ICE and the FBI just captured a dozen Syrians over the last two weeks coming in from Mexico—three of whom are on the terror watch list—means that I can hold you indefinitely if I believe that you're bringing known terrorists into the States."

"Those girls are terrorists?" Leo laughed. "Right."

Noah didn't smile. "I'm not bluffing, Leo. You brought them across the border, I can make the case that you have knowledge of terrorist movements because of your illegal job as a coyote."

Leo stared, weighing if Noah was bluffing.

Noah stepped closer. "I don't like the heat, and you run out here and make me stand in the fucking sun. I don't work here. I'm from DC headquarters. Which means I have a lot more clout than your average fed. One call, and I'll bring the wrath of God down on you. I want to know who those girls were for. Who ordered the facility shut down in order to house them. Where they went. No more games."

He stepped forward. Lucy had never seen Noah be such a hard-ass. But Leo was buying the tough-cop act. *Lucy* was buying it.

"I talk, I'm dead."

"Not my concern."

He glanced at Lucy, then back at Noah. "I really don't—"

Noah shot Lucy a look and a nod. She hoped she read his silent communication right. She said, "Mr. Musgrove, we know that someone is using women, both illegal immigrants and runaways, as breeders. Forcing them to give birth then taking their babies. We have IDs on most of the players, but one. You give us a name, we walk away and no one knows we spoke." She was bluffing about the ID's.

"Everyone will know! Those guys who ran, they're low-level gangbangers with big fucking mouths."

"I want this woman," Lucy said and showed him the photo of the well-dressed woman that Siobhan had taken on Sunday evening. She was the piece of the picture that didn't fit, and she hadn't popped up in any criminal database.

Leo knew exactly who she was. By his expression he would rather take his chances with Noah than this woman.

"Okay, look, yeah, I've brought a few girls in and out of the country. Legal age. They were never prisoners, always wanting to come to the States. You know how it is. Working girls. It's not like we grabbed them off the street. They just wanted a better life, you know? Johns who pay better, don't beat them up. It's a business, that's all it is."

Lucy didn't believe a word. Unless Siobhan didn't know these girls at all, and she didn't believe that, either.

"I just move them. Here to there. No questions asked."

"Where did you move them eight months ago when they left the brothel?" Noah demanded.

"I can tell you, but that ain't going to help you. You think they stay in one place long? Hell no. But I tell you, none of those girls were preggers when I saw them. *None*. And in my business, you don't want them popping out kids, that's why you take care of things before, or after, if you know what I mean."

Noah said, "We know that three months ago, they moved from a place in Laredo to a place outside Freer. Where were they before Laredo?"

It was clear that Leo was surprised they had that intel.

"Hey, I heard they were all laying low."

"Why?"

He shrugged. "Just the word."

"Where did you take them after the brothel closed."

"That's not going to help you now."

"Let me be the judge of that," Noah said.

"Fuck."

Noah raised his chin.

"A property southwest of San Antonio. In the middle of bumfuck nowhere, except that there are a bunch of migrants working the trees."

"A brothel in the middle of nowhere?" Lucy asked. "I don't think so."

"Just saying, that's where I took them. Didn't say it was no brothel."

Lucy held up the photo again. "This woman. Name."

It was clear Leo had hoped she'd forgotten about the photo. He whined, "I don't know."

"Then you can sit in jail for three days," Noah said.

"Fuck that! I did nothing! I don't know her or the girls."

"That's bullshit, Leo."

Leo ran both hands through his dark, greasy hair. "You'll never get her on anything."

"Name!" Noah demanded.

"Jasmine. Jasmine, okay? That's all I know."

"Last name."

"She don't use a last name. You say *Jasmine* that's all, like, you need to know."

Noah said, "Where is she now?"

"Right. Like I would know that. No one knows, except her bodyguard." He motioned toward Lucy, so Lucy figured the suit next to Jasmine was her bodyguard. "I'm pretty fucking stunned you got her photo at all. She's the most paranoid bitch on the planet. Why she doesn't use a fucking last name. She's not going to be easy to find. She has a fucking fortune, fall guys right and left. Including cops. For all I know, you work for her and I'm going to be gutted for talking."

Noah half smiled. "You think I'm on the take?"

Leo shook his head. "Naw. You don't have that edge. I mean, you have an edge, but it's not the *I'm for sale* edge. Believe me, I'd know."

Astute, for a scumbag, Lucy thought.

Leo continued. "You'll never get her. You get close, she'll gut you. Oh God, I'm gonna have to go under. You see what you did to me? Fucking *talk* to me and you ruin my fucking life."

Noah handed Leo his business card. "My cell phone is on the back. You get me good intel, I'll get you out of Del Rio."

Lucy was about to hand Leo her own card out of habit, but an almost imperceptible shake of Noah's head had her simply adjusting the folder in her hand.

Leo looked at Noah's card, then folded it three times and stuffed it way down into his pocket. "You burned me, Armstrong. Give me my gun."

Noah took the .22 out of his pocket and field-stripped it in short order, then tossed it at Leo's feet. "The knife isn't legal."

"Of course it's legal!"

"Not in DC, and those are the only laws I know. I'll leave it at the local FBI office; you can pick it up whenever you want if, like you say, it's legal." Noah walked away but kept Leo in his line of sight until they were almost to the car.

Noah drove away. "Your name—Kincaid. Jack worked down here, didn't he? Against the cartels."

"He specialized in hostage rescue. And he hasn't lived here in years."

"To be on the safe side, I didn't think we should give our boy Leo too much information about you. Rick said that after what happened in June when you took down Nicole Rollins, Tobias Hunt, and the rest of their network, a lot of nasty people became very angry."

"I didn't take them down single-handed."

"No. You, Jack, Sean, your future brother-in-law Kane."

"And the entire San Antonio FBI and DEA offices."

"Right now, considering what we're working on and how it may be connected to human trafficking and possibly the cartels, we need to be cautious." He got on the phone, but it wasn't until he started talking that Lucy realized he'd called Rick Stockton directly.

"Rick, Noah. I'm here with Lucy and going to put you on speaker." He put the phone down and said, "Jasmine. Know the name?"

"Yes."

"A last name?"

"No—but if it's Jasmine in Texas connected to something illegal, I know who you're talking about."

"Have a photo?"

"She's never been photographed. We know that she's in her late forties and the illegitimate daughter of a drug runner—but we don't know which one. Word is she is friendly with her family south of the border, but does mostly her own thing. DEA would know more, she's never seriously been on our radar."

"The blond woman in the photos I sent you last night— we think she's Jasmine. I need more. A last name. Last known address. *Something* to follow up on."

"I'll dig." He hung up.

Noah typed into his GPS. "It's faster to go straight to San Antonio from here. We'll be back before five. The office will thank me—I've been neglecting paperwork for the last two days."

Before he could set his GPS to give him directions, his phone rang again.

"Armstrong." He listened for several minutes. "We'll be there in less than two hours." He hung up and glanced at Lucy. "Dead girl at the morgue in Laredo. She recently gave birth."

CHAPTER FOURTEEN

The resort where Carson Spade had stayed for two nights was one of the best in the region. Acapulco was a tourist city, and as such security was tight; as long as tourists stayed in town, they were relatively safe. Any tourist area had to worry about pickpockets and thieves, but leaving the city could be extremely dangerous.

"Nicco is expecting us."

"Who?" Sean asked.

"Head of security. He pulled tapes for us."

Sean didn't always know how Kane did what he did. For example, there was a jeep waiting for them at the small airport where they landed. Two young men were also waiting, and Kane slipped them money to guard the plane. He didn't want to land at a government-run airport for fear of tripping a security net—the government might search or detain them. Plus, as Kane had warned Sean earlier, having the name Rogan was dangerous in certain areas. The Mexican government had made great strides in stemming police corruption, but it was still a problem and the government itself wasn't squeaky clean. What government was? There was always someone easily bought. That could benefit Kane—or get him killed. That Sean looked like a younger, taller version of Kane didn't help. The luxury resort was on the south side of Puerto Marquez Bay, out of the main Acapulco area, but more expensive than most of the resorts in the region.

"Why didn't she come with him?" Kane asked as he drove onto the resort grounds.

"She said she runs an antiques business in LA. Didn't want to take the time off."

"You believe that?"

"I don't think she would have let her kid go to Mexico with her husband if she suspected he was up to something."

"Hmm."

"Which means what?"

"How's their relationship?"

"She said fine."

"You didn't push."

"The conversation went from awkward to worse when she showed me Jesse's photo." He paused. "I should have pushed."

Sean took another look around. The green, lush foliage; the new, well-maintained structures; the discreet security personnel and cameras. They passed an amazing pool, winding paths, and caught glimpses of an ocean view that would be visible from, it appeared, many of the hotel suites. There were private cabins closer to the shore.

"This place isn't for fathers and sons," Kane said. "She's having marital problems." Sean had begun to suspect the same . . . but not in the way Kane thought. Maybe they'd had an argument. Or maybe Carson took Jesse without her permission. She certainly hadn't wanted Sean and Kane leaving this morning. She either trusted what her husband had told her, or feared for his life. And Jesse's.

"Did you run her business?"

Sean hesitated. "No."

Kane glanced at him as he pulled into temporary

parking near the lobby. "Get your head in the game, Sean. One mistake, I can overlook. Two? That's not like you."

Kane didn't say anything else, but Sean sensed the disappointment. He hadn't thought about researching Madison's business, or asking why she hadn't traveled with her husband and son. He'd covered the basics, but hadn't dug around because he was preoccupied with the fact that he had a son.

But Kane was right. Sean had to focus as if this were a common search and rescue, even though it was anything *but* typical.

Kane didn't enter through the lobby, but used a side entrance that led directly to the security offices. They were just as luxurious and state-of-the-art as the rest of the resort.

"Rogan!" a voice called as soon as they stepped over the threshold.

Kane cracked half a smile at the short, broad-shouldered man who stood in front of them. "Nicco." They shook hands warmly. "My brother, Sean. Nicco Guiterrez, one of the good guys."

"This is Sean? He's bigger than you."

"I can still take him down."

Sean would have argued, but Kane may have wanted to demonstrate, and Sean wasn't sure he could beat his brother. Kane played dirty.

Nicco chuckled. "Come to my office, I have what you need."

Nicco's office was spacious with multiple security screens that duplicated those in the main room. He motioned for Kane and Sean to sit at the conference table. He typed on a keyboard and the lights dimmed and a wall screen appeared showing a frozen image of Carson Spade in the lobby.

"Your subject arrived with his minor son late Thursday

evening. We have him checking in at eight-oh-two p.m. He registered under his name, Carson Spade, with his minor son, Jesse Spade. He was scheduled to stay for three nights, until Sunday."

"When were the reservations made?" Sean asked.

"Same day. I can get the exact time, if you need that."

"Did he make them?"

"He reserved the suite with the same credit card that he used at check-in."

"You're not booked up?"

"Normally, yes. But we always keep a few rooms for VIPs. He's stayed at resorts owned by Diamond Plus LLC many times, and paid a premium for the privilege. He's what we call a platinum guest."

"Were there any other last-minute reservations?"

Nicco glanced from Sean to Kane. "This is getting into my discomfort zone, but for you, Kane, I can say yes. A suite was reserved also at the last minute by a business, Llave de Oro, which also has a platinum membership. Because of the level, we don't require individual names on reservations. Privacy is a premium well paid for."

"You wouldn't share this if you didn't have more on this business," Kane said.

Nicco smiled. "I have no names, but I have photos. Two men and a woman stayed in the suite. Based on what housekeeping informed me, the woman was with one of the men; the other man slept alone. Mr. Spade spent much time in the suite; his son did not. His son spent most of his time on the beach or in the arcade room."

Kane shot a glance at Sean and almost smiled. Sean wasn't smiling.

Nicco slid over a thin folder. "Best shots I have of the men and the woman." Then he added. "I believe, based on my considerable experience, that the boy was under protection by two members of my hotel security. I can't verify that without risking you—however, I have the names of the two men. If you would repay this favor by finding out if these two men have other allegiances, or if they were simply taking money from the father under the table, I would consider us even."

He slid over a small envelope, which Kane pocketed without comment or looking inside.

"Consider it done," Kane said.

Nicco tapped a few buttons on the computer. "This is the only thing suspicious to me—a helicopter flew in on Saturday morning to our helipad. Didn't register, didn't schedule any events. I wasn't informed until after the fact, which is highly irregular. It's not that it hasn't happened, but when it does, it usually means someone who doesn't want any scrutiny. He left two hours later and, according to my staff, spent that two hours in the business suite, along with Mr. Spade and the other two men. The female left in the helicopter with her boyfriend and the new man, and Mr. Spade and the single gentleman, along with the boy, left shortly thereafter in one of our limos. They were dropped at the airport at three forty-five p.m."

"Do you have a photo of the man in the chopper?" Sean asked.

"Unfortunately, he jammed the few cameras he passed. He definitely didn't want to be caught on tape. I can tell you he was a fifty- to sixty-year-old white or Hispanic male who spoke clear, cultured Spanish. High Spanish, some call it."

"Educated?"

"That was the impression of my staff."

"Did Mrs. Spade come down Sunday looking for her husband?" Kane asked.

Nicco nodded. "She caused quite a scene. I let her into the suite he vacated—he took everything with him, checked out, there was no reason to think he'd left a note.

It had already been cleaned. The management gave her one complimentary night. She left for the airport Monday morning."

"What was her state of mind?" Sean asked.

"Worried. Frantic. She was stunned that he'd checked out early. I spoke with her myself. I do believe she didn't know."

"Did you tell her what you told us?" Sean asked. "Did she ask any of these questions?"

"No. Only the time her husband and son arrived, and the time they left for the airport. I confirmed they were dropped off at the airport; however, we have no way of knowing if they got on a plane."

Sean did. It would be tricky, but he could get it if he had to. But tracking the phone number that was used to call Madison earlier would be far less risky.

Sean didn't know why that relieved him—aside from the fact that he didn't want to be used by anyone, least of all his ex-girlfriend. At least she'd been honest with him, up until this morning.

"Do you need a room?" Nicco asked them.

"A conference room with secure Internet is sufficient," Kane said. "We need to make a few calls, but we're leaving within the hour."

"Use my office. I have a staff meeting, then will make rounds. I won't be back until well after the lunch hour."

Kane shook Nicco's hand. "I appreciate it."

"Try not to wander, Kane. We have some guests on site who may recognize you."

"Understood."

Nicco left and Sean shot Kane a look. "Who is that guy?"

"A friend," was all Kane said. He opened the folder and stared at the men. "I don't recognize either of them, though one is familiar." He flipped to the girlfriend. "Well, shit."

Sean looked at the photo. Youngish, very pretty. Familiar. "Who's that?"

"Gabriella Romero, the sister of Dante Romero."

Sean hadn't heard the Romero name in years. "The Romeros?"

Kane nodded. "Those Romeros. Dante is a broker, a middleman, one of the best in the business. Specializes in smuggling, usually money or valuable items, but has been known to arrange drug transportation. He plays many sides. Has given me information only when it suits him. No loyalties. We have an understanding—I stay out of his business, he doesn't fuck with me. An uneasy truce." Kane was thinking.

"But I thought they were friends . . . at least their dad and our dad."

"They were," Kane said. He glanced at Sean. "How much do you really know about what our brother and sister do in Europe?"

"More than I want to know." Liam and Eden were five years older than Sean. They'd been attending university in Europe when their parents were killed. For a time, they worked closely with RCK, but a grave disagreement six years ago, when Sean was just starting to work with RCK, saw them severing ties, and Kane couldn't speak of his brother without scowling. Sean had no idea what exactly had happened, and he didn't ask. It was a sore subject with everyone, and only Kane seemed to know the whole truth.

"Dante and Gabriella are North America's version of Liam and Eden, except while Liam and Eden cross the line on occasion—when it suits them—Dante and Gabriella are mostly rooted on the criminal side. Yet . . . even they have a code of ethics."

Sean was about to ask more about Kane's relationship with Dante and how it might help them now, but Kane said,

"I'll track the helicopter—Nicco put the times of arrival and departure here, though no tail number. You find out everything about Madison Spade's business—because if she's importing antiques, I think she's in as deep as her husband . . . or she's an ignorant fool."

CHAPTER FIFTEEN

It was after five that afternoon before Noah and Lucy arrived back in Webb County. Lucy was surprised that Siobhan was waiting for them in the morgue lobby. Siobhan was naturally fair, but looked ghostly under the harsh artificial lighting. She ran over to Lucy. "It's not Marisol."

"They already let you view the body?"

She shook her head. "I just know. I just know. It can't be." Her voice cracked.

Lucy said, "Noah and I are going in first."

"What? No, no! Don't coddle me. Everyone coddles me—I'm not a child. I can do this."

"I know you can," Lucy said, "but we may be able to take some of the pressure off. Trust me on this."

A man in scrubs walked through the swinging doors. "You must be the agents from San Antonio. I'm Dr. Greg Vasquez, the assistant medical examiner." Vasquez was in his mid-fifties with silver hair and broad shoulders on a stout frame. He wore wire-rimmed glasses.

Noah introduced himself and Lucy. "Thank you for staying late."

"I'm rarely out at five," Vasquez said. "Adam called me and asked that I wait for you."

Siobhan stared at him. Lucy said, "Siobhan, wait here. I promise, we'll come get you in just a few minutes."

She nodded and sat heavily in one of the plastic chairs.

Vasquez motioned for them to follow him back through the swinging doors. "That young lady has been out there for two hours, but I was told not to let anyone view the body until you arrived."

"We appreciate that. She may know the victim," Noah said.

"What did Adam tell you?"

"We know that she was found in an alley early this morning, that she recently gave birth, and that she's Hispanic and approximately twenty years of age," Noah said.

"She was in a Dumpster in an alley. Small miracle she was found so quickly. The alley services a row of small, family-owned restaurants. They all shut down before dark, it's not a great area of town. One of the shops is a mom-and-pop bakery. They get in at four in the morning, before the garbage trucks. They were dumping trash and found her. If they hadn't, the truck would have picked her up and it may have been next to impossible to find out where her body had been dumped. They may not have even noticed her. I had a case early in my career where a body had almost completely decomposed at the dump. Never solved it."

"You've completed the autopsy?"

"Yes, Adam told me not to wait for you on that, and because he said the feds were interested, I performed the autopsy myself." Dr. Vasquez handed them both gloves and paper booties, hats, and gowns. "Usually we prep the body in the viewing room for loved ones, but because she's still in the main holding room, you'll need to cover up."

"We already ran her image through the missing persons database and sent to all law enforcement, federal and within two hundred miles," Dr. Vasquez continued. "But it takes a while to hear back. Adam jumped on it, however, because of the baby."

Lucy stumbled, just a step, as her heart skipped a beat. "The baby is here, too?"

"No, sorry to upset you, sweetheart," he said. "I meant, she died in childbirth, but there is no baby. Whoever dumped her body kept the infant."

Dr. Vasquez led them into the main crypt, where bodies were stored in two areas—drawers if they had to keep the body longer than twenty-four hours or so, and the center aisle for bodies recently transported to the facility, or about to be transported to a funeral home. Lucy had interned at the morgue in DC—this place had a similar look and feel, though smaller and much newer. She didn't know what it said about her that she'd always been comfortable at the morgue, but there was a peace in the process of learning about the dead.

Vasquez had Jane Doe ready for them. "Because we don't have an ID on her, I intend to put her directly into cold storage. We'll keep the body for a year unless identified, then she will be buried in an unmarked grave in the county cemetery." He paused. "We cleaned her up the best we could, but it's not pretty. I can show you just her face if you would prefer."

Lucy shook her head. "I'm a certified pathologist. I'd like the visual to put with your report."

He nodded and pulled down the sheet.

The body was unusually presented. Generally, the ME cut the body open in a very specific pattern to autopsy the remains. This body had several areas that had been cut open and resewed, including her enlarged lower abdomen.

Lucy directed her attention to the woman's features. She was approximately twenty years of age and looked vaguely like Marisol de la Rosa. But it wasn't her. Marisol had a mole on her right cheek; this girl had none. And judging from her height compared with the standard table size, this girl was several inches shorter than either de la Rosa sister.

"This isn't one of the sisters," she said to Noah. "May I see the chart?"

Vasquez dropped the sheet, leaving only her face exposed, and handed Lucy a file. "I made you a copy, but it's preliminary—we're waiting for lab work and, of course, an ID."

"Doctor," Noah said, "why did you cut open her abdomen?"

"I didn't."

"She was found like that?"

The doctor nodded. "Someone performed a very rudimentary but proficient C-section on this girl, but she was either dead or dying at the time. She had preeclampsia—I'm nearly positive, but have to await the lab results before I can confirm. She went into shock and should have been brought immediately to a hospital. Based on her hormone levels and the size of the placenta—which was still inside her body—I believe she was between thirty and thirty-two weeks into the pregnancy."

"What's preeclampsia?" Noah asked.

"A condition during the third trimester that is characterized by high blood pressure. It's routinely screened for during prenatal care, and there are some effective treatments, but the only surefire way to treat it is delivery. When I removed the placenta, the signs of preeclampsia were obvious to me, but I went ahead and ordered additional tests to confirm. In severe cases, the doctor will induce labor early to avoid seizures and dangerously high blood pressure in the mother."

"Doctor," Lucy asked, "do you think someone attempted to induce labor because of her condition?"

"No. There was no sign of any of the standard drugs to induce labor, and those would be difficult for just anyone to procure—a medical professional would be able to get them, but most are used intravenously and under controlled conditions. There were no signs that she had an IV, no sign of any lifesaving procedures. There are indications that she had a seizure—which can happen in severe cases of preeclampsia—based on her brain tissue, and she bit off the tip of her tongue. She was either unresponsive or already dead when they cut open her uterus to remove the fetus."

"But the baby was alive."

"I have no way of knowing that. Except—someone cut the umbilical cord, and I would presume that was to save the baby. Otherwise, why not leave him with his mother?"

"Doesn't a premature baby need special medical attention?" Noah asked.

"Yes. The dangers are primarily in lung development. At thirty weeks, the baby could be as much as three pounds, which is dangerous but survivable with proper medical care. The older the baby, the better his chances."

"His?" Lucy asked.

"I took DNA and blood samples from the mother and the womb. The baby is male." Vasquez took off his glasses and rubbed his eyes.

Lucy turned to the final page of the report. "You should have led with this, Doctor."

"Excuse me?"

"She was shot?"

"I'm sorry, I assumed Adam had told you. Jane Doe died immediately before, during, or after the delivery of her baby. Then someone put a pair of twenty-two-caliber bullets in the back of her head. I suppose they wanted to make certain she died. But she was already deceased."

Lucy handed the file to Noah. Few things made her feel physically ill, but right now she was on the edge.

Someone had cut out this woman's baby, killing her in the process, and then, just for good measure, shot her, too.

Noah said, "You indicate here that whoever delivered the baby had some medical training."

"That is my opinion, yes. An amateur would have a difficult time cutting into the uterus and not injuring the fetus. The uterus is a very strong muscle. The incision was vertical, not horizontal, indicating an emergency delivery. There were no hesitation marks, telling me whoever cut into her had performed this surgery before, likely several times. Therefore, they have medical training. They could be a doctor, a nurse, maybe a midwife."

Lucy stared at the woman's face. She closed her eyes and mentally flipped through the photographs she'd been looking at over the last two days. "Noah," she said quietly, "we need to bring Siobhan in here."

"It's not one of her friends."

"I think it's the girl from the house—the one she tried to help. I can't be sure because of the angle of the photo Siobhan took, but Siobhan saw her close up."

"Fuck." Noah ran his hands through his hair.

"I'll bring her in," Lucy said and left the room.

First, she needed a minute alone.

She found the bathroom, took off her gloves, and splashed cold water on her face.

It had been all she could do to stay in control in the crypt.

Her hands went involuntarily to her stomach. Her barren stomach, that could never grow a child. That someone had torn a baby from that poor woman and left her dead, thrown away like trash, made Lucy ill. It wasn't seeing her on the slab, it was the pictures in the file Dr. Vasquez had handed her. Photos of the girl's womb, cut up, ripped apart, left for garbage. Whoever did this was evil. Lucy didn't throw that word around, but this time it fit. It was a heinous crime, and for what? To sell the baby? A premature baby who needed medical attention?

Lucy leaned against the cool tile wall as waves of nausea washed through her. She'd assisted in hundreds of autopsies, including the autopsies of three infants, one of whom had died of shaken baby syndrome and was by far the worst autopsy she'd witnessed. She'd had a similar reaction then, at the tragic, unnecessary death of another human because of the selfish wants of someone else.

She had to move, but she was rooted in place. She squeezed back her anguish.

Come on, Lucy. You are a professional.

Just one more minute!

She leaned over the sink and splashed more water on her face, then leaned forward and let another wave of nausea pass. Okay, she was better. She had to be. She had a job to do.

She would find Jane Doe's killer.

She would find Jane Doe's baby.

She finally regained her strength and left the restroom. She walked right into Noah.

He stared at her. She couldn't read his expression.

"I'm sorry," she said. "I—I just needed a minute."

He reached out and squeezed her shoulder. "That was hard to hear. I was surprised at how . . . indifferent you seemed. But I knew it was an act. I know you, Lucy. You can't keep all that bottled up. Did you think I would think less of you if you reacted?"

"No." Maybe. "I had to control it, Noah. If I broke down there, over her body, I wouldn't be able to do my job. To see what needed to be seen."

"Lucy, we've been friends for a long time. You know you can trust me. If you ever need to walk away, it's okay."

She nodded. "I trust you, Noah. I don't say that easily, but I *do* trust you. I *am* okay. I want to find these people in the worst way, but I can do the job."

"Dr. Vasquez took Siobhan in; you don't have to go back."

"I should be there for her."

"Think about yourself sometimes, okay?"

Noah dropped his hand, and that's when Lucy realized he'd been holding on to her for the last few minutes. As if he, too, needed to be grounded before he could move on. "How are you doing?" she asked as they walked back to the lobby.

He shrugged. "I don't think I'll be sleeping much tonight."

Siobhan stepped out of the crypt, silent tears running down her cheeks. "That's the girl from Sunday. Dear Lord." She crossed herself. "Lucy, I killed her."

"You did not kill her, Siobhan."

"I went there, I upset her—the doctor said she had a seizure caused by high blood pressure—I set her off. She was screaming at me—"

"Ma'am, I don't believe that's the case," Vasquez said, and Lucy mentally thanked him. "Preeclampsia is a very serious, very dangerous condition. That girl should have been under a doctor's care as soon as it was diagnosed— if it was diagnosed. No one caused it, but whoever delivered her baby killed her in the process. Not you."

It was time to leave.

Marisol couldn't stay here, not when her sister was in such danger. Angelo would be coming soon, and she didn't want the Honeycutts to be in the middle of any of this. These people were dangerous. Angelo would help her rescue Ana and then they could go home.

For the first time in two years she believed she would see her family again. Her village.

George and Nadia didn't want her to go.

Marisol didn't want to leave, either. Rarely had she met two genuinely kind souls, certainly not in the last two years. George and Nadia restored her faith in God, restored her hope that she would survive.

"Wait until John comes back," Nadia said. "He said he would be back tonight, after work. For dinner."

She shook her head. "Angelo is meeting me. You have done so much already."

"Wait until morning. Please, stay one more night."

She wanted to. Nadia reminded Marisol of her grandmother. Last night, she'd told Nadia some of what had happened to her and Ana. When Nadia hugged her, Marisol had cried. She hadn't cried in years, but she cried last night.

Today, she was stronger.

"Angelo knows what to do. These people are very dangerous, I don't want you hurt."

Nadia frowned. "Nonsense, Marisol. You need to let someone help you. There are good people in this world."

She smiled. When was the last time she'd smiled? "You and Mr. Honeycutt are two of the kindest people I've met. But Angelo can help me get my sister back."

She glanced at George. She hoped he hadn't already called the police. Because if he did, they would take her back. She knew it.

Nadia seemed to sense her hesitation. "You are safe here, Marisol. But you're still weak. You had a baby."

She blushed. She hadn't told Nadia about the baby, but she'd known. Maybe it was something women know, once they have a child of their own.

"Please trust me on this," Marisol said. "These are dangerous, bad people. Angelo can protect me, he is a good man. Like John."

"Why don't you have Angelo come here to get you?"

What did she say to that? She didn't know why, it was just her gut feeling. "Because you've done more than can be repaid." She had clean clothes. They were Nadia's, and they hung loose on her, but it felt good to wear something clean that smelled so good.

George walked over and put a phone in her hand, along with money.

She shook her head. "I can't take this."

"I programmed my number in here. If you need anything, any help, call me. John and I will come."

"I—"

"You will take it. It's not much money, but it will feed you."

She hugged them both and tried not to cry again.

Then she left. She had a two-hour walk ahead of her, but she felt so much better now than she had before. Angelo had been emotional when they spoke.

"I didn't know what had happened to you. I looked everywhere, but the policía *said you had gone away. Poof! Just disappeared. I feared the worst. Thank God you're alive. I will be there, just tell me when and where."*

Soon, Ana would be free. Soon, she would have her baby.

I love you, Angelo. Thank you.

Two hours later, while Nadia was preparing dinner and feeling surprisingly sad about Marisol leaving, John burst into the house.

"Wipe your feet," she said out of habit. She'd raised three sons and two daughters. John was the youngest and the only one who still lived close by.

"Where's Marisol?"

"She left."

"What? Why?"

"She spoke to the young man from her home. Angelo. He's coming to get her."

"But why isn't she *here*?"

"Johnny, what's wrong?"

"I talked to Adam after classes ended today."

"You promised you wouldn't go to the police, Johnny. Your word."

"I didn't tell him about her, I just asked hypothetical questions."

"Adam is not a stupid man."

Adam was her son-in-law, a good man, but he was a policeman, and he could be very law-and-order, especially when it came to immigrants. Nadia feared what would happen to Marisol. The girl was scared, terrified about something. Nadia could only guess. The police couldn't help her, not even a good man like Adam.

"An infant was left at a church in Freer. It's under police protection at the hospital. I think it's Marisol's baby."

"She wouldn't hurt a fly!"

"No, Ma, that's not what I mean. I mean that the police think that the baby's mother is in danger. And then Adam said another woman who'd just had a baby was found dead in an alley."

Nadia crossed herself.

"Where did Marisol go?"

"I don't know, she wouldn't tell me."

George came into the kitchen. "I heard her on the phone. I know where she's going. We should be able to catch up with her."

But when they arrived at the intersection fifteen minutes later, there was no sign of Marisol or anyone else.

CHAPTER SIXTEEN

Kane was on edge, which put Sean on edge.

"What haven't you told me?" Sean asked as he secured the plane. They'd landed at a private airstrip outside of Guadalajara. According to Kane, no one used it regularly, and they should be good for a day or two.

"After the cartel used Siobhan to lure me into a trap, I'm wary." Kane double-checked his .45 and slipped a back-up into an ankle holster. "I traced the helicopter and ID'd the guy with Gabriella. I'm pretty sure she's in deep with the Flores Cartel. No one can know our real connection to this rescue."

"No one knows Jesse is mine," Sean said. "I didn't even know until yesterday."

Kane didn't say anything.

"You think Madison set us up?" Sean shook his head. "If that were the case, she would have gone through RCK to ensure you were brought on. No one wants my head."

Kane grunted.

"Not as much as they want your head."

"You can't come with me to Dante's."

"Don't play overprotective big brother with me, not anymore."

"It's complicated. Dante Romero has survived this long in a dangerous business because he's paranoid and cautious. Two Rogans is going to set him off. He can't know that you were approached, that you're the one who was hired. He especially can't know that you have a personal stake. He's smart. He'll figure it out and leverage the information. Old family friends isn't going to buy us shit. The story will be you're my pilot. You've flown for me before, that's not going to raise any flags. But if Dante knows you're primary, he'll want to know why. He's good at math, and he is damn good at getting information. He'll sell it, and that puts the kid at risk."

Against every instinct, Sean reluctantly agreed with Kane. "Keep me in the loop, or I won't stay with the damn plane."

Sean watched Kane slip away, then checked the perimeter. He was going to go stir-crazy.

It was six in the evening. The sun would be going down soon, and Sean felt like they'd wasted the entire day. Half of it was flying time, and while Kane seemed to think the Romeros were the best lead, Sean didn't like to be kept out of the loop. Of course he understood—he didn't want to put Jesse's life at risk because he was a Rogan. But dammit, Carson Spade did it! How could a man bring the boy he called his son into the drug trade?

Sean hadn't had much time to sit and process his emotions, and they'd been churning inside making him physically ill.

He didn't want to think about Jesse, or Madison lying to him, or what Carson Spade was really up to. Because then he started thinking about the future, and what he was going to tell Jesse, and how he could fight for joint custody—if he even had a leg to stand on. He could probably sue for a paternity test if Madison didn't admit that Jesse was his. It was one thing to tell *him*, but it was another to admit to the world that you were a liar. As far as the legal system went, Sean had no rights. This was out of his area of expertise—but there had to be some way to force Madison to do the right thing.

But what if Jesse wanted nothing to do with him? What if he thought Sean hadn't wanted him, or had just walked away from him and his mother? How could Sean convince a twelve-year-old boy that he would never turn his back on his son . . . but Jesse didn't know him. Didn't know what he would or would not do. As far as Sean knew, Jesse didn't think about his real dad, didn't care. He loved Madison and Carson as his parents, and Sean was going to walk in and wreck his perfect life.

But what was perfect about a father who was a criminal? A father who put his son in danger?

Sean opened his laptop to continue his research into the companies Carson Spade worked for—the so-called legitimate company and the illegitimate company. He also needed to dig deeper into Madison's antiques business. A business like that was a great way to smuggle—or launder money.

He couldn't concentrate. He really wanted to talk to Lucy.

The plane had a booster so he had cell reception. He dialed her cell phone.

"Sean?" Lucy answered. "Where are you?"

"Guadalajara. We think we tracked them down—I'm babysitting the plane while Kane talks to someone who may have information. I can't get home soon enough. I miss you."

Tell her, Sean. Just tell her about Jesse.

There was a muffled sound in the background. "Sorry," Lucy said. "We're leaving the morgue."

"You're with Noah or Siobhan?"

"Both." She said something that he couldn't make out. "Okay, I just needed to step away."

"What happened? Why are you at the morgue?"

She didn't say anything for a second, then her all-business, all-cop voice said, "One of the young women in the house Siobhan identified was found dead. She'd just given birth—an emergency C-section. We don't know where, but we know it was late last night. She'd only been dead six to eight hours before her body was found."

"Shit, Lucy—are you okay?" The situation was fucked, and he wasn't there for her.

"It's a mess. The Webb County sheriff's department is working the case, they seem to be very competent. Noah and I are going to head back to San Antonio in a bit. We have one more thing to follow up on first."

"How's Siobhan?"

"As you would expect. Torn up, blames herself. The dead woman had preeclampsia, had a seizure." Lucy paused, her voice lower. "The ME suspected that she seized and someone performed an emergency C-section to save the baby. Then they shot her in the back of the head. Dumped her with the garbage." Her voice cracked.

Sean wanted to be there, right now, for Lucy.

"Say the word and I'll come home."

"I know you would, and I love you for it, but you need to find that little boy. I'm okay. Really."

She didn't sound okay.

"You said they took the baby?"

"The medical examiner believes the baby was about thirty-two weeks' gestation. He would need medical care, but he could survive. Someone with medical training performed the C-section, so we're guessing they could give the baby medical attention. But we don't know if he would need a ventilator, or if they're set up to run any tests. He would have been between three and four pounds." She paused. "They could have brought her to the hospital. Saved her life.

Preeclampsia is dangerous, but they could have saved her and the baby. They didn't care—they only wanted the baby."

"I'm so sorry, Lucy," Sean said. "I'm going to be home as soon as I can. You shouldn't have to be alone at night."

"I'm okay. Really."

She didn't sound it.

"This situation with Jesse is a lot more complicated. It's—" How did he tell her that Jesse was his son? How could he over the phone?

He heard voices in the background.

"Hold on, Sean," she said.

Lucy, Jesse's my son. I didn't know until yesterday.

That sounded so lame.

Madison never told me she was pregnant when I left Stanford, she would never have told me except he's in trouble. I should have told you yesterday . . .

Yes, Sean, you should have. Why didn't you? Dammit, he couldn't do it like this.

"Sean?" Lucy asked.

"I'm here."

"I just got a message from NCMEC—I think we got a hit on one of the girls Siobhan photographed Sunday."

"That's good news."

"I hope so. I'll call you tonight, we can Skype, okay? I love you, Sean. Be safe."

"I love you, too—" Sean began, but she'd already hung up.

Sean's hands were so tight on his phone, he had to flex them several times before he had full mobility. Of all the cases for Lucy to work while he was out of town.

He needed to find Carson Spade and Jesse and bring both of them back to the States, and fast.

Sean continued his research with renewed energy for

the next ten minutes, when his cell phone rang. It was Jaye, the research wizard at RCK.

"You have something," he answered.

"Always. Do you even have to ask?"

"Good news?"

"Maybe. I got a hit on Carson Spade's credit card. He's at the Estadio Omnilife, a soccer stadium. Well, *football*. He used his card at the gift shop. Bought a couple of shirts, a regulation jersey, some other souvenirs."

"He's there *now*?"

"Yep. I checked, the game started at six o'clock your time. Should be going on for a couple of hours."

"Any way you can find out where they're sitting?"

"I'm good, but I'm not psychic. He didn't buy the tickets with his credit card."

"Are these tickets hard to come by?"

"I have no idea, but soccer—I mean *football*—is huge in Mexico. I'd imagine the tickets are popular."

"I have a favor—I would do it, but I need to move. It's going to take me nearly an hour to grab a vehicle and get to the stadium."

"Ask."

"Find out if Dante and Gabriella Romero have season tickets, or anyone in the Flores cartel. You should have the names of the family members somewhere in RCK files."

"That might not be easy, or even possible. Unless—okay, I have a few ideas. I'll text you if I get anything."

"Thank you, Jaye. I owe you big time—again."

"Just come back alive."

"I plan on it."

"I mean, back to RCK. Everyone misses you."

Now was not the time to think about how and why he left RCK last year. "We'll talk later," he said and hung up.

Sean had already hid the plane, but he secured it and

set up an alarm that would alert his phone. Not that it would enable him to get back in time, but he'd be prepared for company. He left a coded note for Kane in case his brother returned before he did.

You should wait for him.

No. he didn't have time. But Kane would be livid. Still, this was a good idea. Sort of. Sean tried to reach Kane by secure phone as he walked toward the main road. No answer. Of course not. When he was working, he didn't answer his damn phone. He sent him a message.

I have a lead on Jesse. I'll be back in a few hours.

Assuming he could locate Jesse at this huge sporting event, he needed to convince his son to come with him. That might even be more difficult.

Madison.

That was it. He'd call Madison, have her talk to Jesse. Tell him to trust Sean. It would work.

It *had* to work.

Dante Romero was eating dinner with his woman of the week when Kane walked into his dining room.

Dante had the same worldly charm as Kane's brother Liam. Attractive, smart, selfish, charismatic. It was no wonder that at one time, Dante and Liam had been the best of friends.

Without taking his eyes off of Kane, Dante addressed the exotic woman sitting across from him. "Darling, would you please leave us for a moment?"

"Of course," she said. She stood gracefully and sauntered out of the room, closing the door behind her.

Dante motioned to the seat she'd vacated. "Sit."

"I'll stand."

"Kane, we're old friends. Family friends. You will sit, you will have a Scotch with me."

Dante rose and walked over to the sideboard. He turned

his back on Kane, which told him that he wasn't concerned Kane had come here to kill him. There might come a day when Kane would put a bullet in Dante Romero, but it wasn't today. He hoped it never came to that, because there were some things Kane liked about Dante. And the fact their fathers had been best friends.

Dante poured two glasses of Scotch and walked over to a small table in the corner framed by two comfortable leather chairs. Kane had sat here before, years ago, when they first negotiated their truce.

"Please, Kane. You can see every entrance from this corner."

Kane crossed the room and sat. He took the Scotch, and Dante raised his glass. "Old friends."

Kane nodded and they both drank until the glasses were empty.

"Did you kill my men?"

"No."

"Good. They're hard to find."

"Look harder. They were easy to take down."

"Who's with you? Ranger? I heard he was still in South America."

"I'm alone."

"You don't travel alone." He paused. "Most of the time."

"My pilot is with my plane. I need information."

"Of course you do. It's the only reason why you visit me." He almost pouted, but there was a light in his eyes that reminded Kane that Dante loved this game. He lived for it.

"I don't have time for the back-and-forth," Kane said.

"You never do."

Kane took out the surveillance photo of Gabriella and the three men, one of whom Kane knew to be Carson Spade. "Your sister stayed with this man"—he tapped the photo—"at an Acapulco resort for two nights. Then she left in a helicopter with him and someone else—an older man."

"You know Gabriella—she's fickle."

Gabriella was anything but fickle, so Kane didn't dignify Dante's lie with a response. "Took me a while, but I traced the helicopter to Borho Enterprises, which we both know is a front for Herme Velasquez. But Herme doesn't operate in this area, per his agreement with the Grande conglomerate, so I suspect he loaned the chopper to the Flores cartel. Herme's niece married into the extended family."

"I was at the wedding."

"Their truce is still in effect. We both know how Gabriella feels about Samuel Flores."

"Of course we do," Dante said, obviously enjoying this conversation. "She wouldn't be in business with them. I take our agreement very seriously."

"Not business. She would, however, go inside in order to assassinate him. I think her boyfriend here is the youngest brother."

"My sweet sister." Dante smiled, but it didn't reach his eyes. "You can't stop her from taking his blood, enacting vengeance. First, you have done the same when it matters to you. And even if you wanted to stop her, you can't. Not this time. Not for this cause."

"I told Gabriella years ago to let me take him down, and she refused. Her games are going to get you both killed, but they are her games. I'm not here to stop her."

"A good revenge plot takes time. Preparation is half the satisfaction."

"I don't want to get involved in that. I need to find this man." He pointed to Carson Spade.

"I don't know him."

"You're lying."

Dante leaned back, his jaw tight. "You come into my

home, for information about my sister, and accuse me of lying."

"His name is Carson Spade. He brought his son with him, then disappeared. The son's mother hired RCK to bring her son home. I don't care about Spade. I want the boy. I am prepared to extract him quietly."

Dante assessed what he said. He didn't relax, but there was a slight shift in his posture. He was contemplating the situation, running over all the facts, and most certainly trying to figure out what Kane was keeping from him. Kane maintained his poker face.

Dante sipped his Scotch. "I don't know Spade, but I know that Flores and his people are on high alert. I do not know why; I do not involve myself in their business out of respect for my sister. If Spade and his son are on their compound, even you won't be able to extract him. Dear friend, you are very good at what you do, but deep down you still have a conscience. That is the only thing that separates you from them."

"I am here to get the boy."

"And I am telling you, it is impossible. You will not penetrate his compound."

"I can if you give me intel on his security."

Dante leaned forward, all humor gone. "I can't, and even if I could, I won't. I will not risk Gabriella's safety for anyone. She is there to do a job, one she has been planning for years. I want her out alive, and that means no mavericks. Any hint that you are here, they will triple security." He stood and walked back to the table. He sat down to resume his dinner.

Kane could see by the tension in Dante's body that he was angry—whether at Kane or Flores, he wasn't certain. He rose, walked back to the entrance. Then he turned around.

"Gabriella is in over her head," Kane said. "There's no

love lost between us, but I know you care for her. I would have taken care of Flores for her. I know what he did."

Dante slowly lowered his fork. He turned to Kane. "You and I are opposite sides of the same coin, Kane. We fight our own wars. You fight yours. And I sincerely hope we never have to battle each other."

He turned back to his food. "I pressed the panic button two minutes ago. You have about ninety seconds to disappear or I'll turn you in for the bounty on your head."

"What bounty?"

He laughed. "There are so many, old friend, I'll probably sell you to the highest bidder."

CHAPTER SEVENTEEN

As soon as they started on the road back to San Antonio, Noah got on the phone. Lucy blocked out his conversation and checked her own email. First thing she opened was an email from her contact at NCMEC. She'd sent him the photos Siobhan had taken of the blond girl with the infant leaving the house in rural Freer on Sunday evening. He'd identified her.

> Lucy:
> Our facial recognition and age maturation program has identified with 89% certainty that the woman in the photo you sent me is Macey Sue Hornthrope from Kansas City, Missouri.
> Macey went missing four and a half years ago shortly after her fifteenth birthday. She is currently nineteen. Police determined that she ran away with her boyfriend, eighteen-year-old high school dropout William "Billy" Randall. While they did minimum due diligence, because of her age and the fact that there was no sign of forced abduction, the police shelved the case as inactive. I've attached a copy of the initial report and investigation into the Hornthrope home situation, but in a nutshell, the parents were in the middle of a nasty

divorce, Macey was the middle of three girls, and there was evidence that Macey had been using drugs for at least a year. When Mrs. Hornthrope forbade Macey from seeing her boyfriend, Macey ran away.

There have been no sightings of Macey, at least none that have come through our office or the federal database. She was considered low-risk—you know how it is. She was over 14, she left voluntarily, she was a drug user.

I've sent you Randall's last known address and contacts for both Macey's parents and Randall's mother. His father is not in the picture.

I contacted the Kansas City police and they indicated that the parents are still looking for her—posting on message boards, social media, contacting the missing persons department regularly for updates. It's my opinion that both parents would welcome their daughter back, no questions, if that will help you convince her to make contact, should you have the opportunity to talk to her.

Let me know what else I can do to help.

I heard through the grapevine—ok, your sister-in-law—that you're getting married. Congrats. Next time you're in DC, let's have coffee.

Sincerely,
Grant Mara
Assistant Director, NCMEC

As soon as Noah got off the phone, Lucy told him the news. "It's a start. I'd like to start by calling Randall's mother—find out where he's living, if she even knows. He could still be with her, maybe pimping her out. Forcing her into prostitution to feed their drug habits." She stared at Macey's current photo, the one Siobhan had taken. She looked scared, not strung out. "Or maybe they split and she didn't think she could go back home."

"We've both seen situations like that before."

"I want to find her. Let her know she has options. Encourage her to cooperate. Explain that she has to help us."

Noah shot her a glance but didn't say anything.

"She's probably a victim, but we don't know, do we? Was she forced into prostitution? Did she go voluntarily? Was it a combination? She may be loyal to these people. Or terrified of them. Or both. We can't trust that she'll turn on them, especially if they've brainwashed her to the extent that she can't see her life any way other than what it is now."

"Like you said, Lucy, we don't know."

Noah was right—and Lucy needed to talk to Macey, assess who she was now. In the past, Lucy always sided with the victims. She still did . . . but she'd learned the hard way that some people pretend to be victims when, in fact, they're predators.

"Grab my phone," Noah said.

Lucy did.

"Look up the SAC in the Kansas City office and send him a memo from me—he can task someone to follow up with the Kansas City police on Randall and Hornthrope and get us current information."

Noah dictated the memo for her to send. The requests coming from Noah would hold far more weight than if they came from a rookie agent, so Lucy was happy Noah thought of it.

"Do you think I've conveyed the necessary urgency?" Noah asked her.

"Oh yes," Lucy said. "Dropping Rick Stockton's name conveys urgency. Speaking of Rick, does he have any more information about this Jasmine?"

"He sent me a message to talk to Brad Donnelly of the DEA. I haven't had a chance to call him—but since you've worked with him, go ahead, call, put him on speaker."

"You've met him, right?"

"Couple of times since I've been here."

Lucy had Brad on speed dial. They hadn't seen much of each other outside of work over the last three months, mostly because Brad was overwhelmed putting the San Antonio DEA back together after a corrupt agent decimated it. He was the acting ASAC for the office, but word was that his position would be permanent by the end of the year.

"Donnelly. Is this Lucy?"

"It is."

"It's about time you called."

"The phone goes both ways, Brad."

"But this isn't a social call."

"It's not. I'm putting you on speaker—I'm with SSA Noah Armstrong."

"Serious?"

"Could be." She put the phone down on the center seat and pressed SPEAKER. "We're all here."

"Armstong," Brad said.

"Hello, Brad. Call me Noah."

"What can I do for you?"

"Jasmine, rumored to be the illegitimate daughter of a drug cartel leader," Noah said. "I don't have a last name, or a family. I hope you have more."

"Yep. I'll tell you what I know—which, frankly, isn't much—but first tell me how she came up in one of your investigations."

Lucy quickly explained the case they were working. "We have a photo, and a CI identified her by her first name only—claimed he didn't know her last name."

"Brave soul—or you have something on him. Here's what I know—I need to give you both a little history lesson first. And to be honest, some of the information I can't verify. It's all rumors, and even the rumors are vague."

"We'll take anything at this point," Noah said. "We have a dead body and two missing women."

"First, the rumor that Jasmine is the illegitimate daughter of someone in the cartel is probably accurate. Don Flores, one of the old-time cartel bosses, had two families—his first and legitimate family in Mexico, and his illegitimate family in Corpus Christi. Some say he was a polygamist, but I doubt it—you and I both know, Luce, that criminals have a weird and twisted view of religion. Flores was very Catholic, four sons with his wife, went to church, the whole nine yards. Sure, keep a piece on the side, but he wouldn't marry her. I can't remember the mistress's name—I can find it if you need it—but she had two daughters. The younger daughter went to college in Massachusetts or Maine and has as far as I know never stepped foot back in Texas. The older daughter—Jasmine—embraced the family legacy. Rumor is that she was Don's favorite, and she learned everything from him."

"Her name isn't Flores?"

"I don't know what she goes by. Legally, her name isn't Flores. She was born Jasmine Constance Ricardo. But she dropped her last name long ago. Married once, the guy's dead under suspicious circumstances, she inherits a small fortune. But this was years ago—when I was a rookie in Arizona. I don't have any more information—but I can get it."

"Was she a suspect?" Lucy asked.

"Not that I know of, but again, I don't have the file handy and I've never had need to read it. Jasmine is one of those names that pops up but never goes anywhere because we don't have a current photo or address for her. Couldn't interview her if we wanted to, and since we've never had even circumstantial evidence against her, no warrants for fishing."

Brad covered the phone and mumbled to someone in the background, then came back. "Sorry, I have like five minutes. But you should know that Don Flores was killed by his own family. It's not a big secret, but it was a long time ago. Fifteen, sixteen years."

Noah said, "So you don't know what she's specifically involved with?"

"No—again, everything is quiet rumors about her. The one rumor is that she's working with her family in Mexico—but because Flores hasn't moved into my jurisdiction, I don't know a lot about their operation. It's possible that now that Tobias's operation is wiped out, they're planning on making a move, but at this point all we're seeing are local turf battles, no big organization coming in. *Yet*—because we all know it's going to happen. Where there's a void and that shit. Oh! One more thing. Even though Jasmine and Don were tight, she's not fond of the drug trade. Go figure. She has her hands in semi-legitimate business enterprises. That's the word, at any rate. Do you want me to ask around?"

Lucy glanced at Noah. He said, "Yeah. And don't be subtle. Maybe we can shake some trees and make her nervous."

"Will do. It'll take me a couple days, but I know exactly how to shake some big trees."

"Would black-market babies be up there on her list of business enterprises?" Noah asked.

Brad swore. "That's what this is? You think she's selling babies?"

"Yes," Lucy said. "We have evidence of four women who were or are pregnant, but suspect there are many more. We don't have a lot to go on right now, but the photo we have of Jasmine seems clear that she's in charge."

"Interesting. Can you shoot me the pic?"

"Yes," Noah said. "Whatever you can learn would help us. You don't have her address, do you?"

Brad laughed. "No. She hides very well. And truthfully, even if we did, it'd mean shit. There's no evidence she's

ever done anything illegal. No proof that she even associates with her brothers. What we *think* and what we can
prove are not the same."

"Our CI acted intimidated," Noah said. "I'm still not
sure it wasn't an act for our benefit."

"Remember—she's smart. She's never even been *questioned* in a DEA operation, and I doubt any other law enforcement agency has interviewed her. She's a lawyer—not
a trial lawyer, but she is well versed in using the law to
both hide and manipulate the system. So mind your P's
and Q's."

"Thanks, Brad," Noah said.

"Lucy," Brad said, "don't be a stranger." He hung up.

"Where do we go from here?" Lucy asked Noah.

"Stay the course. I, for one, would like to get this Jasmine into an interview. She's a material witness at a minimum considering she was in the same house with a
woman who turned up dead."

Lucy didn't say anything. Jasmine was a lawyer—she
could easily manipulate the adoption system. Lucy didn't
know much about the illegal adoption business. She wondered how much parents would pay for a child. Infants
were in high demand.

Still . . . there had to be far more money in trafficking
drugs than infants.

Her heart skipped a beat. There was a demand for
children, children that no one knew existed. They could
be breeding their own armies, indoctrinating young
children their entire lives to serve the cartels, to be fodder
for the militants, to serve in brothels and work in facto-
ries.

"Lucy," Noah said quietly.

"Yeah?" She forced her voice to sound normal but in
doing so sounded like she was suffocating.

"We don't know why Jasmine was at that house. We

don't know what she's doing or how she's doing it, or even if she's doing anything illegal. All we know is that she was at a house where one of the residents turned up dead."

"And her baby missing."

"And no proof that Jasmine killed her. Based on Siobhan's statement, Jane Doe was alive when Jasmine left the house with the others."

Noah was right. What they knew as facts was very little.

"We will find the truth," he said. Noah looked at his phone. "Zach wants to talk to us when we get back—do you think you can spare thirty minutes?"

"As much time as you need. Sean isn't home." She really wished he was. She could talk to him about this. She had promised him that she wouldn't hold everything inside anymore, that when something hit her hard, she'd talk to him. She'd kept so much bottled up inside for so long that having someone to confide in—someone who didn't think she was going to break down at any moment under the weight of tragedy—had freed her.

"But first, let's get some food. Why didn't you tell me you were hungry?"

"I'm not that hungry." She was starving.

"Your stomach is loud."

"Traitor," she mumbled.

Noah grunted a laugh.

An hour later, Noah and Lucy were sitting in the small conference room with Zach Charles, eating Mexican food takeout. "There's plenty," Noah told Zach.

"I ate." But he was eyeing the chips and salsa. Lucy slid them over to him and he took a handful. "Okay, thanks for coming in, because this is hard to explain on the phone."

"You're the one staying late."

"Yeah, well, I don't mind." Zach unfolded the whiteboard on the wall. He'd already drawn a pyramid-type structure with business names, connected by dates and lines.

"So, you both know how shell corporations work, so I'm not going to go into detail, but think about the layers, okay? Because that's really what this is. Layer upon layer upon layer of hollow businesses that were created for the express purpose of making it difficult to find a real person to assign liability. And while there are some legitimate purposes for shell corporations, that's not this. This operation you uncovered down in Laredo is just the tip—I think this goes much bigger."

Zach pointed to the name at the bottom of the chart. "Direct Property Holdings. They manage all the properties you identified. But each of the properties is owned by a different business. And that's key—they're owned by businesses, not individuals. Those businesses are also shell corps and none of them have overlapped—yet." He slid over copies of a printout to both Noah and Lucy.

Lucy stared. She was looking at dozens—hundreds— of business names.

"And they're all anonymous," Noah said. "Shit."

"Okay, maybe I should have led with the good news."

"You think?" Noah said.

"Yeah, well, okay, so all these shells have one thing in common: an address in Las Vegas."

"You've connected them to the same entity? You could have said that on the phone."

"No—they have the same address, but all different corporations. It's just a way to obfuscate the picture. But filing dates are part of the record, so I was able to re-create the order in which these organizations were set up. Maybe whoever organized this didn't realize we'd get so far, or maybe they didn't know what they were doing initially and weren't able to cover their tracks. But the first one was disbanded a year ago—and the appointed director is Gregory Valeria. His address is in San Diego."

"That's really good work, Zach," Noah said. "And fast."

Zach grinned, both out of pride and embarrassment. "Um, yeah, thanks. But I'm not done. The property management company is just a one-room office—I called pretending to have a group of properties and asked about their policies and rates. They told me they are a private company and work only for a group of businesses. They wanted to know how I got the number. I had to do some quick thinking, so I said the Internet, then quickly created a fake page that listed a hundred property management companies in Texas and included them. If they dig deep, they'll see it was created today, but hopefully they don't."

"Smart," Lucy said.

"I need a warrant," Noah said. "I don't want to go in there and tip them off."

"We have cause," Lucy said. "One of their properties was a murder scene."

"We don't know she was killed there."

"We don't know she wasn't."

"The AUSA isn't going to bite on that." Noah snapped his fingers. "The brothel in Del Rio. Illegal prostitution. We have a confidential informant who gave us information, we need the property records and all information on the owner."

"Who? Barrow? He'll never agree."

"Doesn't matter, he already talked to us, he gave us the intel, and we have his investigative report. I think I can convince the AUSA to give us a little room on this." Noah packed up the remaining food. "I'm going to talk to Rick first thing in the morning and we'll work out a strategy. Lucy—follow up with the Kansas City field office about the memo we sent, see if you can find this Randall kid, and be ready to serve the warrant on DPH. Zach—I need you to quietly dig up everything you can about Jasmine Constance Ricardo, born in Corpus Christi, possibly goes by the name Jasmine Flores. Copy in only me and Lucy. Donnelly with the DEA is looking into her as well, and he's making a bigger splash, but I need you to be discreet."

"No problem," Zach said. "Oh—one more thing, on those photos you sent. Finally got a hit late this afternoon on this guy." He slid over the photo of Jasmine's bodyguard. "Lance Dobleman. Dishonorably discharged from the Army six years ago for a variety of charges, including insubordination and assault of a superior officer."

"Why wasn't he court-martialed?" Noah asked.

"I hope you don't mind, but I asked Agent Dunning to look into it, since he's former Army."

"And?"

"Dobleman was sleeping with his commanding officer's wife. Commanding officer caught them in bed, fight ensued, Dobleman got the discharge. But apparently there were a lot of shady things with this guy. Nate couldn't get the details, only that Dobleman was a ladies' man, may have been abusive to the women he was with, and his unit didn't like him. His bunkmate is the one who told their commander about the affair."

Noah said, "Ask Nate to follow up on that, and I'll work on getting his military records and see if we can work that angle. Find out what he's been doing in the last six years and who employs him now."

"I got that part," Zach said with a grin. He handed over a slender file. "I don't have a lot on him, but he works for Gold Key Enterprises, one of the companies in this big shell game." He circled a business in the middle of the chart. "Title is security chief. And I have a residence—thanks to Nate. It's all in the folder."

Lucy opened it. Dobleman lived in Austin, Texas.

"Hold off on interviewing Dobleman until I hear from Stockton about how we're going to handle Jasmine," Noah said. "But Zach—keep working this. The more information we have, the better."

CHAPTER EIGHTEEN

The bad news was that the stadium was crowded and sold out.

That good news was that the stadium was crowded and sold out.

The crowds could help Sean grab Jesse and slip away with minimal attention, but first he had to get in. That wasn't the difficult part—bribing a guard at a back exit did the trick.

But now he had to find Jesse. And Jaye hadn't called him.

On the ride to the stadium—Sean had hot-wired an old motorcycle that was easy to manuever and park close to the stadium—he considered all the ways his plan could go wrong.

In fact, he didn't see it going right.

But what other choice did he have? Kane's idea of appealing to Dante Romero may or may not work. And then they would have to breach the Flores compound, putting both of them—and Jesse—at risk. Grabbing Jesse now and explaining to the kid on the way home what was going on seemed the most logical—and easiest—of solutions.

Sean didn't want to scare Jesse. Hell, that was the *last*

thing he wanted to do. He considered how to explain to his son what was going on . . . and the best way was getting him to talk to his mother. Sean had Madison now programmed on speed dial and he suspected she'd pick up on the first ring. He hoped. After this morning . . .

Focus, Sean. Focus on finding Jesse, then worry about getting him out.

Sean arrived just after halftime ended. People were still moving back to their seats, some agitated, drunk, excited. Sean liked to play sports for fun, but he grew restless as an observer. What was the last major sporting event he'd watched? Was it the Super Bowl? No . . . he missed most of it. He caught one of the games of the World Series last year, only because he'd been with Patrick who loved baseball. How did people have fun here? There was a certain energy and excitement—that he understood—but Sean would much rather be playing on the field than sitting in the stands drinking beer.

He didn't know how much time he had—an hour, take or leave. He walked the entire perimeter of the stadium to get the layout. There were food and souvenir vendors in several strategic locations. The credit card that Jaye had caught only gave the name of the business entity that ran all sales at the stadium, so Sean had no idea which clothing retailer had sold Carson the shirts.

Jaye still hadn't called.

He called her.

"Jaye, I need something."

"Sean, what the hell do you think you're doing?"

"Funny, you don't sound like Jaye." Shit, it was JT.

"You're acting on emotion. For a fucking genius, you're an idiot."

"It's an opportunity."

"You're there without backup!"

"Kane is working his own angle, I'm working mine.

If I can get Jesse tonight, we'll be back in San Antonio before dawn."

"I'm not saying the plan is bad—though it is because you don't even *have* a plan—I'm saying you never go in alone. Kane is on his way. Do not do anything until he gets there."

"I don't even know where Jesse is!"

"Jaye is very good. Flores has season tickets, a box of eight—which means you're not just dealing with some cartel lawyer and a kid; you could be dealing with bodyguards and one or more of the Flores brothers. Wait for Kane. He'll meet you at the top of section one eighteen."

"Okay."

"I'm serious, Sean."

"I said I'd wait for him!" He rubbed his face. He was so close . . . "Look, JT, I get it. But what choice did I have? What if Jesse were your kid?"

"This is why you bring backup—because emotions have no place in hostage rescue. Be safe—and smart."

"I have no intention of dying tonight."

"It's about time," Sean muttered when Kane came up silently next to him twenty minutes after he got off the phone with JT.

Kane was in disguise, of sorts. Black shirt but instead of his military surplus jacket, he had on a worn leather jacket, and he wore a home team baseball cap with sunglasses—even though it was near dark. Sean also wore sunglasses, and Kane pulled an extra cap from his back pocket. Sean put it on.

"You have one chance," Kane said. "If anything goes south, we disappear, got it? Being arrested would really screw with our plans—not to mention being dangerous for both of us. I have a jeep parked outside the perimeter, directly across from the north exit, but it's a quarter-mile walk. I couldn't risk getting caught up in crowds leaving. This place is going to be a zoo." He glanced at the score-board. "Good thing it's tied at one, because if it goes into overtime, no one is going to leave early. This is important, Sean—if you get Jesse, get to the jeep. If I'm not there, leave. I'll meet you at the plane."

"I'm not leaving you behind."

"I have a backup plan. Which is what you should have had before you got here."

"We're close, Kane."

"I know."

"Where is he?"

"The Flores family has a box directly above section one oh three—directly across the stadium from us." He slipped Sean a pair of binoculars. "I already scoped it out when I arrived. The kid is there; so are Carson Spade, Gabriella Romero, and one of the Flores brothers. Four other men, two I pegged as bodyguards, two I believe are associates. I couldn't stay long—this disguise is nonexistent. I'm sure Dante already alerted Gabriella to my presence, and she's a wild card."

"You're going to have to clue me in later," Sean said. He looked through the binoculars and adjusted them. He saw mostly a sea of red and white, the team colors.

And then he saw Jesse.

The kid was watching the game intently. His hair was longer than in the photo Sean had seen, long enough to curl at the ends just like Sean's hair did. He wore a home team jersey that was too big on him, and held a bag of popcorn.

Sean's heart rate increased. That was his son. He should be taking him to games, showing him how to play soccer and baseball. He should be watching him play in Little League or coaching his soccer team.

Focus. Sean turned the binoculars to the rest of the group. Carson wasn't sitting next to Jesse—he was in front of him, next to a relaxed older man. Jesse was sitting between the only female in the group—Gabriella Romero, Sean presumed—and a broad-shouldered dark-skinned man with a mustache. He looked all bodyguard.

"We wait until they leave."

"I hate that plan."

"I've gone through the possibles and this is the *only* way it's going to work. Unless the kid needs to use the bathroom, we're going to wait until the group leaves. I will split him off from his group, using the crowds as a diversion. We need to act fast. Spade or one of the entourage will notice pretty quick if the kid isn't with them. You have to convince him not to make a scene. If he goes quietly, we get out fast. If he argues, we bolt. Without him. You may have authority from his mother, but that doesn't give you rights here in Mexico when Carson Spade is his legal guardian."

Sean wanted to argue, but he didn't. Kane didn't talk much, so when he had a speech, Sean paid attention.

He nodded.

"Follow me."

Sean followed Kane around the south end of the stadium until they reached section 103 where Jesse sat with his group. Cheers erupted when the home team scored a goal, putting them ahead 2–1 with two minutes left. Sean stopped where he had a vantage point, but Kane pushed him forward, around the corner, and up the stairs that led to the upper balcony. After the goal, many people started to leave.

Kane pushed Sean into an alcove—a food stand had once been there, but it was shut down now—and said, "Stay here."

Sean waited. And waited. The stadium roared several minutes later, and thundering applause, shouts, and footfalls filled the arena. Where the hell was Kane?

He almost left. He watched from his vantage point as masses of people filed past him. They didn't seem to be ending. Then suddenly Kane emerged with Jesse by the arm.

"Let me go!" Jesse said. With the noise from the crowd, no one would be able to hear him.

Kane gave Sean a look that said they had little time.

"Jesse," Sean said, "your mother sent me to bring you home."

"No way, she would have told me. Who are you?"

"My name is Sean, and your mother and I were friends years ago. You need to trust me. As soon as we get out of here, you can call her."

"Yeah, and you have a puppy you want me to help you find."

Kane was watching the crowd. "Sean, time."

"Jesse," Sean said, "your stepfather is bad news, and he's put your life in danger. Your mother hired me to find you. You need to come with me now."

He reached for him, took him by the arm, and suddenly Jesse started screaming. "Let me go!"

Sean didn't want to scare him, but what was he supposed to do?

"Carson Spade is working for the drug cartels, and you're not safe with him!" Sean said, pulling Jesse toward him.

Jesse lashed out, scratching Sean. He saw Sean's gun under his jacket and kicked Sean in the balls. Sean fell to his knees and Jesse slipped away.

"Kane! Grab him!"

Kane did and at first Sean was relieved, then Kane said in a low voice, "Jesse, do not tell anyone about this. You will put your mother's life in grave danger. We're coming back for you."

Then he let him go. Jesse ran.

"What the hell?" Sean said. "Why?"

"We have to go, Spade already alerted security. If the kid talks, we're fucked."

Sean slammed his hand against the stone wall and followed Kane.

That didn't go anything like he had planned.

Jesse ran away from the two creeps, but he had no idea where to go. He headed back toward the seats they'd been sitting in, fighting the crowds.

Carson Spade is working for the drug cartels.

That was the stupidest thing Jesse had ever heard. Those men were probably here to kidnap him for ransom. His dad had warned him that it was a real possibility.

Gangs think that all Americans are rich, that they can get money by grabbing kids and families. You have to be careful.

Jesse was almost back to his seat when his dad rushed up to him with Dominick. They both looked angry; his dad also looked scared. "Jesse! Where were you?"

"I—" He saw the gun under Dominick's jacket. "I just got pushed by the crowd, then I couldn't see you."

Why didn't he tell his dad the truth? That two men tried to kidnap him?

Was that really what they were trying to do?

Jesse really wanted to talk to his mom. She would straighten this all out, tell him the truth. And if she said she didn't send anyone for him, he'd tell his dad everything.

"You're not a little kid, Jesse," his dad said.

"You're sure that's all it was?" Dominick said.

Gabriella came up to them with Dominick's brother, Jose, "Dom, he's scared, you're scaring him more. You're okay, little man, right?"

Jesse nodded. Did she know? Had she seen what happened? "Just—I didn't know how to find you so I came back to the seats."

"Smart kid, just like his dad." Gabriella smiled at his dad. "Let's get out of here. The limo should be out front by now."

His dad put his arm around Jesse's shoulders, then kissed him on the top of the head. Normally that would embarrass him in front of people, but right now he was relieved.

His dad would never let anything happen to him.

He almost told him what happened.

Almost.

As soon as he talked to his mom.

Kane took a roundabout way back to the plane not only to ensure they hadn't been followed, but also to check the perimeter of their hiding spot. They were clear.

They set up camp without speaking. They wouldn't sleep in the plane because that would make them an easy target, but they didn't want to be too far from their ride home. Kane did another perimeter check, then they ate sandwiches, washing them down with cool beer that had been in Sean's ice chest.

"I should have pulled the plug," Kane said.

"I shouldn't have gone in the first place." Sean had been thinking about the entire fiasco. "When I was twelve, no way in hell would I go off with two strangers." He paused. "I wanted to tell him who I was, but there's no reason for him to believe me. And there's no reason for him to believe his mother sent me." Sean drained his beer. "Were the Romeros bad news when our dads were friends? Are you on the Flores cartel hit list? You shouldn't be here."

"I'm here because you need me—and Jesse is my blood." Kane pulled out two more beers, handed one to Sean. "My educated guess is that Gabriella Romero has wormed her way into the Flores cartel for the sole purpose of assassinating Samuel Flores." He paused. "Not the sole purpose. She doesn't do anything with a single goal. If she can rip him off before she kills him, that would make her even happier."

"You've already lost me."

"It's a long story, Sean."

Sean didn't say anything.

"Flores killed Gabriella's lover ten years ago."

"Ten years? That's a long time to wait for revenge."

"She's patient."

"And Flores doesn't realize she's out for revenge?"

"He doesn't even know the connection. Few people do. Gabriella is . . . complex."

"Do I hear a hint of admiration?"

Kane shook his head. "Not what you're thinking, little brother."

Sean really hated when Kane did that.

"Dante and Gabriella have helped RCK operations . . . and hindered RCK. They have their own agenda. Their mother died long ago, you know their father was friends with our father. Dante and Liam used to be tight, but they have their own war."

"What else don't I know?"

"A lot. Mom and Dad never wanted you to work with me—I'd already left the Marines by the time they died. They didn't like some of the choices I made, and Duke made sure you didn't follow in the same path. But you made your own choices when you grew up."

"Many of them because Duke pushed me in the opposite direction." Sean rubbed his eyes. He didn't want to think about his complex relationship with his other brother.

"What I'm saying is, I've known Dante and Gabriella for a long time. You were too young to remember them.

But it hasn't always been friendly, especially after Mom and Dad died."

"And their dad?"

"Lives in Louisiana, last I heard. The key point is, I know Gabriella well. Her fiancé was an Army Ranger, Doug Bonelli. He'd been part of Jack's unit when he was still serving."

"Small fucking world," Sean muttered.

"These people we deal with—it seems insurmountable, but there are only two dozen cartels and gangs who are in serious power. There are hundreds of violent gangs and groups, but they don't spread out, they're localized. The most powerful cartels' network have arms in the States and up into Canada and Europe and the Middle East and even China. They pull in gangs as they need, or hire them as protection, but the power centers are mostly controlled by families or family alliances. Sometimes the violent gangs, the rebels, the upstarts, the so-called private businessmen help them . . . sometimes they hinder them."

"Just like the Romeros."

Kane smiled thinly. "You understand."

"So is Gabriella going to help us or not?"

"I don't know. She saw me tonight. She was pissed off, but she won't do anything until she talks to Dante. I'm hoping she'll help—or at least stay out of our way. Until I saw Spade with Dominick Flores, I couldn't confirm that he was working for the Flores cartel, but it's pretty fucking clear he's chummy with him. They were sitting together, heads close—that's not the sign of someone here on legitimate business."

"Dominick is the oldest brother?"

Kane nodded. "The patriarch, now that their dad is dead. But there are three others. They work as a unit. Dominick is in charge, he's the figurehead, but he won't do anything without the agreement of his brothers."

After several minutes of silence, Kane said, "When Bonelli was killed, I offered to take care of Samuel Flores myself. Gabriella said no."

There was far more to that story that Kane wasn't saying.

"She's not going to back down, and Dante isn't going to give me anything that will help. He said that Flores's compound is impenetrable. I reconned the place; he's right. Not without a large team and going in full-force, which puts the kid at risk. I have some specs on the place. Until tonight, we couldn't even confirm Jesse was there—but I'm fairly certain he is. There are no hotel reservations in Carson Spade's name, or either of his business names. Still, we need more information and help in getting inside."

"You think you can convince her?"

Kane didn't say anything.

Sean said, "I have an idea. But you might not like it."

"Shoot straight."

"I need to get Jesse a note. I'll explain everything—can you convince Gabriella to give it to him?"

"Possibly."

"I need proof that Spade is working for Flores. Seeing him with Dominick isn't going to cut it. We get proof, I can then get Madison to tell Jesse to trust me."

"She didn't even want you here. She tried to stop us, Sean."

"Because she's in denial. With proof, she won't be." He shifted on the uncomfortable ground. He doubted he'd be sleeping much tonight.

"Each cartel has their own primary area, right?" Sean continued. "They'll associate with shell corporations and lawyers that Spade associates with. I already have every corporation Spade's firm does business with."

"You've been busy."

"I sent the list to Jaye. She's going to run it against known cartel shell corporations."

"Good, but that's going to take time."

"I'm working on another angle. Pinpointing Jesse's exact location."

"Short of a GPS chip, how?"

Sean reached into his satchel and pulled out a photo that Kane's contact in Acapulco gave them. "This is Jesse—he's playing a handheld video game."

"Okay."

"It's hard to tell which device, but most of the new devices have Wi-Fi. I hacked into the resort Wi-Fi system—not difficult at all, so if you need to pay your friend Nicco for his help, I can plug the holes with a little time and access."

"Access helps us more than the bad guys," Kane said and left it at that.

Sean continued. "Based on the time stamp of this photo, I backtraced Jesse's device. The Wi-Fi system logs specific system information unique to that device, so once that device logs into the system, they don't have to log in again."

"Okay." Kane was sounding more skeptical. Kane was good with tech, though distrustful, but this was the one area where Sean was clearly superior.

"Of course, I've rigged all my devices never to divulge any information, but most people don't do that." Sean almost smiled. "There are many Internet providers, but I figure Flores will want only the best. That leaves two in this area. They are a bit trickier to navigate—the firewall is much better here than at the resort. But if Jesse used his device at all, I will know."

"Wouldn't Flores or Spade have him turn off the Wi-Fi?"

"Possibly, but most adults don't realize the capabilities of handheld video games. You can't download a lot of data from the Internet, for example, because they don't have the storage—the memory is primarily used to play the game and store game progress, but you still need a disk or chip to play. There's no Internet browsing, for example—most are not designed like that. The one Jesse has, though a new model, is primarily for game playing—including multi-player games, on a limited scale.

"But," Sean continued, "even if he turns off the Wi-Fi, he has to open the device to turn it off, which means at one point the device pinged the Wi-Fi system, and that system is serviced by a provider."

"I think I got it."

"Good—because I've already started running my program, and we should have his location in a couple of hours."

"There's a bigger issue here, Sean—getting him out. Even if we know exactly where he is—down to the room, and you can't tell me your tech can pinpoint him to a ten-by-ten spot—we have to get to him, then convince him to leave quietly."

"That's why I need to get him information. I can send him a note on his device—if he's on it."

"Do it."

"And the secondary thing is that once I get the IP address for the wireless system, I can analyze the data and see how they run their security system—whether it's dedicated or not. I suspect it's a combination of both, but even taking out part of the system will help us."

"We need a diversion. If we can get Jesse out of the compound, it would be much easier to grab him."

"Flores will have what? Fifty men or so?"

"Probably less."

Sean shook his head. He should laugh at the absurdity of Kane's matter-of-fact tone, but he was exhausted.

"I'm talking about a diversion he won't expect. Let me think on it. I have a couple of ideas, but none that I'm confident we can survive."

"I need to check on the plane, then get some sleep."
"Say hi to Lucy for me."

Lucy was familiar with death. She'd seen it close up—when she was younger, knowing her cousin and best friend Justin was in a coffin at the front of the church the day of his funeral; when she was eighteen and killed her rapist; when she worked in the morgue and saw the dead every day. And now, on the job, she saw the dead.

But this case . . . it was different than others.

She'd been able to put Jane Doe out of her head when she was in the office with Zach and Noah, talking about shell corporations and property management and legal issues for possible warrants. It helped focus her on the present. But now, as she lay in bed after midnight, she only saw Jane Doe's corpse and the swollen stomach where her baby had once grown.

Jane Doe had died for no reason other than someone had wanted her baby. She could have survived if they'd taken her to the hospital, given her emergency medical care. It was the absolutely senselessness of her death that disturbed Lucy. She should have survived.

But she'd died in childbirth because of the cruelty of those who had her. Then two bullets in the head. Dismissed. Tossed in the garbage. Her son taken. Why? To be sold? To be used? Did that baby have anyone to love him? Did he have a bright future, or was it as bleak as his mother's?

Lucy wanted to believe that someone misguided but desperate for a child would raise the premature little boy who'd been born so violently; but she knew from her experience and training that there were other, darker purposes for children.

She closed her eyes and bit back a cry.

No.

She wouldn't go there, she couldn't and survive. Not now, in the middle of the night, when nightmares were par for the course, followed by insomnia and the overwhelming sense of hopelessness. She'd thought she'd gotten past all that, but after she rescued a group of foster boys who'd been brutalized and used as mules by the drug cartels, the nightmares returned about the ones she couldn't save.

She got up, desperately needing sleep, but mostly needing to clear her mind. It was midnight, but she swam in her pool, thirty hard laps, back and forth, until her muscles ached and her lungs burned. Then she turned and floated on her back, gently pushing herself along. Back and forth. Clearing her mind, focusing on the stars in the sky, the pin lights Sean had put in the trees. She loved her house, but especially the backyard, where she and Sean spent so much time sitting and relaxing. There were balconies and a covered patio outside the poolhouse. They had a small garden, trees and flowers, and of course the pool. Lucy loved swimming, and the pool was large and mostly rectangular so she could swim laps.

Sometimes, she never wanted to leave. She'd been only half joking when she told Sean that they should tell everyone they were going away for their honeymoon, but come back here and stay locked inside for a week, no interruptions, no work, just them.

Paradise.

Finally, she knew she was tired enough to sleep. She climbed out of the pool, went back inside, set the alarm, and took a quick shower to rinse off the chlorine. When she stepped out, her phone was ringing.

Sean.

He was Skyping her, so she accepted the call and smiled when his handsome face came on screen.

"Hello, princess. Did you just get home?"

"About ten. But I couldn't sleep, so I went swimming."

"I wish I were there," he said wistfully.

"Me, too."

Sean's face froze.

"Are you there?" she asked.

"Yes, the connection is poor. Sorry." Suddenly the screen went black. He said, "I cut off video—we're camping out tonight in the middle of nowhere."

"Is everything okay?"

"About as we expected. You sound tired."

"It's been a long couple of days."

"Do you have any leads?"

"You know how these people operate. You'd be proud of Zach—he's really learned how to weed through the information and pull out nuggets."

"The apprentice becomes the master."

She laughed. God, it felt good to laugh. "He did so well, Noah thinks he can get a warrant for the property management company. It might not yield anything, but if we can get a complete list of their clients and properties, we might be able to find the women and babies."

"If you need any help—if Zach needs help—you know I'll be there."

"Dean Hooper from Sacramento is helping. Noah didn't say it explicitly, but I think Hooper is coming to San Antonio."

"He's brilliant. And I don't say that lightly."

"Hooper suggested to Noah that he bring you in, so I think Noah would be receptive to your help—but you need to find that little boy first."

"Yeah . . ." His voice trailed off, and Lucy thought she'd lost him.

"Sean?"

"Here. We know where he is, but it's complicated."

"You sound frustrated."

"I am. It's complicated," he repeated.

"Talk to me."

"I want to—I just . . ." again, he didn't say anything.

"I understand, Sean."

"We're close. But Spade took his son into a dangerous situation. Spade is working for a drug cartel. Madison said he's an accountant, and that's true, but he's also a lawyer. I don't know how deep his involvement goes, and if it'll even be possible to extract him. I just want the kid."

"He took his son into that situation?"

"The kid could be leverage they're using on Spade."

"You don't sound like you believe that."

"I don't. I don't know what to think right now, but the information we've put together tells me that Spade is a willing and proactive partner in whatever is going on." He paused so long that Lucy thought they'd been disconnected.

"Lucy?"

"Right here. I thought I lost you."

"I love you, and I wish I could be there right now to talk to you. I have a lot to explain . . ."

"I'm listening."

"I—not on the phone."

"Are you okay?"

"Yeah. I'll be fine. There's just a lot going on and I wish I were there so we could talk about it."

"I'm always here for you." She paused. "Sean—that's not true. There have been times when I have been so preoccupied with my problems and my job that I forget that you have work that is just as difficult and troublesome. You have always been here for me—and I love you for it. You know that you can talk to me about anything."

"I know I can, Luce—I love you so much. I—I gotta go. We're getting up early, and I need to set up a security trace program on Jesse's game system."

"You're the best, right?"

"Right. Love you." He hung up before Lucy could say another word.

She closed her laptop and turned off the light, but it was a long time before she fell to sleep.

Something was going on with Sean, and she wished she were there to help him.

Sean resisted the urge to hit something—anything. He needed to tell Lucy about Jesse . . . but how could he do it over the phone? How could he just tell her, *Hey, Lucy, I have a kid.*

She needed to know, and he regretted not telling her before he left San Antonio. Why hadn't he? What was he so scared of? That she wouldn't understand? Of course she'd understand! Lucy was the most supportive person he knew. She would always be there for him, just like she said.

But . . . he hated that he couldn't talk about this with her now, about how twisted his gut was knowing that his own son didn't know about him.

Call her back.

No way in hell could he tell her now. He needed to be able to touch her, hold her, talk about it without poor connections. He needed to see her face, answer her questions, show her how much he loved her.

And in the back of his mind he feared that maybe Lucy wouldn't understand. That she wouldn't forgive him. That she wouldn't tell him what she really felt.

I can't have children . . .

He knew, deep down, that Lucy's inability to conceive was a burden she lived with every day. He hadn't really understood the pain until after her nephew was born and he saw the anguish in her eyes when she looked at the baby. He'd convinced her that he didn't love her less—how could he? She was everything to him. But he knew Lucy better than anyone, knew how she internalized her emotions, how she ached and survived.

What do you really fear?

He didn't know. Dammit, he didn't want her to think she was somehow . . . *less* because he had a kid with another woman. It wasn't like he planned it or knew about it. It had happened, and now he was dealing with the truth twelve years later.

It would be okay. It *had* to be okay. Lucy would understand. Sean would show her and tell her how much he loved her, and she would understand that he really didn't have a chance to tell her about Jesse before he left, and that telling her over the phone wasn't an option.

It simply wasn't an option.

CHAPTER NINETEEN

Lucy woke up at dawn. Four hours of sleep. Hardly enough after the last two days, but better than when insomnia plagued her three months ago.

She considered an early-morning swim, but after last night's exercise, she was still physically tired. She went downstairs to Sean's gym and jogged on the treadmill for three miles, working out the kinks and tight muscles, then ran hard for two miles. It helped. By the time she was done, she was starving. She hadn't gone to the store, but a few weeks ago she'd stuck some homemade tamales in the freezer. Who said tamales weren't for breakfast?

She popped them in the oven and went upstairs to shower and dress. By the time she was done, so were the tamales, and she ate two of the three with her morning coffee while reading her email. Carina had sent a message the night before with photos of John Patrick and a note that she and her husband, Nick, would come out a week before the wedding and couldn't wait to see her, Sean, and the house. Which was good, because Sean and Carina hadn't hit it off when they first met. Mostly, Lucy couldn't wait to spend time with her nephew. He'd be nearly five months old by then.

Lucy cleaned up the kitchen, then went upstairs to put on a little makeup, braid her hair, and grab her gun and blazer. She was slipping on her low-heeled boots when the doorbell rang.

Out of habit, she checked the security screen Sean had installed in their bedroom. An attractive blonde stood there, well dressed and obviously upset or angry about something. A neighbor? Maybe. Lucy knew the neighbors to the north, an older retired couple who'd lived in the neighborhood for nearly forty years. Didn't Sean mention a female lawyer across the street? She'd referred a job for Sean at a bank or something.

Lucy went downstairs, cautious but not suspicious. She didn't like always assuming the worst when something unexpected happened. People knocked on doors all the time.

She opened the door. "May I help you?"

"I need to talk to Sean."

"And you are?"

She hesitated, just a minute, before saying, "Madison Spade."

Spade. Sean's ex-girlfriend who'd hired him to find her son and husband. She must be beside herself, and if Sean was deep in the case he might not have had a chance to call. Lucy understood how frustrating that could be. And worrisome.

"Come in," Lucy said. "I'm Lucy Kincaid, Sean's fiancée. Can I get you some coffee?"

She seemed surprised at Lucy's offer. "No, but thank you. I need to talk to Sean and he's not returning my calls."

Lucy led Madison into the living room and motioned for her to take a seat. The woman didn't, but Lucy did to make her feel more comfortable. Madison sat a moment later.

"I have to talk to him now."

"I'm sure he told you that when he's working, there are times he can't call—it may not be safe, he may not have new information. I can assure you that Sean knows what he's doing. Both he and Kane have done this many times."

"But I told him yesterday not to go!"

Lucy was confused. "Why?"

"Carson called me. I *spoke* to him. I talked to my son. They're fine. They'll be home Friday. Sean should never have gone down there!"

Something odd was going on. "You need to trust that Sean knows what he's doing."

"He hates me. That's why he's doing this."

"He doesn't hate you, Madison." Lucy was generally very good at reading people, but she was the first to admit that complex relationships weren't her specialty.

"And you're being so nice to me. You must be a saint."

"No, but I trust Sean. Could it be he thought your husband was still in trouble? Called you in order to protect you? Sean is good at getting information, maybe your husband was forced to call."

"No, no, that's not it." But Madison didn't look at her. There was definitely something more to whatever was going on. "Sean went because of Jesse. I should never have come here. I was just so worried . . . and now my entire life is a mess."

"You're scared. I understand. But your life isn't a mess. Sean and Kane are the best in this business, they will bring back your husband and son, safe." Lucy paused, not sure how much she should say. And she was beginning to worry about Sean as well. They'd spoken last night, and he'd sounded preoccupied, but she expected that. "Sean mentioned your husband may have gotten involved with a shady business deal." That seemed a delicate way to broach it. "Could he have found out that you hired someone to find him? Maybe that's why he called, because he doesn't want anyone knowing where he is until he, well, completes his business. But anytime there are . . . less-than-legal business arrangements, everyone is at risk. Sean isn't going to be concerned about what your husband is doing as much as making sure your family is back, safe."

Madison stared at Lucy. "You really don't know Sean, do you?" She stood up and started pacing. "He's doing this as payback. I told him to stand down, and he won't because he's stubborn and angry. He's going to make me pay because of one little secret, one stupid mistake. I will not lose my son to him. He has no legal recourse to take him from me. You have got to talk to him, tell him to leave this alone and forget I ever came here. If he ever once cared for me . . . please . . . my husband's life—my son's life—depends on it. *Please*. I'm begging you, Lucy."

Lucy might have been naive about interpersonal relationships, but not this. It was as clear as glass.

"I will talk to him," Lucy heard herself saying as she stood up. The room faded around her, and all she saw was a long tunnel. It was like she was swimming through molasses as she walked Madison to the door. "That is all I can promise."

"Thank you. Really, thank you so much. Tell him if he does this for me, if he leaves this whole thing alone, I'll tell Jesse the truth. On my terms, in my way. I'll tell him everything."

"Okay." Lucy walked Madison to the door, said something she didn't quite remember, and closed it behind her.

On autopilot, Lucy walked to Sean's office. She logged into his computer. Sean was super-security-conscious, but he gave Lucy all his access codes in case she needed "the best computer money can buy," as he said.

She didn't need his computer, except for the fact that

all the research he'd done on Carson and Madison Spade would be here.

She didn't need to look far. All she needed was to look at the photograph of Jesse Spade to know that he was Sean's son.

Jesse was up early. Well, maybe because he didn't really sleep much last night. When he was certain his dad was asleep, he snuck into his room and grabbed his cell phone. He tried to call his mom, but the call wouldn't go through. Jesse didn't know why—just that cellular service was unavailable. Then he went downstairs in search of a landline, and couldn't find one. He knew there was one in Dominick's office, but the door was locked. Jesse thought that he might be able to break in, but he was too scared. So he went back upstairs and lay in bed until the sun was up. He might have slept a bit, but when he woke, he was still tired.

His dad was sleeping and the house was quiet. He went swimming, but not for long. Antsy, he returned to his suite and took a shower and played his DS because he didn't have anything else to do. As soon as his dad woke up, he said, "Can I call Mom?"

"Maybe later."

"Can we leave today?"

"I said we might be able to—I have to go to town and set up a new bank account for business. If everything goes well, probably tomorrow. Friday at the latest. Like I said."

"I really miss Mom."

"I talked to her last night, when you were sleeping. She didn't want me to wake you up. You know, she is a little angry with me because you're missing so much school, but she can't wait to hear about the football game. That was fun, right?"

"Yeah." It had been the best night since they'd been here, until those two men grabbed him and tried to tell him his dad was some sort of criminal. "If you talk to her tonight, would you wake me up?"

His dad smiled and ruffled his hair. "Of course. I would have woken you up last night if I knew it was so important to you."

"Can we go do something after you go to the bank? Maybe I can go with you and check out the museum, they have a reptile exhibit—"

"No, this is business, Jesse, you need to stay here where it's safe. I can't keep an eye on you if I'm working with the bank to set up a complex business account."

"I'm twelve, Dad. I don't need to be babysat all the time. I just want to—"

"No," he said. "Jesus, Jess, let it go. We're not in Redondo Beach, California—we're in the middle of Mexico. It's not safe for Americans to just wander around."

"I wouldn't be wandering, just—"

"No."

"Fine." Jesse walked to his bedroom and slammed the door. He was so bored. And a little scared. Because his dad was acting weird, and Jesse didn't like all these guys with guns everywhere, and he thought for certain that Gabriella had seen that guy with the scar on his neck grab him and she didn't say anything . . . what was his name?

Kane.

The guy Sean called him Kane. Who were they? Why had they tried to get him to go with them? Kidnappers? But if they were kidnappers who wanted to ransom him like his dad was afraid of, wouldn't they have like maybe knocked him out and carried him out of the stadium? Or drugged him or something? Why try to talk to him about coming with them? And they sounded American.

It was weird, and Jesse *really* wanted to talk to his mom.

Maybe Gabriella would let him use her phone.

He fell back onto his bed and looked at the clock. It was still early, not even eight in the morning. Gabriella never got up early, but Jesse knew she'd be around later. He'd wait.

It wasn't like he was going anywhere.

CHAPTER TWENTY

Kane left camp before dawn.

Neither he nor Sean had slept well, but now that they'd confirmed Jesse was at the Flores compound, there were really only two options. First—convince Gabriella to let them inside. The chance of that was slim to none. Revenge that had been percolating for ten years wouldn't be set aside for anyone, and especially not for a Rogan.

Which left the second option. One that Sean would never agree to, so Kane needed backup not only to protect him, but to protect his little brother. The risk was great, but Kane had mentally worked through all scenarios, and this was the only one that had a chance.

If Carson Spade was really as deep into the Flores cartel as Kane thought, Dominick wouldn't let him just walk away. He'd require something . . . an action from which there would be no turning back. Kane had seen it before, and because Jesse was here, it would involve Spade's son. Jesse might be allowed back to the States . . . he might return home unharmed . . . but he could become part of something from which there was no return.

Years ago, Kane had witnessed the brutal slaying of a

traitor to one of the cartels. He couldn't have stopped it if he wanted to—he was deep cover, and if he exposed himself, far more people would have died. But the traitor was tortured and killed in front of his own teenage daughter, who had been so traumatized that she committed suicide months later.

Kane couldn't care less about Carson Spade. He was a grown man who had made the wrong choice; whatever the consequences, death or prison, Kane didn't concern himself with it. Jesse was innocent. A child.

Sean's son.

Kane would not allow the kid to become lost, to be forced to witness violence, to live in danger his entire life. He would not allow Jesse to become one of them, because he knew how easy it was to turn a boy. He'd seen that, too. The flip side of violence was the rewards it brought. The money. The toys. And when he was older, the women. The power that the cartels had could be heady to someone who wasn't raised to discern good from evil.

His nephew would not become one of them if Kane had a breath left in his body.

The Flores cartel had its fingers in many pies, which was what made them particularly dangerous. If one route or supply was cut off, they had a dozen more to pick up the slack.

Dominick Flores had been the leader of the family ever since his father died. Murdered, on the vote of his own sons Kane had once heard, back when he and Dante were on better terms. Dom's brother Samuel was far more dangerous—he enjoyed violence. He was the one who had killed Gabriella's fiancé. Tortured and murdered him.

Gabriella had found his butchered body. If it weren't for Jack Kincaid, she would also be dead.

She'd changed since then, as violence often changed

those it touched. Not that the Romeros were pacifists or innocent, but after her fiancé was murdered, the rules of the game changed for them. Kane understood far too well.

Kane hadn't told Sean that he was on the Flores cartel radar because Sean would have sent him away. And Kane could hardly leave now. The cartel wanted Kane's head on a platter, and he was going to give it to them. He just had to convince Gabriella Romero that it would benefit her—and her brother—to take revenge in a different way, and perhaps sooner than she'd planned.

Not him. Gabriella wouldn't listen to him. But there was one person she would listen to.

Jack Kincaid.

Jack rarely took jobs south of the border since he was now married to a fed, but he had a unique skill set and the near two decades he'd spent in the Army came in handy.

And he knew Gabriella very well.

Kane called him from a secure sat phone once he was out of Sean's earshot.

"Kincaid."

"It's Kane. How fast can you get to Guadalajara?"

"Six and a half hours."

"It's dangerous."

"They all are. You have a plan."

"Working on it."

Jack didn't say anything for a long minute. "Who else do you have down there?"

"No one. Blitz, Ranger, and their team are in Honduras. They can't be reached."

"Is this about the kid?"

"Yes. Sean sent everything he uncovered to Jaye—read it on the fly."

"And he's worth risking your lives?"

That was always the question—was an operation worth

the risk, because every time they engaged, they could be killed or captured.

"Yes," Kane said without hesitation. "Look at the file. You'll know why." He wasn't going to spill Sean's secret about Jesse, but Jack had to understand the emotional component.

"We need a team."

Kane didn't want more than he'd counted on, but Jack would do what he felt best, always. And Kane trusted his instincts. "Small and elite. Gabriella is here."

"Well, fuck."

"I'm going to talk to her, but you know what she has planned."

"Ten years. Ten fucking years, Kane."

He didn't say anything. Ten years wasn't that long when someone killed the person you loved.

Siobhan had told him three months ago that she loved him. He replayed that moment every night, every time he closed his eyes. She thought he'd shut her out because he didn't want his life to taint her. That wasn't it.

He could never love her, never call her his own, because when she got killed—and in his line of work, that was almost a certainty—he would become Gabriella. He would hunt down those responsible and slaughter them. Without hesitation. Without remorse.

In fact, he admired Gabriella as much as he was frustrated with her. She'd waited ten years for her revenge. Patience. Kane would slash and burn until he was gunned down, and then he would thank the God he didn't believe in that it was finally over.

Kane said, "I will talk to her, but I may need you to convince her."

"Understood. Are you camped at our primary airstrip?"

"Yes."

"Six and a half hours." Jack disconnected.

Of course Jack knew Gabriella. It had been his soldier who'd fallen in love with her, his soldier who had proposed to her, and his soldier who'd been tortured and killed by Samuel Flores, one of the psycho brothers. Jack had talked her down once before, but after this long, Kane didn't think Gabriella would listen to anyone. He didn't blame her—but when his nephew and his brother both had their lives at stake, he had to make her listen.

Unless, of course, she got exactly what she wanted: Samuel Flores's head on a platter.

And Kane had to figure out a way to do it without Gabriella taking the credit . . . and no RCK fingerprints. RCK didn't do assassinations, it's what kept them off the cartel's most wanted list. Certainly they had caused enough problems over the years that the cartels would kill anyone affiliated if they had an opportunity, but until Tobias Hunt had put a price tag on his head, Kane had been able to work relatively anonymously over the years.

Kane reached the jeep he'd hidden far on the edge of the airstrip. He pushed off the fallen branches and drove into town.

His cell phone rang. It was Gabriella. He'd ignored her first three calls last night.

"The audacity," Gabriella said in her exotic accent.

"Meet me in thirty minutes. You know where."

"No."

"You're going to get yourself killed."

"Do I care?"

"Your brother will."

"Dante understands."

"I can get you what you want and you can walk away."

"I will see this through. Why are you even here? What do you want with Jesse Spade? None of this is your concern."

"I will tell you why when you meet with me. You owe me."

"I owe you nothing, Rogan."

He didn't say anything. She knew exactly what she owed him.

"No promises." She hung up.

Before Kane left that morning, he'd told Sean to write a letter to Jesse—a short note that explained everything. Sean did it, but it hardly seemed adequate. Kane was standing over him. What could he say? How could he say it? Why write it? It was like trying to tell Lucy over the phone that Jesse was his kid . . . he couldn't.

But he did it because Kane said Jesse needed to be on board with them or they would all be killed. Sean understood, but that didn't make it much better.

Now that he was alone—for how long, he didn't know—Sean booted up his computer and started digging through everything Jaye at RCK had found on Carson Spade, his law firm, and his connections to the Flores cartel. Jaye was good—very methodical. Sean worked more intuitively, and had several questions, namely, *Why now?* What happened to bring Spade to Mexico *now*?

Laundering money was both easy and complex. The hard part was setting up the process—layers of bank accounts, shell corporations, moving money from legitimate businesses into shady accounts and finally into the hands of the bad guys. Cartels employed some of the best accountants and lawyers in the business—those with a serious lack of morals—to build the network. Once established, a good network would run seamlessly.

It seemed that Carson Spade had been the lawyer who set up the entire network for the Flores cartel several years ago—based on the dates of the corporations Jaye had identified. His bank and travel records showed only one trip to Mexico a year—likely required by Flores to ensure that Spade was still in his back pocket. Perhaps to handle new business or incorporate a new illegal activity. But this was Spade's third trip to Mexico this year—definitely out of character.

A message from Jaye popped up on his computer.

Jaye: You there?

Sean: Yep.

Jaye: Something weird just happened.

Sean: You're up at dawn?

Jaye: Ha ha. I sent a worm out to gather real-time info on each of the identified corps and three were shut down at the end of business yesterday.

Sean: Shut down how? Money transferred?

Jaye: No money transfers, all shell corps. Closed. The info was posted at midnight ET.

Sean: Influx of cash to Spade?

Jaye: None yet. I'm going to expand the worm, but I suspect they're all being axed. Just closed.

Sean: Why? Did it happen yesterday?

Jaye: No idea why, and they could have been

shut down anytime in the last few days. Not more than a week. They get posted pretty quick. I'll send you what I learn.

Sean: You're an angel.

Sean logged off and wondered what had happened to cause Spade to shut down his shell corps. The most logical reason would be money. These were hollow companies, though—they could let the companies ride and, if they were compromised, just start new ones. On and on. The only way to shut them down would be to completely sever them from the new enterprise. Or maybe there was something there that they wanted to hide.

Sean understood money laundering and finance, but nowhere near as well as he understood computer security and hacking. And he didn't really care what Spade was doing at this point. Associating with Dominick Flores was sufficient for Sean to want his son away from here. After he got Jesse to safety, he would dig into Carson Spade with a magnifying glass and destroy him.

He looked at his watch. Damn, Kane had only been gone for an hour. He said it could take him all morning to set up his plan. A plan he didn't fully explain to Sean. All Sean knew was that it depended on Gabriella getting a note to Jesse. Sean's note. And if that didn't happen, then they were back to square one.

CHAPTER TWENTY-ONE

Siobhan stepped out of the hotel and almost immediately the security chief approached her. "May I summon your driver?"

"I'm just walking to Starbucks. It's only a few blocks."

"It's not a problem."

Before she could argue with him, he was on his radio. Less than a minute later the driver pulled up. Did they have him sitting in his car waiting?

Still, Sean and Lucy had been more than generous in setting her up in this hotel, and she was pretty certain Kane had something to do with the security precautions.

When the driver dropped her off, she said, "I'm meeting a friend—you don't have to stay."

"It's not a problem," the driver said. Apparently, that was the motto of this security team.

"Thanks." What else could she say?

She went inside the Starbucks. She was meeting Eric Barrow, her reporter friend. They'd been friends forever— since high school. He had some problems and could be a complete ass sometimes, but he was all about the truth. He was cynical and would believe the worst about anyone. When he got an idea in his head he would move heaven and earth to prove it, but so far, she'd never caught him printing a lie, and he'd never stabbed her in the back.

The same couldn't be said of other people in Eric's life, which was why Siobhan was probably one of Eric's few friends.

Starbucks was on the corner of one of the most populated business areas of Laredo. Laredo was an old town, depressed; a third of the residents lived below the poverty level. But they still had a Starbucks, Siobhan thought wryly.

It was a treat for her. She even splurged and bought a pastry, something she hadn't done in months. Andie led a simple life as well, but she had her luxuries—and Starbucks was one of them. Siobhan didn't think her sister had gone a day without swinging by the drive-through on her way to Quantico, where she worked as the number two in charge of officer training. When Siobhan pointed out that Andie likely spent $150 a month at Starbucks—more if she added a pastry or sandwich to her triple lattes— Andie wasn't amused.

"I spent thirty-two months in the fucking desert fighting to protect my right to have a goddamn Starbucks latte, and dammit, I'm going to have a goddamn Starbucks latte every fucking day until I die."

Andie had the foul mouth in the Walsh clan.

Siobhan sat down and waited. Eric was habitually late, so she wasn't worried or surprised when he finally came in twenty minutes after he said he'd be there. She had finished her croissant and was nearly done with her coffee.

"You should have warned me about your friends," Eric said.

"Good to see you again, Eric."

He grinned. "Sorry. You know me."

"I do, which is why I'll cut you some slack. But I didn't

know they were going to talk to you. I showed them your article, they followed up. It's important."

"Would you have told me they were coming?"

"Not if I thought you'd disappear." She took his hands. "Eric, this is serious. Marisol and Ana were my friends. Their mother was my friend. I have to find them."

"I know, sugar, I've done everything I can—you know that. But the feds? Really?"

"There's a newborn baby without her mother. Her mother is either Mari or Ana. And now there's another girl, dead, her baby stolen from her womb. This is bigger than us, Eric. Stop—I see your wheels turning. You want a story, and I'll give you a huge story, but don't blow this. Mari and Ana's lives are in danger."

"I'm not, but—"

"No buts. You wanted to meet with me."

"No feds. You gotta shake them."

"I'm not promising you that."

"Dammit, did you know that the girl fed is Jack Kincaid's *sister*? Jack hates me."

"I'm sure Jack barely remembers the time when you nearly got him and his team killed," she said sarcastically.

"I didn't know the information was embargoed."

She wasn't certain she believed him. She wanted to . . . but this was Eric. "Eric—that was then. Let's focus on now. If there is a human trafficking ring targeting pregnant immigrants and stealing their babies, we have to stop them. I'm not here because of my job; I'm here because I fear for their lives."

"Word is that your fed friends made a lot of people nervous in Del Rio. Everyone is laying low. But I have an address. Just . . . be discreet about this, okay? If the feds come out in force, you're not going to get anything from these people." He slid over a folded piece of paper. "This is a midwife who may have information. But I guarantee she will not talk to Kincaid and Armstrong. You talk to her, see what she knows."

Now Siobhan was skeptical. "Why would you give this to me and not pursue it yourself? Since you think there's a story here."

"Because, like you said, this is bigger than the story. You find Mari and Ana, I'll get the story, I know that. I trust you, Siobhan. You're probably the only one." He paused, leaned forward. "I heard about the girl in the morgue. Word's spread on the streets. You don't like my tactics, but people here trust me because I've never burned the little guy. Don't ruin that for me. It's my best source of information."

Siobhan didn't always like it, but she understood. "I can be discreet. But, Eric—don't burn Lucy and Noah. They care, they're good cops. If you burn them, I'll never work with you again."

Eric shook his head and shot her a smile. "You think I'm going to burn a Kincaid who's marrying a Rogan? Hell no, I'm not going to touch her, I promise."

Siobhan wanted to believe him.

Lucy was fifteen minutes late to meet Noah that morning and it was clear that he was irritated. "Let's go," he said as soon as she walked in. "Dunning."

"Sorry," she mumbled.

He glanced at her. "It's been a long couple of days, but you should have let me know you were running late. I would have understood."

She didn't say anything. He was right. Lucy had been late because she'd sent Sean a message to call her when he had a chance . . . he'd responded by text that he would, just didn't know when. She'd then told him his client had come by the house and Lucy had information to share.

Then nothing. *Nothing.*

She was alternately worried about Sean's safety and angry that he didn't respond.

She'd been so blindsided by Madison Spade coming to her house and dropping the bombshell that Jesse was Sean's son that she didn't even think about calling headquarters. It hadn't been intentional—Madison thought that Lucy already knew. Didn't make the news any less shocking.

What's shocking is that Sean didn't tell you.

They'd promised no secrets, they'd promised to be honest with each other. After what happened in June when Sean risked his life to find a wanted fugitive who had already killed several cops—without telling her first—he'd promised not to put her in that situation again. He wanted to protect her, but in his attempt to keep her from worrying, she stressed that much more. Not knowing was worse.

She, too, had a hard time telling Sean what was bothering her, but she'd worked hard to overcome her insecurities and fears. He helped her, and she knew he wanted to share in the good and the bad.

But this was different. Why wouldn't he have told her? What could he have been thinking? That she would be angry with him? For something he didn't know? Or that she would be upset? That she would blame him for not being there? He couldn't have known—that wasn't something he would have ever kept from her, not for the two years they'd been together.

Why? *Why?* Did he not think she could handle the news? That she would fall apart or something? Yes, she was upset—because Sean kept something so important, so personal, from her.

Madison had met with Sean on Monday . . . she'd come home late, but they'd had a late dinner, they'd showered together, they'd made love . . . he could have told her. Any number of times that night. The next morning.

And he hadn't.

She almost didn't notice that Nate had followed her and Noah out of the FBI building. She glanced back and almost asked why, when she remembered hearing Noah call for Dunning. Nate gave her an odd, questioning look. She smiled at him, though it felt unreal. She had no joy inside, nothing. Nate and Sean were close, and if Nate thought something was bothering her, he might talk to Sean about it. That was the last thing she needed.

She had to get her head in the investigation. She couldn't let her personal problems interfere with her job.

Noah tossed Nate the keys, and Lucy climbed into the backseat. "I asked Nate to join us because I don't know what to expect," Noah said. "We're going to the property management first. I have a warrant for limited records—got a friendly judge who liked the argument you put together, Lucy."

"Me?" She barely remembered the conversation.

"Zach came through—he was able to connect the business that owned the brothel property with the business that owns the property outside Freer. I used that to get the AUSA to push a judge—the lawyer didn't want to do it, but I can be persuasive. We can ask for files of all properties managed by the company that are owned by those two businesses, lists of tenants, rents paid or owed, and contact information for the businesses. The management company needs to communicate with them somehow. Zach pulled ownership records—we know the brothel property was bought four years ago from a bank while it was in foreclosure, and shortly after Barrow's article came out it was sold to another business—could still be owned by the same people, just trying to clean the slate. The Freer property was bought six months ago from an estate—the original owner had lived in the place for forty-two years, died, and his lone heir sold it on the cheap after it had been on the market for nearly two years."

"Zach has been busy."

Nate drove in silence. Lucy looked at he phone, checked her email. It was what she didn't see that hurt—no message from Sean.

Noah got on the phone, and it took Lucy several minutes to realize he was talking to Rick Stockton. When he hung up, he said to Nate and Lucy, "We have the clear to interview Lance Dobleman. Nate, let's go there first. It's early, I want to shake him up. I'm going to get two agents to follow him." He got back on the phone. Lucy heard him ask for Abigail Durant, the ASAC who oversaw three units, including the Violent Crimes Squad.

Smart. If they shook him up, a tail may lead them to Jasmine . . . or to the missing girls.

By the tone of the conversation, Noah didn't get the answer he wanted. "Abigail, there is no reason Agent Cook can't handle a simple field assignment. Follow, do not engage." Elizabeth Cook, the agent on their squad who didn't work in the field. The one Juan never assigned to partner with anyone because she handled internal research and the occasional background check.

A moment later Noah said, "Abigail, I need two agents to tail a suspect for at least twenty-four hours, up to seventy-two hours . . . Cook is the only one who isn't assigned to a priority case, and she can go out with one of your . . . I understand, but . . . You have my assignment report in your inbox." He listened for a long minute, then said, "We'll discuss this later, Abigail . . . since you brought it up, yes, I think it's a major issue. Juan is well respected, I am the interloper from HQ." Again, silence. "Honestly, this may sound callous, but I don't care. I needed all hands this week and keeping a senior agent at her desk wasn't going to cut it . . . Yes . . . No . . . I'm happy to meet later this afternoon, but you'll have to give me some flexibility because I don't know how long I'll be out . . . Kincaid and Dunning . . . Yes, I'm aware. I'll take any heat if there's a problem, but I need two agents . . . Fine, I'll send you the details, you send whoever you want."

He hung up. If he could have slammed down the phone, he would have.

"Rick fucking owes me a bottle of twenty-year Scotch," Noah muttered.

Noah rarely, if ever, swore, so Lucy kept her comments to herself.

Nate didn't. "I thought you knew Agent Cook didn't work in the field."

"Juan told me," Noah said. "Active special agents assigned to field offices are required to work in the field. No exceptions."

He didn't say anything more, and Lucy wished she knew what Agent Cook's story was, why Juan let her work only from her desk, and why Noah was pushing it when he was the temporary SSA. She glanced at Nate—he didn't press the conversation, but he clearly knew more of what was going on than she did.

Noah said, "Though you're both rookies, you're going to partner for the duration of this case—at least until I can get freed up. There's no one else, and I can't send an agent back to Laredo solo."

Nate turned into the entrance for a gated community. He didn't say anything as he rolled down his window and showed his badge and identification.

The guard hesitated a moment. He was young. "Can I have the address you're visiting?"

Nate shook his head.

"I, um, I'm supposed to log every visitor."

"Special Agent Nate Dunning," Nate said. He handed the guard his FBI card. "If your boss has a problem, he can call me."

Again, the young guard hesitated, but he took the card and pressed a button. The gate slid open.

Nate drove through before it was completely open. "If they want to intimidate would-be visitors, they should get someone who looks like he already graduated from high school."

The gated community north of I-10 had winding roads, great views of the city, and tree-lined streets. It would be a nice place to live, Lucy thought, though it was clear the neighborhood was relatively new, likely less than ten years old. The developer had done a good job working the custom homes around the existing trees, giving it an older feeling.

Less than two minutes later Nate stopped in front of a large, sprawling two-story home at the end of a cul-de-sac. No cars were on the street or driveway, but an attached four-car garage was behind the house.

Noah said to Nate, "Keep an eye on things."

"Yes, sir."

Noah glanced at him oddly. "Sir?"

"Habit."

Noah shook his head but he was smiling.

Lucy and Noah walked up to the front door. Lucy rang the bell and stepped back. Noah was surveying their surroundings. "Security cameras," Noah said.

The door opened two inches. It was on a security chain. A petite Asian woman stood there. "Hello?" she asked with a heavy accent.

Lucy showed her badge and ID and said, "Special Agents Lucy Kincaid and Noah Armstrong. Is Lance Dobleman here?"

The woman stared at her oddly. "English not good."

"Is Lance Dobleman your husband?"

She hesitated, then nodded. She said something in what Lucy thought was Chinese, but she'd never studied the Far

East languages. She was fluent in Spanish and French, had a basic understand of German, Italian, and Portuguese, but the Eastern languages were far different than the Germanic languages. She wouldn't even know how to communicate.

"Is Lance home?" Lucy gestured to the house. She pointed to herself then at the door. "May we come in?"

The woman shook her head.

"What's your name? I'm Lucy, you are . . . ?"

"Soon Li."

"Soon Li Dobleman?"

She nodded.

"We need to talk to your husband."

"Not home."

"When will your husband be home?"

"Don't know." She said something else in Chinese, then said, "I need go."

Noah handed Soon Li his card. "Tell Lance to call me."

Soon Li's hands shook as she took Noah's card.

"Do you know when he'll be home?" Lucy asked.

"He's not here."

"You said that," Lucy said. "When? When will he be here?"

She looked confused for a moment. "I don't know. Monday."

"He's gone until Monday?"

She made motions with her hands as if she was frustrated she couldn't think of the words.

"He was supposed to be home Monday?"

"Left Monday, not come home."

"Have you talked to him?" Lucy put her hand to her ear to mimic a phone. "Did he call you?"

She shook her head. "Business. Don't know. Business trip. No calls."

"Do you have a number I can call him at? It's very important."

Soon Li narrowed her eyes then shook her head. "No call, no number. I go now." She closed the door.

"She damn well has his number," Noah muttered.

They walked back to the car. "He left on Monday and hasn't returned or talked to his wife. We know he was in Freer on Sunday night. She seemed like she'd expected him, but he didn't return."

"He may know we're looking for him."

They got back into the car. Noah watched the house for a few minutes.

Lucy said, "Siobhan's SD card was stolen from her camera. That means that all the photos we have, they could have."

"Who is *they*, Lucy?"

She didn't know if he was being rhetorical or not. His tone was odd. "Siobhan thought that someone with access to her rental car took the SD card from her camera. That would mean either the deputy who arrested her, the teenager who chased her from the house, or someone they called. Dobleman was there, he could have easily returned, pulled the SD card, realized he could be identified."

"Why not grab the whole camera?" Noah asked.

"They did," Lucy reminded him. "Later that night, with her computer."

"Why not take the camera from her car?"

Lucy didn't know.

"Maybe they were tracking her," Nate suggested. "Didn't know where she was staying. Once they did, they grabbed everything."

"We have to assume they know what we know—who we have on camera, the connection between Siobhan and the de la Rosa sisters."

"That's a big leap," Noah said, but from his expression he was considering it.

"They dropped all charges against Siobhan," Lucy said. "It wasn't even us being there; they had made that decision before we arrived. Maybe it was because of Rick's call . . . or maybe because they were worried that federal attention would get them in trouble. Maybe it's all Deputy Jackson, and he admitted to fondling Siobhan and inciting her to hit him."

"Logical. And the sheriff did seem upset with her deputy, and apologetic."

"A guy like that must have other complaints against him," Lucy said, "or when they realized Siobhan was a photojournalist, they didn't want the bad press."

"Dobleman is an obvious ID," Noah said. "He has a military record, and anyone with half a brain would know we'd have access to basic military records. He could be laying low. Or simply working for Jasmine and unable or unwilling to come home." Noah nodded to Nate. "I want to talk to that security guard at the gate."

The guard had no information because they didn't log when residents came or left. He agreed to call Noah when Dobleman came home and to tell the other guards, but they couldn't count on that information, or that one of the guards wouldn't give Dobleman a heads-up that the FBI was looking for him. Plus, once Dobleman came home and saw Noah's card he might bolt.

Or not. Because what did they really have on him? Nothing. He didn't have to talk to them and they had no reason to arrest him. *Yet.*

Noah got back on the phone and asked Zach to work with ICE on the immigration status of Soon Li Dobleman—if they were in fact married—as well as if she had a job, when she arrived in the country, and if there were any flags.

Nate drove to the property management company atop a high-rise in downtown San Antonio not far from the Riverwalk. But once they got up to the twelfth floor they realized that the office was a small one-room suite. A young woman who looked more like a model than a receptionist, with blond hair swept up into a chignon and an impeccably fitted black suit and white blouse, said, "May I help you?"

Noah flashed his identification and handed her a copy of the warrant. "We would like all files related to those two properties."

She didn't appear flustered by three FBI agents coming in with a search warrant.

"I'm sorry, I can't help you."

"The warrant grants us the right to those files."

"I'm sure it does, but we don't keep any property records on site. Everything we have is digital, and I don't have access to the database."

"Then what do you do here all day?"

She didn't answer. She handed Noah a business card. "This is Direct Property Holdings' law offices. They will, I'm sure, handle your request promptly."

Noah nodded to Nate and Lucy. Lucy said, "Ma'am, if you would please step away from your desk, we need to inspect your workstation."

"Of course," she said and rose. She was taller than Lucy, and that's when Lucy noticed she wore four-inch spike heels. "May I go to the ladies' room?" she asked.

"Not right now," Noah snapped. After the big fat nothing at the Dobleman residence and now this front office, he was clearly angry.

Nate searched the desk. The computer was password-protected. "Password, ma'am?"

"I'm sorry, I can't share that information."

Noah turned to her. "Our warrant—"

"Says you can have two files, which are not in this office. As I said, our lawyer will be happy to provide you with the files. But your warrant doesn't grant you access to the computer system, which has information that isn't covered by your warrant."

This woman was definitely not a receptionist. She was a gatekeeper.

"Are you aware of the penalties for obstruction of justice?" Noah asked.

"I am not obstructing anything," she said. "I'm simply telling you that your warrant does not cover my computer. If you want the files that are covered by your warrant, you will need to talk to the law office, which has access to all records of this company. I wish I could be of more help." Her tone said anything but.

"Identification," Noah asked.

Now she looked a bit flustered. She crossed over to her desk and raised an eyebrow at Nate, who stood behind the desk. "May I?" She gestured toward the bottom drawer.

Nate stepped aside but kept eyes on her hands. She pulled out her wallet and handed her Texas driver's license to Noah. He wrote down the information and handed it back. "Phone number where we can reach you?"

"If it's related to this company, you can contact me through the law office."

Noah clearly wasn't happy with the results of their efforts. He pulled out his cell phone and dialed the number on the card she'd handed him.

"This is Supervisory Special Agent Noah Armstrong with the Federal Bureau of Investigation with a warrant for two properties managed by Direct Property Holdings. I am at your business office and they claim they have no access to the files in question. I want all records including owner information, maintenance, rental agreements, finances, and copies of every check or transaction. And I want them ready immediately."

He listened, then gave the two relevant addresses. He listened again and said, "Next week is not going to work. One hour . . . I don't care if the lawyer who handles DPH is not in the office, I have a federal warrant." He looked at his watch. "One hour."

CHAPTER TWENTY-TWO

Siobhan had the driver take her back to the hotel, then picked up her rental car to drive out to the address Eric had given her. She didn't want to intimidate the midwife by driving up in a black Town Car. Now that she was alert, she was certain she wouldn't put herself in a position of danger.

She appreciated Sean—though she suspected Kane had a lot to do with it—providing her with a secure hotel and transportation, but she'd been a photojournalist for more than a decade and had taken care of herself more often than not. She'd traveled through dangerous countries and was hyperaware of her surroundings. She admitted to herself that being in the States had lulled her into a false sense of security, but now that she was reminded that the States could be as violent as Mexico and Central America, she wasn't going to be caught unawares.

The midwife Eric had identified, Cora Smith, lived in a small two-bedroom, one-bath postwar box house in the middle of a long line of two-bedroom, one-bath postwar box houses. It was late morning, and day laborers who couldn't find work at dawn were now back in their yards, watching Siobhan with cautious, quiet eyes when she stopped the rental car in front of house number 1127. She walked up the short, weed-choked concrete walkway and knocked on the door. The scent of fresh tortillas and chili powder wafted through the air as the door opened. "I've been expecting you," Cora said and opened the door wide.

"You have?"

"I heard a pretty redhead wanted to talk to me. That would be you, right?"

"I'm Siobhan Walsh," she said. "I'm looking for two girls—the daughters of my best friend—and I heard you might have some information."

"Come, I just finished making dinner." In true southern fashion, she called her midday meal dinner, while supper would be a smaller, lighter meal.

Cora wasn't what Siobhan expected. First, she was an octogenarian. And small—not even five feet tall and couldn't possibly weigh a hundred pounds soaking wet. Silver-white hair so short and straight she could have been mistaken for a man. Her house was immaculate but cluttered, with no television that Siobhan could see, and a crucifix over every doorway. An enormous paint-by-numbers of the Last Supper hung in the kitchen's eating area, dwarfing the small room. From a distance, it didn't look half bad.

Two young boys stood in the kitchen at attention. Cora finished filling a dozen lunch boxes with some sort of spicy stew, stacks of fresh tortillas, and small apples. She stacked six lunch boxes into each of two larger cardboard boxes. In Spanish she said, "Thank you, boys. When you return the boxes, I'll pay you. And your lunch will be ready."

The boys stared at Siobhan with wide eyes and nodded at Cora, then left through the back door, each carrying a box that seemed too large for him.

"Good boys," Cora said with a nod. "I prepare meals a

few times a week for some of my older neighbors who can't get around so well. The boys help deliver for me. I'm not as spry as I used to be."

Older neighbors? Must be the ninety-somethings, Siobhan thought.

"Sit, I'll dish some stew."

"You don't have to—"

Cora gave Siobhan a look that told her not to argue. "I don't have to do nothing I don't want to. Sit."

Siobhan sat. "Smells delicious, Ms. Smith."

Cora smiled as she dished bowls of stew and put them on the table, one in front of Siobhan and one at an empty place. She brought out more fresh tortillas and then Cora sat, crossed herself, and said a blessing. Then she smiled when Siobhan said "amen" and motioned for her to eat.

Halfway through the meal Cora said, "You want to know about the dead girl."

Siobhan nearly dropped her spoon. "Yes. I think she'll lead me to Marisol and Ana." She explained who they were and why she was looking for them.

"It's a sad situation, and I don't know exactly how the girls found themselves in it." Cora seemed to be picking her words carefully. Siobhan wondered if she knew more than she planned on saying. "Suffice it to say, I have been a midwife for more than sixty years. I've delivered nearly two thousand babies. Some didn't survive. I know when I can't help, when they need a doctor. Some don't want to go, but I tell them, they go. Because life is precious, and a baby is God's hope in a troubled world."

Siobhan believed Cora had the ability to make anyone do anything even if they didn't want to. She had that quiet, serene confidence that inspired loyalty and trust.

"Two weeks ago, I was called to a house in the middle of the night near Our Lady of Sorrows."

Siobhan's ears perked up. Father Sebastian's church.

"It was far for me to go, but one of my neighborhood boys took me. An old friend, Loretta Martinez, had a complication with one of her clients. I told her go to the hospital. That wasn't an option. Against my better judgment, I went to help."

She sipped black coffee, then continued. "The baby was breech, the girl was unconscious when I got there. There was excessive bleeding and tearing and I thought we'd lose them both. I urged Loretta to call an ambulance and was told that would not happen. This made me suspicious, but there are many young women who come to America illegally in order to deliver their babies. I don't condone it, because who is to help them if they trust no one? But sometimes, life is harder back home. I don't turn my back on God's children when asked to help. I care about the girl, the baby, that's it. Yet, when it's a matter of life or death, I always choose life.

"I would have called, but my phone was taken away and this *man*"—she said *man* as if she were saying the word *Satan*—"threatened me. He said, I will never forget, 'Save the baby, I don't care about the girl.'" Cora's thin jaw clenched, and she rose from her seat. She moved a few bottles, then retrieved what she was looking for and came back to the table. She poured red wine into her empty water glass, then sipped. "He didn't use the word *girl*, but I don't allow swearing in my house."

Siobhan almost couldn't speak. She whispered, "What happened?"

"Loretta is good, but not as good as me. I was able to turn the baby in the womb and deliver a beautiful baby boy. He was a large baby, over nine pounds, and the girl was so small. It's no wonder she tore so miserably."

"Small as in young?"

"She was eighteen, maybe nineteen. I thought we'd lose her, but we didn't. I sewed her up and Loretta and I watched

her for twenty-four hours. She finally regained consciousness."

"Did you have any medical supplies?" Siobhan thought
about the small room in the house that she walked through
Sunday night. The IV, the tools.

"Yes, the house we were in was well stocked, and I have
delivered so many babies and even assisted doctors in difficult births if the mother was one of my clients. We kept
her hydrated, through an IV, and she finally woke up. But
during those twenty-four hours, I learned things I wish I
had never known before I leave this earth. Some things,
you don't want to know. But I trust God, and He wanted
me there to know these difficult things."

Cora took a moment, looking not at Siobhan but into
the past, her wrinkled face troubled. Siobhan didn't push.
She was grateful this woman was talking to her at all.
"Loretta told me that the home was for single mothers,
girls who had been turned out by their families because
they got pregnant out of wedlock. At first, I believed her.
I wanted to. Loretta has been a friend for a long, long time.
She asked me to check on the other women. There were six
pregnant women there, plus the girl who'd just delivered.
All in the second half of their pregnancy. All healthy, fed
well, and they had a small exercise room in the basement
where they walked on a treadmill. But . . . there was
something off. None of the girls were allowed outside, for
example. One of the girls I examined was dangerously ill.
She had high blood pressure and swollen feet. I told
Loretta she had the signs of preeclampsia. She needed to
be in the hospital or both her and her baby would most
likely die. Loretta told the man, the vile man, when they
didn't think I could hear the conversation. He said he
didn't care if she died, as long as the baby lived. What
sort of human being says that? I tell you"—she answered
her own question—"no *human* being says that."

"Cora—why didn't you go to the authorities?" Siobhan asked quietly.

"Because the authorities have not been kind to me and others over the years. A trust issue, I suppose you might say." She paused. "I heard you work with the Sisters of Mercy."

"My mother did. I help them when I can. A few months every year."

She nodded. "A few months a year is more than most people give in their lifetimes. The sisters do God's work, they are good people. Sister Bernadette spoke at my church years ago. I don't have money to spare, but I had I think seven dollars in my purse, and I gave it to her cause."

Siobhan smiled. She could picture the scene so clearly. "Sister Bernadette is very persuasive."

"She came here for supper after the last Mass that day." Cora paused, sipped more wine, then bit off a piece of tortilla. Her teeth were far too large and white to be natural. She changed the subject back to the pregnant girls. "I should have called someone, but Loretta told me not all the authorities could be trusted. And Loretta didn't seem fearful, not after we delivered the boy. She'd been scared when the baby was in danger, but once the baby was well, she relaxed. That struck me as odd, but I didn't press her for more information. I should have.

"When I read the newspaper article about the woman who died of preeclampsia and her baby was missing . . . I just knew in my heart that it was the young woman I saw that week. They called her Jane Doe, in the news. Her name was Eloise. I want her name on her grave, no one should be buried without their name. After I heard about you, and why you are here, I thought you might make that happen."

"I can," Siobhan said. She was practically shaking out of anticipation. She reached into her purse and pulled out the photo of her with Mari and Ana. "Did you see these girls?"

Cora put on her glasses that were hanging on a chain around her neck. She looked at the photo. "Yes, they were both there."

"They were? You saw them?"

"And very pregnant." She pointed to Marisol. "This one, due anytime. Very healthy." She pointed to Ana. "This one, six months' pregnant. With twins. She was having a hard time. They were close, protective."

"Sisters," Siobhan whispered. She was so close . . . so close to finding them. "I need to find them."

"I can tell you where the house is."

"I was there, outside Freer, and they're gone." She reached back into her bag and pulled out the prints she'd downloaded from her cloud account. "Did you see this girl?" She showed her the blonde who was walking and holding a baby.

"This one, yes, she's the one who almost died in child-birth. The breech baby."

"What day was that?"

Cora thought back. "Saturday. Ten days ago. It was very early in the morning, still dark, when we finally delivered the baby. I stayed another night, then my driver picked me up on Sunday. We went to the church there, because I wouldn't get back to Laredo in time to go to my own parish. Loretta warned me not to talk, and I didn't, but it has weighed on me. Loretta is a good woman, a good church-goer. She didn't come with me to church, though I asked her to. This made me worry for her. Guilt, I saw it, I smelled it on her. The guilty don't like to step into God's house. And me . . . I started to feel guilty. That things were not as Loretta had said. That I may have done something, made a bad decision. Not saving the girl and her baby— that was right. But silence can be a sin. I saw that article, and it was God's hand. I do not read the paper, not every day, because it's violent and sad. But I saw it yesterday, I knew I was meant to see it. I called the reporter, and he told me you would want to talk to me. Your presence is divine providence, Siobhan Walsh. God led you to me so I could share my story and ask for forgiveness for not doing something sooner."

Siobhan took the old woman's small, frail hand. "Cora, listen to me. Loretta was right about one thing: You can't trust all the authorities. I was at the house on Sunday, they were moving the last of the girls. The police arrested me, and when I went back on Monday they were all gone. But I have a good friend in the FBI whom I trust with my life. I need to find Loretta, and she needs to tell us what she knows. Mari and Ana disappeared two years ago, and I've been looking for them ever since. I have never been this close."

"I will give you everything I know about Loretta. And"—she pointed to one of the men in the photo with the blonde—"that man is named Raoul. I don't know his last name, but I will never forget him. He is not a godly man."

When Lucy joined Noah to serve the warrant for the property records at the law firm, a thin file was waiting for them at the desk.

Noah looked at it. There was one sheet on each property that listed basic information such as when the property was acquired, how much was paid, the mortgage, balance, and owner.

Each owner was a business.

"Who is the lawyer in charge of this client?" Noah asked the receptionist.

"I do not have that information. The attorney of record

is the law firm—any of our attorneys can work for any of our clients."

"I'd like a list of the attorneys working for this law firm."

"I can't share that information."

"What do you mean you can't share that information?" Noah was on the verge of losing his temper—and it took quite a bit to put Noah on edge.

"Sir, I would need to discuss the situation with the office manager, and she is at lunch right now."

"We'll wait."

"Of course."

"Tell her the FBI is here," Noah said.

Lucy tried to get Noah to sit, but he didn't. Her phone rang—it was Sean.

"I have to take this," she said but didn't wait for Noah to respond. She stepped out of the office and stood in the quiet hall. Security cameras were mounted at both ends— one over the elevator and one over the staircase. She felt like she was on stage and straightened her spine.

You can do this.

She answered her phone. "Sean."

"Hey—I just wanted to check in. I can't talk long, and then we have to go silent."

"I understand, I just wanted to know how you were. And that you got my messages. You didn't respond."

He was silent for a long five seconds. She counted. "I know why Madison came by," Sean said finally. "I'm sorry she dragged you into the middle of this. She's in denial that her husband has put their son in danger."

"Their son?" Lucy asked.

Please tell me the truth. Tell me that it's your son in danger.

He must have had a good reason for not telling her earlier. He wouldn't keep something like this from her.

"It's pretty clear that Spade is laundering money for a drug cartel, and we've already identified the key players. Makes me sick that he brought his kid down here. They're staying at the house of a drug boss."

His kid.

"She said she spoke to her husband and her son and they were both fine," Lucy said, surprised that her voice was steady.

"Carson Spade is a money launderer for one of the cartels. He's here for some reason we don't know yet, but just the fact that he's here with a cartel puts both him and Jesse in danger. I told Madison the same, and she chose not to believe me. She's blinded to the truth, and I'm not going to let her son be caught in the crossfire."

Her son.

Would Sean really go down there to protect Madison's son if he didn't know that Jesse was also his son? Maybe. Because Sean would do anything to protect the innocent.

But he had seen the photo of Jesse Spade. He could do the math just like she had. Jesse would have been conceived when he was at Stanford. When Madison was at Stanford. When they were both young college students. Before Carson Spade. Before Lucy.

That didn't bother her, not really. It bothered her that Madison had never told Sean, it bothered her that Sean didn't know his son.

But it hurt—physically hurt—that Sean wasn't telling her the truth about why he was risking his life in Mexico.

"So you don't believe Madison that they'll be home Friday."

"I don't know what to believe about the call she got from her husband; all I know is that Kane and I located them and we have a plan to get them out without anyone getting hurt. Okay?"

"Okay." She waited.

Tell me the truth, Sean. Please tell me the truth.

"Is something wrong?"

Yes. You're lying to me.

"It's a tough case."

"I wish I could be there for you, princess. You know that, right?"

"I know."

I thought I knew. I thought I knew you better than I know myself.

"I'm hoping this doesn't take much longer, Lucy. I need to see you. I miss you."

You're lying to me, Sean. Why won't you tell me?

She almost asked him. She almost asked if Jesse was his son. But she didn't, because she wasn't certain Sean wouldn't lie to her. She didn't want him to lie to her, it would destroy her.

"Luce? Are you there?" Sean asked.

"Yes. I was distracted."

"Kane's almost back, I need to go—but be careful, okay?"

"You, too."

That was it? Not even *We have to talk about this later . . . There's more going on, but I can't tell you over the phone . . . Jesse's my son, I'll explain everything when I see you.*

"I love you, princess."

"I love you, too," she heard herself saying. Her voice sounded far away.

She hung up. Her chest hurt because she wasn't breathing. Her eyes burned. She wanted to scream, but instead she swallowed her emotions. She locked up everything. The pain would knock her down if she let it out.

There was something fundamentally wrong in her

relationship with Sean that he would keep something so important a secret.

She walked down the hall to the bathroom and slipped inside. She put her head against the cool tile wall. The fan ran quietly, cold, sterile air pushed out into the small washroom. She tried to breathe normally, but each time she drew in air, a stabbing pain had her gasping.

She did not want to cry. She rarely did, and when the tears came she wouldn't be able to stop.

Do not break down. Do not.

Breathe. Focus. Breathe. Again.

She had a case to work, victims who needed her to be at her best. Victims who needed her to be alert or she would miss something. Or, worse, put her life or her partner's life in danger.

Eventually, the pain subsided. She could breathe normally, her eyes no longer threatened a waterfall she wouldn't be able to control. She had no idea how much time had passed, but she didn't care.

She splashed more water on her face. It was splotchy, as if she had been crying, though not one tear had fallen. She just looked crappy. She touched up her makeup and frowned. She was going to have to fake it. She'd faked years of her life, telling her family and the few friends she had that she was fine, just fine. It wasn't until Sean that she finally *was* fine. That she could put the past behind her because Sean taught her that she deserved to be loved, that she deserved a life and a future and a career that she wanted.

She put the mask back on, the cool facade that had saved her time and time again. Why was it so much harder now than in the past?

Because in the past, you never took it off.

She straightened her spine, rolled her shoulders back, and left the bathroom. Noah was still in the law offices, pacing. Only thirteen minutes had passed since she'd stepped out to take Sean's call. It had felt like a lifetime.

Noah glanced at her, but if he noticed anything odd, he didn't react. That helped. She didn't want to explain to him or anyone what was going on with her right now.

A few minutes later a tall Asian woman walked in and said, "Agent Armstrong, was there a problem with the file I prepared for your warrant?"

"Yes. I need to know who owns these businesses, the name of the lawyer in charge of this company, and the name and address of a person—not a business—who is responsible."

"I see. I read the warrant, and it was very clear that you needed the entity or individual who owned those two properties. They are owned by a business. I don't have the information as to who is in that business, but even if I did, that wasn't specifically asked on the warrant."

She was gloating, and Noah knew it.

"The lawyer's name."

"Of course. One moment, I will get you his business card. He is out of the country right now, but I'm sure he'll contact you as soon as he returns."

"Un-fucking-believable," Noah muttered when the office manager walked through a secure door into the back offices. A moment later she returned with a business card and handed it to Noah. Lucy glanced over:

Brian E. Simmons
Attorney

At the bottom was a phone number. The same number as this law office.

"I'll be back with another warrant, and if I find out that anyone here has destroyed records that I want, you'll all be liable."

"There's no need to threaten me," the manager said, looking wholly bored with the conversation. She turned and walked away.

Noah stormed out of the office. Lucy followed. Before they even reached the car, Noah was on the phone. "Hooper, you'd better be as good as Rick Stockton says, because I need you here, ASAP." He listened for a minute, then said, "Good." He hung up and opened the door when Nate pulled up. "Dean Hooper will be here tonight. I have a feeling that not only am I going to get a crash course in money laundering and white-collar crime one oh one, but I'm going to be reminded why I much prefer investigating homicides."

His phone rang and he answered while Nate drove them back to FBI headquarters. Lucy was only partly paying attention to the conversation—her mind was definitely not in this investigation right now. When he got off, he said, "Dunning, you and Lucy need to go back to Laredo. Apparently Ms. Walsh has done some sleuthing on her own and came up with a witness who can ID several of the people in Walsh's photos, and has a name for our Jane Doe."

Lucy leaned forward from the backseat. "What? She does?"

"Weren't you listening?"

"Sorry."

"Yes—she found a midwife who has information. I have to meet with Durant, and when Hooper arrives I'll be briefing him on the case. I wish I could be there— I'll follow as soon as I can. Call if you need backup."

Something was wrong with Lucy. Sean almost called her back . . . did she suspect there was something more about his trip to Mexico than he'd told her? Why didn't she say something? He mentally went through the conversation he'd had, but he'd been distracted. She sounded preoccupied, and he knew why—this case had to be getting to her. An abandoned baby, a dead Jane Doe, two missing women. He should be there for her, dammit.

He was furious with Madison for going to his house—talking to Lucy, bothering her, upsetting her. Lucy didn't need Madison's drama.

Had Madison said something about Jesse? No, she wouldn't. She couldn't have . . . she hadn't even wanted to tell Sean. And if she had, Lucy would have said something about it. She didn't play games, not like Madison.

Sean hit the side of the plane. It was hot, sticky, humid in the middle of the damn day, even with the shade. He didn't want to be here. He wanted to get his son and leave. He needed to talk to Lucy. Tell her everything. Face-to-face. In person. Where he could touch her, hold her, explain everything.

One more day. Two, tops.

Kane walked up to him. He didn't ask Sean what was wrong. Maybe he knew. Maybe Kane was a damn psychic.

"Gabriella will give the letter to Jesse. I pitched her the plan, we'll see if she helps."

"You haven't even told me the plan."

"You're not going to like it."

"This is my operation! Don't keep me in the dark."

"You asked for my help because you need my experience. I'll lay it out: There's only one way to get inside the Flores compound, and it's Trojan Horse–style."

"So we're depending on Gabriella Romero, who you said we can't trust."

"I'm only expecting her to give the letter to Jesse. I'll be inside."

"You're fucking with me, Kane. Just tell me your plan."

As Kane laid it out, Sean shook his head. "No. No. You're going to get yourself killed. I can't let you—"

"It's just as dangerous for you, Sean. But it's the only way."

"We need to pull back. Madison is certain her husband and son will be back on Friday."

"And I'm certain they won't be."

"Why? What happened?"

Kane hesitated.

"Tell me, dammit!"

"Get your shit together, Sean. If you think I'm not aware that you're struggling—between your fear for Jesse and worry about Lucy—then you're an idiot. Emotions are going to get us both killed. Do you know why I don't get involved? Why I don't want you working with me? Why I didn't want Duke working with me years ago? Because you're my brother, I love you, and it would destroy me if you died. You don't remember what it was like after Molly overdosed. You have no idea what I did, what I am capable of doing. My emotions interfered, and I made huge mistakes. I can't afford to make mistakes, and emotions have no place in this business."

Sean took a deep breath. "I get it."

"Jose Flores, the youngest of the four brothers and the one Gabriella is screwing in order to get inside, told her that Dominick isn't happy about something major that messed with their laundering operation. She has no details—and even if she did, she wouldn't share them in case it got out and messed with her revenge plot. But she thinks he blames Spade. Spade's here to fix it, which makes me think he screwed it up to begin with. Do you think that someone like Dom Flores is going to let him walk away? The only reason Gabriella is helping us is because she doesn't want the kid hurt. But make no mistake about it— she will betray us if it saves her own ass."

"So what you're saying is that Flores is going to kill Spade and Jesse?"

"I think Jesse is here as insurance to ensure that Spade doesn't screw up whatever it is he's doing. And if he does—Jesse will pay the price."

"Spade has to know that."

Kane nodded.

"Bastard."

"Are you ready?"

"I hate this plan."

"It's the only way."

"When does Jack arrive?"

"Soon. And then everything will happen very fast."

CHAPTER TWENTY-THREE

After dropping Noah off at FBI headquarters, Nate took Lucy to her house so she could pack an overnight bag. He told her he already had a go-bag in the car.

"Of course you do," she mumbled.

"What's bothering you?"

"Just tired." She went upstairs to avoid any more questions. Nate was Sean's friend, she reminded herself. She didn't need him reporting back to Sean that something was *bothering her*. Hell yes, something was bothering her.

She didn't know if they would need to stay, but since there was a room for them and it was a nearly two-hour drive each way—and they didn't know what they would need to do when they arrived—it was better to plan on staying.

It was after one by the time they got on the road, but they didn't have much traffic to worry about. Lucy called Siobhan to get all the details straight from her, then she called Zach at headquarters to ask him to run Loretta Martinez at the address Siobhan had given her. Then she talked to Noah to give him an update—though she didn't have anything really to tell him. He hung up quickly, no surprise. She wished she had someone else to call to avoid the conversation that Nate had been trying to start with her, but after an hour when Lucy had no one else to call and nothing to pretend to do, Nate said, "You don't have to talk about it, but I know something's wrong. And don't tell me you're tired."

"Don't psychoanalyze me, Nate."

He didn't say anything for several minutes. "You're never late. But you were late this morning."

"I didn't sleep much last night, okay? If Sean told you about my insomnia, that's under control."

"He didn't, but he didn't have to."

Great. So she always looked like something the cat dragged in? Why couldn't people just leave her alone?

"Is Sean okay?"

"Yes."

But he hadn't said anything about Jesse. Not when he found out on Monday, and not last night when they talked for ten minutes, and not this afternoon after he knew that Madison had talked to her this morning. Three chances, and he remained silent.

She wanted to throttle Nate because he was making her wholly uncomfortable. Nate had become Sean's closest friend here in San Antonio. They were two peas in a pod. Just as Sean had bonded with her brother Patrick, he'd bonded with Nate. She was glad—she loved her brother, and she liked Nate, and Sean deserved to have good friends he trusted who had his back. But she'd quickly figured out that Nate would tell Sean anything. He wouldn't share secrets, but he would make Sean aware that she was upset. He had an uncanny way of digging around and coming up with truths that she didn't want to discuss. She didn't like talking about her relationship with Sean, or what was bothering her, or trying to figure out if she was the only one in the dark about Sean's son.

Sean's son Jesse Spade.

"What's really going on with Elizabeth Cook?" she asked. "I've wondered since I got here why she never went in the field, but I didn't really think about it."

Nate said, "It's all hearsay."

"You challenged Noah."

"No I didn't."

"You commented."

"I was fishing. I really don't know what's going on, but I'm curious."

"And?"

"Juan's our boss, Lucy. I'm a soldier at heart, and Juan is my commanding officer. He never sent Cook into the field, and I don't think Noah should shake things up."

"We don't even know if Juan is coming back."

"What makes you say that?"

"I'm the psychologist, remember?" She was trying to make light of the situation, but she didn't feel light.

"I'd like to know your opinion."

"This can't go anywhere else, Nate." If it went to Sean, that was fine—she'd already talked to Sean about it. He'd helped her come to terms with the guilt she'd been harboring over the last few months.

"Lucy, you can trust me. You know that, right? Have I done anything to make you think you can't?"

"No, of course not." *Except that you're Sean's confidant.* "Family is the most important thing to Juan."

"That's not a big secret."

"It's so important that if he thinks they're threatened in any way, he will do anything to minimize the threat."

Nate didn't say anything.

"I'm the threat," Lucy said.

"That is ridiculous," Nate said. When Lucy didn't respond, he added, "You can't believe that."

"Juan said as much to me. When I wanted to visit Nita

and the kids after the baby—after Nita started to feel better—he said no. He made it more than clear that I'm not welcome there, Nate. When I first came to San Antonio, Juan treated me like family. Sean and I went to his house for dinner nearly every week. We enjoyed it. His family reminded me of my family growing up. The noise. The food. The games. It was exactly what I needed to feel like San Antonio was truly my home. And I love Juan's kids. Sean is so good with kids, they all loved him."

Her stomach twisted in a knot. Sean *was* great with kids. And now he had one.

"And I lied to Juan, and Juan knows it. And because of what I did during Operation Heatwave, I brought a cartel battle to Juan's doorstep. Them and us. And people died and were hurt and I know Barry Crawford isn't going to come back, even when he's regained his strength. I'm not naive enough to think that I wasn't one of the targets. It was because of choices I made."

"You were doing your damn job, Lucy."

"Yes, I was, but I went beyond the job, and you know that. And while on the one hand, I've come to terms with what I've done and I'm willing to accept the consequences, on the other, I recognize there were many more consequences to other people that I didn't even consider at the time. I'm dangerous, and I always will be. Nate, you of all people should understand that. I could have separated myself from Jack and Kane's lives fairly easily. Not gone into law enforcement. I could have turned my back on Brad when he was kidnapped by the cartel and never turned the wrath of their anger against the FBI and the DEA. But I became a cop. And I didn't separate myself. And I know, deep down, that I would do it again. Right or wrong, if I was faced with the option of breaking international law and saving a fellow cop or turning my back and knowing he would die, I would break the law. Juan knows, and he can't live with it. So it's either I leave, or he does. And I'm selfish. I want this job. I'm good at this job. I don't want to leave. And I hate that Juan doesn't think he or his family is safe around me."

Nate didn't say anything for a long time. So long, she wondered what he really thought of the situation. Then he said, "Eight years ago Cook had a case with another agent—I don't know his name, he transferred before I got here—investigating a serial killer. Sounds cliché, but it was rather a standard serial killer. Teenage girls, kidnapped, raped, murdered. There was a profile, I don't know the details. Cook had two daughters, was going through a divorce, and she personalized the case. Almost had a nervous breakdown. Our office didn't catch the guy—he was arrested in Arizona. But Cook blames herself because she missed something, and three more girls died after that mistake."

"*Did* she miss something?"

"I don't know. I wasn't here, I heard this from Leo Proctor over drinks one night when I first got here."

"Why didn't she leave?"

"I think Juan sympathized with her. Thought if he gave her some desk time, it would get better. But he never sent her back into the field, over and above basic background checks and paperwork. She's essentially an analyst."

"We have the smallest squad in the office and the highest active caseload." While Lucy had some sympathy for Cook, for eight years the other seven agents had been picking up her slack. "She could have done a lateral move over to analyst, or changed squads. Juan could have made that happen."

"She has friends in high places. I think her daughter is best friends with the SAC's daughter. College roommates or something. So Armstrong walked into the hornets' nest when he didn't follow Juan's directives." He paused. "Sean said you and Armstrong have been friends since DC, that he trained you or something."

"Yes," she said, thinking. "You know, this explains a lot."

"About?"

"Juan. And me. And everything. Juan is a good boss. He wants his team to be happy, to be healthy, to do the job. Crossing t's and dotting i's. He doesn't understand people like me."

"I'm sure he doesn't see you as dangerous."

"He does. And that's one of the reasons he's not coming back. Not because of me alone, but because he realized he can't run this squad and coddle anyone—like Cook. We have a mandate, Nate—we have minimal staff, minimal resources, and a maximum caseload. We have to work hard and work smart. And one of the things I learned from Barry—find a way to turn it off when we go home."

"Is that why you're upset?"

"I'm not upset."

"You don't have to lie about it, just tell me you don't want to talk about it."

"I don't want to talk about it."

"Fair enough."

They drove the last fifteen minutes to Laredo in silence, and Lucy took that time to get her head back into this case. She called Siobhan when they hit the city limits. She was antsy, but promised to wait at the hotel for them.

"Siobhan is jumpy. I don't blame her—she's been looking for Marisol and Ana for two years. She thinks we're close—this midwife, Cora Smith, had seen both the girls at the house in Freer, the one that's now empty. To be this close, I'd be eager as well."

"You don't sound confident we'll find them."

"I'm not confident they'll be the same girls Siobhan remembers." Lucy had been been kidnapped and held captive for two days . . . it had been hell, a time she wished she could forget forever. And while she could put it out of her mind for days—and sometimes weeks—at a time, it was always there, waiting for moments of weakness to creep up on her. To challenge her, taunt her.

But two *years*? Could she have been so strong that she'd be able to endure two years of being prostituted? Humiliated? Used? Forced to deliver babies only to be forced to give them away?

What had these girls endured?

Why hadn't Macey's baby been taken?

"What?"

She glanced at Nate. "What what?"

"You thought of something. Your body leaned forward."

Nate was perceptive. "According to Siobhan's contact, the people holding the girls wanted to make sure the babies were safe, even at the expense of the mothers. Yet there were no babies in the house, no sign of babies having been there—just a delivery room. Ms. Smith helped deliver Macey's baby—the runaway from Kansas City—yet a week later she was carrying the baby out of the house. Why? Why hadn't the baby been taken from her? They didn't care about her life . . . why would they care now?"

Lucy was running through the facts and guesses. "Let's say that Baby Elizabeth was in fact Marisol's baby, and she managed to escape the house and leave the baby at the church. The locket was either because she knew that Siobhan was looking for her, or so that the baby would have something of her heritage." Probably the latter. "But she was found . . . or more likely went back."

"Why would she return?"

"Because her sister was there, pregnant with twins. There would be no other reason for her to return, but she wanted to make sure her baby wasn't taken or sold."

"She didn't go to the authorities."

"She doesn't trust them. Look at what happened to Siobhan on Sunday night."

"She *was* breaking and entering."

"The cop touched her breasts, made lewd comments, very possibly to elicit the reaction she had—assault. The cop didn't believe her story, or if he did, he didn't follow up on it. Her SD card was stolen, and the only way they could have done that without damaging the rental car was if they had the keys. So *someone* in that department is dirty."

"After what happened over the last six months, that wouldn't surprise me."

"So why was Macey still at the house with her baby?"

"Could be they didn't have a buyer until then," Nate said. The acid churned in Lucy's stomach. She drank half a water bottle to settle it down. He was very likely right. Macey delivered, they had a healthy nine-pound baby boy. Seeking a buyer. Or the exchange fell through. Maybe the buyer was out of the country.

"Babies go for ten to twenty-five thousand dollars in illegal adoptions," Lucy said. "But possibly more . . . if the buyer is looking for something specific."

"Or if the buyer can't legally adopt."

"Or if they want the babies for . . ." She couldn't say it. She hated that she could think of the cruel things people could do to the most innocent on earth.

Nate pulled up to the hotel and Siobhan immediately came out and climbed into the backseat. "You made good time, but I'm worried. The midwife gave us everything, but I don't know that she wouldn't warn her friend. I hope not—I asked her not to—but what if she did?"

"I'm glad you waited for us," Lucy said. "I don't think it would be as easy to bail you out of jail again." She was trying to make light of the situation, but the humor fell flat.

"I need to find them," Siobhan said. "I went to the

hospital to sit with Baby Elizabeth after talking to Noah. I had to do something—how could these people steal a woman's baby? Why? And why didn't Mari call me?"

"We'll find out when we find her," Lucy said.

Nate glanced at her. She knew what he was thinking. She wasn't normally optimistic—she faced reality head-on. Maybe she just wanted to believe Marisol was alive. But the chances were, if she had gone back for her sister, Marisol was now dead. That's how these people operated—any disobedience had to be punished to set an example to others.

Loretta lived outside Laredo in a small town with easy access to the highway. They climbed out of the car, and Siobhan frowned at Nate and Lucy.

"You guys are going to scare her off," Siobhan said. "Please, let me talk to her first."

"You're not going in there alone," Nate said.

Lucy agreed. "Siobhan—this is an active federal investigation. You're not interviewing this witness. We're letting you come because you have information and you know these girls. But this is our investigation."

Nate said, "Lucy, you got this, I'll keep an eye out here. Watch the house, make sure this Loretta doesn't bolt."

Thank you, she mouthed and walked up the short walkway to Loretta's front door. They knocked and waited. Knocked again.

"What if she's not home?" Siobhan said.

"She's home." Lucy had already seen her car through the single garage window. She also heard a television inside. She listened carefully and heard movement inside.

It still took Loretta Martinez a full two minutes before she opened the door. She was in no condition to run. Her right arm was in a sling and the side of her face was bruised. By the coloring, Lucy suspected the injuries were five to seven days old. Someone had beaten up this old woman. She was in her sixties, plump, but had a sallow look of someone who didn't feel well. She panicked when she saw them, her eyes darting back and forth, though confusion crossed her expression.

"What happened?" Siobhan said, instantly concerned. "Ms. Martinez, did someone hurt you?"

"Who are you? What do you want?"

"I'm Siobhan Walsh. I volunteer with the Sisters of Mercy."

"Who?"

"They're a religious order of missionaries in Mexico and Central America. Two young women I know were kidnapped two years ago and I think you've seen them. I need your help."

"You're not a nun," she said with a scowl. "You're lying to me." She looked at Lucy. "You look like a cop."

"FBI Special Agent Lucy Kincaid." She showed her identification.

Siobhan said, "I'm not a nun, but I'm not lying. I really am a volunteer for the Sisters of Mercy. Marisol and Ana. I need to find them."

"I can't help you." She started to close the door.

Lucy put her foot in the opening. "Ms. Martinez, you want to help us."

"You're a cop, you can't come in here. That's breaking and entering, I mean, illegal search and seizure." She frowned, as if she couldn't quite think of the words she wanted. "What do you really want?"

Lucy said, "You need to talk to us before anyone else dies."

"Dies? What?"

"The girl with preeclampsia is dead—"

"Eloise," Siobhan interrupted. "Her name was Eloise."

Loretta definitely recognized the name. Lucy continued, "You had access to Eloise and had the medical experience necessary to perform an emergency C-section."

"Oh God—"

Siobhan said, "Someone killed her after taking her baby."

"I—I—" She looked faint and Lucy stepped in and put her arm around her. The woman, though plump, felt soft and weak. She tried to pull away from Lucy but had no strength.

"Have you seen a doctor?" Lucy asked.

"I'm a nurse," Loretta snapped.

Siobhan entered and closed the door behind them. The house smelled of antiseptics and medicine and illness. It was also much too hot.

Lucy helped Loretta to a couch in the living room. She covered her with an afghan. Water bottles and pain pills overflowed on the coffee table. The woman took a pill, her hands shaking so badly that she could barely bring the bottle of water to her lips. Lucy suspected she'd diagnosed herself. "You're far worse off than you want to believe." She assessed her. "This happened about a week ago, didn't it?"

"I fell."

"That's what abused women say."

"I'm not an abused woman!"

"I think whoever you work for beat you." Lucy mentally did the math. It was an educated guess—but she was certain she was right. "One of the girls escaped with her baby, and you were punished for it."

Loretta couldn't hide her shock that Lucy knew.

"Go away. Just go away."

Loretta had limited use of her right arm. She was sore and had shuffled when she walked back to the couch, as if each step pained her. Her right eye had at one point been swollen shut and was now only partly open. The bruises were healing—the ones Lucy could see. But the way she shifted, Lucy wondered if she didn't have a broken rib.

There was no way in her condition that Loretta could have performed an emergency C-section.

"You need a doctor," Lucy said. "A real doctor." She sat next to her and tried to check her vitals.

"Don't touch me! I'll be fine. Just leave me alone."

Lucy dropped her hand. She couldn't force Loretta to get medical help—but there was no way she was leaving without calling the paramedics. She got up and sent Nate a text message.

Siobhan squatted next to Loretta and showed her the photo of Marisol and Ana. "These girls—I know you were with them. Where are they?"

Loretta didn't speak, but it was clear she recognized the girls.

"Cora talked. I knew I shouldn't have trusted her. You don't understand. They're going to kill us."

Siobhan said, "No one else is going to die. Eloise had preeclampsia. She delivered her baby after suffering a seizure. Her body was left in a Dumpster. You have to help us find these people before anyone else dies. For Eloise. For all of them."

"They're all gone." Shaking, Loretta drank more water. It dribbled down her chin and she didn't seem to notice.

"When did you last see Marisol and Ana?" Lucy asked.

She didn't say anything.

"Please, Loretta," Siobhan pleaded, "I've been looking for Mari and Ana for two years. Their family needs them. They have a younger brother and a grandmother who are worried about them. Their mother was my best friend, I have to find them!"

Siobhan was appealing to emotion, but Loretta wasn't biting. She was too old, too jaded, too guilty to say anything.

Lucy cleared her throat. She motioned for Siobhan to

move. Siobhan didn't want to, but Loretta understood only one thing—survival—and Lucy was going to push.

Siobhan stood and walked several feet away. Lucy stood over the beaten woman and said, "Loretta, let me explain what is going to happen from this moment forward. You are at best a material witness to a felony and at worst a co-conspirator. We have a witness who places you in the same house as a woman we later found dead in a Dumpster, her infant ripped out of her womb. We have a witness who identified Eloise at a house on El Gato Street in Freer Sunday night; early Tuesday morning, Eloise was found murdered. Not in Freer, but here, in Laredo. A person with medical training—such as yourself—cut Eloise's baby boy out of her womb, then shot Eloise in the back of the head. They left her body in a trash can."

Lucy used the most blunt, clear language that she could. Every sentence caused Loretta to shrink back, as if slapped. Though recounting the facts sickened Lucy, she put enough venom in her voice to make sure that Loretta Martinez knew that she was deadly serious about this case and that Loretta was not getting a pass on her complicity to kidnapping and murder.

"Three days—they have three days on us. We will find them. We have already identified three of the key players—Jasmine, her bodyguard Lance Dobleman, and the man responsible for keeping these pregnant women locked up, Raoul. We have identified four of the women who were held against their will. We *will* identify the others. And you have two choices. You can either help us and beg the court for leniency, or hinder us and spend the rest of your life in prison. Those are your choices."

Siobhan stared at Lucy. "Lucy, we agreed—"

"No, Siobhan, you *thought*, big difference. You care, I get it. But we're beyond coddling accessories to murder. If we don't find Mari and Ana soon, we won't find them.

These people know how to move their victims in and out of the county, the state, the country. The longer we play these games, the more time they have to disappear."

The pain pill had kicked in; Loretta's eyes were becoming glassy. Lucy frowned. This woman was seriously ill. She pulled down the afghan and Loretta hit her hand. Lucy ignored her and pulled up her nightgown. Her stomach was dark purple. Lucy was stunned that Loretta was still alive.

"Loretta—you have internal bleeding. You need immediate medical attention."

"Go away," Loretta said.

Siobhan was on the phone and Lucy shook her head.

"We have to call an ambulance!" Siobhan said.

"Agent Dunning already called," Lucy said. "I knew she was gravely injured when she opened the door."

Lucy put the blanket back on Loretta. "You're dying, Loretta. Please, if you want to help those girls—if you want to punish the men who beat you—help us. Now."

Loretta was close to talking. Lucy sat on the floor and took her shaking hand. "We know Marisol disappeared with her baby. Did she come back? Where is she? Where is Ana?"

"I didn't know she left it . . . we didn't know. She never came back. I didn't think she'd leave her sister."

She didn't leave her by choice. She must have had a plan . . . it was the only thing that Lucy could think of. But maybe she didn't expect their captors to move the girls so quickly. Maybe she was getting help . . . just not from the authorities.

Or maybe they found her and killed her.

"Why would she leave Ana?" Siobhan asked.

"Ana . . . they were all safe while they were pregnant," Loretta said.

Marisol must have thought she had time, at least enough time to save Ana.

"Raoul was so angry."

"Where would Marisol go?" Lucy asked.

"I don't know."

"You must have an idea."

"She talked about an Angelo. Always, Angelo. I don't know who he is, I don't know anything about him, but she thought he would save her."

Siobhan gasped. "Angelo? Angelo Zapelli?"

"I don't know," Loretta said, her voice weak.

Lucy looked at the pills that Loretta had been taking. Oxycodone, prescribed to someone else. She had no idea how many the woman had taken, but she was loopy and fading rapidly. She heard the ambulance in the distance. She texted Nate to bring them in immediately.

"Who's Angelo Zapelli?" Lucy asked Siobhan.

"Marisol's employer in Monterrey was Antonio Zapelli—his son is Angelo. RCK ran a background on both of them, said the family had no ties to any drug cartels or human trafficking."

"We need to talk to both of them."

"I have his information. I'll call him."

"Not without me," Lucy said. "Siobhan, this has always been serious, but it's gotten much more dangerous. If Loretta is to be believed, Marisol gave birth and left the baby at the church, sought help, and is now looking to get her sister back. She must have an idea of where they are. We have to find her, find these people. They will kill her. They killed Eloise, they've been selling babies, we have no idea how many—"

"Seventy-two," Loretta whispered.

Lucy and Siobhan both looked at the woman. "What?" Lucy said.

"I've delivered seventy-two babies in the last two years. You'll never find them all. Too many women, they're foolish, believe anything because they want to believe."

"Eloise was chained to a bed!" Siobhan said.

"Only after Marisol ran away. Raoul chained them all. But I haven't seen them . . . I came home. Came home to die." Loretta's voice trailed off.

Nate opened the door and escorted the two paramedics inside. Lucy talked to them, showed them the pills that Loretta had been taking, and informed them that the beating happened six to seven days ago, probably on Thursday.

The day Marisol ran away.

While Siobhan was making calls trying to locate Angelo Zapelli in Monterrey, Lucy pulled Nate aside. "I want to place her in custody. Anything to keep her safe and to keep her from running, if she survives. She knows more than what she's said."

"I called the assistant sheriff," Nate said. "Villines."

"Good." She glanced over as the paramedics lifted Loretta onto the gurney. "Seventy-two babies, Nate. She said she delivered seventy-two babies in two years. She wasn't threatened or imprisoned or exploited, she did it for money. Maybe she didn't start out being a criminal, but she figured out what was going on and she remained silent *and* continued to participate in criminal behavior."

"Did she admit that they were selling babies?" Noah asked.

"No, she didn't. If she survives—and honestly, I don't know that she will, she's in bad shape made worse by the fact that she's been popping pills all week—she needs to confess to everything and face consequences for her actions. Let the powers that be decide what to do with her."

Noah asked the paramedics what hospital they were going to, then returned to Lucy. "We don't have a warrant to search her house. Possibly probable cause, but depends on what judge we get. Still, if something is in plain sight—we need to search and clear the house anyway."

Lucy concurred. "If Loretta is telling the truth—and

I'm inclined to believe her, considering she was on so many painkillers I don't think she could have consciously lied—then Marisol went to her old boss for help. Jasmine and her people probably didn't know what Marisol was going to do, so they shut down the house and moved the girls as soon as they could."

"Except Eloise."

"She was sick. Maybe she'd already had a seizure. Maybe they planned on going back for her after Macey and her baby were gone. We don't know, but they might have been short on space if the girls had to be moved quickly."

"And then the FBI comes in and starts asking questions."

"Loretta didn't deliver Eloise's son. She couldn't have, not in her condition. But whoever did it had some medical training. A nurse, possibly. Maybe a doctor, one in a different field who knows the basics but without specialized training."

Siobhan walked over to them. "I just spoke with Antonio Zapelli. He said Angelo left work on Thursday at the regular time, but didn't come in on Friday. He didn't leave a note, just told his mother that he had to help a friend and wouldn't be home for a few days. He's not answering his cell phone."

"But he has one?" Lucy asked.

"His dad said he did. I'll call him—"

"No, not yet. I'm going to check in with Noah. We might be able to trace it."

"But what if he's helping Marisol—maybe he's with her, he can let me talk to her!"

"We don't know, Siobhan, and right now this whole thing seems fishy to me. Just wait a minute, okay?"

Siobhan didn't want to wait, but she pocketed her phone.

Lucy glanced at Nate, and he nodded. Good. He was on the same page as she was. For some reason, she was beginning to doubt her instincts—and her compassion. She'd known almost immediately that Loretta was in bad shape, yet she interrogated her when she could have administered aid. Though, to be honest, there wasn't much she could have done for the woman other than make sure she didn't move around until the paramedics arrived.

Lucy dialed Noah. She wanted to search Loretta's house *now* because there could be vital information in finding Marisol and the others. Noah could trace Angelo's phone, find out when he'd come into the States, maybe even where he was staying.

This was their first real break at finding Marisol, Ana, and the others . . . and learning what happened to all those babies.

Seventy-two. Seventy-two babies taken from their mothers and sold.

CHAPTER TWENTY-FOUR

Noah answered on the fourth ring. "Yes?"

He sounded rushed, so Lucy got to the point. "We have information from a nurse who delivered dozens of babies for Jasmine and a man named Raoul. Marisol disappeared after giving birth and hasn't returned. She contacted a friend in Monterrey—the son of her employer—who disappeared last Friday, according to his father. That would be the day after Marisol left her baby at the church. We have his cell phone number, but I'm skeptical about giving him a heads-up that we're looking for Marisol."

"Why? He may know where she is."

"Because she may run from the authorities. She's scared, Noah. And after what happened to Siobhan on Sunday, I understand why. And honestly . . . why would he drop everything and come here to help her after more than two years? Without telling his father that he heard from her? Or calling Siobhan, who has made it her mission to find the girls? It's just . . . I don't know, my gut is telling me to tread carefully here. Loretta admitted to helping these people deliver seventy-two babies. Where are they? How many girls were used as breeders? What happened to them after they delivered? Were they killed or sent back into the sex trade? How many of these . . . these . . . *breeder* houses are around here? Marisol may have the answers." She stopped herself. Her emotions were getting the better of her, and she had to get them under tight control or she would lose it. She felt that churning, deep down, that she was on edge.

She cleared her throat and continued matter-of-factly. "Loretta Martinez was assaulted last week after Marisol left. She couldn't have performed the C-section on our Jane Doe in the morgue." *Eloise.* "She's on the way to the hospital. I don't think she's going to survive—she has extensive internal injuries and was self-medicating. But I want permission to put a guard on her door and, if she survives, to place her under arrest."

"Talk to Villines, do what needs to be done. You're on the right path. Villines called me a couple of hours ago, said it wasn't urgent but wanted to talk. He might have information, but I'm sitting here waiting to talk to a judge and get an expanded warrant for that damn property management company. Hooper is on his way from Sacramento, and he's already been a huge help with this legal bullshit."

"Do I have probable cause to search Loretta's house?"

"Yes, but we do this by the book. Jasmine is a lawyer. If we find anything on her and she thinks we obtained the information under duress or without a warrant, she'll make our lives hell. I don't want to blow this because we went the easy route." He paused. "Did she let you into the house?"

"Yes." Sort of. She hadn't said no when Lucy came in. *Go away.*

That wasn't an explicit *no.* It was a gray area, and Lucy wouldn't lie on the stand, but Loretta was self-medicating and very sick. "I think Loretta knows exactly where Ana de la Rosa is, or has a good idea. I want to question her as soon as the doctor clears her." Or before, if Lucy could get away with it.

"Because she let you into the house, if you see anything in the open, go for it. But don't tear the place apart. I'll contact Lopez in the local RA and ask them to work on a warrant. You call Villines, get a guard on Martinez, see what information he has for us. Call Zach and have him run this Angelo Zapelli, as well as the father. He may be able to get a procedural warrant to trace his GPS. Then send me a nuts and bolts report. I gotta go, the AUSA needs me." He hung up.

Lucy conveyed the information to Nate and sent an email to Zach about Zapelli. They left Siobhan outside and walked through the house, both of them wearing gloves. They looked carefully, but didn't open drawers or toss any furniture.

This was an older woman. If she kept a record, where would she keep it? A journal? An address book? Lucy looked around for a desk. There was a small stationary desk in the dining room. She itched to go through the drawer, but she didn't. Still, the desk was cluttered, and there were slots at the top of the desk, like an old-fashioned post office. Everything in the slots was in the open. She looked at the mail—bills, some paid, some unpaid, sorted in different slots. An address book—with names and addresses. She flipped through it, but nothing jumped out at her.

There was a book that appeared to be tax records, but when Lucy opened it, she saw that it was a list of dates with notations.

August 2 ~ 5:15 p.m. Boy 6 lbs 6 oz 20 in ~ Cristina
October 4 ~ 3:30 a.m. Girl 5 lbs 14 oz 19 in ~ Joy
December 24 ~ 2:10 p.m. Boy 7 lbs 12 oz 20 in ~ Marisol

There were other notations in each entry, as to the health of the baby and the mother. But Lucy couldn't see any-

thing. She had to get out of here. Clutching the book, she
ran outside, into the humid air. But it was better than the
house. Better than the death that surrounded it. Better than
knowing what had been going on for more than two years.

Marisol. Elizabeth wasn't Marisol's first baby.

It could have been a different Marisol, except that Siobhan had been looking for the sisters for two years. Loretta
had been delivering babies for two years. Twenty-five
months, according to this book.

Nate came out of the house and said, "Hey, you okay?"

She nodded, unable to speak.

He was going to push it, so she cleared her throat and
showed him the book. "Names, dates, births."

He stared. "This is so fucked." He put the book into an
evidence bag, signed and sealed it. Something crossed his
face

"Nate—"

"I was adopted," he said suddenly.

"You know that is completely different."

He stared at Loretta's house, but didn't appear to be
looking at any one thing. "I found my birth mother."

"If you don't want to talk about it—"

He shook his head. "I love my parents. They were good
people. They had my older sister—Jenny. She's a biologist
for a huge pharmaceutical company. Very smart and
nerdy." He smiled. "Anyway, she's twelve years older than
me. They tried for years to have another baby, but my mom
had three miscarriages. Jenny had been a difficult pregnancy, I guess. They had been trying to adopt for more
than a decade. They went through background checks,
medical exams, psych exams—because they were good
people. They did it the right way. And by the time they got
approved, the counselor said that they may not end up with
an infant because they were nearly forty." He scowled.
"They ended up going through a church-run group. All

legitimate. My biological mother was sixteen, her boy-friend got her pregnant. She picked my parents out of over one hundred couples who wanted to adopt. She didn't know their names, just saw their pictures, their facts, and letters that they each wrote about why they wanted to adopt."

"They love you and wanted you."

"I know that."

"What happened when you found her?"

"I found her, I didn't get a chance to talk to her. She died of a drug overdose when she was twenty-three in Chicago. She was pregnant at the time. I got the file from the coroner's office a few years ago. After she had me she ran away from home, got mixed up with lowlifes, started doing hard drugs, and died from it after prostituting her-self to feed her drug habit."

Lucy had nothing to say. Nate wasn't a big talker, and she hadn't realized how difficult this case was for him. She'd only been thinking about herself, the fact that she couldn't have children, that she'd been raped, not that other people had other stories no less powerful.

"I didn't mean to dump that on you."

"I'm glad you did—you needed to get it out."

"You keep things bottled up, too."

"But I have Sean to talk to. And you know, if you ever need to talk to anyone, we're here."

Nate smiled sadly. "I know. Thank you." He cleared his throat. "There's a medical bag on her chair—I didn't go through it, but there may be DNA evidence that tracks to the missing girls. And I found this."

Nate showed her a business card. It was high-quality card stock, blank except for a handwritten phone number. "We'll trace this," he said. "May not lead anywhere."

Neither of them believed that.

Siobhan rushed up to them. "We are so close to finding

Mari! And you're dragging your feet. What are we still doing here? What's going on? Shouldn't we go to the hospital? Call Angelo? *Something?*"

Nate said, "We are doing this the right way. Do not call Angelo—we get a warrant to trace his phone and find out where he is, then hopefully we get to Marisol as well."

"What? She's not a criminal," Siobhan said.

"We didn't say she was," Lucy said. "She's a victim, but she's also in danger. And I don't want either her or Angelo to know that the FBI is looking for her. Not until we bring her into protective custody." She put her hand on Siobhan's arm. "Trust me, Siobhan. We know what we're doing. If she is so scared of the authorities that she wouldn't go to them to save her sister, that she would abandon her baby at a church, she's not going to believe we're here to help her if we talk to her on the phone. We find her, convince her. You can help with that, Siobhan. But you need to do exactly what we say."

Reluctantly, she nodded. But she didn't look happy.

Lucy and Nate met with Assistant Sheriff Adam Villines in his office.

"Thank you for coming down again, I know it's a long drive," Villines said after Lucy introduced him to Nate. "And I appreciate the heads-up about Loretta Martinez. How did you track her down?"

"Siobhan Walsh, the photojournalist, told us she received an anonymous tip."

"Do you believe her?"

"No," Lucy said. Nate raised an eyebrow. "I should clarify, I believe she received a credible tip, and I didn't push her to tell me who it came from. I'm certain it was the reporter Noah and I spoke with earlier this week. They're friends." She'd dug around a bit last night when she couldn't sleep and learned Siobhan and Eric Barrow were the same age and had both been raised in northern Virginia. It stood to reason that they had known each other since high school.

"Were you able to get a guard on Martinez?" Lucy asked. "Our resident agency is working on minimal staff right now, but Noah said they can take over tomorrow."

"We can cover her for the next twenty-four hours. Are you putting her under arrest?"

"Most likely, but I'm going to wait to hear her prognosis and see if I can get more information from her. And jurisdictional issues are between you and my boss," Lucy said. "I don't care who prosecutes her or which facility she's housed in. I just need her to talk."

"I spoke with the hospital staff. She's already in surgery. X-rays showed multiple hairline fractures on her ribs and internal bleeding. She was unresponsive by the time she arrived at the hospital. You very well could have saved her life by showing up when you did."

"Luck."

"Or divine intervention," he said.

Lucy believed, but she didn't have any sympathy for Loretta and didn't know if she wanted her to survive . . . except to interrogate her for information. She felt cold, and the fact that she had no remorse for these cold feelings disturbed her.

She said, "You called Noah with information. He's been at the courthouse all afternoon and since we were here he asked us to stop by."

"You might think this is odd, but if you knew my brother-in-law, you would understand."

"You've lost us already," Nate said. "Your brother-in-law?"

Villines nodded. "Johnny. Johnny Honeycutt. He came to see me yesterday after classes—he teaches math and science at one of the local high schools. A good kid—well, he's not a kid. He's twenty-seven, but he's my wife's youngest brother and was ten when I got married, so I've always thought of him as a kid. He had some hypothetical questions that I don't think were hypothetical. He wanted to know specifically what the law was regarding asylum for foreign nationals who were brought illegally to this country for the purposes of sex trafficking. Now, he didn't ask the question flat-out, he talked around it, but that's what he was looking for. He then saw the photos of Baby Elizabeth on my desk and the photo you brought me of the de la Rosa sisters. He left awfully quick. I called my in-laws last night and my mother-in-law said George and Johnny had gone out and she didn't know when they would be back. Now, you have to understand my mother-in-law. She is as honest as the day is long. The most Christian of Christian women, but with a spine of steel. I pushed a bit, put on my cop attitude you could say, and she lied to me. Told me that they went to fix the tractor and left their cell phones in the house. I know for a fact that they couldn't fix the tractor because Johnny told me the parts he needed were back-ordered. For my ma to lie? No—I didn't want to believe it. But she did."

Lucy asked, "Do they have information about Marisol or the other girls?"

"I don't know. It was really weird. I would have gone out there last night, but it's a goodly drive, and Johnny called me an hour later and said everything was fine. He hedged about the tractor, and then said he was going to stay at Ma's for the night because he and Dad had a couple of beers. That, I would believe—Johnny and George can get to drinking while playing cards after dinner. But Johnny didn't sound like he'd been drinking. He sounded . . . I don't know, different."

"Would you mind giving us their contact information?"

"Go easy on them. My in-laws are good people, salt of

the earth. They would never break the law on purpose."
He paused. "I'd like to go out with you, if you don't mind."

"We'd like to talk to Johnny first. You said he's a teacher?"

Adam nodded, glanced at the clock. "It's after four, I don't know if he'll still be on campus."

"Would you mind calling him and finding out?"

Adam picked up his personal cell phone and dialed a number. "Hey, Johnny, what's up? . . . Are you still at school? . . . Why you going out to the ranch again? . . . Is Ma okay? . . . Fine . . . Yeah, sure. I'll tell her." He hung up. "Okay, he's going back out to the ranch. Johnny is a good son, sees Ma and Dad at least once a week, but this would be the third time this week and it's only Wednesday."

"Lead the way, Deputy," Nate said.

CHAPTER TWENTY-FIVE

On the map, the Honeycutt ranch was eighteen miles as the crow flies from Our Lady of Sorrows Church. Because they were coming from Laredo, it took them much longer to wind through the flat desert roads once they left Highway 59. It was five thirty by the time they arrived. Adam Villines parked next to an older, well-maintained pickup with a high school faculty parking sticker on the rear window. Nate pulled in next to Villines.

The house was a two-story, old-fashioned farmhouse with a wide wraparound porch that had recently been painted. "Five kids, two parents, one bathroom," Adam said with a smile. But he looked worried.

He knocked on the screen. "Ma, it's Adam."

The door opened almost immediately. A young man stood there. John Honeycutt.

"What's going on?" John asked his brother-in-law. He eyed Lucy and Nate.

"Can we come in, John?" Adam said quietly. "It's important."

John was angry, but he swung the door open and let them enter.

Mr. and Mrs. Honeycutt were at the dining room table

with a map of the county in front of them. Both looked startled when Adam walked in with Nate and Lucy behind them. "Adam—what's wrong?" Mrs. Honeycutt said.

Adam took off his hat. "I think you know, Ma. These people here, they're FBI agents. Lucy Kincaid and Nate Dunning. I've been working with them on a case for the last few days." He glanced at John. "And I think you might know something about it."

"I don't know what you think I know," John began, but then Mr. Honeycutt cleared his throat.

"Son, we need to tell them. We can't do this on our own."

John ran his hands through his hair and walked to the far side of the room. "Dad."

They exchanged a look, and John simply looked down, shielding his eyes.

George stood and shook their hands. "I'm George Honeycutt. My wife, Nadia. Please, come in, sit at the table. We've been talking about calling you all day, Adam."

"I wish you had."

Everyone sat at the dining room table, except John. He paced between the dining room and the adjoining living room.

Adam asked, "What happened, George?"

"Monday night Johnny came out to look at the tractor. We found a young woman in the barn. She was sleeping under the hay. Don't know how long she'd been there, at least a night, maybe two. She had some food in a backpack, but she was mighty sick. We brought her inside, fed her, Nadia helped her with her shower. She talked to Nadia."

Nadia nodded, a deep frown on her face. "Poor girl, bless her heart. She didn't really talk to me so much as cry. I don't think she's cried for a long time. She said her sister is in trouble, that she had to find her, get her out of a bad situation. As George said, I had helped her with her shower. Her clothes were bloody, I thought she'd been—I don't know, shot or stabbed." She shook her head. "She'd given birth recently. I could see by her stomach, the way it sagged because she was so very thin. She had a fever, we gave her some antibiotics—I know, we're not supposed to share medicine, but the girl needed it. She was terrified of the police, didn't want us to call anyone, even a doctor. She slept all night, and George, Johnny, and I talked. I told them what she'd said to me—that she and her sister had been kept as prisoners. Well, we all know what that means."

"You should have called me, Ma," Adam said.

"Where is she now?" Lucy asked. Could it be this easy?

"She called someone from her hometown. Someone who she said would have been looking for her."

"She's from a village deep in south-central Mexico. No electricity, no phones."

"It was a man named Angelo," George said. "She called him Tuesday morning and he said he would fly here immediately. After she talked to him, she seemed relieved, like the weight of the world was lifted from her shoulders. We wanted to meet him, but she was adamant. She was very worried that if the people who had her sister found out we helped her, they would hurt us."

"George, these are bad people," Adam said. "You should have called me, you shouldn't have let her stay here. We don't know who she really is."

"Of course she should stay!" Nadia reminded Lucy of her own mother. A petite Latina mother whose word was law. Lucy's mother would give a starving man her last slice of bread and admonish anyone who said she shouldn't. "Johnny came back Tuesday, after she'd already gone, and said there was a baby left at a church, and we're pretty certain that was her baby. She kept talking about having to leave her baby—and then it all made sense."

"She walked nearly twenty miles to this ranch," Lucy said. After giving birth, to save herself and her sister, she'd walked twenty miles in what . . . three days? Four? How long had she been in the barn, sick? "Did she say where she was heading?"

"I think she wanted to get to a town so she could call this Angelo fellow, but didn't want anyone to see her, so she kept to the back roads and ranches," George said.

"When did she leave?" Lucy asked.

"Yesterday at four thirty in the afternoon. She said she was meeting Angelo at seven at an exit on fifty-nine. I wanted to drive her, but she was very jumpy. I gave her my cell phone and told her to call me if she needed anything. I would move heaven and earth for that poor girl."

"She has your cell phone?" Lucy said. "Have you tried calling her?"

John came back into the dining room from where he was listening in the living room. His face was firm and angry. "Yes. She hasn't answered. It's an old flip-phone, no find-your-phone feature."

"John, I couldn't force her to stay," George said.

"You shouldn't have let her leave!"

"Don't yell at your father," Adam said. "This is a difficult situation for everyone."

"We looked for her all night," John said. "We knew where she was meeting him, got there not much after seven, and she wasn't there. We waited, no one showed up. Not Marisol, not this Angelo person."

"But she has your cell phone," Lucy said. "We can trace it."

"But it's an old phone."

"Doesn't matter. If it's on, it will have pinged a cell tower. We might not be able to get it at its exact location, but we'll get close. If you contact your service provider, it will make everything go faster."

"What's her story?" John said. "We wanted to help—she needed it—but she didn't want to take it. She was so scared. And young."

"Marisol and her sister, Ana, disappeared two years ago from Monterrey, Mexico, where they had gone to get jobs," Lucy said. "Marisol speaks three languages and was earning money to help rebuild their village after a flood and mudslide killed their parents and destroyed the village. A photojournalist with ties to the girls has been looking for them, and when the baby showed up at the church with a personalized locket, the priest contacted her. She brought us in." Lucy leaned forward. "This cannot go any further than this, but we believe that Marisol's sister is pregnant and in danger. Marisol most likely left here to rescue her sister."

"She kept talking about Ana, how she was sick and in trouble."

"We believe that the same people who have Ana killed another woman." Lucy didn't mention that Eloise's baby was stolen. There was no reason to give these people more nightmares.

"Tell me what to do," George said. "Tell me how to help."

"Call your service provider," Adam said, "then I'll talk to them."

Lucy felt physically ill. She stepped outside and sat on a bench and put her head between her knees.

Nate followed her and closed the door behind him. "Lucy—what's going on? Are you okay?"

She was so tired of being coddled. Of being asked if she was okay. She was *fine*. She had just browbeat a dying woman into telling her what she needed to know, then dumped sorrow into what had been a happy house. George and Nadia shouldn't have to know these things. But evil . . . it seemed to find Lucy. She drew it to her, like a spider's web.

Worse, she saw the evil. Dissected it. Understood it.

"Angelo," she said through clenched teeth. "He's one of them."

"What do you mean? One of who? The traffickers?"

Lucy hardened her heart, cleared her expression. Reminded herself that this was her job. Even if it wasn't, she would be forever drawn to the evil that people did to one another.

She looked up and faced Nate. "Angelo's father told Siobhan that he was at work on Thursday, but left before work on Friday," Lucy said in a calm, even voice. She didn't recognize it was hers. "Angelo told his mother he was leaving town for a few days because a friend needed his help. Marisol called him on *Tuesday*. Four days later. He told her he would come immediately, but he was already here. She thought she could trust him . . . she thought he was the only one she could trust. But I'll bet my badge that he's the one who sold those two girls to the traffickers in the first place."

Marisol could barely walk. He'd hit her so hard she lost consciousness . . . And when she woke up, she didn't know where she was.

Angelo . . .

She'd loved him. They were going to have a baby. And then . . .

It was him. All along, it was him . . .

It was so dark. So cold. So quiet.

The closet door opened. The mean one, the one she called Doberman because he was mean like the big, hungry dogs that had guarded her and Ana and the others at one of the warehouses they'd been locked in, grabbed her. He yanked her up and scowled. *Growled*. He growled like a mean dog.

"Get up, you stupid bitch. You cost us a small fortune.

You're already a dead woman, but first you're going to fix all of the problems you caused, then you'll die. And you'll die knowing that I will personally make your sister suffer as soon as she delivers those babies. And she'll know it's because of you that she will scream for us to put her out of her misery."

He pulled her out of the filthy house and into an attached garage. The trunk popped open and he pushed her inside and shut the trunk. It hit her in the head and she winced. She was left in darkness. And silence.

Then the ignition turned on and the car burst out of the garage. He slammed on the brakes and her body slammed against the back of the trunk. Metal scraped her, cut her arms, and she felt blood. Then he shifted into drive and pushed the accelerator so her body rolled the other way.

And then they were driving, fast. Away from the girls. Away from Ana.

I'm so sorry, Ana. I thought Angelo was the only one I could trust. I was wrong, and now we're going to die.

CHAPTER TWENTY-SIX

It was dusk when Kane drove off in the jeep. Sean hated this plan, because it meant trusting Gabriella Romero, whom he didn't know and had no reason to trust. Hell, even Kane said he didn't trust her . . . yet their entire plan hinged on her.

Minutes after Kane left, Sean heard gunfire coming from down the road.

No no no!

Sean jumped on the motorcycle he'd stolen earlier, one gun strapped on his back and a handgun within reach. He kept his body low as he sped over the rocky dirt path that led to the main road. He was winding around, he couldn't see far ahead in the twilight, but he heard several trucks and more gunfire. He was forced to slow down when the narrow road made a sharp curve to the right, then another to the left.

As soon as the dirt road widened, he saw Kane's jeep. Several trucks were leaving, but Kane was nowhere to be seen.

Sean couldn't risk shooting at the trucks, not knowing if Kane was inside.

"Dammit!"

How did they know where they were? Someone . . . Gabriella. She betrayed Kane. Which put not only Kane in danger, but Jesse.

Suddenly two men burst out of the bushes, guns on Sean. "Two for one," one of the guys said in Spanish.

Sean didn't hesitate: He took his bike from idle to as fast as it would go toward Kane's jeep, using the vehicle to shield him. They were firing indiscriminately, didn't come close to hitting him. As soon as he was protected by the metal, Sean jumped off the bike and fired at the two men. They returned fire, hitting the jeep. If they hit Sean it would be from luck, because they didn't know what they were doing. Sean focused, aimed, took one then the other down.

He looked down the road. He'd seen the last truck turn right. He assumed going to the Flores compound, but he didn't know. Damn, damn, damn!

"Dammit Kane, what went wrong?" Sean was not going to lose his brother. It wasn't an option. He grabbed his satchel, slung it over his shoulders, and left the marginal safety of the jeep to search the two men he'd taken out. A radio, maybe—anything.

The first guy was dead, and Sean retrieved a handgun and grabbed his AK-47 and slung it over his shoulder. He didn't have a radio, but Sean found a cell phone in his pocket. He avoided looking at the man's face. He was young. Too young to be in the middle of this war.

Maybe it wasn't Gabriella. Kane shouldn't be here at all. Sean should have taken this job on his own. Jesse was his son, his responsibility. There was a bounty on Kane's head; anyone could have spotted him. At the football game last night. When he went to town to meet with Gabriella. Or Dante Romero turned on him.

The bastard. Sean would kill him if anything happened to Kane.

Sean turned to the second guy and stared at a gun in his face.

Blood poured from the guy's leg and arm, but he was close enough to kill Sean. He spoke rapidly in Spanish and Sean didn't know what he was saying.

Suddenly the guy's head caved in from the side and he fell over, dead.

Sean whirled around, gun in hand, heart racing. Then he heard a whistle. Kane's whistle. He lowered his gun just slightly, and Jack Kincaid jumped out of a tree, landing on both feet. Another man came from the opposite direction. JT Caruso. Jack and JT, the other principals of RCK. Sean almost thought he was injured himself and this was all an illusion.

Jack, Lucy's brother, was a lot like Kane in the way he moved and operated. JT, though he, too, had been in the military years ago, rarely worked in the field anymore. He was the face of RCK, looked more like Rick Stockton or a wealthy businessman. Except now, when he was dressed all in black with a Kevlar vest.

"What the fuck?" Sean demanded.

"We don't have time." Jack pulled a radio off the second guy. "You're good, Sean, but you're not a soldier. Never turn your back on the fallen."

Sean didn't need to be lectured, not now. "They have Kane."

"We know."

Then it was clear. "That was the plan?" Sean said. "I told Kane it was a flawed plan from the beginning, and he said he had another way in! They will kill him. Dammit, Jack!"

"Pull it together, Rogan. I get it—Kane is your brother. Now focus, or I'll tie you up in the fucking plane and get your brother and your son back without you."

Sean forced his heart rate to slow. "You know."

"I needed to know." Jack put his hand on Sean's shoulder. "I would have done the same thing. So would Kane or anyone else. But you have to bury those emotions right now. We have a plan, and I need you. I really need you—but we don't have time to argue. Flores is going to weigh turning Kane over for the highest bounty or killing him. The first option gives us time, but once he disappears it will be next to impossible to find him. We have hours, not days."

"They're going to see this is a trap. They'll beef up security."

"That's where you come in," JT said. He walked over and dropped a duffel bag at Sean's feet. "Open it."

Sean did. Inside was cash and bearer bonds. He flipped through the top stack. "That's millions in bearer bonds alone."

"A million in cash and six million in bearer bonds, give or take."

"Where the hell did you get this?"

"An operation years ago. The less you know, the better. But you're going to go in and buy Kane's freedom."

"They'll never agree."

"Seven million is more than three times the highest bounty. It'll at least buy your way into the compound."

"I need more information. I'm not walking in with seven million and no weapons."

"They'll take your weapons, your cell phone, everything. But that bag has a tracker, and if Carson Spade is their accountant and chief money launderer, he'll be given the bag to verify the authenticity of the bonds. Wherever it goes, we'll find it." Jack stared him in the eye. "Do you trust me?"

"Yes, but—"

"No buts. Do you trust me?"

"Yes."

Sean's heart skipped a beat.

"But don't make me tell Lucy that you got yourself killed trying to save my son. It will tear her apart."

"I have no intention of letting any of us die tonight." He looked at his watch and nodded to JT. "It's time."

JT left. Sean wished he had more information. He didn't like going in blind. Without knowing who else was out there, who wanted to kill Kane, how he was going to save his son.

Jack said, "Sean, this is how it's going down. I don't need to tell you that anything can happen, but I trust you, Sean. You're smarter on your feet than anyone I've worked with before."

"I'm not a soldier," he said, quoting what Jack said to him.

"And that is why this is going to work. JT isn't the only backup we have—we have Matt Elliott in the wings."

"The prosecutor?"

"He was a SEAL with JT. They work well together. And if everything goes south, we'll need a diplomat. Now listen. It's important you play this right."

When his dad came back from town, he was in a really bad mood, so Jesse stayed away from him. All he would say was that the bank was fine, but businesses in the States were falling apart.

"Then can't we go home?"

"Jesse, it's not that easy," he said. "Just—just go play your video games."

"Can I call my mom?"

"Later! Jeez, can't you see I have a hundred things to do right now? You're a big boy, do you need to talk to your mom every day?"

He walked away.

"Jesse, I'm sorry—" his dad began.

"It's fine," he mumbled and went back to his room.

Earlier he'd seen Gabriella come in and thought they could play pool—Dominick had a wicked cool pool table in a gigantic room designed like some scene from a James Bond movie. They'd played the first day Jesse was here—him, Gabriella, Jose, and one of the guys who worked for Dominick. They'd had fun.

But Gabriella said, "I can't, Jess, I'm sorry. Maybe later. By the way, I found your game in the atrium. You shouldn't leave your stuff lying around." She handed it to him. "I know you like to play all the time."

He didn't remember leaving it anywhere, but he'd been looking for it.

"Thanks," he mumbled.

So first Gabriella then his dad. *Play your stupid games.* That's what they thought, because no grown-up liked games. Jose did, and he was fun, but he was also . . . well, he wasn't really all that smart. What would his grandmother say? Simple. Yeah, he was simple, but nice. Nothing like his brothers.

Jesse pulled his DS out of its sleeve and a paper fell to the floor. He picked it up. It was folded over, no name on the outside. He hadn't put it there. Had Gabriella slipped him a note? It had to be.

He opened it. It wasn't written in girl writing. Small, clear printing slanted to the right.

Jesse ~
I'm sorry I scared you last night at the football game. I approached you all wrong. Forgive me.
I was asked by your mother Madison to find you and your stepfather and bring you both home. It wasn't until I got to

Acapulco that I learned that Carson Spade launders money for
a drug cartel. Now, my only concern is bringing you back to
the States safe.

You deserve the truth. I don't want to tell you in a letter,
but I need you to trust me and my brother. I am your biological
father. I knew your mother when we were both at Stanford.
She told me Monday that you were born. I didn't even know
she was pregnant. If I had . . . everything would be different.
I hope we get a chance to talk about this soon. But for now
know that I will do everything in my power to get you out of
that house. It's more dangerous than you know.

My brother Kane used to be in the Marines. He's going to
come for you tonight. Be ready. Unlock your window and the
set of French doors into your suite. When he gets there, do
exactly what he says. I trust Kane with my life. More, I trust
him with yours.

I don't know you, Jesse, but I love you. You are my son.
You are a Rogan. And that means you are both strong and
smart. Be both tonight.

                                                    ~ Sean

Sean walked into Dante Romero's house after his thugs
disarmed him.

"I want my gun back," Sean said.

"So you're Little Rogan. How long has it been? Twenty
years?"

"Gun."

"When you leave."

"Your sister betrayed Kane."

"And what? You plan on killing me?" Dante smiled.
"And I heard you were the smart Rogan."

The comparison between Dante Romero and Sean's
brother Liam was right on, he thought. They had the same
innate cockiness and superiority complex . . . and the
same distrustful attitude.

"She promised she would help . . . then turned him over to Flores. I have enough money to buy his freedom."

"I doubt that."

"Don't."

"What I mean is, Kane's head is priceless."

"I will get my brother back."

"You're not like them, are you?"

"What the fuck do you mean?"

Dante waved Sean over into another room. "Relax, Sean. The Romeros and Rogans go way back."

Sean couldn't relax. He was worried about Kane and Jesse and he wanted to kill Carson Spade. Sean didn't like that part of him, the part that would do violence to another. He much preferred destroying people with his brains, not his fists or guns.

Sean hesitated, then followed. Dante was a little older than Liam, who was nearly thirty-six. Just as confident, just as charming. Just as deadly.

Dante led Sean into a well-appointed library. If Sean were in the mood, he would have enjoyed the room, with books and art and a state-of-the-art computer system. Dante waved off his security and closed the door so he and Sean were alone.

"Sit."

"No."

"Kane at least *plays* the game."

Sean grunted out a laugh.

"In his own way." Dante walked over to his desk and leaned back in the leather chair. "You want me to broker a deal."

"I want my brother."

"And your brother wants the kid he was hired to retrieve. Some sort of domestic issue."

"I'm just his pilot."

Now Dante laughed. "Oh, Sean, that is *so* ridiculous.

Do you think I'm an idiot? *Just* a pilot. You think you're immune to this world, flying your brother around and guarding the plane? That anyone would even believe it anymore? The wrong people know *exactly* who you are. You can't be a Rogan on this planet and not have the wrong people keep tabs on you. Your brother did you a grave disservice if he didn't teach you the laws of the universe long ago."

Sean crossed the library and put his hands on Dante's desk. "I want my brother back. I don't care about the kid, I don't care about Flores or your ego or your love–hate relationship with my family. I want Kane. I have seven million dollars—one million in cash and six million in bearer bonds. Call Flores and tell him I want to make a trade."

Dante stared at him for a long minute. Sean could see his brain running through all the possible scenarios. He was definitely intrigued. Then he said, "I want one thing in return."

"What?" Sean said through clenched teeth.

"Not now. But I will call for a favor, and you will not say no."

Sean didn't want to be beholden to this man. He knew nothing about him other than what Kane and Jack had told him. But he knew that Dante was the only one who could broker this deal, and getting that meeting with Flores was crucial to rescuing Kane and Jesse.

"Okay."

Dante smiled. "Kane is a man of his word, and I will assume you are as well. Don't disappoint me."

"Make the call."

"Dear Sean, this is a game I am *exceptionally* good at, do not tell me how to do it. I will call you with a time and place."

"I want my gun back."

"Of course. It's a dangerous city. I would never let you walk out of here unarmed."

Dante made sure Sean Rogan had his weapon and phone returned, then went back to his office.

Six million in bearer bonds.

Kane Rogan was playing a dangerous game, but Dante knew exactly what was going on. Kane, the brilliant fool, had let himself get taken. He wouldn't tell Sean where that money came from, but he knew that as soon as Sean came to him—and who else would Sean go to in Guadalajara who had any information about where Flores was keeping his brother?—that Dante would know exactly what Kane wanted him to do.

But he had Gabriella to think about. His beautiful, smart, revenge-driven sister.

He closed his eyes and played through every scenario he could imagine—something he was exceptionally good at. And in five minutes he realized that Kane must have gotten to Gabriella. Something he said or did or promised had Gabriella helping him.

Possibly. Sometimes, Dante didn't understand his sister. Hell, he didn't understand women. But he did understand Kane Rogan, and he decided that it would be fun to play along and see what happened.

Because Dante knew every party who wanted those bearer bonds. Every. Single. One.

Including the person Kane and JT had originally stolen them from.

It would also greatly benefit him to have Sean Rogan alive.

Sean Rogan who now owed him a favor. A favor that Dante couldn't wait to call in.

Sean Rogan. He hadn't seen him since he was a kid, but

he was everything he expected. A bit hotheaded. Smart. Manipulative. That kid didn't know his value. Or maybe he did . . . which made this deal all the more interesting.

He picked up his secure phone. First he called the eldest Flores brother. Dominick was the only sane one in a family of lunatics. He would take the money over killing Kane—at least, he would be willing to consider it.

It took him a bit of time to get through to Dominick. "What is it, Romero?"

"I've been hired by Rogan's family to negotiate for his return."

"He's not up for negotiation."

"Six million in bearer bonds, plus some cash."

Silence.

"Do you have the money?"

"The family has it."

"Who?"

"Sean Rogan."

"I'll call you back." Dom hung up, but Dante knew the Flores family. They would argue, but they would want the money. So he'd either call back and set up the trade, kill Sean and Kane and take the money, or call back and set up the trade and let Sean negotiate.

This was a dangerous game, because there was no doubt Flores knew that Sean was a computer hacker. These people always wanted the best to help them secure their illegally gotten gains. Of course, Dante understood this because he, too, wanted the best.

Either way, Sean would go to the Flores compound with the money and bonds. And it would happen quickly.

Dante dialed a number he hadn't called in years, but the phone was picked up after two rings.

Dante said, "I found your bonds. And I know who stole them."

He gave the information to his old friend and they discussed what to do about the situation.

Then he made a third call and left a message.

"I have information you want and it's free. You have my number."

He hung up.

Kane Rogan made one fatal mistake. He may know who was looking for the bearer bonds—many people over the years had been looking for them for a variety of reasons—and he may think he would be able to capitalize on that knowledge to create a diversion at the Flores compound. But Dante knew who he'd stolen them from in the first place. And he couldn't wait to expose Kane.

He truly hoped both Kane and Sean survived Dominick Flores and the rest of the Flores clan. Because the real fireworks were to come later.

And Dante, for one, couldn't *wait* to witness that.

CHAPTER TWENTY-SEVEN

Adam Villines walked out onto the porch of Honeycutt's house and told Nate and Lucy, "I have a general location of George's phone."

John came out of the house. "I'm coming with you," he said.

"No," Adam said.

"Adam, you don't understand! This girl—she's been through hell. And now three cops are going to storm her place? She'll be terrified. She needs to see a friendly face!"

Lucy rose from the bench. She still felt queasy, but she was pulling herself together. "John, she will see a friendly face. Siobhan Walsh is a friend of mine. She's been looking for Marisol and Ana ever since they went missing. She'll be with us." Lucy pulled the photo of Marisol, Ana, and Siobhan from her file. "This is Siobhan with the girls when they were younger."

"But—"

Adam put his hand on John's shoulder. They were both tall men, but Adam was broader and more muscular than his brother-in-law. "Johnny, stay with your parents tonight. Keep the house locked up, guns by your side, just in case. Call me if there is anything suspicious going on. And I give you my word, we'll do everything to help those girls."

John nodded, though he still looked unhappy. "Thank you, Adam." He turned to Lucy. "Anything my parents and I can do, we'll do. We don't have a lot of money, but we have this property—a safe place for them to stay. Food. My mom was a school nurse for thirty-five years, she can take care of them. Their—special needs."

The compassion she witnessed helped Lucy more than she could have explained to John or anyone. Here was a family willing to share everything they had to help someone they had just met. Not just Marisol, but *them*. Both the girls. The babies. The Honeycutts were the light in the world, a light Lucy desperately needed right then.

"Thank you," she said quietly. "I'll make sure Marisol knows."

They walked back to the cars after John went back inside. Adam said, "He should have called me when he found her, I'm sorry."

"She's scared of authority, but he's a good man. Don't be hard on him—you have a good family here," Lucy said.

"I do," Adam said with pride. "They just should have trusted me."

"They do. But you and I both know that not all cops are the good guys. And Marisol didn't know if anyone would believe her, or even where she was. She knew there's at least one bad cop in the neighboring county. It would be smart for her captors to bring in one man in uniform to intimidate the girls, so they would be scared to go to the police."

Nate opened his door. "Where are we going?"

Adam gave them the street. "The phone company couldn't pinpoint the exact address, but they gave us a radius downtown. There are several motels in the area, restaurants, some apartments and businesses."

"If Angelo did in fact pick her up, he may have taken her to a motel. Let's check there first, show both their photos." Lucy turned to Nate. "Did Zach come through on Angelo?"

"No known record, at least in the US. Has a Mexican passport, and he used it to fly into Laredo on Friday afternoon."

"He flew? It's a what, four-hour drive or so?"

"About that," Adam said. "So he's been here since Friday." He frowned.

Lucy nodded. "You're on the right path, Adam—he knew she was missing before she called him."

"She could have contacted him before Tuesday morning," Adam said.

"That wasn't my impression after talking to the Honeycutts. They seemed to think she hadn't spoken to him in two years."

Adam rubbed his face. "I'll call in backup."

"And I need to alert Siobhan. John is right, Marisol needs a familiar face, and she'll trust Siobhan."

On the drive back to Laredo, Lucy called Siobhan and told her to meet them at an intersection near the two motels. She didn't give her any more information, though Siobhan had questions. She quickly got off the phone and called Noah. She filled him in on everything they had, and then gave him her theory. He was silent when she was done.

"I'll run Zapelli's name up the food chain. He may not have a record and he may not be flagged, but that doesn't mean he's not on someone's radar. I'm on my way down."

"To Laredo?"

"Hooper arrived and he's working with the AUSA serving warrants and getting things done. I swear, that guy is just brilliant. White collar is over my head, and I'm the first to admit it. I won't know what I'm looking at, and Hooper has done this for years. His specialty is human traffic laundering—his wife is an ICE agent and he's made great inroads in tracking the money with her help in understanding the business of buying and selling humans. Besides, I've already pissed off half the office, why not piss off the other half?"

"Because it's not like you. You're the diplomat."

He laughed. He sounded like he was in a much better mood than when they first were stymied by the law firm. "I try to be, but sometimes it takes too long. Keep me in the loop. I'm already on the road, I'll be there in an hour."

Fifteen minutes later, Noah called Lucy back. "We have a location on Angelo Zapelli."

"That was fast."

"He just checked into the airport in Laredo. Zach had put him on the watch list just five minutes before, and bam, we just got the notification. His flight leaves in forty-two minutes, I'm working on getting him detained, but get there as soon as you can."

It didn't take long for Lucy and Nate to arrive at the airport. Homeland Security had detained Zapelli and he sat in a small room. They stared at him through the one-way glass.

Angelo Zapelli was an attractive twenty-six-year-old with the suave good looks of someone with the perfect blend of Italian and Mexican genes. Lucy could see how the story unfolded—he'd showed Marisol attention, she was flattered and completely unschooled in flirting, and he used that. Got her to trust him, sold her into sex trafficking, covered it up . . . but she *had* trusted him. That meant not only did she not know he was the one who set her up, he had probably been doing it for years.

Siobhan had wanted to confront him, but Lucy told her over the phone to work with Adam Villines. "We traced the cell phone the Honeycutts gave her, she needs a friendly face."

"You're right. Okay."

"I talked to Villines. Do what he says. He's one of the good guys. If you find Marisol, call me."

"You ready?" Nate asked Lucy when she hung up.

Lucy nodded. "If he's really selling young women into the sex business, he's not going to have any respect for me."

"We can play off that."

"He's not going to give it up easily."

"We have some leeway here. He's wanted for questioning and attempting to flee the country."

"He'll say he didn't know he was wanted for questioning."

Her phone rang and she frowned at the interruption. It was Villines. "Yes, Sheriff?"

"We found his motel. They haven't cleaned his room yet, and the motel is giving us permission to search. I also have two officers at the car rental kiosk working on getting the car before they clean it. We have a good chance— if our girl was in that vehicle, I hope to be able to prove it. Just wanted you to know."

"Text me if you find anything useful, particularly if you can prove that Marisol was in the car or the motel. Have you found the phone?"

"Not yet, but I have one of my best guys on it and working with the phone company. They know it's urgent, I will let you know as soon as I know."

"Thanks, Adam." She hung up and relayed the information to Nate.

The officer with the Department of Homeland Security who had detained Zapelli approached them. "We've put Mr. Zapelli on the no-fly list as your boss requested, and we have his passport. We also retrieved his luggage; it's in a secure room with his carry-on."

"Thank you," Nate said. "We're expecting Agent Armstrong shortly, if you can bring him here when he arrives."

"I'll notify the security office."

Lucy said, "Nate, let's search his bags first. I want to make him sit around, it'll make him mad. Angry criminals tend to slip up." They didn't need a warrant because any bags that went through airport security were subject to search and seizure.

"This way," the officer said and led them down a hall.

Zapelli had checked one medium-sized suitcase and had one laptop in a carrying case. The laptop was off. They would need a warrant to access the hard drive, and Lucy sent Noah that information. He seemed to be in a position to expedite these things.

They pulled on gloves and began a thorough search. The DHS officer asked, "Do you know what you're looking for?"

Lucy didn't answer. Nate made small talk.

Zapelli had several changes of clothes appropriate for the weather. He had excessive grooming products, including four kinds of mousse and gel, cologne, expensive shampoo and conditioner. His clothes had been neatly—almost obsessively—folded, and his dirty clothes were in a plastic bag—also folded.

Nothing jumped out at her. She stared at the clothing and toiletries. Nate put the contents of the laptop case next to them. "Receipts for gas, rental car, food, motel. The rental car traveled seven hundred twenty-one miles from when he picked it up on Friday to when he returned it this afternoon."

"That's a lot of miles," Lucy said. She flipped through the receipts. There was a coffee receipt from a coffee shop across from the motel, gas in Laredo and Del Rio. "He was in Del Rio," she said almost to herself. "He filled up Tuesday afternoon there. Only hours after Noah and I talked to

Musgrove." She took the receipts and made a story from them. He may have tossed a few, but there were enough receipts here that she could create a time line. What did he plan on doing, getting reimbursed from someone?

"He arrived in town early Friday afternoon. Checked into the motel, had lunch across the street." She moved a few pieces around. "He had dinner in Freer that night. That would be the closest town to Our Lady of Sorrows." There was nothing for Saturday, nothing to indicate whether he had returned to the motel; they would have to check with motel security—if there was any. "He ate with three other people on Friday," she said, pointing to the items on the receipt. "He paid. Marisol had already left the house, they didn't know where she was. She was traveling across open land until she stumbled into the Honeycutt barn."

Nate slid over a receipt from five o'clock Monday morning. "This is a gas receipt near San Antonio."

She had never heard of the small town, but she believed Nate. "So he comes to Laredo, goes to Freer because that's where Marisol disappeared. Possibly back to Laredo, then to San Antonio at some point, probably Sunday."

Nate moved another receipt. "He wouldn't need to fill up his gas tank just driving from San Antonio to Del Rio, but he was nearly on empty when he filled up in Del Rio on Tuesday morning."

"That's a lot of driving around."

"And the tank was nearly empty when he filled it up this afternoon before turning it in at the airport."

"Del Rio to Laredo, halfway to Freer, back again?"

"Possibly. Maybe with another fifty or sixty miles in there somewhere."

"If we assume he is the one who met Marisol after she called him on Tuesday night, he must have taken her someplace in a fifty-mile radius. The house outside Freer is empty, but we don't yet have the files from the property management company."

Lucy considered their options. "Noah and I only spoke to one person in Del Rio. Leo Musgrove. He was angry, thought we'd exposed him. Slimy bastard. But he'd originally moved the girls to the brothel. What if he works for Zapelli? Or Zapelli knew he was a loose end?" She sent Noah a message that Musgrove might have slipped town or that Zapelli may have talked to him on Tuesday. She moved the papers around. "He was back in Laredo at two p.m.—stopped at the Starbucks off I-35, I remember passing that on our way to Del Rio. Tried to convince Noah to stop, but he said I'd already had too much caffeine." She almost smiled. Then she froze. "What's this?"

She picked up two strands of long black hair that had been entwined in the buckle of the laptop case.

Nate pulled out an evidence bag, and she slipped the hairs inside. "If we can put Marisol with Zapelli, that gives us an edge," Nate said.

"Let's pretend we already did," she said.

As they'd agreed, Nate took the lead. If Zapelli was who they thought he was, he would be more responsive to a male authority figure.

"Mr. Zapelli," Nate said. "I'm Special Agent Dunning and this is Special Agent Kincaid. We're with the Federal Bureau of Investigation and we have a few questions for you." He sat down and took out a pen and small notepad. Lucy sat next to him and focused on watching Zapelli for the small psychological cues that might help them steer the conversation.

Zapelli smiled at her a moment too long, then turned back to Nate. "Agent Dunning, I have been very reasonable with your authorities after I was detained in security.

I have no idea why, my luggage had no paraphernalia, as I'm certain you uncovered when you searched it."

"What was the reason for your visit to the States?"

"Just needed some time away from family and work obligations."

"You told your mother that a friend called and needed your help."

It was immediately clear that Zapelli had not expected that they would have spoken to his family. He covered quickly and said, "My mother is elderly. I couldn't very well tell her I needed a break from her and her constant errands. I am an only son. I'm responsible for many things at my father's business and at home. I gave her an excuse that allowed me to remain a good son."

Nate nodded, made a note. "What did you do while you were in Texas?"

He shrugged. "The usual."

"If you can please be more specific."

Zapelli was suspicious and trying not to act it, Lucy noted. "Is there a reason why you're asking me these questions?"

"Yes," Nate said, and nothing more.

"And?" Zapelli pushed.

"And we'd like to know."

Zapelli leaned back. "I don't like the direction of this conversation."

Lucy's phone vibrated. She glanced down. Villines had sent her the Honeycutts' phone records. Someone had called Zapelli Tuesday at ten-thirty a.m. and spoke to him for six minutes.

Nate gave Lucy a nod, and she said, "We have a record that Marisol de la Rosa called you yesterday morning. You spoke to her for six minutes. Ms. de la Rosa is now missing, and she told witnesses that she was meeting you at seven o'clock last night."

Zapelli may be an arrogant and overly confident criminal, but he couldn't hide his surprise that they had not only that information, but Marisol's name as well. He glared at her, then covered, just not quickly enough.

"Marisol—the girl who worked for my dad? That was ages ago."

"Yet you spoke to her yesterday."

He didn't say anything.

"If you didn't speak to her, who did you talk to for those six minutes?" Lucy asked.

Zapelli turned to Nate. "Yes, I spoke to Marisol. She called me, said she was in trouble. I of course wanted to help. I offered to pick her up—my father has been greatly worried about her and her sister. They left, no notice, nothing. We assumed they went back to their village, but girls like them, they look for the easy way, if you know what I mean." He winked at Lucy.

Through sheer willpower, she kept her poker face. Nate said, "When did you see her?"

"I didn't. She never arrived. I waited for nearly an hour."

"Where?" Lucy demanded. She bit her tongue. She was coming off too strong.

"At a four-way stop on Highway Fifty-Nine."

"Don't you think that was odd?" Nate asked.

"I did, but figured she was on foot. When she didn't come, I assumed she'd gone back to whatever sugar daddy she came to the States with. Like I said, those kind of girls are predictable."

"Why were you in Del Rio yesterday morning?" Nate asked, completely changing the subject to throw Zapelli off-guard.

It did, just for a minute. "Visiting a friend."

"Name?"

Zapelli shook his head. "I don't know what you hope

to find, but I think we're done. I need to get home, my father needs me to help run his business."

"You're not leaving," Nate said.

"You can't detain me."

"You're a material witness in an ongoing investigation."

"I told you, I didn't see Marisol."

"We found strands of long black hair on your laptop case. We're testing it now," Lucy said, "and my guess, it belongs to Ms. de la Rosa."

He stopped talking. Right then and there. "Either arrest me or let me go."

"Very well," Nate said. "You are under arrest."

"Why?"

"We don't need to give you a reason right now. We can hold you for up to seventy-two hours just because you're an asshole."

"I want a lawyer."

"I was just getting to that point." Nate read him his rights.

Zapelli grew increasingly frustrated. "This is bullshit," he said.

"You may exercise your right to remain silent now," Lucy said.

He lunged for her. It happened so fast, Lucy almost missed it. Nate didn't. He was up and between Zapelli and Lucy so fast she barely saw him move. Nate didn't say a word; his expression spoke volumes. Zapelli froze.

"Turn around," Nate said in a low voice. "Put your hands on the back of your head." He got out his cuffs.

"You can't do this," Zapelli said. "I've done nothing. This is bullshit, and you know it. I don't know what that bitch has been saying about me, but I've done *nothing*. I came here to help her. That's all I did."

"Did? So you did see her?" Lucy asked.

"That's not what I said!"

"Yes it is. You helped her how?"

"I don't have to answer your questions without a lawyer!"

"That is correct," Nate said. He searched the guy after he cuffed him.

"They already did that!" Zapelli said.

"Procedure," Nate replied.

The process humiliated Zapelli, making him turn red and even angrier. Angry criminals talked.

"You're all screwed," Zapelli said. "None of you will get out of this alive."

Nate pushed him against the wall. He held him there without much effort. "Is that a threat?"

Zapelli scowled.

Nate held on to him and said to Lucy, "Grab the recording, I want to make sure his threat is loud and clear for the judge when we arraign him. Threatening a federal officer is a felony."

"Yes it is," Lucy said.

Nate turned Zapelli over to two DHS guards and said, "He gets one call, to his attorney, and that's it. You have a cell in this place, right?"

"Yes, sir."

"Put him in it, do not let him out unless I or my boss, Noah Armstrong, authorizes it."

"Yes, sir."

They waited until Zapelli was gone. "I wanted to break his neck," Nate said.

"He didn't slip much. Nothing that we can use with a judge."

"He threatened us. That's good enough for me to arrest him. I didn't even raise my voice."

"You never do."

Villines called. "Kincaid? We hit the lottery. The rental car has a GPS system and guess what? Our number one suspect used it extensively. I'm sending you the printout of everywhere he's been since he picked up the sedan."

CHAPTER TWENTY-EIGHT

By the time they regrouped at Villines's office, Noah had arrived and Villines himself had already mapped out the route Angelo Zapelli had taken. Lucy suspected that because his in-laws were involved, he wanted this done quickly and done right. He had assembled a small group of deputies to help them.

"You are in this room because I know each and every one of you and your families. Because this is a sensitive situation, I want to make sure that whatever we find is handled with complete discretion and sensitivity." He stared at everyone in turn to drive home his point. "I'm turning this over to Supervisory Special Agent Noah Armstrong, who has been instrumental in keeping this office in the loop as far as the FBI investigation goes, which I appreciate."

A stamp of approval for federal involvement in a local office made the whole process run smoother.

Noah stood, thanked Villines, and said, "I'm going to be as brief as possible. I'm not from Texas; you all know this area far better than I do. I'm originally from Colorado Springs, I served ten years in the Air Force, and for the last five years have been working out of the Washington,

DC, Regional FBI Office. I'm running the San Antonio Violent Crimes Squad temporarily while the current SSA is on paternity leave."

Lucy had never known Noah was from Colorado. What else didn't she know about him? She felt awkward, like she should have asked—they'd become friends over the last two years, but she knew so little about him.

"My partner Agent Kincaid and I were sent to Freer to take the statement of a photojournalist who has been looking for two missing young women, Marisol and Ana de la Rosa, who disappeared over two years ago from Monterrey, Mexico. She has known these women their entire lives and believed they had been kidnapped or manipulated into the sex trade. Ms. Walsh followed a trail that led her here, after the abandoned baby known as Baby Elizabeth was left at the door of a Catholic church outside Freer.

"Assistant Sheriff Villines has already distributed photos of the two sisters. However, we believe there are more women who may have been held captive by the same criminal organization. And while they may have started out being trafficked into border cities, we believe that these particular young women have been used as breeders. Agent Kincaid uncovered evidence from a nurse involved in the conspiracy that seventy-two infants were born to women like the de la Rosa sisters and sold into the black market over the last two years. One woman known only as Eloise was found dead in a Dumpster, her baby boy cut from her womb. She was shot in the back of the head."

He let that information sink in. He had everyone's attention.

"Witnesses who found Marisol de la Rosa contacted your office; unfortunately, Marisol met up with a man she believed she could trust, who may have killed her or taken her back to the people she ran from. We believe that Marisol is the mother of Baby Elizabeth, and left her baby at the church in an effort to protect her from a black-market sale.

"What Deputy Villines and I need is for you to assist us in visiting every place that Mr. Zapelli went during his five days in Texas. Mr. Zapelli has been detained and is in custody at the airport pending transport to a federal jail prior to his arraignment. I won't lie to you—we don't have much evidence against him. He has a lawyer and has stopped talking. He gave us no information on the whereabouts of these girls, and denied seeing Marisol. However, physical evidence found on his belongings is being tested to see if it matches the young woman; if so, we will arrest him on felony kidnapping charges. We are going on the assumption that she was with him at some point Tuesday night. Right now, we're holding Zapelli for threatening a federal agent, as a material witness to a felony, and because he's a foreign national and a flight risk. A good lawyer will get him out in a matter of days.

"We need to find Marisol, who can testify against Zapelli. But we are also looking for her sister, who is nearing the end of a high-risk pregnancy with twins, and up to twelve other women whom we believe were impregnated solely to deliver babies into the black market. All the evidence we have uncovered shows that this was done to them against their will. They are the victims, and they need to be treated as such."

There were a few questions, but the assembled force seemed eager to hit the streets. Villines made the assignments, even sending two officers to Del Rio to check out the place Zapelli was parked overnight. He finished by saying, "If you find these girls, contact me immediately. Siobhan Walsh, the photojournalist, personally knows them and she can help facilitate their cooperation so they know we're here to help."

Lucy glanced at Siobhan, who was standing in the back of the room. Siobhan looked like she was running on fumes. Lucy had assumed that Siobhan had seen bad stuff as part of her job. Lucy had seen many of her photos—poverty and pain interspersed with beauty and love and the simple life. The Sisters of Mercy primarily worked on helping poor villages learn to care for themselves in the basics of hygiene, agriculture, building homes, medicine. But in that, there was death and poverty and tragedy, like the mudslide that had killed half the people in the de la Rosas' village. To Lucy, that would be emotionally and physically devastating, yet what was going on here seemed to overwhelm Siobhan, and Lucy didn't understand why.

When Villines was done, Lucy approached her. "Are you okay?"

She nodded, but Lucy didn't believe it.

"What is it?" she pushed.

"Why didn't she call me? Why didn't she come to me for help? Didn't she know I would drop everything, fly from any corner of the world, to help her?"

Lucy didn't know how to respond. All she could say was, "She believed Angelo would help her. She probably was in love with him, trusted him. She was wrong. You don't know what she's been thinking over the last two years. But—she kept your locket. She put it around her baby's neck. That means something."

Siobhan nodded, but her eyes were a million miles away.

Noah said, "Let's go. Siobhan, wait for us here." She didn't answer, but let them go.

Lucy followed Noah out. "Where's Nate?"

"He went with Villines. You and I have two places on our list. Villines gave us a deputy who knows the area."

A young deputy walked up to them. He had the darker skin of a Mexican-Indian and the long black hair to match.

"Deputy Ezekiel Medicine Crow. Call me Ike. I'm a rookie, but I was born and bred here in Laredo. I can get you anywhere."

Noah handed him the map Villines had given him. "These two places. Closest one first."

"Yes, sir."

"I know this address," Lucy said. "This is Loretta Martinez's house."

"It's the first stop he made before going to Freer on Friday," Noah said.

"He may have been the one who beat her up. I just assumed that she was attacked after Marisol escaped."

"You didn't ask?"

Lucy shook her head. "It was a bad assumption. She denied being beaten, said she'd fallen, and I was looking for information about Marisol."

"We'll drive by, see if there's anything else there, then hit the second place."

There was nothing useful at Loretta's house. It was clear no one had been back since the paramedics took her in. Villines had reported that she was still in critical condition, but Lucy didn't know the status of her injuries or if the surgery had been successful.

The second place was a warehouse outside of town that Zapelli had visited right before he went to the airport. It was isolated at the end of a long line of large square buildings, half seemingly abandoned, some with faded FOR LEASE signs, the others a hodgepodge of services: an autobody shop, a moving company, a printing press.

"We have no way of knowing which he visited," Lucy said. The GPS puts him in this general area, but not in an exact spot."

Ike said, "Most of these businesses have been shut down for years. We had some problems out here with gangs, and there was a meth lab running in one of the empty buildings for about eight months before the DEA shut them down, but nothing recent."

They got out and looked around. Talked to the businesses that were open, showed his photo, but no one claimed to know Zapelli.

Lucy was going to suggest they inspect the empty buildings, but Noah put his hand up and answered his phone. "We'll be right there."

He hung up. "That was Villines. They found some of the girls. It's bad."

They were at a house halfway between Laredo and Del Rio. The word *house* was kind. There was what first appeared to be an abandoned warehouse with several trailers and four large, malnourished guard dogs on the other side of the chained-off yard. By the time Lucy and Noah arrived, they'd been tranquilized and Animal Control was taking them to their facility. A fire truck was parked outside as well as two ambulances. Villines's team searched each building. Spotlights had been brought in, and every vehicle had its headlights shining into the fenced area.

Villines approached them and said, "The trailer is on the brink of collapse. We cleared the place—none of the suspects we're looking for are there, but we have five women inside. Two are obviously pregnant; the other two are traumatized and in shock. One is deceased. There are no neighbors, there's nothing in a five-mile radius."

A paramedic came out of the trailer and approached Villines. "Sheriff, the fire chief says there's a gas leak, he wants the women cleared out immediately. But the trailer is listing, we have to do this carefully and with minimal personnel. I've sent for two more gurneys, they should be here ASAP."

"Is the gas leak intentional?" Villines asked. "Were they attempting to kill the women?"

"I can't say. It's probably because the structure is in such awful condition. There's no water, no power, I don't know where the gas is coming from because there isn't service to the house, but it could be a faulty line."

Siobhan arrived with one of Villines's deputies. "I need to help."

"You will," Lucy said, "when we get the girls out. We need a triage area away from this structure."

The paramedic nodded. "We're already set up on the other side of the fire truck. We have two paramedics and two EMTs on site, another ambulance is on its way, and the coroner."

He left to talk to the fire chief.

"Was that bastard Zapelli here?" Siobhan asked. "Left those women in these horrid conditions?"

"They were likely moved after Marisol escaped," Lucy said. "Except for Eloise and Macey, who were left in Freer." She wanted to talk to Loretta again and search her house thoroughly. There had to be a better record of those seventy-two births than the book Lucy found. How many different women . . . where they delivered . . . where they were sent after they gave birth. Lucy wanted to know that they found everyone, that no woman had been left behind to endure more pain and suffering and loss.

"Who died?" Siobhan asked, her voice quivering. "It's not—Marisol? He killed her, didn't he?"

Lucy turned to Siobhan. "We don't know. Go over to the triage area and wait, you can help translate, and they'll want to talk to a woman." Or not talk at all. Lucy hadn't wanted to tell anyone anything after she'd been held captive and raped for two days. She didn't want to talk about it. She still didn't, eight years later.

Lucy glanced at Nate, and he nodded and led Siobhan away. Lucy turned to Noah. "They planned to come back," she said. "Two pregnant women? That's money for them. They wouldn't just leave them here. The other house was clean, sterilized. This place?" She shook her head.

"They had to move fast. Maybe they didn't have another location. Plus, this place is easy to get to on the back roads, no freeways, no neighbors. Temporary."

"And you said you didn't know Texas."

"I can read a map. I'm a quick study. In fact, there's a road that goes almost straight from Freer to here, bypassing Laredo altogether."

"I don't see Zapelli staying here. He was far too neat, too fastidious."

Noah looked at the time line that Villines and Lucy had prepared. "He was here Monday night for thirty minutes, then again Tuesday morning for forty or so minutes. You said he filled up his tank in Del Rio, correct?"

"Tuesday morning."

"We need to track down Leo Musgrove. Want to bet Musgrove called him to tell him we were asking questions?"

"I won't take that bet. The motel he stayed at is less than a mile from the bar we cornered Musgrove in."

Two paramedics were carrying one pregnant woman out on a board because the gurney couldn't fit through the narrow, rotted door frame. A deputy came out escorting a petite young woman who was able to walk. She wasn't pregnant—at least, she didn't appear to be.

Lucy watched as the paramedics and deputies brought out each of the girls.

The last—the last living girl—was very pregnant. The fire chief carried her out himself and put her on a gurney. "Medics! Stat!"

Siobhan was watching closely and cried out, "Ana! It's Ana!" She ran to the edge of the fence as the paramedics came through.

"Siobhan—let them work."

Ana's eyes were full of fear, but they rested on Siobhan as if she were seeing a ghost. "Siobhan?" she whispered. "Siobhan?"

She began to cry. Siobhan took her hand. "Thank God, thank God, you're alive."

"We need to get her to the hospital, *stat*," the paramedic said. He gestured to her legs as he carefully put a blanket over her.

Her right leg was broken. The swelling and bruising were severe.

"I want to go. Please," Siobhan said.

Lucy said, "She's a translator, knows this girl." She showed her badge to the paramedic.

He nodded. "We go now."

Lucy watched as Siobhan left with Ana in the ambulance.

Noah came up to them. "Villines and I are going to check on another property—see if you can talk to the girls before they're transported."

He left, and Lucy walked over to where the two girls who weren't obviously pregnant were being treated by a lone paramedic. The two ambulances had already left. She said in Spanish, "We're getting you help. A doctor."

The paramedic was fluent and had put them both at ease. They were crying, but one of them said in English without any trace of an accent, "I want to call my mom."

"Where are you from?"

Tears streamed down her face. "I—I'm from Houston. I ran away last year with my boyfriend. And . . . and it got bad. He . . . he hit me. And then . . . he left. And I was pregnant and my mom . . . my mom told me if I left with him never to come home."

"Honey, mothers are forgiving. What's your name?"

"Abby Bridger." She drew in a deep breath. "I-I just want my mom."

"How did you end up here?"

"I thought . . . I thought if I had an abortion everything would be better. I could go home, beg my mom to forgive me, never tell anyone. I went to a clinic and they put me under and I woke up somewhere else."

"When was this?"

"February. And . . . and I had my baby last month and I wanted her so badly and begged them not to take her, but they did."

"Why didn't they let you go?"

"I don't know, I didn't ask, I didn't want to go, where would I go?" She squeezed the hand of the girl next to her. "It's all my fault."

"Abby, none of this is your fault. None of it, okay?" Lucy took her other hand, the one that wasn't clutching her friend. Both girls were staring at her with wide, dirty eyes. "These people forced you into this, terrified you, hurt you. Took your baby. Kept you prisoner. They will pay for it." She took out a photo of the house in Freer. "Is this where you were staying?"

Abby nodded. "Since April. First we were someplace else, but it burned down. I think they burned it down on purpose. And then we were there. Until . . ." She stopped talking.

"Until one of the women ran away with a baby."

"They took us all, except Eloise. Did you find her? Is she okay? She was so worried about her baby. She's very sick."

Lucy softened her voice. "Eloise died. I'm sorry. We think her baby survived."

"No. No!"

"We're looking for Marisol. Her sister Ana was here—have you seen her?"

She shook her head. "No one has come for us. They were looking for Marisol."

"Abby, I need you to be strong. You're going to the hospital. There will be a police guard there to protect you—to protect all of you. But honey, we need you to tell us everything you know. We need everything you know about these people, what they said and did and who they are. We need more information to stop them."

"Will—will you call my mom? Explain everything to her? Tell her I'm sorry?"

"Yes—but Abby, the first thing you need to do is remember this. Remember it forever: This is not your fault."

The paramedic took the girls together in the third ambulance and Lucy watched it drive off. Nate said, "One of the deputies confirmed that the dead girl isn't Marisol."

Lucy wanted to be happy about it, but she was so weary.

"I want to show you something." He handed her a photocopy of Loretta's book. "We didn't have time to go through it, but I noticed something. You pointed out that Elizabeth wasn't Marisol's first baby."

"I'm assuming that both Marisols in the book are the same person." Lucy flipped through the pages. "Jasmine and her people picked immigrants—legal or illegal, it didn't matter—who didn't have family connections because they would be the least likely to go to the authorities. Or runaways like Abby who had lost hope."

"How do you know?"

"I don't know as a fact, just an educated guess based on what we've seen already. I thought Macey was an outlier because she was Caucasian, until Abby. Did you notice that the baby boy was Macey's second delivery? Just like Marisol." She frowned.

"That's what I wanted to show you. The dates."

She stared. Marisol was the third delivery in the book,

and the last. Marisol had given birth six months *after* she'd disappeared from Monterrey.

"That bastard."

"You're thinking what I'm thinking."

"Zapelli. Marisol was pregnant in Monterrey. Want to bet it was his kid? That's why she trusted him. How could a father sell his girlfriend and his unborn child into the sex trade?"

"Lucy, you know as well as I do that he probably killed her when he picked her up Tuesday night."

"Then dammit, I want to bury her body."

She flipped through the copy again. The babies were few and far between—some of them months—during the first year. The program must have become lucrative because more than half the seventy-two babies had been born in the last nine months. She took some quick notes. "Nate, there were fourteen girls pregnant at one time just last month—including Marisol and Ana. The house in Freer only had eight beds. There must be another place. More girls."

"Hopefully not like that trailer."

"I think the trailer was a way station. They had to put them someplace, they were angry because Marisol had not only escaped, but had taken her baby with her, and in doing so brought down the authorities. Eight beds—" She gestured toward the trailer where the deputies were bringing out a body bag. "Five girls here. Plus Eloise, Macey, and Marisol."

She paused. "Zapelli had to have known about this baby ring, and when Marisol told him she was pregnant, he sold her—and her baby."

"Then why did she call him?"

"Because she didn't know that he'd done it. I don't think Loretta knew, otherwise she would have rubbed it in—she complained that Marisol went on and on about Angelo saving them. And he was the person she trusted the most to call when she escaped." Shouldn't she have seen the truth? Maybe not. Zapelli was a slimy bastard, but maybe he had a charming side. Marisol and Ana were girls from the country. They might not see the wolf in sheep's clothing.

After finding Marisol, there was nothing Lucy wanted more than to see Angelo in prison. And Marisol would help put him there.

That may give her some satisfaction. Some peace.

Death is the only peace. Would it have given you peace if Adam Scott had been arrested? Prosecuted? Living behind bars? Hardly. You killed him because he was evil and would have raped and murdered again and again until he was dead.

She couldn't go there. Not now. Not when her emotions were so . . . jumbled.

Nate picked up his phone. "It's Noah," he said to Lucy. "Noah, you're on speaker. Lucy's here."

"We traced the Honeycutt phone to a house just outside Laredo, fifteen minutes south from the trailer. I sent you the address. As deputies attempted to reach out to the occupants, they fired shots. Put on your vests if you haven't already done so—we have one cop in critical condition and they have multiple hostages."

CHAPTER TWENTY-NINE

By the time Lucy and Nate arrived at the standoff, the entire block had been evacuated and a dozen police cars, including a SWAT tactical van, were parked around the perimeter. Noah and Villines were both on the phone, and the head of the Webb County SWAT was speaking into a loudspeaker.

"Mr. Dobleman," SWAT said, "please pick up the phone so we can discuss the situation."

Silence.

Noah put his phone down. "We don't know how many hostages they have, but there are at least three gunmen," he told Lucy and Nate. "We're trying to resolve this without any more bloodshed."

Villines said, "My deputy is going in for surgery right now—he made it that far, he's going to pull through." He spoke it as if speaking it would make it so. Lucy hoped he was right.

Less than an hour had passed since the first shots had been fired at the two deputies who had initially approached the house. Zapelli had never driven his rental car to this place, but the phone the Honeycutts gave to Marisol had pinged to this neighborhood. The deputies had been going door-to-door.

"We have one positive ID—Lance Dobleman," Noah said. "He answered the door and fired the first shots. One officer was winged, managed to get his partner to safety, and ID'd him from his photo. Now no one will pick up the phone. There's no way out—we have it surrounded. There's no basement. They know they're out of options."

Villines said, "SWAT wants to get them into negotiation mode to buy time and reduce the tension. If we can develop a dialogue then maybe we can end this without anyone dying."

The sun had long set and the headlights of every cop car were on, illuminating the block in bright, artificial light. Everything seemed sharper, clearer. SWAT was setting up two mobile spotlights at either end of the block aimed straight at the house. There had been no gunfire after the initial burst. Everyone was on edge.

This neighborhood was definitely better maintained than the trailer outside the warehouse. The small houses were older and set far apart from one another. Scraggly fruit trees filled every backyard. Lucy wondered if this was the home of one of the suspects, because it wasn't like the others they'd seen. These houses looked like they had longtime residents who cared about their neighborhood and would notice strangers regularly coming in and out. But this particular house also had an attached garage, unlike most others. It would be easy to pull in a van and close the door, keeping the women out of sight.

"Based on Loretta's notes, there could be up to eight women inside," Lucy said. "She had fourteen women she was seeing who were all pregnant or had recently given birth. I've accounted for the two dead and the four we rescued; that leaves up to eight if Macey and Marisol are also here."

Noah relayed the information to the SWAT team leader.

"No one is picking up the phone. My men are in position."

"Eyes?"

"Negative. Working on it."

Villines said, "SWAT has confirmed one gunman is in the rear. There are at least two female hostages in the rear bedroom."

Lucy had an awful feeling about this. Dobleman and his cohorts knew they couldn't get out of this as free men. Would they rather die?

SWAT got back on the bullhorn. "Lance Dobleman, it's Kyle Brown again. I'd really like to talk to you. We all want the same thing, Lance. We all want to live. You want to live. You have a wife who wants you to live. Let's talk, okay? Just pick up the phone and we can talk about this situation."

Noah shook his head and said to Villines, "He's the bodyguard to a woman known as Jasmine, the illegitimate daughter of a cartel leader. He knows he's dead if he's captured."

"I don't know this Jasmine," Villines said.

"She's the daughter of Don Flores, the dead leader of the Flores crime syndicate out of Mexico. It's being run by his sons, according to my DEA contact. She's a US citizen, hasn't been on anyone's radar except as to her parentage, but she's suspected of running the black-market baby ring. Our white-collar experts are picking apart their shell companies as we speak, but she's in the wind. We don't even have a home address on her."

Villines gestured to the house. "Maybe she's inside."

"Doubtful," Noah said. "She's long gone, probably

bolted as soon as she heard the feds were in town. She was in Freer Sunday night—and that's all we know."

Noah was probably right, Lucy realized.

The SWAT leader was listening into his earpiece, then walked away as he spoke into his radio. "Reports. Alpha."

A moment later there was sudden action as two teams of three, one each north and south of the house, ran around to the back, and another team approached the side of the garage and took cover against the wall.

Shouts from team members over the radio indicated there was movement inside, then a single shot came from inside the house followed by screams.

Noah and Lucy both pulled their weapons and squatted behind the squad car, eyes on the house. Nate was already behind the tactical van with a rifle. She hadn't even seen him grab one.

Villines ran around to squat next to Noah. "They're going to breach the house. SWAT believes they're killing the hostages."

Another gun shot from inside followed by commands from the SWAT team leader to *go, go, go!*

"Garage!" one of Villines's deputies shouted. Whatever he said after was cut off by squealing tires; then the garage door broke apart as a white van burst out. There was no place for the driver to go, but he didn't seem to care. He pressed the gas.

Villines went one way, and Noah and Lucy went the other. The van hit the squad car, the crunch of metal on metal echoing in the night. They ran as fast as they could to get out of the way. Gunfire followed from the back of the house, a burst then single shots then another burst.

Before the van completely stopped, the driver began to spray bullets indiscriminately from the driver's window into the perimeter. Almost immediately multiple deputies fired at him and he slumped forward over the steering wheel. The van continued to roll forward, pushing the demolished squad car with it, until they were both wedged against a sheriff's truck.

A swarm of SWAT officers surrounded the vehicle, guns drawn. There were screams from the back of the van. One cop opened the driver's door while another held a rifle on the slumped-over body. He was clearly dead. They pulled the gun he'd used from the vehicle. Four other officers opened the back of the van. Lucy couldn't hear their commands, but they were ordering whoever was inside to exit the vehicle.

Silence filled the air; only the sobs of women in the back of the van could be heard. SWAT started toward the front door when it opened.

Dobleman stood there on the small porch. He held a very pregnant woman in front of him. She was sobbing. Blood stained her dress and her face.

"Back away!" Dobleman screamed. He looked frantically about, left and right, wide-eyed. SWAT had him surrounded; they'd secured the house, and it appeared that Dobleman was the only remaining threat.

"Back off! I mean it!" He stopped at the edge of the porch. The .45 he carried was buried into the woman's neck. "I'm leaving, right now, you're going to let me go."

The SWAT leader said, "Lance, it's over. Put the gun down and you will live. Cooperate, it'll help you."

"Fuck you!"

He shot the woman and pushed her from the short staircase into the front yard.

Lucy screamed from the shock and surprise of Dobleman's sudden violence.

He aimed the gun at the cops in front of him, but didn't get off another shot. Multiple gunshots rang out and Dobleman fell backward against the house, dead.

"No!" Lucy didn't know if she'd spoken out loud or if the shout was simply echoing in her head. She jumped up but Noah pulled her back down.

"Don't be stupid!"

She stayed low. Noah was right. But dammit, she couldn't just sit here. Maybe that poor girl was alive. Lucy had to help her. She was practically crawling toward the fallen woman, Noah at her side.

"House secure! Multiple casualties!" SWAT called over the radio. "Every medic inside, stat!"

Lucy jumped up again and this time Noah followed her.

Lucy, Noah, and one of the SWAT officers surrounded the woman on the lawn. The bullet had gone through her upper right shoulder just below the back of her neck. She was bleeding profusely. She opened her mouth over and over but no sound came out. Her hands flailed about and she suddenly grabbed Lucy's arm.

"*Bebé, por favor, bebé.*" Her voice was weak. Then her eyes rolled back into her head and her body began to convulse.

The SWAT medic said, "I can't stop the bleeding."

"Put pressure on it!" Lucy took off her jacket and folded it, putting as much pressure as she could on the wound. In seconds the jacket was wet and sticky with blood.

"She's not going to make it, Luce," Noah said.

"She has to! Her baby."

Lucy put her other hand on the woman's stomach and felt the baby kick multiple times. She bit back a sob. "No. No. No!"

Noah said, "Can you deliver it?"

"I—maybe." She had to try. "Where's the paramedics? We need someone!"

The SWAT medic called in the ambulance that was waiting down the street. "House is secure. We need a paramedic stat." He then pulled out a small emergency kit from his belt. He cut open the woman's dress and liberally sprayed an antiseptic over her skin. "I've assisted in one emergency C-section when I was an EMT. We have to do it fast. She's gone. I have no pulse. The baby won't survive more than a couple minutes, if at all."

He took out a scalpel and said, "This is all I have." He hesitated.

"Do it," Lucy said. "We don't have much time."

"I can't. Not without authorization." He looked pained. Damn rules!

Lucy took the scalpel, took a deep breath, forced her heart rate to slow. She'd never cut into a living person before, but she'd cut into the dead. She knew how the body was designed, how the uterus expanded and thinned during pregnancy. It was a strong muscle, it needed a sure and firm hand.

At the top of the belly, she pushed down with the scalpel until she felt the muscle give. Then she made a smooth vertical incision down, across the large stomach, all the way down to her pelvis.

Thank God she'd cut through the uterus on the first try. She pulled it apart, separating it. There was very little blood. She saw the baby in the amniotic sac. She carefully punctured the sac, reached in and took hold of the infant.

"Scissors—we have to cut the umbilical cord before the toxins from the mother reach her. We need a clamp. Something to seal it."

"Scissors?" The medic held surgical scissors in his hand.

Lucy nodded and without hesitating pulled the baby out. The medic cut the umbilical cord. Then he twisted the end still attached to the baby around the scissors and created a temporary clamp.

"She's not breathing." Lucy turned the small infant over, supporting her stomach with her hand and arm, and spanked her lightly. She was so small. So tiny. But she was perfect.

"She could have a blockage," the medic said. He reached over and rubbed the infant's back, then gave one light slap below her shoulder blades. He did it again. The legs kicked and suddenly a faint cry came out.

"Oh God," Lucy said. "Oh God, thank you." Noah took off his jacket and put it over the baby. Carefully, Lucy wrapped her up. "She's small, about four pounds. We have to get her to a hospital."

The paramedics rolled up with a gurney. They first saw the woman on the ground. "She's gone," the SWAT medic said. "But we have her baby."

The paramedics ordered Lucy to put the baby on the gurney. Quickly, they wiped out her mouth then wrapped her in clean towels. "We'll take her to the children's hospital in Laredo," one said. "Do you know anything about the mother? The infant?"

"No," Lucy said. "The mother was dying, the baby would have died if we didn't get her out. She wasn't breathing at first . . ."

"That's common in an emergency C-section. Good work." They strapped the baby in.

"I want to go with her—" Lucy said.

"Meet us there," the paramedic said and they rushed toward the ambulance.

Lucy stared after the baby. She couldn't move. Suddenly her knees buckled, and she would have collapsed if Noah hadn't caught her.

"You saved her baby," he whispered in her ear. "It's okay to feel, Lucy. It's okay to cry."

Lucy stared at the dead mother, then turned her head and buried her face into Noah's chest. She clutched at him as if she were drowning.

She couldn't think, she couldn't put together a sentence.

Waves of grief washed through her. Grief and anger. That so many human beings could hurt others with no remorse, no punishment. A baby who had no mother, no father. Alive, but what would happen to her?

Grief. Anger. And then a sudden relief that it was over. The last three days had been the second worst three days of her life. She wasn't the victim this time, but she saw herself in the eyes of the woman who'd begged her to save her baby. She saw herself in the eyes of all these women. She could have been one of them.

There but for the grace of God go I . . .

She let Noah hold her. He sat on the ground and pulled her to him, his hand gripping her tight. She felt his chest, the sobs he was trying to hold inside. Suddenly, the tears came. Tears she'd never shed because she feared they would never stop.

They came.

CHAPTER THIRTY

It was nearly midnight when Lucy sat on the edge of the exam table. She'd washed off the blood, and Noah had insisted a doctor check her out. She was fine, she'd said. But she was drained.

"We should go to the hotel," Noah said.

"Where's Nate?"

"He's still with Villines at the house."

"I should have stayed. Done my job."

"You did your job, Lucy."

"I fell apart."

"I would have worried more if you didn't. Lucy—no apologies. You did what had to be done and saved that little girl. The SWAT medic told the story to everyone, including the nurses. They're calling her Lucia."

The tears threatened again and she shook her head to clear her thoughts. She couldn't do this, not now.

Noah sat down on the doctor's stool and took her hands. "Hey, Luce, it's over."

"It's not. I overheard you talking to Villines. Marisol wasn't in the house."

"We found the Honeycutts' phone in a closet, and it's clear someone had been restrained inside. I'm going to make a run at Zapelli and see what he can tell us. His lawyer is raising Cain about unlawful detention and false arrest and whatnot, so we're probably going to have to cut him loose."

"You can't!"

"You think I want to? I'm fighting hard to make sure we can keep him here, but I may not have a choice. We pushed the boundaries on this case. I told you to push, you did everything right, but we have to remember that we have rules for a reason. We don't have cause. But I'm going to run at him, see what he can give us. The AUSA is staying up all night to see if she can make a case against him. But it'll be up to a judge in the morning as to whether we cut him loose."

Sometimes, she hated the system.

"They killed her," Lucy said. "They must have killed her."

"There was no evidence that she died at that house." His phone rang. "It's Dean Hooper, I have to take it. Then I'll take you to the hotel." He kissed her forehead.

"Armstrong," he answered. He listened for a full minute, then said, "Where is he? I'll pick him up tonight."

He listened again, then swore under his breath. "Are you sure? Did he flee because he knew we were going to uncover this? . . . *Really?* Last week? . . . I'll talk to his wife . . . This isn't a joke, is it? Yeah, I know, you don't joke about serious shit. Okay, I'll be there first thing in the morning. I need a couple hours' sleep before I can make the drive back, it's been a fucking long day." He hung up.

"What happened?" Lucy asked. "Hooper found something?"

"Hooper found Jasmine's legal name—Jasmine Flores-King. King was her married name and she still uses it. "Then he found the lawyer who set up all the shell corporations for her. Once we uncovered her legal name, he said it got a bit easier, but I still think the guy's next to God when it comes to this stuff. Hooper knows what to look for and he found it."

"That's great. I need good news right now."

"But get this, the lawyer left the country last week. Went down to Acapulco according to flight records. But his wife is in San Antonio, flew here on Monday from—get this— Acapulco. So we'll talk to her, see if she knows what her husband is doing. If he fled the country to avoid prosecution or what. After the week we've had, I'm going to push her hard. No one is walking away from this bloodbath."

As Noah spoke, Lucy's stomach fell. She stared at him.

"Hey, do you need a doctor? You look pale. I'm sorry—I shouldn't have dumped that on you tonight."

"Spade," she said.

Noah froze. "How did you know their name?"

"Sean. Sean was hired by his wife, Madison Spade, to go to Mexico and find her husband Carson and her son Jesse. She said they weren't in Acapulco and she feared they'd been hurt or kidnapped. That's why Sean and Kane went down there."

"Has he found them? Does he know this guy is a fugitive?"

She nodded. "I haven't spoken to Sean since . . ." When? Was it really this morning? "I talked to him briefly when we were at the property management office. Noon, I guess." She rubbed her eyes. "He located them in Guadalajara and were working on an extraction plan. Sean suspected that Spade was laundering money after he dug around as Sean generally does . . . but he would have told me if he'd known it connected to my case." She paused.

"What else?"

"I haven't told Sean much about the case. We haven't had much time to talk since he left."

"Call him."

She pulled out her cell phone and dialed. It went straight to voice mail.

She sent him a text message.

Call me. It's urgent.

She watched as the text started to send. Then her phone beeped back a message.

Text undeliverable.

Marisol woke up because she was cold. She shivered, tried to reach for a blanket, and couldn't move her hands.

She opened her eyes, panicked, but saw nothing in the dark. She heard nothing. She tried to shift but tight bindings cut into her wrists and ankles. She bit her lip to keep from crying out.

Everything was so fuzzy. She remembered the car . . . the trunk . . . the fear.

The fear was still with her. The fear would never leave. Until she died.

No, dear God, I can't die. I have to save Ana.

They would kill Ana because of her. Take her babies and kill her. A cry escaped her parched lips.

Where had Dobleman taken her? She squeezed her eyes closed, tried to remember . . . she'd been groggy when he opened the trunk. Had he drugged her? Was she sick from the exhaust? All she remembered was he carried her into a house. It was dark. The middle of the night. And silence.

Flashes returned, of the big man, of him touching her. Tying her up. She didn't remember much. Her stomach was empty, her head spun, and she knew, right then, that she would be dead very soon. If not by the big man then out of thirst or hunger or the sick she felt.

Heavy footsteps crossed the ceiling above her and she whimpered.

Then they stopped.

Hope didn't last long.

They crossed the floor again and she heard a lock turn.
No. No!
The creak of the stairs. Then blinding light.
She closed her eyes and turned her head.
"I knew you were awake. I'm so lucky they gave you to me to punish. I'm going to have so much fun."

CHAPTER THIRTY-ONE

Sean didn't dare contact Lucy, though he desperately wanted to.

His confidence level was usually high on ops like this, but tonight he wasn't certain he would survive. He didn't generally get involved this deep in the cartel battles—that was the domain of Jack and Kane and their teams of highly trained former military soldiers. Sean was the guy behind the curtain, the geek, the computer wiz, the pilot. He could shoot and fight if he had to, but he did much better using his brains instead of his brawn.

Instead, he wrote Lucy a letter, addressed it, and put it in his laptop case. He hid the laptop on the plane. If anything happened, he could only hope someone would find the plane, find the laptop, and send her the letter.

"Do you have any questions?" Jack asked him.

Sean had a million questions, but he knew the answer to all of them.

He glared at Jack. "You should never have let Kane do this."

Jack didn't smile, but his eyebrow rose just a bit. "Have you ever successfully talked Kane out of a plan?"

Good point.

"And if Dante betrays us?"

Jack stared at him with dark eyes that reminded Sean of Lucy.

"I'll kill him."

Jack was deadly serious.

Dante sent Sean a text message.

Meet is on. No weapons.

Sean showed the message to Jack. He nodded and disappeared into the dark.

Sean had the bag of money and bearer bonds. He put the backpack over his shoulders and took the ATV that he'd procured earlier. Being silent no longer mattered; they were expecting him.

He hit the dirt road two miles from where the plane was hidden, and turned toward the compound. He feared someone would take a shot at him, that Flores—who knew Sean had the money—would take him out en route, take the money, and then kill Kane. But none of that happened.

Sean hid the ATV a mile from the compound. If they had to foot it back to the plane, it was a fifteen-mile hike through unfamiliar terrain. He hid the duffel bag with the bearer bonds a good hundred yards from his ATV, then walked the rest of the way up the road. The night was hot and humid. His T-shirt stuck to his skin under the jacket he wore.

He already knew where the security cameras were, but he had rigged his tablet to give him information as he walked through. Wireless intel that he could use to hack into the system. Information was power, and Sean wasn't going to go in completely blind.

Movement to his right and left stopped Sean in his tracks. He reached for his gun, then remembered he'd hid it in the bottom of the money bag—and slowly put his hands up.

"Smart move, Mr. Rogan," an accented voice said.

Four men came into view, all with guns pointed at Sean. He twitched. Any one of them could have nervous fingers. The guns were crap, but that didn't mean the bullets were faulty. And the closer they were, the more likely they'd hit their target.

"Where's the money?"

"Hidden."

"That wasn't your orders."

"I'll tell your boss where to find the money when I know that Kane is alive and well."

The guard hit Sean across the cheek with the back of his hand. Sean barely resisted hitting him back. He spit bloody saliva on the dirt road.

"Search him," the leader ordered.

The other three men patted him down, turned out his pockets, took his burn phone and his small tablet, which were the only things on him.

"Walk."

Sean complied.

The compound entrance was a hundred yards from where Flores's goons picked Sean up. It was gated with two guards standing outside. Yesterday, when Kane first reconned the place, there had been only one.

Jack knows what he's doing.

Sean was uncomfortable depending on anyone else for his safety. He'd always gotten himself in and out of jams as needed. But he felt out of his element, and not for the first time over the last forty-eight hours. It wasn't like he had much choice.

The Flores compound was really a mansion surrounded by twelve-foot-high chain-link fences topped with barbed wire, interspersed with wide stone columns for strength. As they walked up the long drive, Sean noted that there were two wings to the house and several outbuildings, plus a barn, an eight-car garage, and a four-car garage. Sean loved cars, but a dozen?

Was Jesse in the main house or was there a guesthouse Sean couldn't see? He'd guess the main house, where Flores could keep his eye on Carson Spade.

Anger burned in his veins. That Carson Spade had brought Jesse here, with these criminals—violent thugs who would kill anyone who thwarted their plans. A twelve-year-old boy. Sean had known a lot about the world at twelve. Kane had just left the Marines and was starting Rogan-Caruso with JT. Their first big assignment was a hostage rescue when the sister of one of their friends had been kidnapped along with her professor and three other students during a study-abroad program in Honduras. They'd been held for ransom, and Kane and JT had retrieved four of the five safely. One of the students had been killed, and Sean knew that had bothered both of them greatly. They went through extensive training, both professional and self-taught; expanded the business; brought on Duke to handle computer security after he did his stint in the Army; hired former cops, FBI agents, and soldiers to fill their ranks.

Sean's parents had been inventors—his dad had served in the military for ten years before a training exercise left him partially disabled. But he loved the military, and came up with new and innovative equipment designed primarily for troop safety. Long-range night-vision goggles, early drone technology, and a state-of-the-art tracking system—at least twenty years ago—had put Paul and Sheila Rogan at the top of the government contractor list. Who knows what they could have accomplished had they not died in a plane crash that nearly killed Sean as well?

His parents never shielded him from the evil in the world, or from the heroes who battled the villains. They were blunt, honest, and dedicated. They worked constantly, and that was one of the things Sean would always remember. In some ways he envied Lucy and her family . . . her dad had been career military, but Lucy said her happiest moments growing up were family outings—to the beach, camping, or holiday dinners at home. When her parents came to watch her swim meets, when her older sister took her to Patrick's baseball games, when Patrick took her for ice cream "just because." But the best, she said, were the family dinners. Even after the older Kincaid kids left home, even after tragedy struck and her nephew was murdered, Sunday night was family night. No matter how busy, they made the time. Sean never had that, even when his parents were alive.

Yet when he was Jesse's age, he knew what drug cartels were; he knew how to shoot a gun and field-strip it; he could hot-wire a car even though he wasn't old enough to drive. He could tell almost just by looking whether someone was carrying a weapon under their jacket, and he had a knack for spotting drug deals going down at school.

What about Jesse? His mother was Madison McAllister. She'd caved in to the pressure that her father placed on her and didn't tell Sean that she was pregnant thirteen years ago. She did everything her dad wanted . . . did she do everything her husband wanted, without question? Without argument? Had she been ignorant of her husband's criminal behavior? Was Jesse sheltered and blind? Would he get himself into trouble simply by asking the wrong questions? Would Flores keep Jesse to ensure that Carson Spade did what he was supposed to do? Was Carson here voluntarily . . . or had he been forced to come? Had they grabbed Jesse first to ensure compliance? Was Kane right and would both Carson and Jesse be dead as soon as Carson did his job?

The guard opened the main doors. Motioning for the other three men to leave, he led Sean straight across the wide, opulent foyer and through one of a dozen sets of ten-foot-tall French doors. The center of the mansion was an atrium, covered from the elements but with a glass roof. It was humid in here as well, likely to keep the many plants thriving. A narrow lap pool had been installed dead center, and a smaller, but more opulent black-bottomed pool with a waterfall and Jacuzzi was off to the right. Four sets of staircases went up to landings north and south.

The main house had to be, minimum, thirty thousand square feet. The atrium itself was about half a narrow football field with nooks and crannies and lots of places for the bad guys to hide and take a shot at his head when they had a chance.

A short, trim man of fifty with dark graying hair wearing white pants and a red floral shirt sat at a table next to a fully stocked bar. The bar had its own bartender.

He smiled when he saw Sean. "Thank you, Romie, you can leave."

The guard said, "He hid the bag."

"Of course he did. He wants to see his brother first." He motioned for Sean to take a seat, which he did. There was no good place to sit and see every angle of the atrium. "I'm Dominick Flores. It's good to finally meet you, Sean Rogan. I've heard a few stories about you, never know exactly what to believe and not believe. But since I know most of the stories about your brother are true, I would be impressed if even half of yours are true. What would you like to drink?"

Jack had already warned him that refusing to drink with Dominick Flores would be insulting.

"A cold beer would be nice," he said.

Dominick laughed. "A beer? Are you a lightweight?"

He didn't wait for an answer. "Bernie, two *cerveza, por favor.* And two shots of the Fortaleza reserve." He smiled at Sean. "Just one," he said. "You've earned it."

Sean raised an eyebrow. "Earned it?"

"You have balls, I admire that. You must be aware that your brother has a bounty on his head. More than one bounty."

"And I'm prepared to pay for him."

He dismissed Sean's comment with a flip of his hand. "We'll get to that."

Bernie brought out two cold bottles of Negra Modelo, two shot glasses, and a bottle of Fortaleza tequila. Dominick poured the shots and slid one over to Sean. "Salute," he said and held up his shot.

Sean went along with it, picked up the glass and said, "*Salud.*"

They drank together and slammed the shot glasses back down on the table. If Sean wasn't so tense, he would have enjoyed the drink—he would be hard-pressed to remember a better tequila.

He opened his bottle of beer and sipped. "Thank you."

Dominick smiled then snapped his fingers. "Your brother."

Sean looked around. At first he didn't see anything; then on the landing directly across from the bar, a door opened. Kane was brought out. He was cuffed and his face was swollen. A cut on his cheek would most certainly scar. Sean tensed.

"He put up a fight, but they're all superficial wounds," Dominick said. He waved his hand and Kane was forced back through the door. It closed.

"The money?"

Sean said, "Paper and pen."

Dominick snapped his fingers again, and Bernie brought over a notepad and pen. Sean drew a line on the top. "This is your gate." He then drew the road. "Point six mile down the road there's a fallen oak tree—I think it's an oak, it's distinctive because two new growths are coming out of the base."

"I know the tree."

Sean drew a stick tree, then another line to the west. "There's an overgrown path here. About one hundred steps there's a thorny hedge that's completely overgrown. The bag is in the hedge. It's black, so they'll need some lights, but it's almost dead center."

Dominick looked at the bartender, who approached and took the paper from Sean. He left the atrium.

Dominick leaned back. "How do you know Dante?"

"Kane."

"Friends?"

"I wouldn't say that."

"Enemy?"

"I wouldn't say that, either."

"I've always wondered why Kane never slit his throat."

Sean shrugged. "If you know anything about me, you know I'm just the pilot."

Dominick laughed. "Just the pilot. Is that like the Hollywood movie, the one where the guy is *just the cook*?"

"I don't go to the movies much."

"Is it true that you escaped under intense gunfire outside Santiago a few months ago?"

"They were bad shots."

"I'm sure they were. But your plane was totaled, was it not?"

Sean didn't like how Dominick knew these things about him. If he knew about Sean, he knew about Lucy.

A man in jeans, a polo shirt, and Nikes ran into the atrium. Dominick looked irritated.

"Dom, Jasmine is here."

Dominick tensed. "At the house?"

"On her way. She landed thirty minutes ago with a fake passport. She has a girl and baby with her."

Dominick spoke in rapid Spanish. He was not happy, but Sean's Spanish wasn't good enough to translate, especially not so fast. But Sean caught the end. "When will she arrive?"

"Ten minutes."

"Is this Alberto's kid?"

"I guess so. Jasmine hasn't been chatty lately, she's really pissed off."

"Fuck."

Dominick looked at Sean. He wished he could read the crime lord's mind, but he couldn't. He had no idea who Jasmine was, or why Dominick would be scared of her—which he clearly was.

"What do you want to do about her?" the guy asked. He was taller than Dominick but had the same basic facial structure—a brother? Very possible.

"Greet her at the gate. She likes you the best, Jose. Keep her away from Samuel. Oh—and tell your girlfriend to disappear for a while. Jasmine hates the Romeros."

"Why?" Jose asked.

Dominick looked at Sean pointedly, then said, "No need to air family business in front of our guest."

Jose was so young that for a minute Sean thought he might be Dominick's son, but he didn't call him *Dad* and was more likely the youngest brother.

"She'll understand," Jose said. "Where do you want me to put Jasmine?"

"She'll want to see me first, but try and convince her to rest. I don't need to have her interfering with tonight's business arrangement." He paused a moment, looked around the atrium, then said to Jose, "Tell Flora to prepare the Rose Suite."

"And the girl and baby?"

"Alberto's whore and kid, he can put them in his rooms." Dominick swore again, profusely, then said, "Have Alberto go to the gate with you. I don't want to see the girl. I told Jasmine not to bring her and her bastard here."

"Alberto wanted her."

"Alberto can't fucking keep his dick in his pants, he wants every damn whore he sees."

Dominick was deeply angry. In fact, Sean suspected that Dominick was doing his best to keep his temper in check. Just what Sean needed—an angry crime lord who might decide to keep the money and kill them all because he was pissed off at family drama.

"I'll take care of it, Dom." Jose left. Typical younger brother, wanting to keep his older brothers happy.

Sean could relate.

But now he had more information, which was always good. Jose was the brother Gabriella had seduced in order to get into the Flores operation. Jose actually seemed like a genuine guy—but he was still in a crime family, and one thing Sean knew better than anything, blood won.

"Once you have confirmation that the money is where I said it was, perhaps you can let Kane and I slip out," Sean said. "We don't need to interrupt whatever it is that's going on here."

"You have more family than Kane, do you not?"

Of course Dominick would know, so Sean nodded.

"Yes, your brother and sister in Europe. Interesting fellow, that Liam. And the other one, I don't remember his name. He doesn't come down here."

Sean didn't tell him.

"Family is complicated," Dom said.

"But you love them anyway."

Dominick relaxed, just a bit. "Yes. We understand each other. Which is why it's difficult for me to simply let you and Kane slip out of here."

"I've heard you are a man of your word. I wouldn't have made this deal if I didn't believe that."

"I am, true, but Kane has been a thorn in the side of me and my allies for years. I'm sure you're aware of that."

"Like I said, I'm just the pilot."

"We had a vote. It was split. As it generally is when it's an even number of voters."

"Yet you agreed to take my money."

"Kane is no longer welcome south of the border."

"He never was."

"But this time, I have you." Dominick stared at Sean, his face hard. The killer beneath the suave businessman showed himself, and if Sean were alone in this plan, he would have been terrified. As it was, it took all his control to bury the fear and hope Dominick couldn't see his nerves. "If Kane interferes with my business again—*any* of my businesses, including the business of my allies— not only will the bounty on his head increase, but I will put a bounty on the head of every Rogan. Including you. Including your fiancée."

Sean saw red. The fear turned to rage. He wanted to strangle Dominick where he sat.

"It's not a bluff," Dominick continued. "I know everything about you. I know everything about Lucy Kincaid."

Through clenched teeth Sean said, "Then you know who her brother is."

"Of course. And you know he no longer travels south of the border. The Kincaids are off-limits, as long as Jack minds his own business. But Miss Lucy is going to be a Rogan, so she is fair game, whichever side of the border she is on."

Sean leaned forward and whispered, "If anyone touches her, the wrath of a thousand gods will rain down on you and yours."

"Now you know how I feel if your brother continues to interfere with me." He didn't break eye contact, but leaned forward, almost as if he were going to kiss Sean. "I could kill you both and be done with you, but like you said, there are others who may seek retribution. This is the agreement. Take it, or die."

CHAPTER THIRTY-TWO

Kane picked the handcuffs with the pin Gabriella had slipped him earlier. Flores wasn't stupid—he hadn't left Kane alone in the room. A guard inside and a guard outside.

But still, only one to deal with at a time. Small consolation.

Sean had given Kane the signal—by requiring proof of life. When Kane saw Sean with Dom, he knew the plan was on. That his little brother got this far was a testament to his talents, but they were far from out of the woods. Even if this was an even exchange, they were still at risk. That Kane intended to destroy the Flores crime family tonight just added another element of danger. Because in no scenario that he and Jack could conceive would they be allowed to walk away with Jesse Spade without a distraction. Not with the fortress the Flores family had built and the people they'd bought. If they could have grabbed him at the stadium, it would have been much easier.

Little in Kane's life was easy.

The outside guard came in. He said, "Jasmine is here."

"No shit?" the inside guard said. "Fuck, I wish I could go home."

"You and me both. Dom is furious. He didn't know."

"He didn't?"

The guards found that interesting, and it weakened their boss in their eyes. Dominick Flores was supposed to be all-knowing, all-seeing . . . that his own sister was here without his knowledge would taint his authority.

Kane didn't know much about Jasmine, the illegitimate daughter of Don Flores. She lived in the States; her mother had been a nurse in Corpus Christi when the elder Flores met her forty-plus years ago. Flores had kept the nurse in style for years, and had apparently loved her so much that her death from cancer when Jasmine was in college had devastated him greatly. He'd left a substantial settlement to Jasmine and her younger sister in his will. As far as he knew, the younger Flores had no connection to the family, moving far away to the Northeast. But while Kane had heard that Jasmine had a relationship with her half brothers, he'd never heard that she was involved in their business affairs.

But if she was here, chances were she was as involved as any of them, just better at staying beneath the radar. And she lived in the States. Not his battlefield.

The two guards chatted a bit longer, but Kane only paid attention with one ear. He'd already unlocked the cuffs, but he didn't dare take them off with both of the men in the room. He wished they'd wrap up the gossip session because, while it was interesting, Kane didn't have much time.

The outside guard heard something in his earpiece a few minutes later, and walked out.

The inside guard smirked at Kane. "Your brother came through," he said in broken English. Did he actually think that Kane wasn't fluent in Spanish? Fool. "Dom isn't going to let you live, you know that, right?"

Kane didn't believe anything this idiot said because he

was a gossip, and Dominick Flores was too smart to trust his expendable men with key information.

Of course, if Dominick found out that Kane had set this whole plan into motion, he would certainly attempt to have him killed.

Kane hoped he wasn't around at that point.

The inside guard was small and wiry. He also had an earpiece, but for listening only—if the wearer wanted to speak, they had to press the SPEAK button on their lapel, otherwise there'd be too much interference. Good equipment, but definitely not state-of-the-art.

"Bathroom," Kane said.

"Hold it," the guard said.

"Asshole," Kane muttered.

The guard scowled and crossed the room to show Kane who was in charge . . . he raised his hand to smack him.

Kane jumped up, grabbed his arm with his left hand, twisted it around his back, used his right arm to reach around and grab him by the neck and *snap*.

He was dead.

Kane removed the earpiece and put it in his own ear. He disabled the microphone, so he could hear what was going on without fear of anyone hearing him. He took the guard's weapon, a shoddy-looking 9mm that wouldn't do much damage unless it was up close and personal. He searched him further and found a switchblade—not bad. Kane pocketed the 9mm and kept the knife in hand. A quieter way to silence someone if he had to.

The door was locked; a fail-safe, he supposed, but hardly one that would keep anyone in or out. Besides, he had no plans on using the door.

While Flores had outstanding external security, his internal security was less than adequate. There were no alarms on the windows or doors—and being on the second-floor south wing provided additional cover. He opened the window and slipped out. The decorative ledge was narrow and Kane wasn't positive it would hold him, but the drop wouldn't kill him.

Though the patrolling guards would if they heard him fall.

He put the knife in his mouth and shimmied over two windows until he reached a balcony.

Kane quietly climbed over the metal railing. A creak had him stopping, listening. He heard voices outside and down below—he couldn't make out what they were saying, but they were definitely a two-man patrol. Again, smart on Dominick's part. He should have had two men guarding him on the inside. While Kane would have been able to take them both out, it would have been noisy, cutting down his lead time.

He listened again—they were moving away. Good. He didn't have much time.

He carefully ran on light feet to the opposite end of the balcony, past two sets of French doors and two windows. They were partly lit, so he had to be quiet. He then put his hand on the handle of the third set of French doors. There was a light on, but he watched through the thin curtains and didn't see anyone. He had the blueprints of the house firmly in mind, thanks to Gabriella. Of course she could be lying to him. She could have set him up.

But he didn't think so. Not this time.

He pushed down on the handle. It clicked open. It didn't mean anything, it could have simply been unlocked . . . or it could be a trap. But it was a small sign of hope.

He slipped into the room. It was a small sitting room. This was the suite Carson Spade shared with Jesse. Carson had a bedroom and den to the left, the windows that Kane had just passed. Jesse had a room on the right.

This all depended on Jesse now.

Kane walked to the door. He heard something behind

him, in Carson's room. Then nothing. Carson was up, but he wasn't coming to the door. Kane opened Jesse's door and closed it immediately behind him.

Jesse sat on the end of the bed playing a handheld video game. He was fully dressed. He had a backpack at his feet. For a split second, he looked so much like how Kane remembered Sean as a kid—hair too long, dimples that could get him out of trouble, but the tense jaw that said he was ready for a fight.

Jesse looked up. He whispered, "Sean was right."

"He usually is, kid."

Kane only marginally relaxed. Gabriella had done the two things Kane needed her to do—tell him which room was Jesse's, and deliver Sean's message.

"I saw you yesterday. Who are you?"

"Kane. Sean's brother."

Jesse tilted his head. Again, that inquisitive, too-smart look that Sean always wore. "My uncle."

"Call me Kane." He half smiled. "Less weird."

"What now?"

"You can't bring anything."

Jesse glanced down at the backpack and nodded. He tossed the video game on the bed.

Kane reached under the mattress and retrieved a phone. *Thanks, G.*

Okay, she had come through. Kane was going to owe her big time if they got out of this alive.

"Wow—I didn't know that was there."

He put his fingers to his lips. He sent Jack a message. *Got the package.*

Kane listened. There were footsteps in the hall. They weren't rushing, but that didn't mean anything. He turned on the earpiece. No chatter about his escape.

Jack responded.

In position. We have company.

That must be Jasmine Flores, the half sister the guards were talking about.

"Now what?" Jesse asked.

"We wait."

"Okay." Jesse said. "I'm not good at being patient."

"Neither is your dad," Kane said. "Your real dad." He took a good look at the kid. He was family. He was a Rogan.

Kane would die to save him.

Sean had counted down in his head after he signaled Kane. He'd seen the guard at the door go into the room for three minutes before exiting; that was going to cut everything far too close. But Sean trusted Kane.

It would take ten to twelve minutes for the guards to find the bag, assuming they drove the mile to the oak tree, then walked the hundred yards to the hedge. Give them a few minutes to look, though they might locate it immediately if they were competent. They'd call it in. By that point, Kane should be out of the room and with Jesse.

Thirteen minutes had passed, according to Sean's internal clock, by the time Dominick's phone rang. He didn't say anything, just listened.

"Very good," he said.

He smiled at Sean. "We have the bag. It appears intact."

"I'm also a man of my word. You can bring my brother down."

"I'll wait."

"For what?"

"To ensure that you don't have a team ready to storm the fence when my men return."

Sean laughed. "Okay, I suppose that wouldn't have been outside of reason. But there's a storm coming in at dawn, and I don't like flying through storms."

"I'm sure you can handle it. Or stick around for the rest of the night. I have plenty of room."

Sean wasn't positive he was joking.

There was some commotion in the foyer and Sean jumped up.

"Sit," Dominick ordered.

Sean tensed. He complied, only because he needed to give Kane more time. Two more minutes.

The doors opened into the atrium. A striking woman with dyed honey-blond hair walking in heels that could kill a man strode through the cobbled floor right over to Dominick. Jose was behind her along with another man—Alberto, most likely—who had his arm around a young blonde carrying a baby. The girl couldn't be more than twenty, and she looked physically sick.

Sean recognized all of them from Siobhan Walsh's photos. This woman, the one Lucy suspected of selling black-market babies, was Jasmine Flores.

In that moment, Sean put it all together. Carson Spade's urgent trip to Mexico came the day after Marisol de la Rosa left her baby at the church. Jasmine moved all the girls out as fast as she could, suspecting what? That Marisol would go to the police? Or maybe the fear came after Siobhan Walsh started asking questions. They would know that if the FBI was involved, they might be able to burn a few of their shell corporations, so they'd need their accountant and lawyer—Carson Spade—to create a new set of corporations. And because they wouldn't trust him—no one wanted to be working against the clock when the FBI was breathing down their neck—they wanted to keep an eye on him. It would also be easier for Spade to set up bank accounts from a home base in Guadalajara than from a home base in Los Angeles.

There's no way that Carson told Dominick that Madison had sent Sean down here . . . in fact, Madison didn't tell Carson who she'd sent because otherwise Dominick would never have agreed to this meeting.

Unless it was a trap.

Sean watched the Flores family carefully. They weren't overly concerned with him; Dominick was focused on Jasmine.

But he spoke his first words to Alberto. "Take the girl and your kid to your suite. I'm in the middle of a business transaction, and they're a distraction."

Alberto sneered at Sean, but he was focused more on the blonde. "It's a boy, Dom. The first Flores heir."

Dom was more than a little angry, but he said, "Congratulations, Alberto. We'll arrange for the christening next week."

"Marcus," he said. "Marcus Alberto Donald Flores."

Dom glared at Alberto until he walked up the stairs opposite from where Kane was being held—or had been held, if all had gone well.

"I'm not happy," Jasmine said.

"Can we discuss this in the morning?"

"No. Where's Carson?"

"I assume sleeping. It's after one in the morning."

"Wake. Him. Up."

"He's set up a parallel structure, moved all the money, shut down the compromised corporations, and I verified the funds were transferred. What *is* the fucking problem, Jasmine?"

"The fucking FBI is the fucking problem, Dominick," she snapped. "Some bitch photographer turned over her photos to the FBI. Including one of me. They didn't *have* a photo of me! Until now."

"They don't know it's you."

"They will. You know people won't keep their fucking mouths shut. It's just a matter of time. They raided the law office this afternoon. They'll eventually trace the companies to me. My name has been clean for years. Why do you think I kept the King name?"

"Your name is Flores; it's never been clean, so don't play the innocent card, Jasmine."

"And then I land here after a horrific flight and get a call—Lance is dead. So is his entire team. The fucking FBI found both houses where we stashed the girls after I had to shut down the safe house. So not only did I lose my investment, I have no fucking staff!"

"Jasmine, we have company, calm down."

Jasmine turned to Sean and scowled. "I don't know you."

"And," Dominick said, "you won't see him again after tonight. I had Flora prepare the Rose Suite for you. I'm sure you're exhausted."

"Have you listened to anything I've said?" Jasmine paced. She was acting wired—as if she had partaken in some of the illegal substances that the Flores family was known for smuggling.

Or maybe she was fueled on anger. Either way, Sean couldn't let this woman know who he was, who his family was. She was too volatile, and even if she didn't put it together right away, she most certainly would know Kane. If not by sight, by name and reputation.

"Have a drink." Dominick snapped his fingers and the bartender brought out a bottle of French Cabernet that went for easily three hundred dollars a pop.

Jasmine smiled. "Thank you, Bernie, you remembered."

"Always, Ms. Jasmine."

He opened the bottle and poured her a glass. Dominick glanced at Sean, but Sean couldn't read his expression.

Jasmine sipped, then pulled out her phone. She had a number on speed dial, and waited. "Carson, were you sleeping? Good. Then come down to the courtyard. We need a plan, and we need it now." She hung up.

"I don't need to be part of this," Sean said to Dominick.

"And you are who?" Jasmine snapped.

Dominick reddened. "Jasmine, a word." He walked across the atrium and Jasmine hesitated, then followed, a bit more nervous. Sean couldn't hear what they were saying, but he was ready. He hoped. He had the exits identified, but chances were they were covered. And anyone on the landing above would have a clear target.

Shit. They had two plans—the first, for Sean to get out the front entrance, then head around to the southeast corner, on the assumption that they'd bring Kane to him. The second, if Dominick stalled or didn't bring Kane out, Sean was to slip out a side door that Gabriella was supposed to have cleared for him. He stared at it. It was partly obscured by the bar, but she'd told Jack it would lead directly into the kitchen, and the service entrance off the kitchen would be unmanned. Sean didn't know what Gabriella planned to do—probably kill the guard and assume Kane and crew would be blamed. But a kitchen would have knives, and Sean could arm himself.

Dominick walked back to Sean. Jasmine sat on a lounge chair, kicked off her heels, and sipped her wine, purposefully ignoring them. "My sister is justifiably angry. Your money has cleared the gate. Wait in the foyer; I'll have my men bring your brother down the back way." He glanced at Jasmine. Dominick hated her. It was clear as day. But she was family. Blood.

Blood always wins.

Kane had told him that over and over again.

Dominick extended his hand and Sean took it. A sign of respect that Sean didn't feel, and Dominick could see that, but it still pleased him that Sean went through the motions. "You hope I never see you again."

"Ditto."

He started toward the foyer. As soon as he reached

the double doors, they opened and in walked Carson Spade.

Carson stared at him and Sean pretended he didn't recognize him, but the moment passed quickly. Carson hit Sean in the jaw. Sean was able to duck, but Carson still grazed his chin.

"Flores! Do you know who this—" Carson stopped mid-sentence and ran across the atrium.

"Carson!" Jasmine shouted. "What are you doing?"

"He's here for my son!"

It was clear both Jasmine and Dominick were confused. But as Carson ran up the stairs, a guard emerged from Kane's room. "He's gone!" the man shouted.

Sean didn't wait. He bolted. Someone fired a gun, but he didn't know if it was at him or Carson. All he knew was that the bullet didn't hit him.

He almost ran out the front door, but three armed men were running up the drive toward the house, so Sean went right, around to where he hoped the kitchen was, based on the intel they had.

This place was a maze, but he ran through a dining room and the kitchen was straight ahead. It was huge. There were no knives sitting on the counter, and he didn't have time to search. He ran out the service door expecting to be attacked, but no one was there. Two steps later the yard burst alive with spotlights shining from what seemed like every corner of the house. Shouts came from everywhere. There was no place to hide.

Two men rounded the corner, guns drawn, aimed at Sean.

A small explosion shook the ground, and every light went off simultaneously—the spotlights and the houselights. Adrenaline made his ears ring and Sean hesitated, just for a moment . . . what if Kane and Jesse were still inside?

Trust your brother. That's why you brought him.

A second small explosion came thirty seconds later and propelled Sean toward the rendezvous point in the southeast corner.

Sean couldn't see anything, but he'd memorized the layout of the house and the compound grounds. He knew exactly where he had to be. And prayed Kane was there, with Jesse.

Gunfire behind him was closer than he expected. There was no place to hide, but the shooters couldn't see him, either. He was in the middle of a sick game of Russian roulette. Anything that hit him would be out of sheer luck, but there was still the chance that a bullet would hit the back of his head and he'd be dead, here in Guadalajara.

Not tonight. You're not going to die tonight.

He zigzagged, kept as low as he possibly could, stumbled, kept moving toward the southeast corner. But in the dark and with all the noise, he was losing his sense of direction. Was he heading to the right corner? Had he messed up? Shouldn't he be there by now?

He slowed down, listened, and heard a whistle. Kane's unique whistle.

He turned to the right and bolted through the new hole in Flores's stone and metal wall, courtesy of Jack and JT.

"We have a problem," Jack said.

"Jesse," was the only thing Sean could say as he gasped for air.

Please don't tell me he's dead. Please don't.

"He's here," Kane said.

Sean glanced over. Standing behind Kane was his son. *His son.*

He didn't know what to say. *Thank you* to Kane was inadequate. *Hello* to Jesse, likewise. He just stared.

"We need to retrieve Spade," JT said.

"What the hell for?" Sean snapped back to attention. "He made his bed, let him die in it."

Then he looked at Jesse. This boy considered Carson his father. The man who had raised him. The only father he knew.

"Rick Stockton needs him in the States," JT said. "Rick has covered our ass many times and asks for little in return; we're doing this. There's no way they'll get him extradited before he slips away. He has far too many assets and properties. He's not just a small-time accountant laundering money for a crime boss. He's the only accountant for the entire Flores crime syndicate. He knows everything."

"But we're on a clock," Kane said. "If Dante did what I expected him to do, the Velasquez crime family has sent a team to take care of business. We don't want to be here for that battle."

A female voice said, "You made a promise to me, Jack Kincaid."

Sean looked over and saw Gabriella Romero. Tall, slender, beautiful. *Exotic* would be the right word.

Jack said, "Sean, Matt Elliott is at the rendezvous point, and he has the coordinates you need to pick us up."

JT handed Sean a .45. "You'll have a tricky landing and takeoff, but you're the best."

"That I am," Sean said, though he didn't feel at all confident at this moment. Then he spotted the duffel bag that had the bearer bonds and cash. "What—you got it back."

"Took out Flores's goons before they arrived at the gate. We can't let anyone have these bonds. Take them with you. The cash is going to Romero—he earned it."

Kane grunted. Sean didn't know what Dante actually had done, but clearly JT and Kane didn't see eye-to-eye on this.

"Go," Kane told Sean. He glanced down at Jesse. "Trust

us, kid." He handed Jesse a phone. "When this beeps, call Carson's cell phone."

Jesse nodded. He was pale as a ghost, but he stood tall.

Kane, Jack, JT, and Gabriella went back into the compound. Sean wanted to go with them.

But it was just him and Jesse, and he would do anything to protect his son.

CHAPTER THIRTY-THREE

For all her flaws—mostly criminal flaws—Gabriella had done everything she said she would and more. It had been Jack's plan to take out the lights, but Gabriella had taken care of the backup generators first. Kane was going to owe her and Dante big time, and he didn't like owing criminals anything. He and Dante were going to have a heart-to-heart when this was all said and done. If Dante could recuse himself from some of the shadier businesses, Kane could look away from the other shit. But he didn't think Dante could turn down the money. He wasn't a distributor, smuggler, or grower . . . he was a moneyman. A negotiator. The arbitrator when two crime families—like the Flores and the Velasquez families—had a disagreement.

And sometimes, like now, it paid for Dante to know everyone's secrets.

But Kane sure as hell didn't like him knowing the Rogan family secrets.

Kane and JT split off from Gabriella and Jack. They had their own plan, and it didn't include grabbing Carson Spade.

JT didn't work in the field anymore, but there were some things that were so ingrained, it was like they'd been work-

ing together for years. They didn't need words. A nod,
subtle body movement, hand signs. It was like old times,
but Kane was acutely aware that JT was rusty. Just because
he had once been among the elite didn't mean his reaction
time was the same. Kane hadn't thought Jack would bring
in JT and Matt Elliott to implement Kane's plan—Matt
was a fucking *prosecutor* and hadn't run an op since he
left the Navy SEALs umpteen years ago. JT—he was more
in the game, but not from this side of the war.

But that was a conversation for another day. Today was
about survival. And finding that bastard Carson Spade.

He looked at the countdown on his watch. When Jesse
called Carson, whether or not he answered his phone, Kane
would have his exact location. Sean was brilliant, though
Kane stopped telling him that long ago. Why inflate his
ego any more? Sean had created an app so that even if the
person had GPS turned off, if they were called from a
phone with the app, any other phone with that app could
track them to a ten-foot radius. If they answered the phone,
a virus wormed its way in so the individual could be
tracked even when they terminated the call.

Unless of course they took out the battery. But Kane
didn't think Carson would suspect anything. And he would
absolutely answer a phone when the caller ID had been
programmed to show the name JESSE.

JT held up his hand and Kane stopped. They were flush
against the back wall of the house, partly obscured by
scraggly oak trees. Kane looked at the watch again. One
minute. He held up one finger to JT, who nodded.

A group of four guards ran past them toward the back
wall.

Thirty seconds.

Kane and JT entered through the same service door that
Sean had escaped from. A guard stood there as sentry, but
hesitated just a second, surprised that the man who had

escaped had returned. Kane hit him in his neck and broke his windpipe. Quiet, effective, deadly.

They ran through the kitchen and stood in the butler's pantry. Kane looked at his watch. Ten seconds. He took out the small tablet Sean had given him. The light was so dim he almost couldn't see the screen, but he didn't dare turn it up. He launched the app and waited. Listened. There was still chaos outside, but inside the atrium there was only a shouting match between Jasmine and Dominick.

He caught parts of the fight because the atrium echoed.

Rogan! How dare you!

Bitch.

Fool.

They won't get out of Jalisco alive.

They're not here, are they?

The app showed Kane as a white dot and Carson's phone as a green dot. It was moving, about twenty feet from them and walking rapidly away.

Kane motioned down the hall that marked the atrium's northern perimeter. JT nodded. They both moved down the hall and pursued Carson. They were getting closer when a shout and gunfire had them taking cover.

"Get him," JT said. "I got you."

Kane didn't like leaving his partner, but he also couldn't let Carson Spade get away. He bolted down the hall and into a room.

Carson had a gun on him. Kane reached out and disarmed him immediately. Fucking accountant and *lawyer*, not a soldier.

Carson stared at him wild-eyed. "You took my son!"

"My nephew," Kane said in a low voice, "never forget it."

Carson made the connection immediately, opened his mouth, then closed it. "You'll never get out of here."

"Shut the fuck up. I planned to kill you, but others want

you alive. They won the coin toss." Kane enjoyed the panic written all over Carson's face.

"What? What do you mean?"

Kane didn't answer. He looked around the room. They were on the ground floor, which was good. Where was JT?

Gunfire erupted, very close, and JT ran in the door. He was favoring his right arm.

"Fuck it, J!"

"Flesh wound. Let's go." JT pushed a table in front of the door.

"I'm not going with you!" Carson shouted purposefully to alert anyone in the house where they were.

Kane hit him. Damn, that felt good. He whispered in his ear as he pulled the bastard's arm behind his back until he winced, "If you say one more word, I'll stab you in the kidney and leave you here to die slowly and in agony."

JT pushed open the window and climbed out. Kane pushed Carson toward the window as someone started hitting at the door. The table moved.

"Now!" Kane ordered.

Carson went through. Kane followed as the guards broke through the barrier. He pulled a grenade out of his pocket, pulled the pin, and tossed it back through the window.

"Run!" he commanded.

Ten seconds later the explosion sent them all to their knees. Screams echoed behind them, but Kane couldn't be concerned with casualties.

He hoped Jack and Gabriella had been successful, because the plan had them splitting up until they reached the plane.

Provided Sean made it safely to the plane. And was able to land at the right coordinates in the dark with the pending storm.

They couldn't escape the same way Sean had; by now the perimeter guards would have found the breach. They had to go through the main gate. And the best way was to create another distraction.

"J, now."

JT pulled a detonator out of his pocket, flipped the switch, then pressed two buttons simultaneously. Every corner of the compound perimeter exploded simultaneously. The bombs had been placed outside the gates because they couldn't access the inside until Kane had found Jesse. But the distraction was just what they needed. All the guards rushed toward the house to protect the structure. And Kane, JT, and a reluctant but terrified Carson Spade ran toward the road.

The jeep was right where they'd left it, hiding two hundred yards from the entrance. Kane cuffed Carson to the vehicle because if he didn't, he might have killed him.

He didn't like criminals as a general rule, but he despised criminals who put kids in danger.

Especially when the kid was family.

Everything that had happened from the moment that Sean had cornered him at the football game had seemed surreal. But tonight . . . Jesse was living an action movie, only it wasn't as exciting as he'd thought it might be.

In fact, he'd been scared to death. He still was.

"Explain that again, Matt?" Sean asked the driver.

"I said, you only have 1500 feet to land and take off. But it's secure."

"That's next to impossible. Not the landing part, but we're going to have what, seven—no, eight—passengers. I need more room."

"We don't have more room."

"We'll have to dump everything."

"Okay."

"And half the fuel."

"Um, is that a good idea?"

"Do you want to fly or crash?"

"I see your point." Matt didn't talk for a while. "Are you going to have enough fuel to make it to Hidalgo?"

"No. Kane better know a place where we can refuel before we hit Monterrey."

Jesse had flown many times, but never in a small plane. He was scared. And excited.

But mostly scared.

"Jesse, you good?" Sean asked. He looked back at him, winked. "We'll be fine."

Fine? He didn't know if he'd done the right thing. Well, he did . . . but he didn't. When Carson didn't let him call his mom . . . and then he got the letter from Sean . . . he thought okay, this was going to happen, Sean was his real dad.

But his real dad was a jerk. His mom said so. His mom said he'd told her he didn't want a kid and why not just get an abortion. So why would he swoop in and save him now? Risk his life? It didn't make any sense.

"Seriously, you aren't hurt or anything, are you? Jesse, talk to me."

"I'm fine." He bit his lip. "My mom told me you didn't want her to have a baby."

Sean turned in his seat and stared at him. Sean looked really upset. Angry and sad all together.

"Jesse, I don't know why Madison said or did any of the things that she did. All I can say is this: She was nineteen and pregnant and in college. She made decisions based on what she thought was best for her. I'm not going to fault her for that. But I'm going to tell you this once, and it's the truth. I never knew you existed until this week. I didn't know your mom was pregnant. If I had, I would have been there. I wish I had been. God, Jess, I love you." He looked away. For a second Jesse thought Sean was crying, but maybe not.

He shifted in the seat so he could see Sean better. Yeah,

his eyes were wet, Jesse could see that even in the near-dark. Sean put the palms of his hands against his eyes, pressed hard.

Jesse didn't know what to say. Everything he'd believed for his entire life was a lie. His mom lied to him . . . and Carson. He couldn't call Carson *Dad* anymore. Carson lied to him, too. Told him he couldn't call his mom, took away his phone, said he'd talked to her. Had he? Had he really talked to her?

And then there was that conversation this morning.

"I heard Carson talking to Mr. Flores this morning," Jesse said quietly.

"You don't have to tell me."

"You were right. About everything you said in your message. And more. He . . . he talked about it. About how he was moving money around so Dominick could access it. I didn't understand a lot . . . but Dominick was angry with my dad. With Carson," he corrected himself. "Carson kept saying it wasn't his fault, that he set up these bank accounts and companies or whatever perfectly. But Dominick said, 'Fix it or else.' And I knew Carson was scared that the *or else* meant he'd be killed." What would that have meant for him? Would they have killed Jesse, too? His mom?

"Carson worked for dangerous people," Sean said.

"Criminals," Jesse said. "You said they were criminals."

"They are," Sean said. "Flores and his family run a drug and human trafficking organization, and Carson set up their money-laundering operation. The FBI has proof, and that's why my brother went back to get him."

"Would Dominick have killed him?"

"Yes," Sean answered. Matt cleared his throat. "Matt, I know what you're thinking, but I'm not going to lie to my son."

Sean looked back at Jesse. "Jesse, you're young and

you've had a quick and violent education in the last three days. I'm never going to lie to you, okay? Maybe I'm too blunt sometimes, and I'll work on that—but I was raised by my brothers, and they never sugarcoated anything. Ignorance is never an option."

"So Kane is my uncle."

"Yes he is." Sean smiled.

"And is Jack my other uncle? You said brothers."

"Jack I guess would be your uncle-in-law. He's almost my brother-in-law. JT is Jack and Kane's partner. I'll draw you a flowchart and teach you about Rogan-Caruso-Kincaid and what we do. Well, what they do. I don't work for them anymore."

The fear started to fade, and curiosity grew. Jesse had a lot to learn about his dad and his new family. It was, well, really kinda cool and exciting.

"Is Carson going to jail?"

"I hope so," Sean said. "I'm sorry, but that's the truth."

"I hope so, too." Jesse paused. The fear came back. He didn't know quite how to say it, to explain it.

I hope Dominick doesn't get so mad that he kills me and my mom.

But he would be brave. Because his uncle Kane and his dad—his real dad—were brave.

And he hoped they would protect his mom even though she'd been lying to everyone ever since he was born.

CHAPTER THIRTY-FOUR

Noah brought Lucy back to the hotel at two that morning. She felt like a zombie. She was cried out, exhausted, barely able to put two thoughts together.

Ana was stable and the babies were healthy, but the doctor put her on bed rest. Siobhan was sleeping in Ana's room, her two years of searching finally over. The baby girl Lucy had delivered was in the NICU, but the doctor expected her to be just fine. She was nearly five pounds, almost full term, and she'd make it. Abby had called her mother, who was driving all night to be here for her daughter.

She said there was nothing to forgive and she loves me.

Lucy was an emotional basket case. They hadn't found Marisol. Four women had been killed in that slaughterhouse. There were seventy-one babies unaccounted for—all sold, all gone.

"It's over," Noah said. "Sit down before you collapse."

The hotel rooms were a suite—two rooms on either side of a living area. Lucy sat on the couch and Noah sat next to her. She put her head on his shoulder and closed her eyes. "It's not over."

"For now."

"We have to find Marisol. Bury her." Her voice cracked.

"Not tonight."

She had never been so exhausted. Emotionally, physically. Noah put his arm around her shoulders.

"Lucy," Noah said.

"Yeah?"

"I need to tell you something. It's important."

"Okay."

"When I told Rick about Carson Spade and what Sean and Kane were doing in Guadalajara, he told me he already knew about the rescue mission, though he didn't know it connected to our case. He asked RCK to bring Carson Spade back to the States. I guess everyone's down there."

Lucy sat up. "What? Everyone who?"

"Your brother. JT Caruso. Someone else, I don't remember his name. Have you heard anything?"

She shook her head. She hadn't even thought about Sean or Jesse or the rescue. With everything that had happened tonight, to save her sanity she had blocked it from her mind.

"Rick said he'd keep me in the loop. I saw the file."

"The file." Lucy rubbed her eyes. "What file?"

Noah swore under his breath. "Dear God, Lucy, I shouldn't have said anything."

She was tired, but she realized what Noah was saying. "Jesse."

"I thought—sorry. Of course you knew."

"No. I didn't. I mean, I found out Tuesday by accident."

Do not cry.

She had no more tears inside. Not tonight.

"I don't know why he didn't tell me. I can't think about it anymore. I just want . . . I don't know. I don't know anything anymore. I'm so tired, Noah. Just . . . tired."

"Hey, come here." He put her head back on his shoulder

and she closed her eyes. She felt his arm wrap around her again and she felt safe.

Seconds later she was asleep.

Lucy's phone vibrated. She opened her eyes and panicked. Where was she?

She sat up. Her body was sore and her head fuzzy from lack of sleep. Her stomach growled and she didn't remember the last time she ate. The digital clock glowed red: 7:17. The room was dark, thick curtains pulled over windows.

Hotel. You're at the hotel.

She'd fallen asleep on the couch and had no idea how she got here. She was wearing only her panties and a tank top—the same top she'd worn under her clothes the day before. Noah—had he taken off her clothes and put her to bed?

A normal girl probably wouldn't care—there was nothing sexual about their relationship—but Lucy felt her face heat.

But you trust him.

She took a deep breath, let it out. Yes, she trusted Noah. He might be the last person she could trust after everything that had happened this week.

She reached for her phone assuming it was Noah who'd texted her. Instead, it was a message from an unfamiliar number.

We're refueling in the middle of nowhere. Home this afternoon. I have to turn off this phone, it's for emergencies only. Everyone is okay. I know you're worried. I miss you. I love you ~ Sean

Relief flowed through her. Sean was alive. Everyone was safe. Her brother. Kane. The innocent boy.

Sean's son.

She shut down her emotions. She could be happy they were safe and still hurt and angry that everyone knew Sean had a son except for her.

Well, she knew, but he hadn't told her.

She didn't know if she could forgive him. She wanted to, but . . . what could he say to make it right? Lies of omission were just as bad as outright lies.

You promised me . . . you promised you would never lie to me.

She had work to do. She got up, took a shower, and felt almost human again. She left the bedroom and saw Nate clean and dressed, sitting on the couch typing on his laptop.

"I got a message from Sean. He's okay. They all are."

Nate smiled, and she saw the relief in his posture. He'd also been worried.

"I'm kind of hungry," she said.

"This place is supposed to have a great free breakfast."

She sent Noah a message that she and Nate were up and eating breakfast if he wanted to join them. He didn't respond.

But he still hadn't returned her message when they were done. They checked out at eight thirty, and went back to the hospital.

Lucy tracked down Dr. Laurel Davidson while Nate went to the lobby to call Noah and Villines and find out what the next step was. The doctor looked as tired as Lucy had felt last night. "I'm just getting off a thirty-six-hour shift," Davidson said, "but I thought you might want an update, so I hung around."

"How do you do that? Work thirty-six hours straight?" Lucy asked.

"I get naps here and there. But I'm looking forward to ten hours of lights-out. I'll be back to check on the infants, though, and I'll be on call." She motioned for Lucy and

Nate to follow her to an alcove. "Baby Elizabeth is doing great. I have no reason to keep her here, no medical reason, but Agent Armstrong said you're close to finding her mother?"

Lucy nodded, though it seemed impossible at the moment. Unlikely. "Ana de la Rosa is her family, too."

"Children's Services wants to put her in a foster home, but Agent Armstrong was quite emphatic that she wasn't to leave this hospital for her own safety, so I ordered some more tests just to keep her awhile longer. Baby Lucia is in the neonatal unit."

Lucy's heart skipped a beat. It hadn't really sunk in that the nurses had named her Lucia. Lucy's given name.

"She was just under five pounds when she came in. I'm guessing based on her development that she was about thirty-six weeks into the pregnancy. She's perfectly developed, just small, and her lungs are immature. She can breathe on her own, but it's a struggle, so we've put her in an oxygen-rich environment. She's having a hard time keeping formula down, so we're feeding her every hour in small quantities."

The doctor reached out and took her hand. "Are you okay, Agent Kincaid?"

Lucy nodded, out of habit more than anything. "Did I . . . do something wrong?"

"No. She would have died if you waited to get her mother to a hospital. The toxins from the mother's body would have made their way into her bloodstream, if the lack of oxygenated blood didn't kill her first. She's alive because of you. She'll be here for at least a week."

"And then what happens to her?" Lucy asked.

"That's out of my hands. It's up to Children's Services."

For a moment, just a moment, Lucy wanted to say, *I want her.* And she did. Desperately. Lucy couldn't have her own children, but Baby Lucia was as close as she'd come to delivering a child.

But her life was a mess. And dangerous. She was twenty-six and ill prepared to be a mother. She was unmarried, and while she and Sean had talked about adopting . . . they didn't lead calm lives. Could they? Could they settle down, move to a mountain in the middle of nowhere, and raise an infant?

And yet . . . right now, at this moment, Lucy didn't even know what was going to happen between her and Sean. A baby wouldn't solve any of their problems. And they had many. Far more than Lucy had thought. For nearly two years, she'd thought their relationship was perfect. Ups and downs but they, together, were a constant. She trusted Sean explicitly with everything, with her heart and her thoughts and her fears.

Trust. It all came down to trust. She couldn't marry Sean if she didn't trust him anymore.

And she couldn't possibly raise a child on her own. Women did it all the time. And maybe, if she were a different woman, she could do it. But Lucy didn't want to taint a baby with the horrors of the world, and those horrors were a part of her life. For the first time, she considered what Nate had told her months ago, that he never wanted to bring children into the world because the world was a screwed-up place. And Lucy had said it was up to people like them to raise the future leaders to clean it up.

But maybe that wasn't in the cards for Lucy. Maybe she was the one who had to clean up the world so her nieces and nephews had a safer place to live.

For the first time, Lucy didn't see the light of the future. With all the darkness she'd witnessed over the last three days, the light was gone. It was all darkness, all hopelessness, and how could she taint Baby Lucia with that?

Davidson was talking to her, and it took Lucy a few moments to realize she was giving her a status on the women they'd rescued. "I'm sorry, you said something about Ana de la Rosa?"

"She's on mandatory bed rest. She's twenty-eight weeks' pregnant with twins, and her body is weak. Not from lack of nutrition—her blood work is good. But her heart is struggling. She went into premature labor last night, which we stopped. Her leg was shattered and she's going in for surgery to repair it, but she'll have a severe limp for the rest of her life. We're going to try and keep her resting for at least four to six weeks before we schedule a C-section. If she improves, we'll see if she can carry them longer."

"Thank you, Doctor."

"Would you like to see Baby Lucia? You're on the approved list, you just need to show the head nurse a photo ID."

"No."

The doctor looked at her oddly. "I thought—"

"I can't. Not now."

"Is something wrong?"

Everything.

"I need to find Baby Elizabeth's mother. And then . . . maybe I'll be back."

But she wouldn't. She couldn't hold that baby and think again about everything she could never have.

She thanked the doctor and went to find Nate.

Nate was waiting for her. He didn't look happy.

"Noah is negotiating with Zapelli about the where-abouts of Marisol."

"He can't let that bastard go, that's not what you mean, is it?"

"We actually don't have a choice—the AUSA said the judge is going to toss everything we have. His statement, the search of his luggage, everything. But Zapelli doesn't know that yet. The judge is angry, but he also understands the situation and postponed the hearing until one this afternoon."

"Which means what?"

"We have a few hours to pressure Zapelli. Offer a deal to let him go because he doesn't know we're going to have to cut him loose anyway."

"That's not good enough. He sold her!"

"We can't prove it."

"We can if we find Marisol."

If we find her alive.

An hour later, Noah met Nate and Lucy at the sheriff's department.

"I have something."

"Did you cut him loose?" Lucy asked.

"He will be released after the hearing." Noah caught her eye, didn't say anything, but he didn't have to. She was personalizing this case, and she had to stop. She had to remember that not all the bad guys could be stopped.

"Okay," she said quietly.

"It sucks, Luce, I know it does, but I think she's still alive."

Adam said, "Where is she?"

"We need to go through Dobleman's phone records. Zapelli said that he delivered Marisol to Lance Dobleman on Tuesday night. They met in a parking garage and moved her from his trunk to Dobleman's. He overheard Dobleman talking to a man he believes was going to buy Marisol."

Lucy sat down heavily in the closest chair. Would this nightmare ever end? Marisol had lost two children, had been prostituted, and was now being sold to another man?

"I have the records." Adam flipped through several folders, pulled out one and handed it to Noah. "That's it," Adam said, pointing to something.

"Run it," Noah said. Then added, "Please."

Adam waved away the formalities. "The faster the better." He got on his computer.

Noah sat next to Lucy and put his hand on her forearm. "Hey."

"Hey."

"You good?"

"Yes."

"You can stay here."

"No."

"Lucy—you don't have to be superwoman all the time."

She tilted her chin up and looked Noah in the eye. "I know, and I'm not. I'm going to see this through."

"I think she's alive, but . . . we have to expect the worst."

"I do." *Always.*

"Okay."

"I heard from Sean this morning. They're on their way back."

"That's really good. Rick didn't have a time line. I assume they have everyone?"

"Yes." And that was all she could say about that.

"Got it!" Adam scribbled an address on a notepad. "And it's close by. You want backup?"

"Yes," Noah said. "As many as you can spare. We don't know what we're facing."

While Adam put together three units to assist, Noah called Quantico for information. "I have an address and a phone number, I need everything you have about the person or persons who live there. Immediately."

Five minutes later Adam's team was ready and Noah briefed him as they walked out to the vehicles.

"The house is owned by—guess who?—one of the shell

corporations that Carson Spade set up. But the phone is personal. It's registered to a forty-nine-year-old man named Alastair Holmes. He's a registered sex offender who went off the grid years ago."

"Yet he has a phone in his name."

"Probably a different social, but my people at the FBI think it's the same Alastair Holmes based on probabilities and location. Holmes is originally from Del Rio, which isn't far from here. He served three years for forcible rape in Oklahoma City, and then got ten years, served five, for a series of three violent rapes in Baton Rouge. He's on the registry in Louisiana and Oklahoma, but he never registered in Texas."

"He got smart," Lucy said. "Instead of targeting just any woman, he buys them from Dobleman. Women who won't say anything."

"You're probably right."

"But he's escalated."

"What makes you say that?" Adam asked as they climbed into his sheriff's Bronco.

"Dobleman doesn't want Marisol to live. Why give her to someone who will only hurt her? He's going to kill her. I'll bet it's not his first murder." She glanced at Noah. "Do you have his file?"

"Nuts and bolts."

"You said violent rapes."

He didn't look at her. "Yes."

"Age?"

"College age."

"How?"

"You don't need to—"

"How, Noah?"

"He raped them with foreign objects." He paused. "If you want the details, you can read them, but I'm not going to talk about it here."

"I'm trying to get into his head, Noah. You know that."

"He enjoys hurting women."

"And my guess? He's now hurting women until they die. And that's why no victims have come forward, because they're dead. And he pays Dobleman for the privilege. Or Dobleman pays *him* to get rid of their problem women, like Marisol."

It was Thursday morning. Holmes had her for the last thirty-six hours. She could already be dead. How much could she have endured? Giving birth a week ago. Walking twenty miles. And now being raped and tortured by a sick pervert.

"Five years," Adam mumbled. "Pathetic."

They didn't know what they were facing at Holmes's place. One of Adam's units did a drive-by and then called in.

"House appears quiet. Drapes pulled, no lights. Street is quiet, houses far apart. Target is a single-story ranch, and my knowledge of this neighborhood is that the homes all have basements."

Adam thanked him then said, "How do you want to proceed? If the guy is on the registry, we have the right to inspect his property, talk to him about any crimes in the neighborhood."

"He won't answer the door, and that puts Marisol in danger." *If she isn't already dead.*

Noah was about to speak, but Lucy interrupted. "A female cop needs to go to the door. Not in uniform. Ring the bell. Get access to the house."

"I'll have Officer Gorman change," Adam said. "She's with one of the units I deployed."

Lucy shook her head. "I met her last night. She doesn't fit his profile. She's close to fifty. I can get him to open the door."

Noah didn't say anything.

And Lucy was not going to tell him that she was *fine*. She was sick and tired of telling people that she was *okay*.

"Villines?" Noah asked.

"Fine with me."

"We walk in," Noah said. "Dunning and me, two of your people. As soon as he opens the door to Lucy, we go in. Do you have a wire?"

"I'll keep my phone on an open line. If I get a feeling, I'll let you know."

"A feeling?" Villines said, his nose wrinkled.

"Instincts," Lucy said. She almost smiled, but she had no humor inside. "Not a psychic."

"Sometimes I wonder," Noah said. "You got this, Lucy."

Lucy took off her blazer and hesitated, then unbuttoned her blouse.

"You don't—"

She glared at Noah. He stopped talking.

She had on a tank top under her Kevlar vest. She took off the vest. She rarely wore jeans for work, but her black slacks had been stained with blood, and the jeans were all she had with her. She took her hair out of her braid and shook it out, then put it in a loose, sloppy ponytail. She took off her holster and handed her gun to Nate, then checked her ankle holster. No way was she going in without a weapon. Anything could happen. She slipped her badge in her back pocket.

"You look five years younger," Noah said.

"That was the goal." She stretched her jaw and smiled, trying to loosen up. She dialed Noah's phone, he answered, and she put him on speaker then locked her phone so that she couldn't accidentally hang up on him. "Put yours on mute so he can't hear anything on your end."

She got out of the Bronco at the end of the street, out of line of sight of the house. Shook off her nerves. It was hot already and she was sweating, not just from her nerves.

Don't be nervous.

Holmes's house looked like every other house on the street. None of the houses looked like anyone was home, but they were all small, unfenced, and set far apart from the street, lined with scraggling trees. The problem was there was no easy way for Noah and the others to approach the house. Not until she got him to open the door; then they could come around from behind.

She glanced behind her and saw that Nate and Noah were running parallel and behind her through the back-yards.

That meant Adam and one of his people were approaching from the other side, though she couldn't see them.

She stopped in front of the house. Looked around as if she were lost, then walked up the narrow cement walk. Holmes's yard was immaculate. The lawn was a sickly green color from the drought, but it was cut short and there were no weeds. The small porch had been swept, and matching pottery with cacti framed the door. The house was well maintained—the roof, for example, had a few new shingles, neatly patched.

Fastidious. Methodical.

She knocked on the door, then rang the bell. It buzzed loudly, which surprised her.

She had the distinct impression that she was being watched. At first she dismissed it as Noah and Nate getting into position, but she stepped back a foot and glanced around, not like she was intentionally looking for something, just casual.

But she saw the camera mounted under the narrow eave of the roof.

Holmes was watching her.

She wiped the sweat off her forehead, then stretched, which had the added effect of stretching her tank top tight over her breasts. Her cotton shirt was damp, which made her uncomfortable, but it would intrigue Holmes. She fanned herself and rang the bell one more time.

He was inside. Why wasn't he coming to the door?

Then she heard footsteps. "I'm so glad someone's home," she said for Noah's benefit. She kept her voice light, young.

The door opened. The security screen was still locked. She couldn't see into the dark house, and the screen made it difficult to make out any details. "Hello?" she said. "I'm sort of lost. I mean, not really, I know I'm in the right neighborhood. My grandpa moved in last month, and this is the first day off I've had in *forever*. He told me his address was 11678 Diablo. But *two* street signs are missing. I've been to four houses, no one answers. Do you know where Diablo is?"

He didn't say anything for a second. "I think I do."

"Oh, thank you. I'm *so* hot. I can't wait for winter, you know?"

He still didn't open the screen. He said. "I think Diablo is the street two over from here."

"Two over which way?" She turned, not completely putting her back to Holmes, but trying to get him to step out and point. "Two streets over parallel? Perpendicular?"

"Go to the corner, turn left, two blocks." He looked around. "You don't have a car."

"I parked under a tree down the block, hoping someone was home to help." She fanned herself. "Thanks." She coughed.

"Hey, you want some water?"

"Oh, I don't want to trouble you." She coughed again.

"No trouble. Come on in." He unlocked the screen and opened it.

"I don't want to put you out."

But she held the screen open, not giving him a chance to close and lock it.

"It's not a problem." Holmes was staring at her breasts. "You can stay here, I'll bring it to you. Icy water."

"Okay, thank you so much. I'll wait right here."

He walked away. She had the screen open, and turned her back to the camera, took out her phone, and whispered. "He's going to the back. There's a camera on the porch." Then she saw there was a second camera. If he was watching, he would have seen her talking into her phone. "Shit," she said, "two cameras."

Noah and Nate both ran from the yard next door and toward the porch. Inside, she heard a door slam. "He knows," she said.

She pulled the gun from her ankle holster and went inside. Noah and Nate were right behind her. Noah was talking through a mike in his sleeve to Villines. "We're inside, need cover."

Stairs went down to the dark basement. The door was open—this wasn't where he'd gone.

Lucy gestured. Noah nodded, motioned to Nate to lead. Noah stayed at the top of the stairs—they didn't know where Holmes was.

Lucy followed Nate down. It was darker than upstairs, but ground-level windows let in some natural light.

She smelled blood. Urine. Bile.

In the corner, a naked woman hung by her wrists from a hook on the ceiling.

No no no no!

Lucy made a move toward her, but Nate put up his hand and stopped her.

The basement had nearly as large a footprint as the house. Nate motioned to a switch on the wall. Lucy nodded, turned it on.

A weak light gave them more visibility. The basement was one large room and they quickly cleared it.

Nate said into his com, "We have her. Basement secure."

He helped Lucy cut Marisol off the hook, then he stood guard because there was no word as to where Holmes had gone.

Marisol moaned. She was alive. Lucy said, "You're safe. You're safe, Marisol." She looked around for something to cover her. There was nothing.

"Ana. My sister."

"She's safe. She's in the hospital, she's going to be okay. The babies—they are healthy."

Marisol began to sob. "I'm so sorry, so sorry."

"You saved them, Mari," Lucy said as she hugged the shaking woman. "You saved them because you had the courage to escape."

"It's my fault. I . . . I called Angelo. I thought . . . He . . ."

"I know," Lucy said. "He lied to you. He used you. That's not your fault, Mari. That's on him."

A single gunshot made Marisol jump. Nate said, "Stay with her," and ran up the stairs. There were several voices and footsteps above them. Then Nate came back down with a blanket. "Holmes killed himself," he said.

"Where was he? We cleared the house."

"There's a false wall in the second bedroom. And there's evidence of his crimes. A wall of photos."

Lucy felt ill and closed her eyes. "Good riddance."

Lucy watched from the doorway as Marisol was reunited with her sister, her baby, and Siobhan. She was relieved, more than anything, that they'd found Marisol alive. She'd been abused, but she was a survivor. Lucy would give her a bit of time, then come back and talk to her.

Marisol would need someone to talk to. Someone who

understood what she'd suffered. Someone who could help her overcome the worst of her trauma. For now, she needed her sister.

Lucy turned and walked away. She needed to go home. Home. What home? Did she even have a home anymore?

"Lucy!"

Lucy stopped and waited for Siobhan to catch up. John Honeycutt was right behind her. "They're safe because of you," Lucy told Siobhan. "You never gave up."

Siobhan hugged her tightly. "You saved them. What you did . . . What you do . . . Thank you."

Lucy accepted Siobhan's hug, but she was so emotionally drained that she couldn't muster a smile or a tear.

Lucy turned to John. "Thank you, John. You and your family are a light in this world that we all need."

As she spoke, she believed it—yet the light was fading. She saw it here, but what about outside? What about her life? She hadn't felt this lost and alone in a long time.

"I—um—Adam told me I might be able to see Marisol." He held up a pink gift bag. "My mom made Baby Elizabeth something."

"Looks like a lot of somethings," Siobhan said.

"My mom knits when she's worried."

Siobhan said, "Let me tell Marisol you're here. I'm sure she wants to see you." She went down the hall.

Lucy watched as John adjusted his collar. "You care for her," she said.

"I—I'm just relieved. I was scared for her. Adam said you found her, saved her. Thank you."

"It's my job."

"You went above and beyond. Adam told us about the baby last night. He's down in the neonatal unit right now checking on her."

Siobhan came out of the sister's room and said, "You can come in, John."

Lucy intended to leave the hospital, but she found herself in the neonatal unit. She wanted to see Baby Lucia one last time.

Adam Villines was watching Baby Lucia being fed by a nurse. He was beaming. When he saw Lucy, he said, "She's perfect. Dr. Davidson said she's going to be fine. She still needs extra oxygen, but not for much longer." He took her hand. Lucy felt uncomfortable with the intimacy. "Do you want to hold her?"

Lucy shook her head.

"That's my wife in there."

"Feeding her?"

Adam nodded. "We talked about it last night and this morning. If Children's Services can't find her family, we want to adopt her. We have three girls, one more would be a blessing. She needs someone who will love her unconditionally. Protect her. And my family is strong. Mine and the Honeycutts."

Lucy's heart skipped a beat. She wanted to say no. She wanted to say Baby Lucia was hers.

But Lucia wasn't her baby. And right now, Lucy wouldn't make a good mother. She didn't know if she ever would.

Sean, on the other hand, would make a great dad.

He's the light in your life. Without him, you're nothing but dark.

But she didn't have Sean anymore, did she? Because she didn't know him. And he didn't trust her.

Whatever happened, she would continue to survive.

"She's a lucky baby," Lucy heard herself saying. "You'll love her?"

"I already do." He hugged Lucy.

Noah was staring at her. She hadn't even seen him walk in. The look on his face . . . He saw more than she wanted him to see. She averted her eyes.

"I talked to Nate," Noah said. "He's going to stay here and wrap things up over the next day or two. Let me take you home."

She didn't argue. All she wanted was to go home.

Even though she didn't know what she would find there, or if she even had a real home anymore. Because home wasn't just a place, it was a person. It was family. She thought her home was Sean.

She just didn't know anything anymore.

CHAPTER THIRTY-FIVE

After the last seventy-two hours, the flight back to Texas was relatively uneventful.

Sean needed uneventful.

They made two stops. One to refuel in the middle of nowhere—how Kane had friends in the oddest, most remote places always surprised Sean. The other was in Hidalgo, where the FBI was waiting to take Carson Spade into custody. Sean didn't know the agents, but JT did. He took responsibility for the official RCK statement on the extraction of Carson Spade. No one at RCK talked officially to any law enforcement agency except JT.

Jesse had slept almost the entire plane ride, even through a few rough patches when they were low on fuel and hitting some turbulence. But he woke up when they landed in Hidalgo and watched as his stepfather was taken into custody.

Kane put his hand on Jesse's shoulder. "It's going to be okay, kid."

"I know. Thank you."

Kane cracked a grin. "He's already more polite than you ever were, Sean."

Carson Spade practically growled. "Madison will never let you near him, not after what you've done."

Sean glared at Spade. He was in deep. Could the feds even trust him? That wasn't Sean's concern.

He glanced down at Jesse. Yes, Carson Spade was Sean's concern, because he was in his son's life. Even if Spade went to prison for the rest of his life, he had worked for some very bad people, and those people may seek retribution on Spade's family.

Sean's son.

Kane caught his eye. His expression was hard, as if he knew exactly what Sean was thinking. Kane put his arm around Jesse's shoulders, silently showing Spade—and Sean—that Jesse was under their wing. That the Rogan family would protect him.

The FBI agents drove away with Spade, and JT came over to them. "Sean, do you have a minute?"

Sean followed JT away from the others. Jack and Matt were refueling the plane and talking. Sean had learned that Matt was Jack's brother-in-law. That, more than the fact that Matt was a prosecutor and JT's closest friend, was probably why he'd come to help. Because he was family. It was truly a small world.

"First, the feds are going to want to talk to Jesse, but I convinced them to let you bring him back to his mother in San Antonio. Madison Spade has been told not to leave town until after she and Jesse are both deposed. I thought you might want some alone time with your son first."

"Thank you." He cleared his throat, surprised at the emotions that ran through him. It was like he was one big emotional balloon that could burst at any moment.

"Sean, I want you to come back full-time with RCK."

Sean hadn't expected that. He didn't know what to expect—maybe a lecture, or a warning. For years he'd wanted to please his brothers—and JT, who was the next closest thing to a brother—but he always felt like he'd fallen short. That he'd disappointed them. When he left, he left on his terms, because he realized that his brother Duke—his guardian, his mentor, his tormentor—would never think of him as an equal. Sean would always be the problem child, the kid who got in trouble and tried to charm his way out of it.

Duke never gave him the benefit of the doubt.

"You know why I left."

"Yes." JT looked Sean squarely in the eye. "Family is complicated, and while we love our family unconditionally, there are still . . . long memories. Deep resentments. Sometimes we can't overcome our own insecurities, guilt, failures, or fears. Duke is a good man, but he has a blind spot when it comes to you. He's trying. I want you back in RCK. Me. And Jack. You've already been working freelance, but I want you under our umbrella. You're an asset, one I don't think any of us appreciated until you were gone. You won't be working under Duke. You may have to work with him, because when you two partnered on security systems it was truly a sight to behold. You work well together . . . But you would be a full partner. Like Jack. Like Duke. Like Kane. Like me. Equals."

Sean was speechless. He hadn't been expecting the offer, and he didn't really know what to think about it. He missed his old assignments, but he didn't miss the tension.

If he was really a full partner, an equal, maybe he could find a way to work with Duke.

JT continued. "It won't be easy. Jack and Duke are both married to federal agents, you soon will be, and there are times when we won't necessarily see eye-to-eye. But I know we'll make it work. I want to make it work."

"I need to talk to Lucy. I need a few days."

JT nodded. He slapped Sean on the back and said, "You were good back there. Truly good. Even with the personal stakes. But it's not because of this operation that I'm asking you back. It's because you make RCK better."

"I appreciate it."

"One more thing." He put up his finger to have Sean wait, and walked over to the plane. He spoke briefly to Jack and Matt, then went inside and came out empty-handed. Odd.

This week had surprised him. JT and Jack had Kane's back. They didn't work south of the border anymore, but when Kane and Sean needed them, they were there. That kind of brotherhood went beyond blood. And for the first time, Sean felt like he was really one of them. Not just Duke Rogan's smart-aleck troublemaking little brother, but one of the team.

Returning to RCK had a lot of pros, more pros than cons. The only big hurdle might be Sean himself—whether he could forgive his brother Duke, whether he could pull himself out of the role of the troublemaking little brother, whether he could get over his insecurities and resentments. Maybe his entire problem with RCK in the first place had been psychological.

JT came back over to him. "The bearer bonds. They're in the lock chest on the plane. I need you to take them to your house. You have a safe, correct?"

"Yes."

"State of the art, I assume."

Sean smiled. "Yes."

"Those bonds are hot right now. There are a lot of people who want those bonds for a variety of reasons. Until things cool down, I'd like you to keep them in your safe."

"Okay," Sean said, skeptical. "Though RCK has a safe, too. Bigger. Better."

"It's complicated. But Rick Stockton and I have an agreement—and it works for us. One of the terms is that we don't keep certain information from each other. After the operation, he heard about the bonds . . . and asked me if I had them. I said not anymore. So I can't have them, at least not right now. When things settle down, we'll arrange a time for you to bring them back to RCK."

"Okay." Sean was curious—more than a little curious—but he would do research on the bonds later. Talk to Kane.

First things first. Reunite Jesse with Madison. See Lucy.

"You're good here?" JT said. "Kane's going to go with you to San Antonio, just in case. I don't expect trouble, but . . ."

He didn't need to say anything else.

Sean asked, "Do we have a report on casualties?"

"All I know for certain is that Samuel Flores is a confirmed kill and Jose Flores is alive and well. He's the least of my concerns."

"There was a girl, with Alberto. Young. And an infant."

"Gabriella got the girl and baby out, but I don't know where they are. The Romeros will try to get them back to the States. I don't have a report on Alberto, Dominick, or Jasmine, but we have people down there. We'll have intel soon."

"Thank you."

"Watch your back, Sean. Until we get a full and confirmed report, we all have targets on our back."

JT left with Jack and Matt. Kane walked over with Jesse. "Ready?"

"We're fueled, let me just check over the plane and we can go."

"What's going to happen now?" Jesse asked Sean.

"The FBI will talk to Carson. Decide if they have enough to arrest him. There'll be a trial. Your mom will be questioned about how much she knew. You may be questioned."

"My mom didn't know anything. She wouldn't have let me go if she did."

Maybe, maybe not. Maybe she was willfully blind to the truth.

"Carson isn't all bad," Jesse said.

"No one is all bad." That wasn't true. Sean had promised never to lie to Jesse, and he'd just lied. "Well, there are some people who are mostly bad, but let me tell you something. When Carson recognized me last night, the first thing he thought about was you. He was worried about you."

"But you weren't going to hurt me."

"No, never. But he didn't know what the plan was, and he knew that whatever it was it would be dangerous. And he didn't know if I was there to take you away from your mother."

"Would you?"

"I thought about it for half a minute." Sean stared at Jesse. He hadn't been there for him. Through no fault of his own, he hadn't been there. But would he have made a good father? He didn't know. "Look, right or wrong, your mother did what she did and we can't change that. But she loves you. She was there for you every day since you were born. I wouldn't take you away from her. Okay? Don't worry about what's going to happen."

"I can't help it."

"I get that. But you can't affect it. It's going to happen, good or bad, based on the courts and the FBI and lawyers and everyone except you and me. But we're good, Jesse, I hope. I want—I want to get to know you. Is that okay?"

"Yeah. I want that, too." He bit his lip. "Can I call my mom? Let her know I'm okay?"

"I already sent her a message, but yeah, it's safe to call now."

Sean wanted to take Jesse back to Madison and then go to Lucy. He had an uneasy feeling that something was very wrong.

* * *

Two hours later, Sean knocked on Madison's hotel room. She opened the door.

Madison looked like a wreck. She threw her arms around Jesse and began to cry. "Oh my God, oh my God, Jesse, are you okay?" She held him at arm's length, brushed the hair away from his face, then hugged him again.

"I'm okay, Mom. Mom, I can't breathe."

"You can't breathe? Do you need a doctor?"

"You're squeezing me."

She let go. But she couldn't stop touching him. His face. His hair.

"You're okay." She took a deep breath. Then she turned to Sean and slapped him. "I told you not to go!"

Sean stared at her and controlled his anger. "Don't."

"I told you they were okay. You put my son's life in danger!"

Sean stepped into the hotel room. Kane was outside the door. He gave Sean a look of confidence before Sean closed the door.

"Jesse was in a house owned by a crime family."

"There's no proof of that. You're making it up to make me look bad."

"You? No. Carson? Yes. The FBI has plenty on him. He's not getting out of this."

"No. You did this, somehow. When I came to you, you found a way to discredit me . . ." As she spoke she realized how idiotic she sounded, so Sean didn't say a word.

"How could this have happened?" she said, wiping tears from her face.

"Carson wanted to give you everything you wanted," Jesse said.

Madison stared at her son as if he were a stranger. "What? You mean your father."

"He's not my father," Jesse said.

Madison turned to Sean. "You promised you wouldn't tell him!"

"No, I didn't."

"Carson raised you, Jesse. He loves you. He loves us. He *wanted* us."

"Mom, he's a criminal. He launders money for the drug cartels."

"You can't believe what Sean tells you. He'll say anything to hurt me. I'm sorry, Jesse, but Sean and I were very young when we met. He was wild, he'd been expelled from Stanford and was almost put in prison for computer hacking! I didn't want you around that. I wanted to protect you."

Sean wanted to hit her. How dare she bring that up—here, now. Like this.

"There are two sides to every story," Sean said, his voice low. He caught Madison's eye. She was in full panic. She was afraid of losing everything, of losing her son.

Jesse said, "Mom, stop. Sean didn't tell me anything I didn't already know."

Madison looked like she was going to faint. Or puke. Or both. Sean still had no sympathy for her.

"Honey, this is just mixed up in your head. I'm sure there's a logical explanation for everything, and when Carson gets here, he'll explain."

"They arrested him at the airport."

"What? No!" She grabbed her purse. "I have to go see him. Come on, Jesse."

"I don't want to go. I don't want to see him right now."

"I'll stay with him," Sean said. He didn't want to stay. He wanted to go home and see Lucy. But he could bring Jesse with him. "He can come home with me."

"No way. Absolutely not."

"Why not, Mom?"

"Because! He's not your father!"

Jesse looked from Sean to his mom. "But—what?"

"Madison!" Sean snapped. "Tell him the truth. Now, or dammit, I will get a paternity test and prove it."

"I mean to say, he's your biological father, but he didn't raise you."

"Because you didn't tell him about me. Right, Mom? You kept it a secret."

"I—" She was going to lie again, Sean could see it in her eyes. "We were young. He wasn't ready to be a father."

"That might have been the case then," Sean said, "but I'm not a teenager anymore. And you didn't give me a chance to prove myself to you, or to Jesse."

"We'll talk about this later. I need to see my husband."

Jesse sat down on the bed. "I'm not going."

Sean didn't want to see Jesse start taking this whole thing out on his mother—no matter how much she deserved it. He said to Madison, "It's been a long couple of days. And the FBI isn't going to let you see Carson, not yet. My advice? Find him a good lawyer."

"He already has one."

"Maybe find him a lawyer who doesn't also work for the drug cartels. They're known to eat their own when threatened."

She paled, and Sean felt guilty for being so blunt. But the truth was, Madison had to grow up and face the music. Her husband was a money launderer for some very nasty people. He was going to prison. There was no way around it.

"I'll find him a lawyer," she said.

Sean turned to Jesse. "I'll see you later."

Jesse ran over and hugged him. He whispered, "I was really scared the whole time."

Sean's heart tightened. "You know what?" he whispered back. "So was I."

CHAPTER THIRTY-SIX

It was Thursday afternoon before Sean made it home. He walked into his house and Lucy was there, in the living room, curled up on the couch. His heart quickened.

He was home. He was truly home.

She sat up when he closed the door. She looked so exhausted. For the first time, Sean didn't know anything about what had happened on a case of hers. He had known it was a bad one, and he knew now that they'd solved it and stopped a black-market baby ring, but it was clear from the way Lucy looked that she'd gone through hell and back.

And he hadn't been here.

He practically ran over to her, kissed her, hugged her. She felt so good, so right here in his arms.

"I missed you so much," he said. He buried his face in her hair. Her neck. He kissed her over and over.

She kissed him back lightly, then sat down again. He sat next to her, grabbing her hands. He never wanted to let her go.

"Our cases intersected," Lucy said.

"Yes. But Carson Spade is in custody and Jesse is back with his mother. And you found the missing sisters. It's over." He kissed her. "Can we talk about it tomorrow? I just want to think of nothing but us. You. Me. A hot shower." He kissed her again.

She wasn't kissing him back.

"Lucy, what's wrong?"

"I saw Jesse's photo."

He blinked.

She continued. "I wish you had told me, Sean."

"That Jesse is my son."

She nodded.

That was when Sean saw what was underneath Lucy's exhaustion. She was blank. Cool. She was assessing him. How he responded mattered.

"I didn't know about him."

"I know. Not until Madison told you."

"Right. And I couldn't just tell you over the phone. I wanted to, but I needed to be here with you. She never told me she was pregnant. She never told Jesse that I was his father. It was . . . a shock. But that doesn't change anything, not for us. We'll work through it."

She extracted her hands from his and stood up.

"It's not Jesse. It's not that you have a son. You lied to me, Sean."

"What?"

"Just now. You lied to me. I wanted—needed—to hear you tell me why you didn't explain everything on Monday before you left. You knew Monday, when Madison came here and told you everything. And yet . . . You didn't tell me. So I've been thinking and trying to figure out why you kept that from me, why you went to Mexico to rescue your son without even explaining to me the real reason you took the job. Nothing I thought of made sense. But I love you, and I knew you would have a good reason that I would understand.

"And then you lied to me."

"I didn't. That's not what I meant!"

"You did. Why didn't you tell me when you had the chance?"

He stared at her. This could not be happening. Lucy was emotionless. It was like she already had walked out on him. His chest tightened. "I—there wasn't a good time. You had a tough case, an abandoned infant, missing girls, and I didn't want you to worry about me. I had Kane—"

"Kane and everyone else knew. Everyone." Now there was a flash of anger. Anger was good, right? That meant she still loved him. That she cared. "Kane knew. Jack knew. JT Caruso knew. Rick Stockton knew. They knew because they needed to know, because they were all part of this extraction in one way or the other. But not me. I didn't need to know, did I?"

"Lucy—"

"I love you, Sean, and this has been the hardest three days of my life. Your attempt to once again protect me by keeping information from me hurts more than anything. It comes down to trust. I trust you explicitly. But you don't trust me."

"That's nonsense! Lucy—"

"Is it nonsense? Because if you trusted me—my emotions, my ability to compartmentalize, my sanity—then you would have told me the truth and we would have worked through it. But you kept it from me because somewhere deep inside you think that I'm fragile. That I need protecting from, what, *life*? That lying to me, keeping secrets from me, is your way of loving me. That's not love, Sean. It's pity."

"God no, Lucy, you're wrong." This was not happening. Lucy couldn't be thinking like this. Sean began to panic.

"I was once broken. I know what it's like to be in a million pieces. But I'm not broken anymore. I'm no longer fragile. You gave me hope. You gave me back the piece of me I was missing before I met you. You told me once that we were stronger together."

"We *are*."

"You don't believe it. Because you don't trust me to not break again under the weight of life. Life is cruel, Sean. It's dark. It's violent. Innocent people die and we can't save them all. You were my light, my hope, my sanctuary."

"I still am. Lucy, please don't—we need to talk, we need to sleep, we need—" He couldn't talk. The room was spinning. It was whirling away and Lucy was going with it.

"I need time, Sean. I have to think. I don't know who I am without you. I have to find out. One thing I know, I'm not the broken girl I once was. I'm not going to be lied to or treated with kid gloves. I'm tired of telling people that I'm fine, I'm okay, I'm not falling apart because life becomes messy or the case I'm working is brutal."

Sean couldn't stop the tears. He did not cry, he never cried, but the tears flowed. "Don't leave me."

He saw the tears in Lucy's eyes, and there was hope.

"Forgive me, Lucy. I love you so much."

"I love you, Sean." Her voice cracked. "I need time. I need—just—I'm going to pack a bag. I need to go away."

"No. No! You can't!" He grabbed her by the arms. "Don't walk out, we have to fix this!"

"It can't be fixed overnight." She pulled away from him and walked up the stairs.

He started after her, then stopped, sat on the bottom step.

Lucy was leaving him. And it was all his fault.

Lucy closed the bedroom door and collapsed against the wall. She put her head on her knees and forced herself to breathe.

Walking away from Sean had been a lot harder than she

thought. She focused on the lie he told—a lie she still didn't understand. She wished she understood what he'd been thinking.

She loved him. He loved her. Why would he not tell her the truth? And then . . . lie about it? Lie that he didn't have a chance to tell her? That's what bothered her the most.

She didn't want to leave, but she needed time and space. Distance. She had a key and the security codes to Jack's house in Hidalgo. No . . . she couldn't do that. She couldn't leave work for a few days, and she was in no condition to drive anywhere today.

The security panel beeped. She looked up—Sean had left the house.

What was she supposed to do? Forgive him? Just like that? She wanted to, desperately, but there was that doubt in the back of her mind that he would do it all again. That his regret was only that she'd figured out he knew about Jesse before he left.

Time. Time and distance and then maybe they could find a way to pick up the pieces.

Or not. Because right now, she didn't know if she could forgive . . . because she didn't know how Sean thought of her.

She was too tired to think, too tired to do anything, really, but she had to leave before he came back. Tomorrow maybe there would be perspective. She'd get a hotel room. Noah already told her not to come in tomorrow morning. She'd sleep . . . if she could. Go to work. Bury herself in her job. It would save her.

It would have to.

She went down the hall to the storage closet and pulled out her travel suitcase. She packed up enough clothes for the weekend, a couple of work outfits, her toiletries. The faster she got out, the faster she could figure out what to do about . . . everything.

It was after six by the time Lucy walked down the stairs with her bag. She couldn't bear to look at her house . . . it might be the last time she saw it. She didn't want to leave.

She had to.

She went down the hall to the kitchen. Considered leaving Sean a note as to where she'd be, but he might not respect her wish for time. Maybe it would be better if he didn't know where she was.

His laptop case and overnight bag were on the floor by the garage door. She picked them up and put them on the breakfast nook table.

She needed to leave him a note. Brief. Something like, *We'll talk tomorrow*. Though she didn't know what she could say. She'd said it all.

She grabbed a notepad that was next to the house phone and searched for a pen. She unzipped the side of Sean's laptop case and felt inside for a pen. Attached to the clip was a folded piece of paper with her name on it.

Slowly, she opened it. It was dated Wednesday. Yesterday.

Dearest Lucy ~
    In case everything goes sideways tonight, I need you to
know that I loved you with a passion and joy that knows
no bounds.

Lucy sat down. He went into the rescue thinking he might die.

    You are everything to me. My beginning and my ending.
You have made me a better person, a better man, a better
brother, a better friend. You are my strength. I see in you a
glow that humbles me, and always makes me want to do
better.
    I'm gone now, but you're not. You have an amazing life

ahead of you. You have family and friends who love you. But
more than that, you have you. You are stronger than you know;
you are braver than you think. You have always told me that
I am the light in your darkness; princess, you are my light. You
are my life.

You're going to learn that Jesse Spade is my son. I didn't
know until Monday when Madison told me; I wanted to tell you,
I don't know what stopped me. I think . . . deep down . . . that
you would think I was a lesser person. That I should have
known that I had a son. That I should have talked to my
ex-girlfriend, figured it out. But I didn't know, and I hate that
I didn't know.

And I think in the back of my mind, I knew you had a tough
case. I didn't want you to worry about me. Or be thinking that
this was anything but a normal rescue situation. I wanted you
to focus 100% on your case. I wanted you to find the lost girls.
Distractions can mess with our heads, they can lead to
mistakes—I should know. I have made many mistakes.

None of this means anything anymore. The only thing that
matters is that you know I loved you with every cell in my
body. That now that I'm gone, I want you to live and love
again. You deserve it.

Yours now and always,
Sean

Lucy didn't realize she was crying until her tears hit the
paper.

CHAPTER THIRTY-SEVEN

Sean didn't want to see Dean Hooper or Noah Armstrong tonight, but they'd both left urgent messages for him that he had been ignoring all afternoon.

He was on autopilot. Lucy was leaving him, and he didn't know how to make it right. He didn't know what to do. She loved him . . . but she was walking away.

When he finally checked his messages, he knew he had to go into FBI headquarters. He didn't want to leave the house . . . would Lucy be there when he returned? But what could he do? There was a lot of fallout from what happened in Mexico. Some things he needed to clean up himself. And he didn't know what else he could say to Lucy.

He arrived at FBI headquarters at six that night. When had he last slept? A bit on the plane when Jack took over flying.

He didn't care. His life was falling apart around him.

Noah greeted him at the door. "You look like shit."

"Good to see you, too, Noah."

Noah almost said something else, but didn't. "I would have waited until tomorrow, but we have a time crunch, and I need my ducks in a row before I talk to the judge tomorrow. But the most important component is Jesse."

Sean pushed Lucy out of his head—as much as he could. His fears still clouded his head, but if Jesse was in trouble . . . He had to be able to fix one thing in his life.

"What happened?"

"Hooper and I took his statement. Do you know what he knows?"

"Some."

"He figured out what Spade was doing and has some dangerous information. He's a witness. Hooper doesn't think we need him to testify against the Flores crime family, but they're going to know he could potentially testify."

"RCK will do everything to protect him."

"Spade agreed to turn state's evidence. He's working with the AUSA now putting together his statement. He's going to testify so Jesse doesn't have to—on the condition that he and his family are put into witness protection."

Sean stared at him. He might be slow tonight, but he knew what that meant.

"That bastard."

"Sean—he knows a lot. We can take down not only the remaining Flores cartel members, but others."

But if Jesse was in witness protection, Sean would never see him again.

He was losing both the love of his life and the son he barely knew.

"Let's sit down," Noah said and steered Sean into his office. He closed the door. "What's going on?"

There was no way in hell Sean was telling Noah about what had happened between him and Lucy.

"It's been a long fucking week."

"Jesse had a lot to say."

Sean didn't say anything.

"He sees you and Kane as practically superheroes."

"We didn't do anything we wouldn't have done for another kid in trouble."

"He doesn't want to go into witness protection. He refused, in fact. Had some choice things to say about his stepfather. But at the core, he realized that if he goes into witness protection, he'll never see you again."

Sean had no idea what to do or say. He didn't know how to fix this. He didn't know how to protect Jesse and get Lucy back.

"Hooper is bringing Madison and Jesse here. I think you are the only one who can convince Jesse that this is the best thing for him." Noah paused. "Sean—RCK is the best in the business, but can you honestly say you can protect Jesse *and* his mother? Because Madison made it clear if Jesse doesn't go, she won't go. And Carson Spade made it clear if his wife and stepson aren't with him, he'll go to prison before turning state's evidence."

"Which puts Jesse in danger because he knows too much. Goddamn that bastard."

"Where's Lucy?" Noah asked.

I don't know.

"Home."

Noah stared at him. What did he know? That Sean had fucked up? That he was losing the only good thing in his life? Sean couldn't stop thinking about what he'd said, what he'd done, how he'd screwed up. He thought . . . Hell, he didn't know what he was thinking. When he was in Mexico, it was so easy to believe that when he told Lucy, she would understand. She'd listen, she'd realize that he hadn't had a good opportunity to explain before he left . . .

He'd lied to himself. Just like he lied to Lucy. He *knew* he should have told her the truth from the beginning, but he was scared. He didn't know why. Lucy would never have left him because of Jesse. She'd never have walked away.

She's leaving you because you lied to her.

He wanted to take it all back. He didn't know how to fix it.

"Are you okay, Sean?"

"No."

He didn't elaborate. He couldn't. This was Noah Armstrong. He was half in love with Lucy; he'd told Sean before he didn't think Sean was good enough for her.

"Did Lucy tell you what happened in Laredo?"

"I don't want to talk to you about Lucy."

"I don't care what you want, Sean. You need to listen."

"You were just waiting for me to fuck up."

"Get over yourself. *You* did this, Sean. You fucked this up. But Lucy loves you."

"Don't. Just . . . stop." Every muscle in Sean's body was coiled and ready to pop.

"I'm not your rival. I'm your friend. More, I'm Lucy's friend. She went through hell these last three days. You went through your own crucible. I'm not judging you. I was in college once. I've made mistakes. We all screw up, Sean. But right now, this isn't about you. It's about Lucy. This case was horrific. It affected me, and cases don't affect me. None of us working this have slept much in four days. But through it all, Lucy went above and beyond. She needs time. She needs you."

"I fucked up, Noah."

"I know. Fix it."

"I don't know how."

"You'll figure it out. You always do." He slid over a newspaper. "The unidentified FBI agent in the article is Lucy. I'm going to check on Hooper. I'll get you when they're here."

Noah left Sean alone in his office. Sean picked up the newspaper and read the article Noah pointed to.

Laredo, TX—A violent shootout Wednesday night resulted in seven dead, six injured—including two Webb County sheriff's deputies, one of whom is in stable but critical condition—and three arrests.

Webb County Assistant Sheriff Adam Villines reported that at approximately 0900 hours, he and two officers canvassed a neighborhood where they believed a woman was being held against her will. When they approached a ranch house on the 1800 block of Westwood Avenue, they were fired upon. Officer Tom Franz was shot twice point-blank in the chest and thigh. He's in critical but stable condition following surgery.

After a short but tense standoff, the suspects began to shoot hostages. Three of the six hostages were killed before SWAT was able to secure the scene. During the assault, four suspects were shot and killed and three were taken into custody. Two were transported to the hospital but are expected to make full recoveries.

But the hero of the night was a rookie FBI agent whose name was withheld for her safety. One of the hostages was a pregnant woman who was used as a shield by Lance Dobleman, one of the suspects. According to witnesses, Dobleman shot the unidentified pregnant woman in her neck before SWAT officers immobilized him. With her dying breath, she begged the officers to save her baby. The paramedics were en route, but the life of the infant was at stake. The rookie FBI agent, who has had some medical training according to her commanding

*officer, performed an emergency C-section with
the assistance of the SWAT medic. According to
Dr. Laurel Davidson with the children's hospital,
the quick thinking of the officers saved the baby's
life. Unfortunately, the mother died from her
injuries.*

*"If the FBI agent didn't perform the surgery
immediately, even in the horrific conditions, that
baby would have died," Davidson said. "Even so,
it's a miracle that the baby survived."*

*The nurses at the hospital are calling the miracle
baby Lucia.*

*Villines said that this is the end of a black-market
baby criminal organization that has resulted in the
sale of more than six dozen infants over the last two
years. The FBI and Webb County Sheriff's Department have been working together . . .*

Noah brought Sean to where Jesse was sitting in one of the
FBI conference rooms. It was late, so no one was in the
office except for them and the small team Dean Hooper
was working with in the White Collar Crimes Division.
"Hooper is talking to Madison. You have about ten
minutes."

Sean looked Noah in the eye and said, "Thank you."

Noah squeezed his shoulder. "Sean, it's going to be
okay. Things will work out the way they are supposed to."

Sean closed the door and sat down next to Jesse. He
looked tired, scared, and determined.

"Hey."

Jesse looked at him. "I'm not going."

"They can't make you."

He seemed surprised by Sean's comment. "Exactly."

Sean wanted to tell him about Carson Spade's selfish

ultimatum. He wanted to tell Jesse that he could live with him. He wanted it . . . but in the back of his mind, he knew that wasn't the right call. There were too many things going on, too many people involved, too many dangers.

"You have to want into the program, follow it, or it doesn't work."

"I hate Carson."

"You don't."

"Don't tell me what I think. You know what he said? He said he talked to my mom all week. But he *didn't*. And then he said the phones weren't working so I couldn't call her. He just didn't want me to talk to her *at all*. To ask about you or tell her what was going on. And now I know he's a criminal, that he was working with those people. And that they do really bad things."

"He's going to risk his life to testify against them."

"Only because he was caught. Why should he go free?"

Good question.

"Jesse, I'm not going to defend what your stepfather did."

"Carson. He's not my stepfather. I refuse to call him anything. It's not *fair*."

"Life isn't fair, Jess. It's not. It sucks sometimes." He didn't know how to get through to him. "Look, Carson did some shitty things. But there are worse people out there, and what Carson knows will help catch them. Put *them* in prison."

"But why do I have to go? Why can't my mom and I just leave him?"

Because Carson is an asshole.

"You and your mom will always be in danger." Sean paused, assessed his son. When he was growing up, he hated when people talked around the real issues. Like the overdose of his older sister, Molly. Or why Kane left the Marines to become a mercenary. Things Sean may have been too young to know, but that he should have been told. "Did anyone tell you the danger you are in?"

"Because of Carson."

"Because of what you know. You, Jesse. You witnessed things . . . saw people you probably should not have seen. Heard things. We don't know the fallout from what happened at the Flores compound, but we do know from past experience that there is always someone to fill the void. Carson put you in a dangerous situation, but you're a smart kid, and you know too much. Things that could put you and your mother in danger. I don't know that I can protect you."

Jesse's lip quivered. "I . . . I don't want to never see you again."

"It won't be like that."

He slammed his fist on the table. "Yes it will!"

"We'll work something out. I have friends in high places." Sean couldn't bear the thought of losing Jesse. He'd just found him.

"My mom said I can't see anyone I know, that we'll be moving someplace, a different city, different names, different everything—and I would never see you again."

Sean wanted to throttle Madison, and not for the first time.

"Jesse, I won't let that happen."

"You won't have a choice. Only I have a choice. I . . . I . . . I want to see you again. I mean, I guess it sounds weird, but I feel like, I don't know, I don't really know myself because I never knew my real dad."

Sean's heart was breaking. He had to be strong. "It doesn't sound weird."

"I don't know what to do."

Sean put his hand on Jesse's arm, and then he said, "Can I hug you?"

Jesse put his arms around Sean's neck and Sean squeezed him tight. Tears burned, and he didn't know how he was going to fix anything. He didn't even know if he could promise Jesse anything. But dammit, something had to go right for once. Something had to work.

Sean took a deep breath and settled Jesse back in his chair. "I can't promise anything, but if this is important to you, as important to you as it is to me, I'll move heaven and earth for visitation. The US Marshals must have dealt with something like this before."

Jesse sniffed and wiped his eyes.

"You'd do that for me?"

"Yes—I'm doing it for me and you. I just found you, Jess, and I don't want to lose you."

"Okay."

"Okay?"

"I'll go. I'll do the stupid program—on one condition. I get to talk to you. I get to visit."

"I think that sounds reasonable. And fair."

"You said life wasn't fair."

"It's not. That's why you always have to work to make things right."

It was nearly midnight before Sean got home. He hadn't heard from Lucy, hadn't talked to her or seen her; he didn't know where she was going or who she was staying with.

Her car was in the garage. For a split second he had hope . . . but what if she had a taxi pick her up? Or a friend? Who would do that?

Anyone in her office. Or Brad Donnelly, the DEA agent she worked closely with.

That twinge of jealousy hit him again—the same kind of jealousy he had with Noah. Two federal agents who had more in common with Lucy, who liked her, who would move right in if Sean walked out.

But Sean wasn't walking out. Lucy was.

But her car was there.

Please, God—I haven't talked to you since I was a kid, but please, I need her.

The lights were off downstairs. He walked to his bedroom—their bedroom—and Lucy wasn't there.

But a dim light came from the small room off their bedroom, the sitting room that Lucy liked to use as her office.

He opened the door.

She sat in her comfy chair looking out the dark window. The comfy chair she read in, she worked in, and sometimes she fell asleep in. She was fully dressed, but her shoes were kicked off into the corner.

Maybe she was a mirage. Maybe he just wanted to see her, so he did. Tonight he'd been hollowed out, torn apart, and he feasted on her with his eyes.

He had so many things to say to her.

I thought you were leaving me.

I'm sorry.

I failed you.

Instead, he said, "I love you so much." His voice cracked and tears that had been burning inside poured out.

She got up and walked to him. She kissed him. He grabbed her, held on tight, and cried. "I can't lose you," he said. "I hate myself for hurting you."

"Shh," she murmured and led him to her chair. She sat him down and climbed into his lap.

"Don't leave me." He didn't want to beg . . . but yes, he would beg. He was wrong. He had to convince her he regretted everything.

"I love you, Sean. We'll work through this."

She held him close, like he'd often held her, and he ached. How could he explain anything he felt? Lucy was the most important thing in his life. More important than his life. Without her, he was an empty shell without meaning. He'd been searching for something intangible for so long, and when he found Lucy he knew she was it. She was his beginning and his ending; she gave him hope and purpose and a deep joy he couldn't explain. And he'd fucked it up.

But she had forgiven him. Or she was forgiving him. Maybe it would take him time, but he would spend every moment of the rest of his life showing her that her forgiveness was warranted.

It was several minutes before Sean could speak. "They're going into witness protection." His voice was a squeak.

"The Spades."

"I want to be in Jesse's life." He took a deep breath, trying again to control the intensity of his feelings. "I may never see him again."

"You will."

He could hope, but if Madison didn't agree to it, it would never happen. He wasn't even on Jesse's damn birth certificate. As far as the world was concerned, he had no rights to Jesse. No rights as a father. Anything he got now would be because of Madison, and that pained him. Sean had promised Jesse he would do everything he could to ensure that he had visitation rights, that the marshals could make it happen . . . but Noah and Dean weren't certain they could make it work.

They would try, though. They wanted to make it work, almost as much as Sean did.

Lucy shifted and he grabbed her and pulled her closer. "Don't leave."

"I'm not leaving," she said. "I think we should make dinner or something."

"I'm not hungry."

"Sean, why are you so terrified that I'm going to leave you?"

"Because you said you were."

"I was hurt and angry," she said. "I was ready to walk away to clear my head. But you know I love you. You've always known, from that first moment when I came to your house in DC in the blizzard almost two years ago."

"Nothing sticks to me."

"I don't understand."

He was already an emotional wreck. But saying it out loud . . . it was still hard. "You know my parents died in a plane crash. What I've never told you was that I was also in the plane."

"In the plane crash?"

"My mom died on impact. My dad was . . . broken. I had bumps and bruises but that was it. The plane was a goner, but I salvaged what I could. I worked day and night on the radio and fixed it. I purified water, I killed rabbits to eat, and I made a fire. I fixed everything, except my dad. He died three days later. I didn't know how to fix him. We were in the middle of nowhere, and I couldn't fix anything. If only I was smarter, if I could have fixed the radio faster, if I knew what to do to help my dad . . ." He took a deep breath, trying to stop the waves of guilt and regret and pain that rushed over him. "I buried them together."

"You never told me."

"No one knows, except Duke and Kane. And . . . I never told them my father survived for three days. I couldn't accept that I couldn't help him.

"I think that's why Duke has always been hard on me. Not just because I was a fuckup as a teenager and in and out of trouble, but because he blamed me somehow for what happened."

"He does not," Lucy said emphatically.

"I don't know," he said, suddenly exhausted. He pulled Lucy back down to him. "Just stay with me, Lucy. Please forgive me. I will never let you down again."

She pulled back and for a minute he thought he'd lost her. She stared at him, her dark eyes full of something unreadable. He'd always been able to read her . . . but she'd changed. Something fundamental inside her had changed. For better? For worse? He didn't know.

"Sean, we can't make promises we can't keep. Neither of us. If you put that weight on your shoulders, you will suffer for it. I will disappoint you. You will disappoint me. We will both say and do things in anger or sadness or pain that will hurt. But I know that you love me. That you take me for who I am. That you aren't going to try and change me or fix me, but you'll always pick me up and make me stronger. You will carry me when I can't walk. And I'm just as much to blame for you lying to me about Jesse."

"No, Lucy, that's all on me."

She smiled, just a bit. "Okay, most of it. But part of it is my responsibility. For the last two years, I have leaned on you for everything. I have depended on you for my sanity when things overwhelmed me. You have always been here for me. *Always.*"

"I wasn't—not this week. When you needed me the most."

"And that's it—because you weren't here, you thought you were protecting me by keeping this information to yourself, but I learned that even though this case was the hardest case I hope I ever have, and even though I wanted you here to lean on, I made it through. There were a few moments I didn't think I could . . . but I did. That's because of *you.* I am stronger because of you, but you don't have to coddle me and nurse me back to emotional health every night. You enabled me to stand on my own feet, to take the good with the bad. To survive."

He touched her cheek. This woman was incredible in every way. "You have always been a survivor."

"Physically, yes. But emotionally, everything is locked up tight. And it needs to be, most of the time, so I can do my job. But I survived this week *emotionally* because of you."

"I will *try* never to disappoint you."

She smiled. There was a glimmer of light in her eyes. Just a small beacon of hope, but suddenly the weight of Lucy leaving disappeared. She wasn't leaving him. She was here.

She'd stayed.

"That's better," she said. "We're going to need to talk."

"Isn't that what we've been doing?"

She climbed off his lap and pulled him out of the chair. She wrapped her arms around his neck and kissed him. "We're going to talk about how you gain parental rights."

His heart skipped a beat. "Lucy—you don't have to do this. You don't have to be part of this if you don't want to. I—"

She put her finger to his lips. "Of course I want to be part of this because it is your life. The good and the bad. We're getting married in six weeks. For better or worse." She kissed him. "Jesse is your son. He deserves to know you, to know Kane, to know the Rogans. More important, you deserve to be part of his life. We're going to find a way to ensure you can see him."

Sean pulled Lucy to him so tight he was afraid he'd break her. Except she wasn't breakable. Not anymore. "I love you, Lucy."

She took his hand and pulled him away from her office. Then she stopped and smiled. "I don't have to be at head-quarters until noon tomorrow."

"Eat. Sleep."

She lay back on the bed, pulling him down to her. "Make love. Then maybe food and sleep. And then repeat."

She put her hands on his face and held him above her. He saw the truth in her eyes. She had changed. Something fundamental, deep inside. But she was here, she hadn't left him even though he had screwed up. She hadn't left him, and he would never give her another reason to even consider it.

"That sounds like the perfect plan." His voice was rough around the edges.

"I've missed you, Sean. In every way."

Sean kissed Lucy as if it were the last time.

Read on for an excerpt from

MAKE THEM PAY

by Allison Brennan

Available in March 2017 from St. Martin's Paperbacks

CHAPTER ONE

Kane Rogan had been a Marine and a mercenary, and had devoted his life to Rogan-Caruso-Kincaid Protective Services. He was ruthless when necessary, but preferred clandestine operations to violent encounters. He wasn't a soft man, but he wasn't cruel.

Still, he had a deep-seated anger for those who hurt innocent people. And a violent rage against those who bought and sold human beings like property.

If Kane had known that the FBI had that bastard Angelo Zapelli in custody, then let him go, Kane would have taken him out before he crossed the border. He didn't care about any rights Zapelli claimed to have, or a supposed illegal search and seizure—which resulted in saving dozens of lives. He didn't care that Zapelli was a Mexican citizen or that he had been detained without probable cause or any of that other legal bullshit which separated Kane from some of his closest friends.

Angelo Zapelli had sold his pregnant girlfriend and her sister into the sex trade where they suffered at the hands of brutal men and women, all for sick thrills and profit. Zapelli didn't deserve to live, he didn't deserve to breathe the same air as the women he betrayed.

For the two weeks Kane Rogan watched him, Zapelli clearly felt no remorse for his actions. But it wasn't until Zapelli started talking up a young and obviously under-age girl that Kane knew the bastard hadn't changed. That he would once again sell girls into the sex trade, or abuse them himself.

Neither of which was acceptable.

Which was why Angelo Zapelli now sat tied to a wooden chair in the middle of a decrepit barn outside Monterrey, Mexico. His face bled—from his mouth and a cut across his cheek and a gash on his forehead that would scar if Kane didn't kill him. A tooth that must have already been loose lay in a ring of bloody saliva on the ground in front of Zapelli. Kane hadn't tortured him, not yet, but Zapelli had put up a fight and Kane enjoyed taking him to the ground. Kane planned on killing him and he wouldn't bring his team or his family into it.

Not this action. Not this time.

Zapelli tried to put up a tough front, but he was soft. Strong and powerful around young women he could ma-nipulate, use, and bully; but he was weak inside, with clean hands and manicured nails. He fought, but now he cried. He'd lost his rage because he wanted to live.

Zapelli knew exactly who Kane Rogan was and what he could do.

"I swear," Zapelli pleaded, "I'm not doing anything wrong!"

Kane remained silent. He sat on a chair in front of Zapelli, gun in hand. Silence drew confessions from the weak better than torture.

Kane rubbed his jaw. Zapelli had gotten in one left cross, but that was it. Sore, a little bruised, but the punch hadn't even broken his skin. He stared at Zapelli. Sweat dripped down his face, mingling with the drying blood. He pontificated, lied, begged. Then lost it.

"Fuck you, fuck you!" Zapelli screamed. "You'll be sorry. If I die, everyone in your fucking family will die. You think I don't know who you are? Do you think I don't know that fed is your fucking sister-in-law? Do you think she's unreachable?"

Kane kicked the chair over. Zapelli fell hard, unable to brace himself against the hard-packed dirt. He was stunned into silence.

"You won't do anything because you'll be dead," Kane said calmly.

His family had been threatened before; they knew the risks. Kane had read Lucy into the program, she had made many of her own enemies, she was cautious and she had Sean. A low-level prick like Angelo Zapelli wouldn't be able to get to her.

But it wasn't only Zapelli that Kane wanted.

Kane had spent the last few weeks putting together the players in the human trafficking organization that Zapelli fed. The Flores Cartel who ran it were wiped out, their accountant was turning state's evidence, all but two of the family members were confirmed dead, and their organization was decimated. Kane had someone on the inside making sure the youngest Flores brother didn't start up the operation again.

But Kane understood this business well enough to know that there were others who would fill the gaps, and that the Flores Cartel was the head. Kane might have cut off the head, but those who answered to them would be taking over, and Kane wanted to make it clear that there would be no more black market babies. The sex trade was bad enough, but to use these women as breeders, sell their babies, put them back into the business . . . it was worse than cruel. It was evil.

Kane would not tolerate it.

He rose from his chair, walked behind Zapelli where he still lay stunned on the ground, and pulled up his chair. When he was sitting up again, Kane re-secured his restraints, then returned to his own chair. He had all day. Hell, he'd stay here all week and watch Zapelli die of dehydration.

"What the fuck do you want?" Zapelli sobbed.

"Your contacts."

"They'll kill me!"

Kane just stared at him.

Sweat dripped into his eyes and he blinked, full panic. *Yes, asshole, you should be very scared.*

Zapelli continued to beg, swear, argue, threaten, plead . . . he tried every tactic and Kane sat there.

Kane wanted to kill him. He'd planned to kill him.

But he'd promised he wouldn't.

He never made promises like that, and it bothered him on more than one level. Not only because it tied his hands in an operation, but because Siobhan Walsh had figured out his plan without him so much as saying a word.

Since when had the infuriating, sexy, too-smart-for-her-own-good redhead been able to read his mind?

"I know what you're going to do, and I won't stop you," Siobhan said the night he left.

Kane stared at her. *"You know nothing."*

"I want to kill him, too. Marisol wants to kill him. But remember what you told her, just two days ago? You can't come back from murder."

"He wouldn't be the first man I killed." He'd said it to scare her, but Siobhan didn't scare easy.

"You need information, you'll get it from him. But he's

not worth another piece of your soul." She stepped toward him. He didn't move. He didn't dare move.

Siobhan whispered, "I still love you, Kane." She kissed him. He stood rigid, willing himself not to respond to her. She stepped back and smiled, just a little turn of her lips, and he itched to take her to bed, right then, show her that he wasn't the man she thought he was. That he took what he wanted, and he had wanted her for years.

But Siobhan wasn't a one-night stand. She wasn't a woman he could screw, then walk away. She was a woman who demanded lovemaking, not mere sex. She knew it, and still she pushed him. "I will love you no matter what you do in Monterrey. But you're better than Zapelli. You're better than all of them. I'm not letting you disappear on me again, not anymore. I will hunt you down and make you realize that you are the man I see, not the man you think you are."

And then she walked away. Siobhan walked out of his bunk and left him shaking with a hard-on.

He didn't want to love anyone; love was dangerous.

He especially didn't want to love Siobhan Walsh.

It looked like he had no choice in the matter, because as soon as she walked away, he craved her even more.

It didn't take long for Angelo Zapelli to break, and Kane Rogan didn't have to say another word.

"Fuck you." But there was no venom, no fight. He was resigned.

"Names."

Zapelli gave up three names, and after continued questioning, Kane was fairly certain those were the only players Zapelli knew. Kane had heard of two of them. One he was certain was dead. The other in hiding when he found out Kane was looking for him. And the third . . . a new player? Or an alias?

Kane would find out. He stood.

Zapelli started to cry. "I don't want to die. Please."

Had the women he sold as sex slaves cried and pleaded for their lives? Zapelli hadn't cared about them, and Kane cared less about the whiny, sniveling bastard in front of him. Angelo Zapelli was a waste of oxygen.

But he'd made a promise. Even though he didn't explicitly say he wouldn't kill Zapelli, Siobhan had walked away believing he had.

He should shoot Zapelli now to prove to Siobhan that he was unworthy of her and her love.

But Kane was tired. Tired of the violence and the heartache and the misery that he'd been fighting for well over twenty years.

"Is Jasmine alive?"

"I don't know! I swear, I don't. I . . . I think so, but I haven't seen her, I swear! I'm out of the business. I only work for my dad now. I swear."

He was blubbering, but Kane didn't believe him—Zappelli wasn't out of the business. Maybe this beating would change him, but Kane wasn't holding his breath.

"If you want to live, tell me one thing."

"Anything. Anything."

"Who bought your son?"

Zapelli's mouth opened and closed and no sound came out, until a gut-wrenching sob. "No. They'll know it was me."

Kane raised his gun.

"New York! That's all I know, someone in New York, a business tycoon who has four daughters and wanted a son. He's powerful and has money. My son will have everything, everything! Why do you care? He's not yours! Marisol can't give him shit, she's nothing!"

Kane pistol-whipped Zapelli and he fell over again. He holstered his gun and took out his knife.

It took all his willpower not to slit the bastard's throat.

Instead, he cut the binds at his wrists, leaned down, and said, "I will kill you if you ever threaten my people again."

He rose and walked away. It might take the sobbing asshole a few hours to get out of his leg restraints, but Kane lived up to his promise. He didn't kill him.

In fact, he lived up to both promises. He'd promised Marisol that he would find her son, and now he had a lead.

Time to call in the cavalry.

And time to go home.

Home.

CHAPTER TWO

Lucy Kincaid heard her fiancé Sean slip out of bed at four that morning. Monday. She groaned, then stretched and sat up.

He walked over and kissed her. "Go back to sleep."

"I can't."

"I didn't mean to wake you up."

"You didn't."

She hadn't slept well as it was, and neither had Sean. On Saturday he'd received an email from his son Jesse and immediately knew something was wrong, but it was against the rules of witness protection for Sean to contact Jesse outside of the Marshals' office. Then yesterday, Jesse's handler in the U.S. Marshals service called because of the email—Jesse had violated the terms of the program by contacting Sean. Sean convinced Jesse's handler to let him talk to Jesse, and they agreed that a face-to-face meeting might help the twelve-year-old understand the gravity of the situation.

If Jesse left witness protection, he would have a target on his back. And it pained Sean that he couldn't protect his own son.

Sean sat next to her on the edge of the bed and took her hand. He played with her fingers out of nerves more than anything. "What do I tell him, Luce?"

"The truth," she said. "He's just like you, Sean. He's a smart kid. Honesty is the only way to convince him to do what's right."

Lucy had met Jesse briefly before he and his family went into witness protection. It had been bittersweet—Sean had to say good-bye. He'd found his son and lost him in a matter of days, and now, only a month later, he was still having a difficult time accepting the situation. And, evidently, so was Jesse.

"I wish it didn't have to be like this." Sean was on edge, emotional and in pain.

Lucy took his hand, kissed it. "Jesse knows this isn't your call, Sean, but it's for his safety. Just think how you would feel if you were in the same situation."

"Helpless."

"Yes, but also angry and betrayed and scared. He loves you."

"He doesn't even know me."

"That doesn't mean anything, and you know it. You saved his life. He wants to get to know his father, and right now it can't happen." Didn't Sean see what she saw? "He's been emailing you—against the rules—because he's trying to see how far he can go. He doesn't understand that the rules—at least, these rules—can't be broken. It's too dangerous."

"I don't know how to fix this."

"You'll find a way." She kissed him. "You don't have a lot of time."

"I hate traveling commercial, and they're making me fly all over the damn country. I don't even know where he is."

Lucy didn't have to explain to Sean why the Marshals were setting such protocols. They both knew it was to keep the Spade family safe.

Sean pulled Lucy into a tight hug. "I love you, Lucy. I'll be back tomorrow."

She smiled, trying to show a brave front for Sean. He didn't need her worries and anxiety when he was so stressed himself. "It's going to work out."

He nodded, kissed her. "Twelve days."

Her heart skipped a beat. They'd discussed eloping, considering everything that was going on in their lives. They'd even gone so far as to talk to Father Mateo about the prospect—the priest who would be marrying them at St. Catherine's. He'd talked them out of it.

"You've earned this wedding. What you two have been through these last two years, you deserve this one day of joy and love in front of God, family, and friend. And Lucy," Mateo added, *"your mother scares me. She calls me twice a week about details, and if she can't see you get married, she'll probably curse or haunt me for the rest of my life."*

The wedding would be small and intimate, but those they cared about the most—friends and family—would be there. For the celebration. It was a new beginning, and they both needed that confirmation. That whatever life threw at them, they weren't running away or hiding. That together, they were stronger.

"Twelve days," she whispered.

She walked Sean to the garage, kissed him good-bye, and watched through the kitchen window as he drove off in his black Mustang.

Once he was out of sight, Lucy started the coffee, then went back upstairs to take a long, hot shower. She figured she'd get into FBI headquarters early this morning, considering that she had a lot on her plate she needed to clear in the next twelve days. She wanted to locate as many of the black market babies—sold in the human trafficking ring she'd helped stop last month—as she could before she left.

But after her shower, she got caught up in reading the news while eating a bagel and drinking her coffee and suddenly she didn't have as much time as she'd thought.

"Shoot," she said and rushed back upstairs to finish getting ready. Sean texted her that the first of his short flights was done, but he was turning off his phone and removing the battery per orders of the Marshals. Truth was, he'd been told not to bring a cell phone at all and this process was a compromise.

She sent him an emoji kiss.

I love you.

They'd had a recent setback in their relationship and for a short time, Lucy wasn't even certain they would survive the events. But instead of tearing them apart, they'd found a way to not only stay together, but love stronger. For nearly two years, Sean had been her rock of support. She'd leaned on him, he'd carried her when the weight of her life threatened to bury her. Now, she was strong enough to be Sean's support when he needed it the most. Two years ago, she would have failed. Now, because of Sean, she could be the rock he needed.

Lucy had just strapped on her gun when the doorbell rang. She pressed the security screen in the bedroom to see who was on the front porch so early. Sean was more than a little security conscious, especially after he helped the FBI catch a money launderer last month. Now, as soon as anyone crossed onto the property, the sensors alerted them. It took Sean a week to adjust them so every squirrel that scampered up a tree didn't set them off. She'd turned off what she called the "hyper-alert" system when Sean left for the airport earlier that morning.

An impeccably dressed, attractive woman with long sun-streaked, dark-blonde hair swept up into a loose bun stood waiting. She had a large shoulder bag and a small suitcase. She looked familiar, but Lucy couldn't remember meeting her. It didn't help that she wore large sunglasses. A neighbor?

While the visitor didn't look suspicious or dangerous, after the past month Lucy had become edgy. It didn't help that Sean was nervous; he rarely showed any stress, but this last month had been even more difficult for him.

Lucy pressed the intercom speaker. "Who is it?"

"Hello? I'm Eden. Eden Rogan. Sean's sister."

Eden Rogan? Lucy stared again at the screen. She had only seen photos of Eden and her twin brother Liam, most of them more than a decade old. It could easily be her.

"I'll be right down," Lucy said. She grabbed her blazer and slipped it on as she walked down the stairs. She disengaged the alarm and unlocked the door.

Eden smiled and pushed her large dark glasses up to the top of her head. Immediately, Lucy saw the resemblance—the dark blue eyes that she shared with both Sean and Kane stood out the most. But there were other little things, like her smile and her strong jawline, tempered by her femininity, and the way she tilted her head, just a bit, as she assessed Lucy, that was very Roganesque. "So you're the girl who tamed the wild beast."

Lucy said, "Come in. We didn't know you were coming."

"My baby brother is getting *married*? Of course I couldn't stay away!"

The wedding was still two weeks off—well, twelve days as Sean reminded her this morning. When they were going over the guest list this weekend, they'd taken Liam and Eden off—they hadn't responded yes or no. Lucy had suggested that Sean call them—he said no.

"I haven't seen either of them in years. Something bad went down between Liam and Kane. I used to want to know what happened . . . now? I don't care. Especially since they couldn't even RSVP. I'm staying out of it."

"I'm glad you're here," Lucy heard herself saying, though she wasn't sure she was happy. With everything that Sean had been dealt this last month, he didn't need surprise guests.

Eden walked in and looked around the large foyer with a half-smile that was so much like Sean it was a bit un-nerving. She openly assessed Lucy. Her face appeared open but her eyes were cool. Calculating.

Lucy needed to stop being so suspicious.

"So, you're Lucy."

Then she walked across the wide, open hall to the living room and stepped down the two steps. She surveyed the high ceilings, the furnishings, the multiple French doors that went out to the pool. "This place is really great. I never imagined that Sean would settle down, but well, stranger things have happened." She put her bag down on the floor and dropped her shoulder bag. "It's Kincaid, right?" Eden smiled and shook her head almost in disbelief. "Is that how you met? Because of your . . . brother, right? New partner at Rogan-Caruso."

Lucy wouldn't exactly say *new*. Jack had joined Rogan-Caruso Protective Services six years ago and they'd changed the name to Rogan-Caruso-Kincaid. Patrick had joined two years later.

"Not so new," she said.

"Time really flies, doesn't it? I haven't been back to the States in *years*. No reason to, until now."

"Do you have a place to stay?"

"Not yet—I wasn't sure I could get away, so I planned this sort of last minute. I came here straight from the airport. I've been traveling nonstop for the last eighteen hours. Milan to Heathrow and then just *waiting*. Wishing I'd been as smart as Sean and got my pilot's license. And then I was stuck in customs at JFK for hours. I'm not a good traveller. I hate flying."

Eighteen hours of traveling and she couldn't send Sean a message that she was on her way? Lucy wasn't buying it, not completely.

That's when Lucy saw it, the tension under Eden's perfect makeup. She was a stunning woman—beautiful, really. But there were fine lines around her eyes, which were a little too bright. Either fatigue or fear or both. Lucy had a little sympathy for her, considering the transatlantic flight. Two years ago she wouldn't have thought twice about inviting her to stay. But now, she hesitated.

"Where *is* Sean?" Eden asked. "He's never been one for sleeping in."

"He had to leave early. A case he's working on."

And just like that, the tension eased. It was subtle, and if Lucy wasn't so focused on Eden, she would have missed it. It was like Eden was relieved Sean wasn't there. Had she thought there would be a confrontation?

"Well, I'll be around for a while, I'll catch him when he gets back," Eden said. "Would you mind if I stayed here with you this morning? I don't have a hotel reservation, I need to call around, find a suite for the next two weeks. And truly, I really want to get to know you. I hate that Sean and I have gotten out of touch, but weddings are new beginnings."

"Stay here," she said. It just came out, and it was probably a bad idea. "At least for a day or two. My sister and her family won't be here until Sunday, we have plenty of room."

Lucy hoped Sean wouldn't be upset at her spontaneous invitation. But this was his sister. He hadn't seen her in years, and when he was nostalgic, he talked about the time when he was young, before Liam and Eden went to Europe where they'd stayed since college. When he sent them wedding invitations he'd said they wouldn't come, but he wanted to reach out anyway . . . maybe this was Eden's way of trying to fix their relationship. Sean wouldn't have sent the invites if he didn't want to mend fences.

Spontaneously flying halfway across the world and dropping by unannounced? Something was up.

She wanted to talk to Sean about this, but he'd turned off his phone. He wouldn't turn it back on until after he left Jesse. Maybe not until he arrived back in San Antonio. She'd send him a message that he'd get as soon as he turned on his phone—at least that way he wouldn't be blindsided when he got home.

"Are you sure?" Eden asked. "Call Sean, please, make sure it's okay with him. It *has* been a long time. But he sent the invite, and I thought . . . " Her voice trailed off and she looked nervous.

"He's traveling, I won't be able to reach him until tonight. Let me show you around." Lucy gave Eden a quick tour of the downstairs—the living room, dining room, kitchen, family room. She skipped the other rooms—like Sean's office—and led Eden down the hall to the guest rooms. There were two on the main floor, each with its own bathroom. Next week, Carina and her family would have one, and Lucy's brother Dillon and his wife would have the other. Upstairs was another guest suite, and Sean

ALLISON BRENNAN

had partially finished the large space above the garage. It wasn't fancy, but had a working bathroom. Lucy wished she could put Eden there because then she could secure the house—the garage apartment was on its own security system with its own entrance. The pool house was Kane's when he visited—he liked being separate from the house with his own space, and he'd been coming and going a lot over the last month. It was one of the reasons Sean started renovating the garage apartment—he wanted to offer Kane a permanent place. But for the wedding, they needed it for family.

Just two days ago, Sean had treated her to breakfast in bed and announced, *"This is the lull before the storm. We'll be overrun with Kincaids and Rogans in a week. Enjoy the peace."*

Lucy had the distinct impression that Eden was the beginning of a hurricane.

"This place is *amazing*," Eden said. "I love it. Thank you *so* much, Lucy. I won't be a bother. I'll be out of your hair tomorrow."

Lucy showed Eden the security panel. Eden frowned. "Is something wrong?"

"Wrong?" Lucy asked.

"Sean has always loved his toys, but this system is . . . rather advanced. Overkill."

"We've both worked cases that have made us cautious," Lucy said carefully. "I work for the FBI."

"Oh, I know," she said with an almost dismissive wave of her hand. "Surprised, though, since Sean has never particularly liked authority. I suppose true love knows no bounds."

Lucy decided to leave the comment alone. She didn't know Eden, and she didn't really know much about her relationship with the rest of the family, other than that there had been a falling-out and Liam and Eden had walked away from RCK when it was still Rogan-Caruso Protective Services. "Is Liam also coming to the wedding?"

"I doubt it," she said. "I really tried, but . . . well, some things can't be fixed."

Why did Lucy think she was lying? Why would she? Because she knew that Liam still had problems with his brothers? She probably spoke the truth, but there was more to the story, and Sean would get it out of his sister. Still, this visit was odd, especially with Sean out of town. She couldn't possibly have known—Sean didn't even know he was leaving until last night. Eden would have already been on a flight by the time Sean got the approval from the Marshals to visit his son, Jesse.

Lucy was now *really* late to work. She said, "I have to go. I'll try to get off early, take you to dinner. I'm not a very good cook."

"I would really *love* getting to know you better." Eden smiled and hugged her lightly. "Thank you for letting me stay. I promise, I'll be out by tomorrow. There are several nice hotels in the area, and a resort I've heard *fabulous* things about. I'll find something."

"You don't have to leave tomorrow. I'm serious—wait until Sean gets home, you two need to catch up."

"We'll play it by ear."

Lucy grabbed the rest of her things and hesitated in the kitchen. Maybe she should take the day off. Except . . . she had no time to take. She'd taken so much time off already this year that she didn't even have vacation for her honeymoon. She'd told Sean they would have to postpone the secret trip. Sean had been planning it for months, but kept Lucy in the dark, which was fine with her. But her fellow agents on the Violent Crimes squad had each given up one of their vacation days to her as a wedding present so she could have a honeymoon. She almost cried when they'd taken her out to lunch and told her. She hadn't made the best first impression on her team. She got along with some of them, and others were wary. She didn't blame them. Trouble followed her, and unfortunately touched everyone else. But all of them, including her temporary boss, Noah, had given her time.

Eden stepped into the kitchen and said, "I'm going to take a shower and sleep. I really am exhausted."

"Give me your phone number and I'll call you later, see if you need anything." Lucy wrote down her cell phone on a notepad.

"Great." Eden rattled off her number for Lucy. "It's a US number, I have both—comes in handy when traveling."

Odd, considering how she said she hadn't been in the States in years.

Lucy left after showing Eden once again how to set and reset the alarm, and reminding her to keep it engaged even when she was inside.

From her car, she sent Sean an email to call her when he had an opportunity. She didn't want him to worry, so added:

Nothing serious, just have some information for you.

Then she called FBI headquarters to tell them she was running late. As she drove, she was still apprehensive, so she called Sean's oldest brother, Kane. He didn't answer, which was par for the course. She left a message to call her. "It's not urgent, just call when you get a chance."

Put it out of your head.

She had a full day ahead of her, and worrying about Sean's sister wasn't going to help.

But she really hoped Kane called her back soon.